To: MK&C
From THE CLIENT

THE PRODUCT: MARIJUANA
The next President of the
United States will legalize
marijuana. We want to sell it
to the American people.

THE MOTIVE: MILLIONS OF DOLLARS
The race is on. We're ready to
grow and ship it. Can you sell
marijuana like cigarettes? And
can you do it first?

Read what happens in an advertising agency
when it gets the jump on the promotion of the
first legal marijuana cigarettes. And, read what
happens to the creative director handling the
account, torn between the exciting campaign
that would make history and his fears that, reports to the contrary, he is actually selling a dangerous drug.

Books By Edwin Corley

Acapulco Gold
The Jesus Factor

Published By
WARNER PAPERBACK LIBRARY

ACAPULCO GOLD

Edwin Corley

**WARNER
PAPERBACK
LIBRARY**

A Warner Communications Company

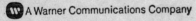

ACAPULCO GOLD

EXECUTIVE OFFICE

November 14

C O N F I D E N T I A L

To: All Creative and Account Personnel

As you know, in the past two years, Professor Harold
McClintlock of Northwestern University has become
well-known for his in-depth investigations of contem-
porary business practices. Operating in much the same
way as the famous Nader's Raiders of the late Sixties,
McClintlock's Mob first provided a piercing analysis
of the newspaper business and, last year, the broadcast media. Now, although it has not yet been formally
announced, Professor McClintlock soon plans to turn
his attentions to the advertising industry. Normally,
his study--which involves placement of some 50 or 60
graduate students in the working structure of the
industry involved--begins early in January and
continues for several months.

However, since we as an industry--and particularly we
of MK&C--have nothing to hide, I have taken the
unprecedented step of suggesting to Professor
McClintlock that he assign a team to us at his
earliest convenience to conduct somewhat of a pilot
study. The advantages to taking this step are obvious:
if the Professor finds that the unfavorable rumors
and speculations about advertising are essentially
false, the chances are quite good that the larger
study might be cancelled in order to turn the Mob's
attention to other areas where investigation is more
obviously called for.

You do not have to worry about being "spied on" by
McClintlock's people. They do not sneak aboard in
undercover jobs, but stand up and announce clearly
who they are and what they are doing. In response,
I request that you do the same. We have nothing to
hide. Be candid and honest.

When I learn definitely when the McClintlock team is
reporting, I will so advise the agency.

Hamilton Keyes,
President

HK/sg

I sighed and filed Keyes's memo in the wastebasket. Monday mornings are bad enough without being treated to the rah-rah stuff. Especially from Hamilton Keyes, who, despite a couple of years fighting our little brown brothers in Asia, hadn't learned yet how to talk straight to us common folks. I'm not knocking Ham—but I believed his memo just as completely as he did, which means about one word in three.

It had been waiting for me on top of my IN basket, sealed in the blue MK&C envelope that is used only by Hamilton Keyes. Once, the story goes, *Time* magazine made the mistake of sending Keyes a personal invitation to an executive luncheon in a *blue* envelope, and not only did he boycott the luncheon, he cut the pages of *Time* from the schedules of all MK&C clients for three months. Perhaps the story is apocryphal, but in the Ad Game, anything is possible. One thing is sure: at MK&C, *nobody* but Ham uses blue envelopes.

I leaned out of my office door, nearly tipping my chair over in the process, and shouted, "Effie! Where's my coffee?"

Unflappably, Effie shouted back, "I sent the boy away with it."

"What the hell do you mean you sent him away with it? Don't you know this is Monday morning? I've got a ten-thirty meeting with a client. I'm not *ready* for the meeting. If I don't get my heart started, I'll *never* be ready for it."

"Simmer down, Clyde," she replied in dulcet-tones Mississippi. Effie is the best secretary I've ever had. She studied creative writing at Ole Miss, came to New York at twenty-two, took a week to look the field over, and then decided she would rather be a secretary than a copywriter, although the money was far less. Effie was unpredictable then, and she has remained so. For one thing, my name is not Clyde. It is Mike. Michael Evans. And for another, taking a job as a secretary had in no way diminished Effie's ambition to become a successful writer. It was merely that she had no interest whatsoever in becoming a successful *advertising* writer, no reflection on Mary Wells. Effie wasn't snobbish about it. In fact, in occasional moments of candor she admitted that the job of an advertising executive was no bed of roses, a metaphor I quarrel with because I have often discovered Madison Avenue to be lined with very sharp and prickly thorns.

"Mike," she explained one evening over drinks in the Beef and Brew, "the trouble is, you never get away from your work. You take it everywhere with you. When you see a play, you're thinking, 'How can I use this dramatic effect in a commercial?' You listen to music the same way. How can I *use* it? You even listen to *people* that way. How can I use *them?* You earn every dime MK&C pays you. Well, at five in the evening us poor little slavey secretaries put down the tops of our desks and walk out the door and it's goodbye to old MK&C until nine A.M."

"You never made it in at nine A.M. one morning in your life," I grumbled, but my heart wasn't in it. Because what she had said was true. Being really successful in advertising is a full-time job. Full-time meaning twenty-four hours a day. Twenty-five when we set the clock back for daylight saving. But hell, isn't being successful at *anything* the same?

In this business you get the rewards fast. And they are ample. Today, at the ripe age of thirty-two, I have my own

2

window office, two windows, not just one—a, don't think the number of windows you have makes a ference, you never heard of pecking orders or milk-cow lineups. My office is my home away from home, my badge of honor, my fortress. A framed certificate hanging on the wall just over my *Mad* magazine portrait of Alfred E. Neumann as Teddy Roosevelt proclaims me a vice president with all the rights and privileges accruing thereto, which means that I can take a month's vacation—except that if I ever took a month off, everything would go to hell so fast that I would probably return from my safari just in time to get fired. I earn $28,500 a year, which isn't the highest paycheck in the land, particularly after Uncle Sam and an ex-wife in Los Angeles get through with it, but which isn't exactly Green Stamps either. I have had my photograph on the advertising page of *The New York Times* (thereby getting me on the permanent mailing and phone lists of every mutual funds salesman in the world), and my campaign for Coronet Cigarettes won me an Andy award last year.

But I still didn't have any coffee. And it was nine minutes after ten, with a Coronet meeting looming up at ten-thirty.

"There I will be," I warned Effie, "standing before the client, unable to speak a single word, not even my name. They will drum me out of the business. But while my shame will be bottomless, it will be as nothing compared to your own. They will point fingers at you on the street, the other secretaries, and whisper, '*She's* the one who let her boss go into a client meeting without his morning coffee!' Your exile will be so complete that you will have an entire car of the A train to yourself during the rush hour."

"Everything's under control, General," she said. "The coffee shop messed up the order and sent it up with cream. I gave the boy twenty lashes and he'll be back in a jiffy with the real stuff. Black, just like your Yankee heart."

"If you speak the truth," I said, "then you're forgiven."

"God bless you," she said. "My day is made."

I sighed once more and leaned back inside my office. My two-window office fortress with a framed certificate signed by Hamilton Keyes and a portrait of Alfred E. Neumann and a bottle of Irish in the desk drawer to liven

3

coffee. And—in the middle section of the ... I had promoted to store my storyboards ...hotograph of Janice taken during our honey- ...Montego Bay. I'd had a two-foot photostat made ...nning to use it as a dartboard, but by the time it c... back from the stat house the whole idea seemed pretty silly, so I stuck the photo in the taboret and now, every so often, I run across it while looking for a lost, strayed, or stolen storyboard and sometimes I sit there for a few minutes looking at it, feeling an indefinable kind of sadness that is mixed with anger. I don't know why I didn't just tear the damned thing up.

"Coffee, master," said Effie, putting the styrofoam cup down on my desk. I don't like coffee in styrofoam cups, but it doesn't do any good to pour it out into a mug, something I tried for a while, because even when you are drinking from the mug, you can't help remembering that the coffee *came* in the styrofoam cup and it spoils any improvement the mug might provide. I don't understand why I detest styrofoam cups so much. Maybe it's because they're so damned *inert*. I mean, with a cardboard cup you at least have the bitter taste of cardboard to remind you that you're not in Mama's kitchen any longer.

I sipped the coffee. "Ten-fifteen and all is well. Have you seen Phil or Mark?"

"They're both in Mark's office, looking at dirty pictures," Effie said. "Shall I send them in?"

"No," I said. "I'll catch up with them."

"You just want to catch up with that new *Playboy* centerfold. You are becoming a dirty old man."

"A dirty *young* man," I corrected. "Don't you know that in this business anybody under fifty is described as a vigorous young executive?"

"Not by his wife," Effie said, and left.

"Decadent Southern catfish-eater!" I called after her, and sipped my coffee again. My hand was shaking a little. The back-and-forth with Effie had helped, but I was still nervous. I always am just before a meeting. Once an account executive noticed and said, "My God, Mike, you're a nervous wreck. Do you want me to present the advertising today?" I told him no, went in, and sold three million

4

dollars' worth of television commercials, and afterward, over drinks in Ratazzi's, he asked, "How could you be so nervous this morning and so goddamned *cool* during the actual meeting?" I told him the truth: "I just don't know. But if I'm not nervous before a presentation, I'm not really *up,* and if I'm not up, I won't be any good. It's hard on the ulcer, but it's the only way I know how to work." He thought that over a minute, then lifted his fishbowl of a martini and said, "Keep trembling, Mike. Keep trembling."

Okay, I was trembling. Ten-twenty. Time to start moving. I make it a point never to be early for the meeting. It's bad psychology to be sitting there, waiting, when the client arrives. I walk into the room right on the dot, and if the client got there early and *he's* the one waiting, that's even better. In a business like advertising, which is one-tenth business, one-tenth art, one-tenth luck—and the rest personal salesmanship—you need all the help you can get.

I don't know how many stories you may have heard or read about Madison Avenue, which is what the business is called despite the fact that there are more agencies on Fifth Avenue, and Lexington, and in Chicago and San Francisco and Detroit and Atlanta than there are *buildings* on Madison Avenue, but whatever you think you know about advertising, the chances are it's mostly baloney. I entered the business eager to be initiated into the wild parties and the sex at lunch and the flights to Rome on a moment's notice. Instead, I found that practically everybody on the executive level runs like hell to catch the 5:17 to Larchmont, or Scarborough, or whever the 5:17 goes. And as for the secretaries and research girls, they all had boyfriends who were construction workers, or cops, or bus drivers, all of whom had large muscles designed for stretching the neck of any young ad man foolish enough to mess around. As for the lady copywriters, of which there were many, they were either happily married or else so neurotic that you couldn't stand being alone with them for more than two drinks, or else so obviously sharp and desirable that it was already too late, Charlie, because there were waiting lines around the block, composed of suitors who had nice little goodies like private airplanes and

5

shares in a good ski lodge and all the stuff that $9000-a-year junior copywriters only dream of. So much for the wild life on Madison Avenue.

I took my coffee and went down the hall to Mark Hedin's office. Mark was my senior copywriter now that I had gotten the certificate from Hamilton Keyes and become a group copy supervisor. The only reason that the names of Samuel Morton and Frank Cooper do not also appear on my veep certificate is that Frank Cooper keeled over with a massive coronary right in the middle of a presentation to General Motors. He did not survive, and MK&C did not get the business either, so it was a dark day all the way around. As for Samuel Morton, he ruminated for a year or so about Cooper's dramatic exit, decided enough was enough, sold his MK&C stock back to the company, took almost two million bucks in capital gains, and moved to Sarasota, where he now fishes for yellowtail and counts his money. So, at the age of fifty-one Hamilton Keyes inherited the whole big ball of wax and, surprisingly for a product of Groton and Harvard, succeeded within four years in building the agency into a ninety-four-million-dollar operation. Spelled out, that doesn't look too impressive, so look at it like this: $94,000,000.00.

Mark's door was open and I went in. Phil McKenna, my art director, was sitting on the edge of Mark's desk, holding up the *Playboy* centerfold.

Joyously, he said, "Cunt hair!"

"*Pubic* hair," I corrected, examining the photograph. "And a darling thing she is too. What the hell's happening out there in the Windy City? Has Hugh Heffner lost his airbrush?"

"Lower your voice," said Phil. "You are speaking of a farseeing man who believes in giving the public what it wants. A benefactor of mankind."

"Since you raise the benefacting of mankind," I said, "how about our meeting? Are the layouts done?"

"They'd better be," Phil said. "Otherwise we're all in deep trouble."

"How deep?" I asked. "Where are they?"

"Out in the bullpen being mounted."

"I thought we did that on Friday. Hey, troops, what the hell's going on?"

"We came in on the weekend and made some changes," Phil said. "Mark and I decided that the whole frigging cowboy motif was too much like Marlboro Country."

"Great," I said. "Forgive me for asking, but as supervisor on this account do I get to see the new work before our meeting or shall I hold my breath and be just as surprised as the client?"

"We took the backup idea," Mark said. "You remember, the deep-sea stuff. I would have called you, but since you'd already agreed it was a good followup idea, it didn't seem worth disturbing your weekend."

"Bless you, my son," I said. "I shall remark on your kindness to the receptionist on the unemployment line when I go down to draw my benefits. Jesus, Mark, what are you trying to pull? All I said about deep-sea stuff was that Phillip Morris Commanders died a miserable death years ago with that briny-deep stuff."

"Don't worry, Mike," said Phil. "We've still got the Wild West layouts. If you want to show them after seeing the new stuff, that's your option. Either way, you've got a backup stack in case Uncle Norman's cooled on the cowboy jazz."

Norman Barnes, the brand manager on the Coronet account, had never been west of the Mississippi, but he always came to New York wearing a big black cowboy hat and pointy-toed boots with high heels. "Since when does Marlboro own the Old West?" he had demanded at our last meeting. "Goddamnit, Zane Grey doesn't own the Old West, and Mack Brand doesn't own the Old West, so how the hell does Marlboro get away trying to grab it?"

"I think it's Max Brand," I said, "and Marlboro gets away with it because they've spent umpteen million bucks a year for fifteen years, and with that kind of dough they could own the Lone Ranger and Tonto and throw in all the silver bullets."

Now it looked as if I was being mousetrapped into putting my layouts where my mouth was, and that way could lie unemployment. I wasn't too happy with my team just then. "You could have called me," I told Mark.

"And have you miss watching the Jets getting slaughtered by Oakland?" he answered as Phil went down the hall toward the pasteup room that, since time immemorial,

7

has been called the bullpen—in honor of the tiny cubicles around the edges of the room in which junior art directors labored over such minor tasks as lettering headlines and drawing in clients' logotypes.

"It was San Diego, not Oakland," I said. "And anyway, the Jets scored in the last quarter."

"Yeah, a field goal. Making the tab twenty-one to three. Go Jets!"

Mark Hedin, at twenty-seven, was considered the agency's hottest young writer, and I knew I was lucky to have him in my group. We jointly supervised three other writers —two men in their early twenties and a female copy trainee who had come up through the secretarial pool. My job was now more salesman than active writer—I talked directly with the account people, with the agency's management, and presented copy to the client, listened to his criticisms, suggestions, hopes, and dreams. Also, when the meetings were in New York, I shared with the account team the inevitable wining and dining, although since the recent recession, such entertainment had become more sensible: no more hundred-and-forty-dollar tabs at the Spanish Pavilion. Now it is time for you to ask, "But what *work* do you do?" and my answer will just have to be, "It's *all* work." Until you stand up in a room full of cigar-smoking men and try to convince them that the piece of paper in your hand is worth their spending six million dollars on during the coming year, you don't know the meaning of the word "work." Anyway, that's how the business operates. It's a paradox that when a writer wins respect and the big thou through his creative efforts, he is then promoted out of the writing area into supervisory work, presumably on the assumption that he will be able to pass along his charisma to a team of younger writers. Often it just doesn't work out that way; he may be unable to communicate ideas to others, although able to execute the work himself, he may stammer trying to sell a perfectly good idea to the client, he may prove to be a disaster when pulled out from behind his typewriter. In short, like so many, he may have been promoted beyond his capacity to function. In which case does the Big Typewriter in the Corner Office recognize the error and allow our writer to go back to doing what he does well? Not on your life. Instead, the complaint is voiced: "Irving's a lousy group head," and he gets his ass canned—usually during the Christmas holidays. Not because management has been taking lessons from Scrooge, but because after the holidays comes the first of the year, and that is when new budget periods begin, and nobody wants to carry poor Irving into a brand-new budget.

So, when Phil came back with the layouts, I looked at them hard. And he had been right. The sea stuff was good. Which proved once more that one of the things wrong with intangible work such as advertising is that you can sit around and talk a good idea to death without ever knowing what you missed, because when I say "sea stuff," I am seeing one thing in my head and Phil is seeing something else, and Norman Barnes sees yet a third set of visuals. You actually have to look at it, rendered on the layout, the way Phil had done it this time: a virile, gutsy campaign that made our Western series seem derivative and tame.

"The hell with Uncle Norman," I decided. "We'll show the sea stuff."

"Twenty-nine after," said Mark. "The apes are having their coronaries. Shall we let them off the hook?"

"Ape" was one of our many semiaffectionate terms for the account executives, who are the men supposed to represent the agency to the client and, in turn, the client to the agency. In practice it never works out that way. Most of their time is spent in worrying about "keeping the client happy," and since I have rarely observed apes worrying about "keeping the agency happy," my personal view toward the account executive's schizoid role is somewhat jaundiced.

The AE on the Coronet account, Howard Porter, was one of the rare apes with a sense of humor about his job. In fact, it was Porter who coined the title "empty suits" as a synonym for "ape." It was during a wild drinking session in Louisville while awaiting the outcome of a nine-million-dollar recommendation we had made to the Coronet Tobacco Company. If they bought, MK&C would have a deliciously profitable year. If they stalled or, worse, fired us off the account because of the slump in sales that had followed the removal of cigarette advertising from radio and television, we would have no Christmas bonus and a

9

number of unsmiling men in Brooks suits would be hustling down to the dean of job-placement agents, Jerry Fields.

I remember warning Porter, "Take it easy on the booze, Howard. Tomorrow's meeting is a big one. Uncle Norman's been reading the sales figures and he doesn't like what they're saying."

"Screw Uncle Norman," said Porter. "I'll just send my empty suit to the meeting and nobody'll know the difference."

When we managed to stop laughing, account executives at Morton, Keyes and Cooper had become "empty suits." And so they will remain for all time until summoned to their reward by that Great Client in the Sky.

I tucked the Coronet layouts under my arm and nodded at Phil and Mark. "Let's go."

"Body text is all set," Mark said, holding up a manila folder. "Copy's the same word for word except that we talk about the fresh expanses of the sea instead of the plains."

"Okay," I said, fighting down the wave of nausea that always grips me just before I walk into the conference room. "Another day, another million dollars. Let's go get them."

I led the way down the hall to Conference Room 661, where Howard Porter and two of his assistants waited, with or without the august presence of Norman Barnes of the Coronet Tobacco Company of Louisville, Kentucky. As we passed the cubicle of Allen Meyer, one of our junior writers, he looked up and said in an awed voice, "Jeeze, Killer, I hope when my time comes to go through that Big Door, I handle myself with as much guts as you do."

"Screw you," I said, and opened the door to Conference Room 661.

10

CALL REPORT

DATE: November 14

PLACE: New York

PRODUCT: Coronet Cigarettes

PRESENT FOR
AGENCY: H. Porter, M. Evans,
             P. McKenna, M. Hedin

PRESENT FOR
CLIENT: N. Barnes

Meeting convened at 10:31 a.m.

Agenda included presentation of new bi-annual print refresher campaign, Agency recommendation for media and point-of-sale budgets, and suggested format for coupon redemption.

Before any scheduled business was introduced, Client requested the floor for an announcement, which is covered in separate, confidential memo.

Meeting was adjourned at 10:40 a.m.

Writers who ought to know better are always presenting a false picture of Madison Avenue. Despite the novels of Frederick Wakeman (*The Hucksters*), Herman Wouk (*Aurora Dawn*), and Sloan Wilson (*The Man in the Gray Flannel Suit*), the bare and obvious purpose of an advertising agency meeting room is merely to provide a room in which to have a meeting. There are no stained-glass windows, no knee-deep carpets or reclining lounges to rest the client's weary back. Few, if any, have built-in bars. There may be a motheaten TV set, but it is hooked up to the closed-circuit television system down in the projection room and usually doesn't work anyway. There may be a rickety easel on which to prop visual aids, but the chances are excellent that it will fall down during the crucial part of the presentation. Rarely is there any slide or movie projection equipment, or even a piano, and almost never are there live performers singing, "Doo-dah, doo-dah, buy Fluffy Flakes." In short, conference rooms are mostly functional, workaday type rooms for functional, workaday guys.

The walls are often lined with corkboard, with long chalk trays running around the circumference of the room, about three feet off the floor. They're used to prop up art directors' layouts and storyboards. The cork wall itself is useful for pinning things to, such as tissue overlays for layouts. And they are very handy for throwing pushpins into. A pushpin is a super thumbtack with a tiny handle that looks like a square mushroom and a long, very sharp point perhaps half an inch in length. Longtime ad men have learned the trick of throwing these unlikely darts all the way across a room, imbedding them half their length in the cork wall. Uncle Norman was a master of the push-pin. His specialty was the underarm throw, with which he was able to pitch a dozen pushpins inside the edges of a sheet of typing paper from the far side of the room. Secretly, I practiced for months and one day when Norman was particularly hot with his throws, I ambled up to the chalk tray, scooped into the pushpin box, selected three straight and true missiles, turned my back to the wall and, without looking, threw all three over my shoulder into the corkboard. They landed within inches of each other, imbedded deep in the wall. Without a word Norman put down his own handful of pushpins and the meeting continued as if nothing unusual had happened. But it was weeks before he touched another pushpin.

This morning we walked into the conference room at exactly ten-thirty. Howard Porter looked at his watch and said, "Ah, Mike's made it again. Right on time." We all shook hands as if we hadn't seen each other in the elevator, sneaking into the office at the crack of ten. Norman Barnes was already there too, sitting quietly at the far end of the big conference table. His only greeting was a casual wave of his hand in my direction. His eyes were puffy and I didn't like the way his hand trembled as he sipped black coffee from a genuine cup. While I am always uptight before a meeting, Norman never is. That he was nervous now didn't bode fair for the Mike Evans team.

"Guys," said Porter (he can say "guys" in a way that would dislocate my jaw if I tried it), "Norman has to catch an early plane back to Louisville, so why don't we get with it? Norman, we want to present the new advertising for magazines and newspapers, some point-of-sale col-

13

lateral, and then I plan to go into media and suggestions for a coupon offer. Is that okay with everyone?"

"Fine by me," I said. "Except, Norman, the creative group has done some fresh thinking since our last meeting, so let's allow a little extra time to bat new layouts around."

Norman put both hands on the table and said, "Mike, I think I can save us all some time. Howard, what I've got to say makes your whole agenda redundant."

Puzzled, Howard Porter asked, "What's that, Norm?"

"I had to come in here first, before I went upstairs," Norman Barnes said slowly. "Listen, I've worked with you characters for five years. I don't buy that formal crap of telegrams and registered letters. You owe it to a man to give it to him in person. I haven't even been up to see Ham Keyes yet. I don't know Ham Keyes. I know you guys. And that's why I flew up here myself instead of letting Coronet's eminent president communicate with his opposite number."

"Norman," Howard Porter said tightly, "are you trying to say what I think you're trying to say?"

"I'm afraid I am," said the client. "You're the first to hear it, but effective as of now MK&C is fired as Coronet's advertising agency."

"Jesus Christ," said the account man. "Can I ask why?"

"You can ask," said Norman Barnes, "but I can't answer you. I don't know why. The order came down from the top. Wild Bill himself initiated it. Listen, buddy, I fought him. I put my ass on the line for you guys."

"I know you did," said Porter, and from his voice I knew that he believed Norman. "But what the hell happened? I know we've had some minor reverses this year, but so has the whole damned cigarette market. We've held our share points. Sales haven't gone up, but they haven't gone down, either, and that's more than American Tobacco can say."

"You're only recapping what I've already told Wild Bill," Barnes said. "Look, Howard, I don't know what happened. Nobody consulted me, and if you don't think my nose isn't out of joint over that, you're sadly mistaken. For all I know I don't even have a job myself any more.

14

Believe me, I really laid it on the old man, but it did just about as much good as pissing into the wind. So that's it. I was told that MK&C was canned. I wanted to know why the decision and I was told it wasn't any of my business, that I'd get new instructions when management was ready to let me have them. Period."

"That just doesn't sound like Wild Bill," Porter said. "He's a bastard, but he's a shrewd bastard. This isn't his style."

"What can I say, Howard? I'm as shocked and mad as you. But I was given my orders. Nobody told me why. I'm just the good soldier who got sent out to inform the rearguard that they're expendable. Sorry, and all that shit. And I mean it." Norman looked at his watch. "Okay, I'm going upstairs to give the word to Ham Keyes, and if he doesn't cut my throat with one of those decorative cutlasses on his wall, I'll see you guys in Reuben's and I promise to buy you all the martinis you can drink."

"Jesus," said Howard Porter. "Do you know how many people we're going to have to put out on the street for losing that twelve million bucks?"

"I'm sorry," Norman repeated.

Nine minutes after it had begun the meeting adjourned.

November 14

11:30 a.m.

C O N F I D E N T I A L

RUSH--DELIVER BY HAND FOR SIGNED RECEIPT

TO: All Department Heads, Group Copy Supervisors
and Head Art Directors

There will be a meeting in Mr. Keyes' office
promptly at 2:30 this afternoon. Attendance is
mandatory. Please rearrange your luncheon and meeting
schedules accordingly.

If you have client meetings or trips scheduled,
they must be postponed without indicating to your
client that the reason for postponement is other than
routine. This is most urgent; under no circumstances
is any MK&C client to be told of this afternoon's
meeting.

Please be on time.

S. G.

Stella Green

(For Mr. Keyes)

"Big Stella writes a mean letter," I said, sitting at the bar in Reuben's, the noisy restaurant on East Fifty-eighth Street. You've heard of the Reuben's Sandwich? Same place.

Glumly, Howard Porter said, "Hamilton's reacting to the bad news from Louisville. This afternoon's when he'll give us the word to cut twenty percent from our budget. I'll have to let a couple of my guys go. And so will you, Mike."

"I'll be lucky if they don't let *me* go," I said. "What the hell. It was too good to be true anyway. I can always buy a ski lodge and starve on the slopes."

We were waiting for Norman Barnes to show up and were one martini into our vigil. Needless to say, neither of us was overflowing with joy and good fellowship. The loss of a twelve-million-dollar account is serious business. This one account represented more than ten percent of the agency's billing, but even that hard fact needs some interpretation. One *twelve*-million-dollar account is always more profitable than twelve *one*-million-dollar accounts. That's because twelve different accounts demand twelve

17

times as many meetings, twelve marketing plans to be drawn up instead of one, and while maybe not twelve times the personnel, at least six or seven times as many guys, all spread pretty thin. But the single twelve-million-buck Coronet account was staffed by a small crew of hard-core professionals. Even if the agency were to fire every single person who had anything to do with the Coronet account, MK&C would still be behind the financial eight ball, because the overflow of profit from Coronet sweetened the pot for a lot of other marginal accounts.

"You're a million miles away," said Porter.

"Sorry," I said. "I was thinking gloomy thoughts." I waved for another martini. "I hope Uncle Norman gets here soon or we're going to have to face Ham Keyes on an empty stomach."

He stared at me. "You weren't thinking of *eating!* My God, Mike, I couldn't get down a poached egg. My plan is to numb the upper cortex with a few of these silver bullets and go up to Ham's office and take my punishment like a man."

"You'll be all right," I said. "They can't fire you. You're a senior vice president, and more than that, you're in the club. Guys in the club don't get fired. Firing is reserved for peasants like me."

"Let me tell you about guys in the club," he said. "A few years back, over at one of the big shops, they brought in a hotshot management supervisor. Stole him away from Leo Burnett out in Chicago. He was an instant club member. The poor sap even moved to Westchester so he could ride down on the eight-sixteen with the agency president and two other wheels. He made senior veep, had options on preferred stock. He could even sign his own expense account, that's how important he was."

"Don't tell me," I said. "A major client said, 'Get that shit-kicking hillbilly off my business,' so they fired him, stock options and all."

"Right on part one, wrong on part two. Like you said, Mike, they don't fire guys in the club. All they did was stop playing bridge with him on the commuter train."

"They *what?*"

"It's God's own truth. In fact, to make sure that there

18

would never even be room in the coach for him to sit down, they actually had one of the bachelor account executives move into a motel in Ossining so that all four seats would be filled."

"I'd have said screw them. Who wants to win their money anyway?"

Porter shook his head. "That was just the beginning. He got evicted from his office. Oh, not formally. They were 'redecorating.' For three months they redecorated. Then they tore it all out and started over again. And there wasn't any big rush to put him on a new account. He was assigned to 'Special Projects.' Makework. Reading reports on which were more economical in the johns—cloth rollers or paper towels. And he couldn't approve his own expense account any more. It had to be sent upstairs, where a *secretary* in accounting questioned every luncheon and every sixty-cent cab ride. He lasted five months, finally got a job with N. W. Ayer down in Philadelphia, and sped off on the Metroliner, shaking his fist back at the Big City. He's still there, happy as a clam and signing his own expense account again."

"I didn't think things like that really happened."

"They haven't at MK&C. Yet. Let's hope Ham doesn't break the mold this afternoon. I'd hate to have the new regime start with me."

We drank silently for a few minutes. The martinis were icy and very smooth, with just a trace of vermouth. "Silver bullets" we call them. With good reason. Deadly.

I said, "If they tell me to cut back, I don't know what the hell to do. We can't fire Mark. He's one of the best men in the shop. And even if we dumped both junior writers and a trainee, I'd only save around twenty grand in payroll. Besides which, who would do all that picky day-to-day dog work?"

"Mike," Porter said softly, "in a couple of days, there isn't going to *be* any of that picky day-to-day dog work."

"Yeah," I said. "I forgot."

"You might as well make up your mind about it," he said. "You're going to have to fire somebody. Hell, I've fired a couple of my best friends over the years, and they're still my friends. The facts are that when a shop

19

blows a twelve-million-buck account, that's a million eight hundred thousand of gross income to us that vanishes. And the only way to really trim costs is to cut on payroll."

"Where is twenty grand of lower-echelon payroll going to help much?"

"Multiply that by twenty cuts around the whole shop and that's almost half a million in salaries. But the important thing is the saving in benefits like insurance and welfare and office space and even telephone calls. It all adds up. Fifty people out of the pension fund saves us a cool two hundred thou a year right there."

Bitterly I said, "People are our most important product. And the most expendable."

"Sure. Know what at least half of that big salary check we get is? Combat pay, pal."

I looked at my watch. "Where the hell is Uncle Norman?"

"He'll be here. He's probably in the john, tossing his cookies."

"A client barfing? I thought that that was strictly for agency copywriters."

"Norman's badly shaken. I knew it this morning when he first walked in. I saw he wasn't wearing that silly damned cowboy hat. And he had on shoes. Real Adlers."

"I didn't have time to notice. The shit started flying so fast it was all I could do to duck."

I spread some of the soft cheddar on a cracker. Howard Porter shuddered. "Please," he said. "Not while I'm drinking."

I ate the cheese anyway. It tasted soapy. I said, "It's days like this that I wish I'd followed my early calling and become a matinee idol."

Howard toasted at me. "Here's to Michael Evans, America's Heartthrob." He sipped. "Are you putting me on, Mike? Did you ever act?"

"What do you think I do in every one of those goddamned client meetings?"

"I'm serious. You know, we never talked much about what you did before you came to MK&C."

"There wasn't much to talk about. I put two years in the service, got out, and took my GI Bill to the Columbia

School of Drama. At the age of twenty-one, my burning ambition in life was to play King Lear."

Porter smiled broadly. "I have often said, scratch a writer and you will reveal a frustrated actor. How did you end up in the ad biz?"

"Please," I said. "Such familiarities are passé. The advertising *profession*. And I got in it the same way everyone else does—out of fear, desperation, and hunger."

"You didn't get to play Lear?"

"I starved my ass off for three years in summer stock and Off-Broadway, doing an occasional walkon in a TV commercial to pay the bills. In fact, although I've never breathed this to a soul, I once appeared in a Coronet Cigarette spot, when Benton and Bowles had the business. That was back when cigarette commercials still ran on TV."

"Something tells me you weren't the standup announcer."

"Something is right. Remember that corny campaign with the country music? I was one of a dozen farmer-type chorus boys doing a barn dance while some fag baritone sang, 'Get rich new-flavored Cor-o-nets, the ones that smoke clean country style.' Those goddamned words still echo through my nightmares. I think, in a sense, they were responsible for me becoming a copywriter. A guy I was rooming with at the time worked for Compton, and he got sick of my constant bitching about the lousy commercials I had to audition for, and dared me to put up or shut up. So I wrote a couple of my own—I'd had two semesters of playwriting at Columbia. Jack, he was my friend, showed the spots to the creative director over there, I had an interview, and, by God, they hired me. Eight thousand a year, and I never knew there was that kind of money in the world. Well, I put in two years writing on Procter & Gamble. Crisco, Tide, Duncan Hines. All package goods. And I got married—"

"I know about that," he said.

"Well, it didn't take. Nobody's fault, I guess. I was running out of my class, that's all. Janice's family owned half of Nob Hill. I met her when I was out in San Francisco, shooting a pool of cake commercials. She was in one of

21

the TV spots, we did the North Beach bit together over the weekend, I pulled a week's vacation and we went down to Vegas, and then over to Tahoe and got married, and then . . . *only* then . . . did I learn that she was loaded with the green stuff."

My drink was gone. I ordered another. This would make three. If I wasn't careful, they'd have to carry me up to Ham Keyes's firing squad.

Porter was frowning. "Since when is money a communicable disease?"

"It isn't. But when you're twenty-six, and proud as hell, you sometimes don't have all the smarts in the world. We had our first big fight when Janice's old man decided to buy us a co-op apartment for our wedding present. Hey, what's twenty stories high, green on the outside and red on the inside, and goes for five hundred bucks a month?"

"What?"

"A Park Avenue co-op watermelon."

Porter swore softly. "You weren't kidding about being proud."

"Looking back, arrogant is more like it. Anyway, I had to make more money, and Compton wouldn't give it to me, so I looked around and ended up over here at twelve thousand. But you have to understand, that was just walking-around money for Janice. Oh, she gave it the old North Beach try. She bought clothes in thrift shops—except she took cabs to get there. She shopped at the Key supermarket, and we sponged theater tickets from my friends appearing Off-Broadway, and our first Christmas we did the whole poor bit, you know, making little gifts for each other and so on. Then things really went bad. She got to running with that rich crowd, the ones who find the new joints before they're popular, and she couldn't understand why I wouldn't crawl First Avenue with her. Shit, Howard, picking up one of those tabs would have wrecked a week's pay. And you can't just sponge off the crowd, even if they do have all the money in the world. So I got very self-righteous and started handing out lectures about the gimme generation. I said everything except 'they toil not, neither do they spin.' Jesus, I was a snotty little bastard. But my pride was hurt. Hell, I couldn't compete with that crowd, not on any level except one—I worked, and

22

they didn't. So I played that one to the hilt, and I got just what I deserved. She stuck it in and broke it off. Do you know, I'm still paying her alimony?"

"Alimony? Why, for God's sake?"

"She said if I wanted to play it middle class, I could play it all the way. I had insisted she live on my money while we were married. Well, now I could treat her the same as any other divorced woman. Two hundred bucks a month. That doesn't hurt much now, but it was a big chunk then."

Porter swore again. "You sure must have had some sonofabitch of a hanging judge."

"In New York State they all are. Anyway, it's only money, right? Who cares? Don't you see, I lost a hell of a lot more than money."

He was silent for a moment, then: "Yeah, kid. I guess you did."

Norman Barnes arrived. "Shit, I'm sorry," he said. "I was on the horn with the old man trying to make sense out of this mess."

"Martini, sir?" asked the bartender, already mixing our next round, unbidden.

"Let me have a beer first," Norman said. "Jeez, my gut feels like a washing machine. This is not my day." He turned back to us. "I still don't know what's really going on. I picked up a rumor that the account's going to Esty. I asked Wild Bill about that, and he informed me that *he'd* tell me when it was time for me to know. I reminded him that I'm carried as advertising manager on the brand, and he said that if I didn't stop pushing, that might be corrected. Crap. I think the whole world's coming to an end."

Carefully, Porter asked, "How did you make out with Keyes?"

Norman gulped down half a glass of beer. "That's the goddamnest thing. The news didn't faze him. He didn't even look surprised. He just thanked me for coming to him personally instead of copping out with the telegram bit. And he asked me if I'd told you guys. I said yes, I felt I had to. So he thanked me again and that was it." He finished the beer. "Man, this ain't doing it. Let me have that martini," he called to the bartender.

"Well, Ham's got something on his mind," Porter said.

"He's called a big meeting this afternoon. We figure it to be termination time."

"I hope not," said Norman. "I'd hate that. I'll do anything I can, you know that. I'll tell the whole goddamned world that we didn't yank the business because of bad work on the creative or account end. The only thing is, I may be right there standing in the breadline alongside you."

The three of us sat there sourly and worked joylessly on our drinks. Like most of the Madison Avenue stories you hear, the martini-at-lunch bit is generally overdone. There is certainly a small clan of devoted lushes who enjoy a liquid lunch, but it usually catches up with them just about the time they reach middle management. Then, if they're lucky enought to be in the club, they will often be sheltered and protected, allowed to hang on—but their careers are effectively over. The average business luncheon calls for just a drink or two, usually unfelt because inner tension is running so high that alcohol is instantly converted to energy and bad jokes.

On the other hand, there is much after-hours carousing. I have always secretly believed that clients go into training three or four days before a New York trip. Because after pub-crawling until two A.M., I am a washed-out case the next morning, while they arrive chipper and full of energy for destroying my advertising copy. Storyboards which looked so good the day before in the privacy of my office stare sullenly at me from the cork-lined walls of the conference room, while the alert client pounds away at my leaden hangover with questions I am too tired to answer.

Somewhere distantly I can hear a quiet little voice questioning, "Do you call pub-crawling *work?*" to which I reply snarling, "Hell, yes, it's work!" One thing you should never confuse with fun is a night on the town with the client. You may be swapping girlfriends and drinking from the same cup, but never, *never* get the idea that you are good buddies together and that these festivities are "off the record." Nothing is off the record. Whatever you say in your cups will come back to haunt you. So you spend those gin-hazed nights wheeling and dealing, and if the net result of six hours on the town and ninety bucks on the expense account is to prepare the client for the fact that, in the morning, he is going to see a campaign considerably different from the one he expected but that he should keep his mind open about because it is *good,* and if he accepts that premise, you are way ahead of the game.

Now, of course, in Reuben's, the client/agency relationship had broken down completely. We were all three the walking wounded, huddling together for warmth. Later, if we survived, we would never speak of these moments— nor would we ever presume on the temporary camaraderie they had brought. We were in a backwash of the perpetual war for position, and anything we said today was just for now, not for keeps.

"What are you doing the rest of the day?" I asked Norman.

He tossed an American Airlines ticket folder onto the bar. "Flying home. I'm on the five-fifty out of La Guardia."

Howard Porter raised his fourth martini.

"Have a nice trip," he said, and hiccoughed.

Advertising: Coronet Sheds MK&C

by BILLIPS DOHERTY

In a surprise announcement that rocked advertising circles late yesterday, William P. Haney, president of the Coronet Tobacco Company, revealed that the Coronet Cigarette account, consisting of regular, king-sized, 100's, and menthols, is being moved from Morton, Keyes and Cooper to William Esty, effective in 90 days. The account bills in excess of twelve million yearly, and has been with MK&C for almost five years. Before that, Coronet had used several agencies, including Benton and Bowles, Young and Rubicam and Kudner.

Hamilton Keyes, president of MK&C, was unavailable for comment. However, Mr. Haney stated that the parting was "amicable" and had been brought about by a basic division of opinion on the role of full-service agency responsibilities in long-range planning." "MK&C did some fine work for us on the creative level," said Mr. Haney in a tele-phone interview. "I regard them as an outstanding agency. So much, in fact, that for the time being we intend to continue using their basic campaign line, 'Coronet for the crowning taste in flavor' unless the new team at Esty can top it with the work they're engaged in right now."

Mr. Haney denied that there had been secret new-business presentations by several of the larger package goods shops. "I picked Esty because I like their style. They've done very fine work for cigarettes in the past. But they never created a single speculative layout for me."

Significantly, Coronet Advertising Manager Norman Barnes was not mentioned in either the announcement from Louisville, or the subsequent interview. Mr. Barnes was unavailable for comment, but it is known that he flew to New York personally to deliver the decision to top management at MK&C.

In case the previous few pages have given you a somewhat grubby impression of advertising offices, which is all too often true, don't despair. I have at least one morsel of glamour to hold out. The office housing Hamilton Keyes is everything that MGM would specify, and then some. Whereas a humble group copy supervisor such as I may have two windows, and a management supervisor like Howard Porter may have four, and Charles Stewart, the creative director, will have six in his corner office, Hamilton Keyes has twelve. Twelve! And four of those are stained glass, genuine stained glass from Florence, depicting the Four Seasons. Keyes does not have a regular office desk; he has a rewrite desk cannibalized from the defunct New York *Journal-American,* and when he has a work session, he stations himself in the city editor's slot with everyone else seated around the horseshoe-shaped desk and scoots back and forth on his ball-bearing secretary's chair, confronting each of us in turn.

The walls are hung with old pirate trappings: cutlasses, maps, a tattered Jolly Roger flag, and what purports to be the original privateer charter issued to Sir Walter Raleigh by a grateful (and dry-footed) Queen.

Today, at twenty-nine minutes after two of a gloomy Monday afternoon, the room was filled with nervous men and women, puffing twitchingly at Coronet cigarettes. Once, a few years ago, a hapless account executive was riding up in the elevator with Hamilton Keyes and absent-mindedly reached into his pocket and took out a package of Lucky Strikes. Alarmed by Ham's baleful stare, the poor ape stammered, "Hell, I must have picked up my wife's pack by mistake this morning," to which Ham replied coldly, "Oh? And does your wife have a separate income?" From that day on part of the standard prework checklist included being sure one's pockets did not contain enemy cigarettes.

There is a tomtom rumor system in any advertising agency that would do the CIA proud. I had warned Mark and Phil to keep their traps shut about this morning's announcement, Porter and I hadn't talked, and I doubt that Norman or Ham Keyes had been spreading the evil word. But there was still an unspoken awareness in the big office that somebody was the carrier of a deadly disease, and from the way our former working buddies inched away from Porter and me, it was equally obvious that we were *it*.

Taking a leaf from my own strategy book, Keyes strode into his office at precisely two-thirty. He nodded at several of the copy and account supervisors. Porter and I were not included. Were we being snubbed? Or were we merely out of his line of vision?

He punched a button on the intercom. "Stella, no phonecalls, no visitors, no interruptions."

Hamilton Keyes is Oak Park, Illinois, Groton, and Harvard, in that order. He put in a tour in the Navy as public relations officer aboard the carrier *Enterprise* during the Korean War, and picked up a Navy Cross for pulling an injured pilot out of a flaming Hellcat that had tumbled a barrier. With all of the seagoing knick-knacks on his walls, both in the office and in his Dobbs Ferry home, the one thing not in view is that Navy Cross. But now, more than twenty years later, the white crisscross of burn scars still twist their way up his wrists and forearms, disappearing inside the smartly snapped Sulka cuffs.

Ham is a slight man, with thinning hair that is almost artificially gray along the temples and sideburns. He looks something like a skinny Stewart Granger and talks like John Daly used to on *What's My Line?*

He leaned on the rewrite desk and held out a printed sheet of paper. "Ladies and gentlemen, this is an advance proof of a piece that's appearing on the advertising page of tomorrow's *New York Times*."

Then he read the headline: " 'Coronet sheds MK&C, shifts twelve-million-dollar account to William Esty.' "

Porter and I were confirmed as plague carriers. As Keyes read the rest of the *Times* article a gap gradually opened between us and the rest of the assembled troops. No one looked at us. They even seemed to be trying to avoid breathing the same air.

"Well," said Keyes, folding the galley proof and putting it in his pocket, "we've all been through this before. Every man and woman in this room has worked at an agency that lost a major account, and you all know what to expect. Am I right?"

There was a subdued murmur that might have been assent. Keyes nodded. "Sure. We know what happens. Budget cuts in every department. No Christmas bonus. Terminations. Maybe even a salary trim for everyone earning over ten thousand a year. And worst of all, anxiety. Uncertainty. Jealousy. Infighting. Whose head is going to roll? Mine? Or his? And maybe a little subtle maneuvering to make sure it *is* his, not mine." Keyes scowled down at us. "Well, hear this. That's not the way it's going to be at this shop. Did you hear what I said? That's not the way it's going to be at MK&C!" He patted the pocket that held the *New York Times* advance proof. "I'm sorry the news about Coronet had to break this way. It isn't what I intended to happen. Yes, the client was in my office this morning and he told me of the shift, but that wasn't any surprise to me. I've known for more than a week that the Coronet business was being moved out of the shop."

He sensed a movement from Howard Porter and held up his hand quickly. "Howard, it's no reflection on you or on your creative and account teams. I had my reason for keeping quiet and, believe me, Haney meant it when he said the work in both account and copy was topflight. Just bear with me and I'll get back to that in a minute."

Keyes scanned the room. "All right," he said. "Here's what's going to happen around here." He ticked the points off on his fingers. "There will be no terminations. I repeat, nobody is getting fired. There will be no budget cutbacks, no downward salary adjustments, no curtailment of expense accounts. Business is not only going to go on as usual, it is going to go on better than usual."

"Holy shit," said Porter, "he's come up with another cigarette account."

Keyes heard him. "Not exactly, Howard. Haney's put us in a bind with his premature announcement to the press. Now it's going to be up to us to retrieve the situation. Yes, I do have a new piece of business on the string. But we've got to keep that string from breaking, and we've got to land that baby before we can have it mounted as a trophy. I can tell you, I had second thoughts about what I've told you this afternoon. Leveling with you like this may cost us this new business I'm dickering for, because— and hear this good—if word leaks out before we're ready, the whole thing could blow up right in our faces, and then we *would* be having the meeting you expected today. But I just couldn't see putting you people through weeks of needless anxiety. And, selfishly, it's likely that many of you would have gone out and found new jobs in anticipation of needing them, and I don't want to lose any of you. If this thing comes off, I'm going to need every last one of you, and a detail of new recruits besides."

He ran his hand through his thinning hair. "I've played it straight with you. But you've got to keep your traps shut. Shut. Not a word. Not a peep over drinks. No 'Oh, things aren't so bad, why if I could only tell you' crap. Excuse me, ladies. It's that important. In fact, if you want to look around for other jobs, go right ahead. Just don't take them. Not without seeing me. If you get a bona-fide offer at more money, let me know and we'll discuss it." He smiled wearily. "This is one time you can blackjack management and get away with it."

There was an equally weary laugh from the group.

Keyes looked around. "Any questions?"

One of the art directors said, "Ham, this is going to sound fishy, but I had an offer from Bates just this morning."

"How much?"

"Another five."

"Will you stay for a three-thousand raise?"

The art director nodded. He seemed to be dazed.

"Okay," said Keyes, "you've got it." He put his scarred hands on his hips. "Anyone else think I'm kidding?"

Silence. Keyes jumped down from the rewrite desk. "Okay," he said. "Take the rest of the day off. Get drunk. But keep your big mouths shut."

We turned to leave. He leaned over and touched my arm. "Mike, will you stay behind for a moment?"

Zappo. Amnesty for everyone but the guy last seen with the body. Send my personal belongings home to mother, but first screen out the dirty pictures. . . .

"Sure," I said weakly.

Morton, Keyes and Cooper

Advertising
629 Madison Avenue

FROM: H. Keyes

TO: M. Evans

Mike: This morning I sent out a general memo about the team from the McClintlock organization at Northwestern. Later in the morning, I received a call from Professor McClintlock accepting my offer and informing me that he has assigned one researcher, a Gene Patrick, to the shop for an indefinite period of time.

The trouble is, in view of what happened with Coronet this morning, that McClintlock specifically requested Patrick be allowed to monitor the activities of the cigarette group. After all my protestations of permitting complete access and information, I couldn't very well tell the Professor that since we were losing the business, it was off limits. So I'm afraid you're going to have one of McClintlock's Mob underfoot at this difficult time.

Don't put on any act. Do your job the same way you always do, answer any questions honestly, give complete cooperation, and call me if anything seems to be too much for you to handle.

Best,

Ham

HK/sg

I gave the memo back to Hamilton Keyes. "Is this why you asked me to stay behind?"

"Of course." He squinted at me. "Why, Mike? What did you think I was going to do? Fire you?"

"Yes," I said slowly, "that's exactly what I expected."

He gestured toward the rewrite desk. "Could you use a drink?"

I shook my head. "I had more than enough at lunch. I'm stoned."

"No one can blame you. If I hadn't known what I do, I might have been over there slurping them down with the rest of you."

"What *do* you know, Ham?"

"Mike, I'd tell you if I could. And as soon as I can I *will,* because you're one of the guys I'm counting on to help me pull it off. But I meant it when I said that it could be disastrous if anything leaked out."

I nodded toward the hall outside his closed door. "Then you made a big mistake telling that bunch as much as you did. It's bound to get out."

"I know. But what else could I do? Keep them guessing

—and stabbing each other in the back, trying to survive the purge? I took a calculated risk. If we get to Thursday —maybe even Wednesday—it won't matter."

"What happens Thursday?"

"You'll know when you see it."

"Okay," I said. "I'll watch out for this Patrick guy and give him the full treatment."

"Play it straight," he told me. "I think it's a good omen, McClintlock only assigning one researcher. Maybe he's already figuring the project isn't really as hot as the consumer groups would have people think. And, Mike," he added, touching my arm, "I meant what I said. Don't bail out on me. I need you."

"I won't touch the ripcord without checking with you," I said.

"Fair enough. I'd tell you to take tomorrow off, but your McClintlock researcher will probably be looking for you by then."

"That's all right," I said. "I'll get my drinking done tonight." I started for the door, paused. "Ham, what's going to happen to Norm Barnes?"

Keyes shrugged. "I don't know for sure," he said. "Right now, I'd say it's in the lap of the gods."

"Meaning to say, in the lap of Colonel William P. Haney."

Ham gave me a tight smile. "It's much the same thing," isn't it?"

I nodded and left. Howard Porter was waiting outside, talking to Stella Green, Ham's personal secretary. Stella is around fifty, easily goes two hundred pounds, and has a mind like an IBM computer. She looked up, spoke before Howard could. "Is everything all right, Mike?"

"That's what the man says."

"Then it is," she said, beaming. "I don't know why that pleases me. I suppose it's because I enjoy reading your expense accounts so much. They're the most creative things you write."

"Wait until you see tonight's," I said.

Howard and I walked slowly toward the elevators. "What happened?" he asked.

"Ham gave me more of the same. Hang in there, don't panic, it's all going to be fine."

"Do you believe him?"

"Hell, I don't know. He gave Denny a three-thou raise, didn't he?"

"Maybe that three grand was well spent, if it keeps everybody working instead of running all over town with their sample books. Meanwhile he and Charlie Stewart can quietly figure out who they want to keep and who they want to can."

I pushed the DOWN button. "Then why would he suggest that we put on a show of looking for other jobs?"

"Honesty, maybe. Ham's no bastard, you know. He may find himself in the same spot you were in over at Reuben's—torn between what he wants to do and what he *has* to do."

The elevator arrived. I got in. Howard didn't. His office was here on the ninth floor, the executive floor. I rode down to six—creative—where, perhaps appropriately, the little light over the elevator door never lights up the way it does on the other floors.

Everyone appeared to be working very hard. The doors to several of the offices were closed. I could well imagine the conversations burning up the phone wires.

Effie Fowlkes looked up as I came around the corner. Her brow was furrowed and her eyes were anxious.

"Don't worry, sweetheart," I told her. "I think I'm still among the living."

Desperately, she said, "I was just going to phone down for your coffee."

"Do that. In fact, let's go hog wild. Order a cheese Danish too. I just got my appetite back."

She picked up the phone, put it down again. "Oh," she said, "I almost forgot. You've got a visitor."

"Don't tell me," I said. "Gene Patrick from Northwestern University?" Effie nodded. "Where is he?" I asked.

She gave me a surprised look, then said, "Waiting in your office. I—"

"Make that two coffees," I said. "Cream on the side, just in case Mr. Patrick hasn't been weaned. And hold any phone-calls."

"But, Mike—" she started. I shook my head and growled, "When Mike Evans drinks coffee, everybody drinks coffee. To your duty, woman. You can be replaced."

She was dialing the phone when I went around her desk and through the open door of my office, saying, "I'm sorry I wasn't here when you got in, but—"

My voice trailed off.

Gene Patrick was *Jean* Patrick, a tall, gawky, colt-legged girl.

MK&C EXPENSE VOUCHER

9/4	Taxis	6.85
"	Dinner (J. Patrick, NWU)	14.10
"	Refreshments (J. Patrick, NWU)	18.50
"	Tips	6.00
		45.45

Charge to JPO 6001, Special Research Project

Mike Evans

MICHAEL EVANS

Approved.

C.S.

C. STEWART

It was only nine-thirty when I got to the office on Tuesday. I immediately began making up my expense-account voucher. When Effie came back from the ladies' room, where she had obviously been putting on her face, she stared at me in surprise.

"My gracious, it's Early Evans. What brings you in at this ungodly hour?"

"Mind the impertinence, wench," I said. "Order my coffee and then hustle this chit over to Charlie Stewart, get it approved, and draw my money from the cashier."

"You sound desperate," she said, taking the voucher. "You even typed it yourself."

"I *am* desperate," I said. "I heard strange voices in the night. They whispered, 'Don't go in hock to MK&C for one thin dime. Get it all out in front.' That's what I intend to do."

Without looking at the voucher, she said, "Are you still worried about what happened yesterday?"

"You bet your BP I'm worried about yesterday. Aren't you?"

Subdued, she answered, "Yes."

"I think everything's probably going to be fine," I said. "But why take chances? The agency's still got more money than you and me put together. Let MK&C finance our expeditions to the Top of the Six's from now on. Starting today, we always draw a cash advance. Let them try to get *that* back."

Effie laughed and started toward her desk.

"Get that in to Mr. Charlie before he gets tied up in a copy review board meeting or something," I said. "I'll phone down for the coffee."

"Okay," she said, glancing down at the chit. "J. Patrick. Isn't that—isn't she—"

"Yeah, the one from McClintlock's Mob."

Effie went past her desk, stopped, turned, and, surprisingly, yelled, "She's too goddamned skinny!" and vanished around the corner with her heels clicking on the tiles like a boozed-up drummer.

Women. I phoned for the coffee and then began going through my mail. A bill from the Literary Guild. I threw it in the wastebasket. One of these days Effie would intercept one, write a check, I'd sign it, then, Lo! back in the Guild's good graces, I would receive yet another copy of *The Making of the President 19—*, whatever year it was Teddy White was reporting this time. Three form letters from my friendly neighborhood mutual fund salesman. Wastebasket. A letter from the Mutual of Omaha informing me that the undersigned had taken the liberty of having a handsome desk calendar imprinted with my name and would be happy to drop it off at my convenience, no obligation. A stamped self-addressed envelope is enclosed. . . .

Wastebasket.

I rarely get too upset any more by the constant barrage of direct-mail solicitation. But once, shortly after I made vice president and got my picture in the *Times,* one particular insurance salesman persisted beyond the point of all reason. I received a special delivery letter complaining that after all of the letters he had written and the phonecalls he had made, none of which I had ever responded to, the least I could do out of common courtesy was to grant him an interview.

Furious, I drafted a letter apologizing for my silence,

explaining that I had been out sick—hovering, in fact, near death's door—for several weeks, and that most certainly I would be happy to have him drop by because ever since a team of specialists in Houston had transplanted the heart of a male gorilla in place of my own failing ticker, I had been unable to buy insurance anywhere, and that it was wonderful to find a company willing to take a chance on me. I suggested a policy with a face value of one million dollars, and inquired if I might pay the premium monthly, since there was little likelihood that I would have to meet more than two or three payments that way, thanks to the chronic rejection symptoms I had been experiencing. I further informed him that I was enclosing a list of other advertising personnel who also probably had difficulty in getting insured, suffering as they did from ulcers, alcoholism, drug addiction, and acute anxiety. I had the letter packed up with a copy of the *Advertising Red Book,* which is a huge directory listing every agency in the country, along with their key personnel and which weighs at least ten pounds, and had the whole mess shipped to the insurance salesman, first class, special handling, insured for $1500. Collect, of course. The bill came to $19.61, and not only did the salesman accept the package when it arrived, he wrote me a nice letter saying that under the circumstances, he did not think it would be a profitable expenditure of his valuable time to visit me, the longevity of gorilla transplants being what they were. But he thanked me for the new leads, which he planned to follow up. "After all," he pointed out, "there is a considerable difference in the actuarial tables for a simple ulcer case and the receiver of a gorilla heart transplant.

If Mr. Insurance Man was putting me on, he came out in front, hands down.

My phone rang. I picked it up.

"Mike, this is Charlie Stewart."

"What's up?"

"This expense voucher of yours."

"I've got receipts for everything but the cabs, Charlie."

"That isn't it. Are you sure this was business, Mike?"

"Why do you ask?"

"Your girl told my secretary something about this J. Patrick being a skinny dried-up old maid on the make.

Look, Mike, I know what Ham said yesterday, but even if we hadn't lost Coronet, we'd still be watching vouchers a little closer what with the new IRS rulings on entertainment and—"

"Charlie," I said patiently, "that dried-up old maid is a twenty-two-year-old graduate student from Northwestern University—"

"So *that's* what NWU means?"

"That's what NWU means, Charlie. And I have been specifically instructed by Mr. Hamilton Keyes to give J. Patrick anything she wants with the exception of my fair white body, which is, I'm afraid, what my secretary thinks I'm doing. Check with Ham, if you want. This is all kosher, and it wasn't my idea anyway, and you're lucky I'm not billing you for services above and beyond the call of duty."

There was a pause. Then, with an attempt to be flippant, "Wow, Mike. Is she *that* bad?"

I thought about it for a moment. "No," I said finally, "I was joking. She's not really that bad."

"All right, Mike," he said. "I'll approve it. But lay down the law to that girl of yours, will you? She misrepresented this whole thing."

"I'll handle it," I said, and hung up.

Effie came in. "Here's your coffee," she said sharply, slapping the brown paper bag down on my desk.

"Did you put the hemlock in it?"

"Go to hell," she told me, and stood there waiting. "Well?"

"Well what?"

"I suppose I'm fired."

"No, you're not fired. Sweetheart, please don't bug me. I had a long night and I have the hangover to prove it."

"Good," she snapped, and left.

This was definitely not my week for women. It had started very badly and was going nowhere fast.

For instance, yesterday, the first words out of Jean Patrick's mouth when I barged into my own office, apologizing for not having been there when she arrived, were, "Why, you're drunk!"

Stupidly, I said, "Are you Jean Patrick? Jean with a J and not with a G?"

Remember the young Katharine Hepburn in films like *Bill of Divorcement* and *Holiday*? That's who this girl reminded me of—except, of course, she had the new mod look instead of the cool handsomeness of early Hepburn. Instead of boyish, I guess you'd describe my visitor as looking as if she was a member of *unisex*.

"Don't think I'm a prude, Mr. Evans," she said, "but I can smell gin all the way across this room. It seems those stories about Madison Avenue lunches weren't exaggerated."

"It's a long story," I said. "But you're right. I *am* half in the bag. It doesn't happen very often, but when it does happen, it happens good. Do you mind if I sit down before I fall down?"

Alarmed, she said, "Are you going to be sick?"

"Not unless you keep treating me like Irving Lushwell. Look, this is all going very badly. Why don't I go outside, come in again, and we'll pretend none of this happened and begin anew."

"Oh, come now, Mr. Evans. This isn't a Doris Day-Rock Hudson movie. I don't mean to make value judgments on you personally. It simply seemed a little amusing to arrive here and in my first five minutes at an advertising agency become involved with a Madison Avenue stereotype."

"Well, I'm glad I made your day," I said, mad. "Without going into the qualifications of any college student to make value judgments about matters she knows nothing about, I'll just try to appeal to whatever sense of fair play you may have picked up in your ethics course out at good old NWU. You have me at a complete disadvantage and you seem to be enjoying it to the hilt. I'm under strict instructions to be helpful and cooperative toward you, while you apparently have no such restrictions on your own behavior toward me. On top of that, you happen to be a female, which is the only thing that has kept you from being dumped on your flat little ass, Miss Mob!"

I must have raised my voice, because I heard Effie's chair scrape back outside, but she got to the door just in time to have it closed in her face by Jean Patrick, who did not see her. When the college student turned to me, the tone of her voice was different.

42

"You're extremely upset," she said. "And not with me. I've merely provided a focus. I'm sorry, Mr. Evans. Is it something personal? If so, I'll leave. I have no right to intrude on your personal affairs. My job is to observe the business of advertising, not"—and here she smiled tightly —"not plop my flat ass down where it isn't welcome."

There wasn't anywhere sensible this conversation could go. So I said, "I think you hit my secretary in the nose when you closed the door."

"Oh!" she said, and opened it. Effie reappeared. "Coffee," she said, putting a paper bag in Jean Patrick's unprepared hand like a quarterback executing an improvised handoff. The girl almost dropped it, then recovered.

"You might as well have some coffee, Miss Patrick," I said. "Coffee time is as much a part of advertising as cost per thousand and Nielson ratings."

"If you have enough," she said.

"I ordered that one especially for you. You can even have half a cheese Danish."

"I had lunch," she said.

"Well, I drank mine," I said, pushing one of the white styrofoam cups across the desk to her. "You want cream?"

"No, it puts on weight."

I had to smile. "You don't look as if you have any problems in that area."

She did not return the smile. "When I was sixteen, I weighed more than a hundred and fifty pounds. Then I had an—operation—and came out of the hospital at a hundred and nine. I've never been over that weight since and, if humanly possible, I never intend to be."

"Do you drink?"

"Moderately."

"Would putting a little Irish in the coffee to sweeten it be considered moderate?"

"Are you using some?"

"Yes."

"All right. Just half an ounce."

I gave her a good shot. If she noticed, she did not protest. I sweetened my own and nodded a gentle toast. "Health."

"Yours too," she said. Somehow I was oddly pleased

43

that she hadn't come back with "Cheers" or "Skoal" or any of the other cuties.

"Okay, Miss Patrick," I said, "what do you want from me?"

"To start off, call me Jean."

"Mike, then."

"Okay, Mike. Next, try to trust me. It's only natural that there be some suspicion and antagonism toward what we're doing. But believe me, Mike, we aren't out to tear things down. The role of ombudsman—"

"Om-who?"

She laughed. "Don't play the uneducated huckster with me, Mike. I had you checked out."

"Okay, I know what an ombudsman is. He represents the people to the establishment, or to the government, or whatever. What do you mean you had me checked out? How long have you known we'd be working together?"

"Since Friday. We have access to most of the computer files and an extremely efficient retrieval system. I didn't know for sure I'd be working directly with you, but we had requested the cigarette account, so I found out as much as I could about those of you who work on it."

"What did the magic machine say about me? Do I pass?"

She actually blushed. "It just gives facts. Education. Columbia, drama major. Your Off-Broadway acting credits. The listing in *Who's Who in Advertising*. And the usual personal background."

So that explained the blush. "Ah," I said. "Including my brief bout with matrimony?"

"I didn't request such personal information," she said. "But it was part of the computer readout and there wasn't any way to exclude it."

"Don't apologize," I said. "I'm resigned to the fact that from the day they invented magnetic tape, the life of every human being became public property."

"There's nothing wrong with being divorced," she said. "It's better to admit a mistake and get out while there's still time, rather than cripple two lives—or more, if there are children."

"Really?" I said. "Were your parents divorced?"

"That's none of your business!" she shot back. Then,

44

softly, "No. No. But they should have been. Oh, God, they should have been."

Embarrassed, I said, "Now *I'm* throwing the low ones. I'm sorry."

"Accepted," she said. "Let's get back to the study. You're familiar with the previous work Professor McClintlock has done?"

"Vaguely. I remember his report on the television networks. Program directors were jumping out of windows all over town."

She frowned. "That's precisely the attitude we have to fight. You assume automatically that we're out to *get* you."

"Aren't you?"

"Only if there are real abuses against the public that ought to be corrected. In the case of the television networks, our—the Professor's, rather, because I wasn't working with him then—conclusion was that the networks have become obsolete. In attempting to please an audience of more than two hundred million, they're really able to please no one, *serve* no one. So a new system is called for."

"You couldn't expect CBS to be overjoyed by the Professor telling them to go out of business."

"We didn't say go out of business, we. . . ." She stopped. "Well, Mike, that's not the issue here. We're discussing my working relationship with you and with the rest of the agency. Are you going to help or—"

"We'll cooperate. All the way." I smiled at her. "Not my idea, Miss Mob. Orders from the top. Believe it or not, the boss doesn't think we have anything to hide."

"*Do* you?"

"Doesn't everybody?"

She looked away. Took out a small notebook. "I'll leave it up to you to explain to your co-workers what I'm doing here, or not, as you choose. As I told you earlier, my job isn't to make value judgments. At this early stage of the study my position is to be merely a recorder. I will gather material and others will evaluate my raw data and decide which areas should be followed up."

"And there is nothing personal about it. This is a recording. This is a recording."

45

She snapped the notebook shut. "That wasn't necessary."

"Sorry. I just felt like your last speech was canned and that you've given it a dozen times before."

"Well, I haven't!" Then, more softly, "I mean, not for real. This is my first field assignment. But you're right. I did memorize something like it for the class practice sessions."

"What did they tell you in class about having dinner with one of your subjects?"

"They advised that personal relationships between researchers and subjects are to be avoided."

"You don't sound like you really mean that. After all, how do you imagine you're going to find out what I really do around this place if all you see is what happens from nine to five and all you know about me is my job description?"

"We're only interested in the business of making and selling advertising, not what happens after hours—"

"For your information, Miss Mob, half of the most important decisions in this business are made after hours, in crummy Third Avenue bars or in posh traps like Twenty-One. We're very democratic about where we drink. We spread the business around. But client entertainment is certainly one of the stereotypes of Madison Avenue that you ought to investigate."

Smiling a little, she said, "You're very persuasive."

"That's my business, being persuasive."

"All right," she said. "But we'll go Dutch."

I leaned back and choked. "We'll what?"

"What's so funny about that?"

"Jean, you're the one who said this isn't one of those Doris Day-Rock Hudson movies. Nobody goes *Dutch!* Hell, even buddies who work at the same shop don't make like the little old ladies at Schrafft's, divvying up the check."

Stiffly, she asked, "What *do* they do?"

"It's split up on a different basis. I'll pay one time and my friend'll pay next. Or we might put our Diner's Club cards face down on the table, shuffle them around, and have the waiter pick one."

"In which case the loser reports the bill to the IRS as a business expense?"

"You bet your"—I stopped, made a fast recovery—"your sweet life we do. And who's to say it's *not* business?"

"But you both work for the same company."

"And that's why we can't turn it in here. But we got a hell of a lot of work done at those lunches, in between the lies and the gossip and the bad jokes." I noticed that she was looking at her wristwatch, a slim, sensible Timex. "Are you in a hurry?"

"It's just that I have to check in where I'm staying before five or they might not hold the room."

"You mean you came here straight from the airplane? Where's your luggage?"

"I sent it down by taxi."

I groaned. "And you expect it to be there? Don't you know about New York cab drivers?"

"I wrote down his number and tipped him well. He saw me take the number. I think everything will be all right."

It probably would. I couldn't see any cabbie with the nerve to cross this one.

"Where are you staying?"

"The Hotel Claremont, on West Eleventh Street, near—"

"I know the place well," I said. " 'Marrying Sam's' we called it in my own Greenwich Village days. It's where all the nice girls from the Middle West get sent to preserve their virtue. They've even got a eunuch for a doorman."

Straight-faced, she said, "That's probably why I ended up there. The Professor is very strict." She held out her hand. "After thinking it over, I believe I'd better unpack this evening instead of going out. Suppose I see you here at nine in the morning?"

"If you're here at nine, all you'll see are window washers. Quarter of ten's more like it."

"Banker's hours, Mr. Evans?"

"I thought it was supposed to be Mike. And if bankers work until seven or eight a couple of times a week, and stay out until four A.M. with clients at least two times a month, why yes, you could call them banker's hours."

47

"I see," she said coldly. I stood up to lead her out the door, but she waved me away. "That's all right, I remember the way out. Nine-forty-five tomorrow, then."

When she was gone, I sat there for a moment, contemplating my empty coffee cup. Then I dialed Ham Keyes's number. Stella answered. I said, "This is Mike Evans. Is the big boss there?"

"Just a minute, Mike."

"That's a good girl."

There was a click, and Keyes said, "Yes, Mike?"

"Your McClintlock investigator is here."

"Have you spoken with him?"

"It's a her, and yes, I've already had a session down here. I'd say that your Professor is not exactly sending out his first team."

"What do you mean?"

"She's just a kid, Ham, green as grass. This is her first field trip."

A pause, then he said, "That might be good. It *could* mean that McClintlock doesn't think there's much here to be investigated."

"It could also mean that he thinks we're such pushovers that he can throw in the rookies. And even if that's not so, it's not the best deal having someone around who's never held a job. You have to remember that some of those kids think there's something dreadfully immoral about earning a buck, especially if their old man already got his and sends them regular checks to finance their protests."

"No lectures, Mike. And what I said still goes. Cooperation all the way. We can't expect to pick and choose who McClintlock sends out."

"Right on. But can I spend money?"

"What?"

"Can I put this broad on the expense account? If it was a guy, I wouldn't even ask. But Accounting doesn't like writers slipping their girlfriends on the old swindle sheet, and that's just the way it'll look if you don't give them the word. After all, I can't let her pay for her own coffee and Danish. Somebody's got to pick up the tab, and right now my own personal bank account is down to zilch."

"All right, call Accounting and have them assign a JPO. Call it a Special Research Project."

"Right. I'll keep you posted."

He hung up without answering. I wasn't upset. He always does. That and his blue envelopes. Two minor flaws in an otherwise consistent character. Would that I had so few inconsistencies.

I went out and told Effie to get the JPO, and then to have Personnel free up an office on our floor for Jean Evans.

Puzzled, Effie asked, "Is she a new copywriter?"

To Effie's greater confusion, I said, "No, she's a paid spy, representing the union of American consumers."

I put on my London Fog and went down to try and get a cab before the rush. I wanted to take a Bromo, shower, and try to sober up. I had big plans for this evening.

Telegram

NYC L2L4 NY210 1B FR NEW YORK NY 14

MISS JEAN PATRICK HOTEL CLAREMONT
WEST 11 ST & AVE OF AMERICAS NEW YORK CITY NY

RE PROJECT URGENT YOU ARRIVE MINETTA TAVERN 8 PM SHARP
TODAY MONDAY NOVEMBER 14 ASK FOR PACKAGE YOUR NAME.
DETAILS ENCLOSED WITHIN GOOD LUCK

MCCLINTLOCK

WU 1261 (R 8-00)

Minetta Lane is a narrow interstice running vaguely from Macdougal Street to Sixth Avenue, which—twenty-some-odd years after it was renamed—everybody still refuses to call Avenue of the Americas. The lane is named after an underground stream that originally meandered through the area when Greenwich Village was just what its name implied—a bucolic bit of countryside between the hurlyburly of downtown Manhattan and the newly burgeoning Forty-second Street area.

In recent years the quiet-paced coffeehouses that originally lined Macdougal have given way to flamboyant head shops with psychedelic posters and peace emblems plastered all over the dirty windows. Off-Broadway theaters that used to showcase Ibsen and Shaw and Chekhov now offer jarringly offensive homosexual plays with the act of sodomy simulated in the nude; with sex revues building on the candor and occasional wit of *Oh! Calcutta!* but with candor replaced by lechery and wit pushed aside by vulgarity; where beatniks chanted "Ommmm" and sketched bearded portraits in charcoal, pushers now shove sticks of weed and black cowboys flaunt their young blonde girl-friends.

But amidst this tawdry display there is still an oasis of quiet and taste: the Minetta Tavern, a genuine family restaurant squeezed in between the honkytonk joints and the Blimpie hero-sandwich shops. If ever the Minetta Tavern closes its doors, the last remaining vestige of genuine Greenwich Village will be gone as far as I am concerned.

Caricatures of favorite customers—many from the forties and fifties—line the wall behind the bar: Maxwell Bodenheim, the tragic poet who was a frequent visitor before meeting bloody death at the knife of a crazed sailor in a cheap East Side rooming house; Maurice, town crier of the artistic and literary crowd at midcentury who was often to be found just inside the door on cold winter nights, peddling a late copy of *The Paris Review* or *Off-Broadway Magazine* or perhaps *The Realist*. Maurice, too, is gone—as are most of the faces that smile down from the wall through the boozy mist of some long-ago beer bust.

But the drinks are still good and the food in the back dining room is rich and garlicky, for the cuisine is predominantly Italian, and superbly so. I go there often and am always pleased.

I was nursing a martini on the rocks when Jean came in shortly after eight. She looked around, not seeing me in the corner near the cigarette machine, then approached the bar and asked, "Excuse me? Do you have a package for me? Miss Jean Patrick?"

Without rancor the bartender said, "Have you tried the post office?" I signaled him over her shoulder and he nodded and walked down to the other end of the bar. I stood behind her and said, "Package for Miss Jean Patrick."

She turned, starting to thank me, and froze.

"I suppose you think this is funny," she said.

"I really *do* have a package," I said, handing her the single white orchid in its plastic box.

She held it awkwardly, not sure whether to shove it back at me, keep it, or put it down on the bar.

"You forged that telegram," she accused.

"Guilty," I said. "Look, Jean, I'm sorry for making that crack about the Claremont. I was trying to be funny, and when I try too hard, I rarely succeed. But you must have observed that I have changed into my sincere necktie in honor of this occasion, and I have chewed half a roll of Clorets, and while I may not make any more sense now in trying to explain myself, at least I'm no longer bouncing off the walls. I'm hungry, and I don't like to eat alone, and I *do* want to talk with you, and this is probably the best restaurant within ten miles—"

"Stop!" she laughed. "I was sold way back there when you mentioned the sincere necktie. But just this one time, Mike. And only because we haven't really started the project yet."

"Let's wait until later to argue about that," I said. "But I'll tell you this, Nader's Raiders didn't hesitate to hoist a few with the boys after work."

"That's because they were boys themselves," she said. "When you're a girl—" She stopped. "May I have a Scotch and water?"

I beckoned the bartender. "White Label all right?"

Jean nodded, slipping onto one of the leather stools. I took the shoulders of her woolen coat and she shrugged out of the arms. Beneath she wore a white blouse and a colored scarf tied around her neck, all violent reds and oranges and blues. She had on slacks and sensible-looking black boots.

I draped the coat over a wooden peg. It seemed heavy on one side. I touched the left pocket. There was a square, weighty object inside. Probably one of the little Sony cassette recorders.

When I went back to the bar, she had opened the plastic box and was gently touching the orchid. She looked up at me and said, "Thank you. That was sweet."

"Put it on. There's a pin in there somewhere."

She held the box out to me. "You do it."

My hands shook slightly as I slipped the pin through the flower. It was the old pre-meeting syndrome. Then, as I hung the orchid on, I knew that I had stuck her in the breast with its sharp pinpoint. "Whoops," I said. "Sorry." She didn't react, didn't seem to notice that I'd jabbed her, just looked over and said, "That's fine. I love flowers."

"I didn't mean to stick you," I said.

"You didn't—" she began, then stopped. She looked

down at her drink. "You didn't stick me," she said softly. She drank. Deeply. Too deeply, I thought, for a quiet little girl from the Midwest who believes in being moderate. I wondered what I had done or said.

"Look," I told her, "I paid for the orchid myself. But from here on in you're a JPO, so let's not have any more of that Dutch nonsense."

"What's a JPO?"

"Job Project Order. Your number is six-oh-oh-one."

She smiled. "Do you mean there have been six thousand before me? You're a busy man, Mike."

"Perish the thought. No, a JPO is just for cost accounting on any particular project."

"What kind of project am I?"

"Public relations, we hope. You see, Ham—Hamilton Keyes, our eminent president—really believes in advertising. He doesn't think we have anything at all to hide. I don't agree. Everybody's got a closet stuffed with skeletons. But I take orders. So relax and enjoy it. You're going to get the same treatment as any other VIP in town."

Jean studied her drink. "I'm not a VIP. I'm just a graduate student doing a pilot study on an industry which may or may not come under full investigation by the McClintlock Commission. I have no axe to grind either way. My mind is open, I hope. But it won't do any good to try to soft-soap me or buy me off with either luxury or flattery. I'm immune to both, Mike."

"Look, Jean, nobody's trying to buy you off. I'm merely following my master's orders right out the window. Full and complete cooperation, he said, and that's what you'll get. If you think your price is so low that you can be bought by a bowl of linguine with white clam sauce, that's your problem. I may be old-fashioned, but I want to like the people I work with, so I try to see more of them than hello in the elevator. And what's more, I have this terrible weakness for good looking females, and if our ubiquitous JPO is willing to indulge my weakness, who am I to fight the inevitable?"

"I said flattery wouldn't work either, remember?"

"What flattery?"

"I've got a long way to go to qualify as what you'd call a good-looking female. And—"

54

"Hold it right there, lady," I said. "Who are you to judge what *I* consider good-looking? Beauty is in the eye of the beholder. Maybe the Revlon Company would like me to think that two pounds of glop, some dragon-wing eyelashes, and a nylon stretch wig is beauty, but, sweetheart, they lost me on the first curve. Methinks thou dost protest too much. I know every chick likes to be told over and over again how great she looks, but I only serve one to a customer, and you just had yours."

She didn't try to cute it up. Instead, she touched my hand and said, "In that case, thank you very much, Mike. Now, what did this JPO of yours say about dinner?"

"It said time's awasting."

At the table I did the magic fan act with the big menu and heaved it over my shoulder at Pete, who caught it deftly, as he always does. "Let us throw ourselves on the mercy of the management," I said.

Jean Patrick laughed, and for a second there she really *was* beautiful.

<u>MK&C TRAVEL REQUISITION</u>

NAME(S): H. Porter, M. Evans, J. Patrick

DESTINATION: Montego Bay, Jamaica, West Indies

DEPARTURE DATE: 9 a.m. November 16, Pan Am Flight
               TK 102

RETURN: Open

CLASS OF TRAVEL: First Class

BILL: Client

H. Porter

H. Porter

APPROVED

H.K.

Hamilton Keyes
(by Stella Green)

I had been daydreaming, remembering last night. When Effie came back from upstairs with my cash for the evening's expenses, I was over being mad at her. "Sit down for a minute," I said. She did. "Listen, have I ever made you promises?"

Grimly, she said, "You've been careful not to."

"Then where do you get off going down to Charlie Stewart's office and shooting off your mouth? Listen, Miss Jean Patrick is business, plain and simple, and even if she weren't, it's frankly none of your concern. You and I had a couple of laughs, and that's all there was and all there ever will be. I'm sorry your nose is out of joint now, but for Christ's sake, keep your cool. We've got troubles enough around here."

As if I hadn't said a word, she told me, "Mr. Keyes wants you to call. Karen took the message on my line while you were talking on yours."

"Is that all you have to say?"

"Yes." She got up and went back to her desk.

Well, I'd asked for it. Rule Number One is never, never play around in the office. Because if it doesn't work out, or even if it does, you've got an extra layer of problems. I admired Effie, and we had a few drinks every now and then, and one night after the Feast of San Gennaro down on Mulberry Street we somehow ended up in my apartment in Chelsea, and it wasn't planned, and it was softly delicious and gently sad, and finished with the dawn, no encores called for. But it had been churning around down there all these months, just waiting for the right time to boil over, and that time just had to be now. I groaned and reached for the phone.

"Stella, is Ham there?"

"Hold on, Mike."

Keyes came on. "Mike, it's happened sooner than I thought. Get yourself packed, be sure to have proof of citizenship, and be ready to take off from JFK at nine A.M. tomorrow."

"Take off? Where are we going?"

"Jamaica. Listen, I'm juggling two calls at once. Get together with Howard Porter. He's been briefed already. He'll give you the scoop."

"Hey, hey!" I yelled. "Don't hang up." I didn't hear a click, so I figured he was still there. "What the hell do I do with Miss Jean Patrick? She's assigned to me, remember?"

There was a pause. Then, "Jesus, Mike, we can't have *her* along. Think of something. Tell her you're going on vacation."

"You don't know this girl, Ham. She'll go back to Northwestern and they'll send the Mafia after us."

"This project is too delicate," he said, hesitating.

"What's so delicate, Ham? I thought we didn't have anything to hide."

Angrily, he said, "Whose side are you on, anyway?"

"*My* side. Listen, this was your idea, boss man. What did you get me into it for if you didn't mean to let me play it straight?"

Some executives would have cut you down for handing it to them like that. But Hamilton Keyes was one of the good ones. He thought it over for a few seconds and said, "You're right, Mike. Okay, put it to her like this. We're making a new business pitch on the Dodge Truck account this Friday. She can stay around with Harry Smith's group and get in on that. Or she can come along with us for some dull meetings which have nothing at all to do with Coronet Cigarettes and which may or may not result in a piece of new business coming into the agency. Give her the fair choice. Hell, McClintock ought to be interested in the background of car advertising. Nader was. Be sure to tell her our trip has nothing to do with tobacco, and that may get you off the hook. She *does* know we've lost the Coronet account, doesn't she?"

"Yes," I said remembering last night, "she knows."

We had left Minetta's early, around ten-thirty, and her idea was to go back to the Claremont, but my own ideas were different.

"Have you ever heard of McSorley's Wonderful Saloon?" I asked.

"Joseph Mitchell wrote a book about it, didn't he?" she said, as we walked slowly up Macdougal toward Washington Square. The night air was crisp and we could see our breaths, and there was a feeling of snow in the air.

"Right. It used to be a hangout for old Irishmen and young NYU students. It's over on the East Side, just below Cooper Union. Until 1970 it was for men only. For over a hundred years only men could get in. Hell, a woman *owned* it, and if she wanted a beer, she had to come to the back door, tap on the window, and they'd hand one out to her. Well, Women's Lib fixed that. They integrated McSorley's. The Supreme Court, in its wisdom, handed down a decision that opened McSorley's dingy doors to all comers."

"That's sad," Jean said.

I stopped and looked at her. "Funny," I said. "Somehow, I would have imagined that you'd be in favor of the Court's decision."

"Why?" she asked, not without a tinge of bitterness. "Because I know how to handle myself, do you think I despise femininity—or its opposite, masculinity? Can't I be an effective person without wanting to grab all a man's prerogatives and private jujus? After all, we women have a few of our own, you know."

"Strike one against Evans," I said. "I take it no McSorley's."

"I think you're trying to prove something," she said, "and I don't want to play that game."

59

"Maybe I was," I said. "Okay. Yonder comes that rarest beast of all on a chilly evening, a New York taxicab, and we are going to get into it and I will show you something that proves nothing at all except that even ugliness can be beautiful if seen from the right vantage point."

She was bewildered, but she got into the cab. "Six Sixty-six Fifth Avenue," I told the driver.

"What's there?" Jean asked as we headed up Sixth Avenue.

"Around five advertising agencies," I said, "including Ted Bates and Benton and Bowles. And a great joint called the Top of the Six's, with so-so-food, pretty good drinks, and the greatest view in the world on a clear night. We call it Client Heaven. They all mumble about wanting to be treated just like one of the boys, but when we really want to impress one of them, we haul him up to the Top and it knocks his eyes out. I bet they have some neat conversations about it back in Louisville."

"That division is always very apparent, isn't it?" she asked.

"Which division is that?"

"Client/agency. They're two different kinds of people, from the tone of your voice. I get the impression that you look down on clients."

I thought about what she'd said for a moment. "No," I answered slowly, "that's not really so. There is a division, that's true. But my attitude is a two-part thing. First, the client has the power of life and death over me. A whim can put me on the unemployment line, no matter how good my work is and how nice a guy I am. And since, like anything else, clients come in bad sizes as well as good ones, we tend to remember the times we got stung by the bad ones. So the term 'client' isn't what you'd use for a dear friend. Then, even the good ones are going to have to beat you up every now and then, often for reasons you can't understand. They will be mousetrapped by their own management, maybe, and have to give you the dirty end without even being able to tell you why. Like today. . . ."

"What *did* happen today, Mike?"

What the hell? I'd been told to conceal nothing. Besides, I *wanted* to talk about it.

60

"We got fired off the Coronet Cigarette account. No warning, no reason, no notice. Just zappo."

"How can that be? Aren't you part of the product's company, or whatever they call it?"

I shook my head. "Freshman advertising lecture number one: the ad biz is a relatively young industry. It got started in the last part of the eighteen hundreds. Oh, there were guys around before that, with their snake-oil wagons, waving big colorful signs urging the populace to 'Drink Dr. Newton's Magic Elixir,' but that was small potatoes. It wasn't until after the Civil War that advertising became a big thing, because of the thousands of newspapers that were printing. The catch was, there were ten thousand different papers, each operating in its own crazy way, with ad rate cards that meant about as much as the ravings of a drunken Ouija board. They might be quoting a dime a column inch and be happy to settle for three cents. What's more, it was a hell of a job contacting all of those papers, making arrangements for buying the space, paying for it—and then *checking* to be sure the publisher hadn't simply spent your dough without actually running the ad."

"Hey, Mac," said the taxi driver, "you mind if I stop for a pack of cigarettes?" His voice emphasized "pack" and I suspected what was really his problem.

"Not if you shut off the meter," I said.

"Would I cheat you?" he said in a hurt voice. He pulled over to a White Rose bar, turned off the engine, and hurried inside. The meter clicked happily onward.

"What happened then?" asked Jean.

"The good knight kicked the hell out of the black dragon and his fast meter," I said.

"I mean when the advertising business was getting started. I've read all of the history, of course, but it sounds different when you tell it."

"Oh. Well, let's see. All was confusion and mess. So enter the advertising agent. Notice the key word, '*agent.*' You see, in those days, and for that matter even down to the present time, the advertising agent did not work for the client. He worked instead for the *media,* for the newspaper, then the magazine, then the radio or television broad-

61

caster. And for his efforts in selling the space or the air time he received a commission which started at ten per cent but which was now more or less stabilized at fifteen percent of the total space cost. Remember, this dough came from the media in which the ads were placed, and the client was in essence getting the agent's services for nothing."

The meter clicked over. I was paying for the driver's lengthy leak and probably a quick shot besides.

"Yes?" said Jean.

"Okay, there came the day when the client said, 'I'd like to run an ad this week, Charlie, but I haven't got time to write it.' So the agent said, 'I'll write it for you, Sam,' and he did, and the next thing you know advertising agencies were in the business of creating the ads they placed."

"Without getting paid for the work?"

"Oh, the client's quick enough today to say, 'You guys better be good, for all the money I'm paying you,' but the truth is the client isn't actually paying the agency one thin dime. He's only letting the agency collect a commission from the media—and that commission is something no client can get kicked back by the media, not without some crooked under-the-table deals at any rate. Say Brand X places an ad that costs ten thousand bucks. The agency gets fifteen hundred as its commission for placing the space. And, incidentally, for doing most of the work. But if the client, Mr. Brand X, bought that same space direct, he'd pay the full ten thousand and have to do all the work himself."

Jean said, "But if it costs him ten thousand either way, he doesn't really need an agency, does he?"

"Yes he does," I said. "He needs somebody to do the work, and most of all he needs somebody he can fire when things go wrong. That's us. All for fifteen percent, tax-deductible."

"Thanks, Mac," said the driver, sliding into his seat. The meter said click and I said nothing.

As we drove up Sixth, Jean asked, "Well, what does it mean that you've been fired off the Coronet account?"

"It means my client's boss told him to tie the can to MK&C, and so the poor bastard had to fly up here this morning and chop off our feet without even knowing why he was doing it. That's why we were lushing it up at lunch. Incidentally, the client lushed better than any of us. So it looks like you picked a loser when you elected to sign up with the Coronet crowd. Unless you want to follow the account over to its new agency, wherever that may be."

Concerned, she asked, "Does this mean you're out of a job? Isn't that what happens when you lose an account?"

"Ordinarily, yes. But don't look so worried. Not for yours truly anyway. I'm the kind of guy a little unemployment doesn't hurt. My running expenses are rock bottom, except for a couple of hundred bucks a month alimony, which I'd dearly love to have a reason not to pay."

"But you were so upset this afternoon."

" 'Drunk' was the word you used, and an accurate one. But not for myself, Jean. I can find another job fairly easy, because I honestly don't *care*."

"That seems an odd qualification."

"You have to understand that this business is nine-tenths front," I said. "Down on my working level it doesn't matter so much, but once you're up in senior management, you've got to act the part. That means a big house in Westchester, and memberships in the right clubs, and entertaining at the right restaurants, and your kids in the right schools. All of these things cost real money. You may be pulling in eighty grand a year and living at the rate of a hundred. Well, a guy on top is so success-oriented that he can't abide the lack of it in anyone else. So no matter what my track record has been, if I come in looking like I *need* a job, I'm poison. There has to be something wrong with me, don't you see, or I'd be *successful*. But if I just don't give a damn, and my attitude shows it, I might even get a nice jump in salary. Because, oddly enough, that way I would probably end up doing a better job at the new place than if I were running scared."

"Then why are you so upset?"

"Because when an account as big as Coronet leaves a shop, twenty or thirty guys who *do* need a job usually end up on the street. And the hell of it is, they may have had nothing at all to do with the account that got away. But when management's deciding who to let go, they pick the guys they're not too happy with anyway, or maybe the guys who have been around quite a while in middle-authority jobs but whose salaries have climbed as a result of yearly increases to where they can probably be replaced by younger men at two-thirds of their price. Take a forty-year-old art director, a good one but nothing to set the world on fire: he's got a house to keep up—not in Westchester, but maybe in Greenwich—and two kids ready to start college, and a couple of car payments, and all the rest. Yank the rug on him and you've got a frightened man. And that fear can destroy him, because they'll smell it at job interviews, and he may be on the beach for months, eating away at savings and capital before he finally gets located again. Some of them never do. They end up trying to use their old friendships in the business as prospects for mutual funds or insurance plans. It's a rough business, baby, if you let yourself care too much."

"It sounds to me," Jean said, "that what you're really saying is that you can't afford responsibilities outside the business if you're going to be successful *in* it. I just can't agree with that, Mike. Wasn't it John F. Kennedy who quoted Sir Francis Bacon when he said that if you have children, you've given hostages to fortune? A person automatically assumes various responsibilities as he moves through life. And perhaps those responsibilities make him more vulnerable than he would be without them. But you can't just cop out on everything because you're afraid you might get hurt later."

"I didn't invent the system," I said. "I'm merely trying to explain it to you as I see it. Whatever you would like to believe, that won't change the fact that the guys who are afraid are the guys who would have a hell of a hard time getting relocated favorably, and that's why we were slugging down the silver bullets at lunch today."

The cab arrived at 666 Fifth Avenue and I traded a seventy-five-cent tip for a grunted "Thanks, Mac" from the driver, and we took the fast elevator up to the restaurant. Phillip, the new headwaiter, was at the rope, and he waved me through ahead of a sixpack of tourists.

"We're just drinking tonight, Phil," I told him. "But the lady would like to see the view. Crowded?"

He shrugged. "So-so. But not too much to take care of old friends." He led us past the bar in the center of the room. "The south view, so Madame can see the World Trade Center."

How the world turns. It used to be the south view so you could look at the Empire State Building.

"Brandy?" I asked.

"Drambuie," Jean said, staring out at the night view with undisguised fascination.

The skyline vista of New York City still qualifies as one of the real wonders of the world. During the day the city is grimy and smog-shrouded, with ugly construction holes ripped from nearly every block. But when night covers the ugliness with healing darkness, a hundred million Christmas trees seem to go on, and when seen from a great height, such as the Top of the Six's, their effect is breathtaking.

Our drinks came, and Jean said, "Thank you for bringing me here, Mike. It's really lovely."

"The view from my apartment is even better," I said. She laughed and I knew she could tell I was only kidding.

Or was I? How much kidding is there, really, under the banter and the idle flirtation talk? Are we always throwing out little lines, so tiny that if they are rebuffed you can say, "See? I was only joking?" but strong enough that an acceptance of one can lead to the weaving of several, and the creation of a skein capable of tying two lives together for a moment, however brief?

"Mike," Jean Patrick said slowly, "you said, about those other people, something like they were the ones who would have trouble relocating. Would, not *will*. Does that mean they won't be fired after all?"

Deeper water here. I decided to level all the way. "Could be," I said. "Keyes thinks he's got another piece of business coming in to take up the slack. If so, they call off the firing squad."

Looking down over the twinkling lights of the city, she said, "You make it all sound like some kind of war."

"For me," I said, "it is."

INTERNATIONAL
EMBARKATION/DISEMBARKATION CARD

1. (Please Print)

Mr
Mrs
Miss

EVANS
....
(Surname)

....
(Maiden name)
MICHAEL
....
(Given names)

2. Date of birth   22   OCT.   1940
                  (Day)   (Month)   (Year)

3. Place of birth   DOVER, N. J.

4. Nationality   U.S.A.

5. Occupation   ADVERTISING WRITER

6. Permanent address   611 W. 28 ST., NYC USA

7. For arriving passengers: port of embarkation   NYC
   For passengers leaving: port of debarkation

8. Passport number   F 7837805

(FOR OFFICIAL USE ONLY)

Cleared Customs
Wexford Court
        Mo. Bay

   Long Pine

Nine A.M. is a gruesome hour to fly out of John F. Kennedy International Airport, especially on an international flight for which you must arrive early. The timetable requires either arranging for a thirty-dollar limousine to pick you up—and even then you are never completely sure he will actually arrive—or hoping you will be able to catch a cab at six A.M. If you choose the latter, you can depend on considerable swearing on the part of the driver when he is directed to the airport, an attitude hard to understand when you know all too well the meter is going to read around sixteen dollars for the haul, and that the grumbler can reasonably count on the rest of the twenty dollars you hand him as a tip, all for an easy forty-five-minute drive against the rush-hour traffic flow, making the trip swift and painless. Sometimes I think New York taxi drivers resent having to carry passengers at all. Their chief joy in life seems to be barreling around choking sidestreets, lighted off-duty signs blaring their independence to all who are foolish enough to want to hire them. And I realize that what I've just said may offend those drivers who *are* courteous, helpful, and fair—so I apologize in advance to them. Both of them.

Ham Keyes and Howard Porter both lived in Westchester and would be driving across the Whitestone Bridge, bypassing Manhattan. I didn't feel like spending thirty-five bucks, with tip, of the company's money on a limo service, so I elected the cab routine with all its attendant risks. And my decision was complicated by the fact that Jean Patrick would be riding to the airport with me.

I don't know what she told Professor McClintlock to convince him that a week in Montego Bay came under the heading of business. I had a hard enough time with Effie, especially when she learned that Jean was going too. I felt bad about having chewed Effie out, but she was behaving in a most unsecretarylike way, and I was just as glad to be away for a few days. I didn't really want to have her transferred to some other group. Had I tried, she probably would have quit anyway. A good secretary can just about name her own terms on Madison Avenue, and except for her present case of office-wife jitters, Effie was one of the best around.

Ham's Dodge Truck new-business-pitch ploy didn't have a chance of working with Jean. She cut me off in the middle of it and said, "Listen, Mike, this sounds like a fast shuffle to get me away from something you don't want me to see."

"Not true," I told her. We were sitting in the cubicle Personnel had lent for her stay at the agency. "It's just that all activity on Coronet has, as you know, come to a sudden stop. So if you want to see what really happens when we pitch an account, this Dodge thing might be the answer."

Stubbornly, she said, "The only way I'm going to find out what I came here for is to pick one team of subjects and stick with them. If that conflicts with your instructions, I'm sure Professor McClintlock will be glad to learn that your cooperation is limited to those areas which you choose to designate."

I held up my hands in surrender. "Hold it down. Remember who you're talking to? Old Honest Mike, souls unbared at the drop of a martini? If you want to hang in there with us, fine. I was just giving you an alternative, sweetheart."

"Another thing," she flared, still angry, "why all the 'sweetheart' and 'baby' stuff? My name is Jean."

"Enough already! I guess it's because, in this racket, we're on the outer fringes of show business and we end up imitating them. As for why *they* do it, I'd say it's because they rarely remember anyone else's name, and 'baby' is safe when you don't know who you're talking to."

"Well, you know who I am, so please use my name."

So then we argued for a while about who was going to pay for her plane ticket to Jamaica, and since she didn't have the cash anyway, it was another victory for good old JPO 6001.

When I explained the cab situation, she said, "It's silly for you to go twenty blocks out of your way to pick me up. I'll get a cab and come by for you."

"Baby," I said. *"Jean.* Things have changed in the Village. Six-thirty in the morning is a very lonely time for a girl to be looking for a cab."

"I'll get the eunuch doorman to do the looking," she said, and that was that, and at seven sharp the next morning there came three quick rings on my downstairs doorbell, and when I looked out the front window, she was on the curb, waving up at me.

I waved back, scooped up my canvas suitcase, double-locked the front door with the Fox Police Lock, and hurried downstairs. The morning was gray and chilly, and down the street a garbage truck was grinding up the trash. I remember, when I first came to the city, asking a friend why the garbage grinders were marked with the Civil Defense symbol. "After all," I said, "the trucks are closed up. You can't haul anything in them. All they're good for is grinding stuff up and compressing it to be hauled away."

And my friend, a child of the twentieth century, answered calmly, "What do you think they'd have to do with all the bodies?"

I heaved my bag into the taxi's front seat beside the driver, got in next to Jean, and said, "Kennedy. We're flying Pan Am."

"Juan's English isn't very good," Jean said. She leaned

forward and sprayed a couple of pounds of Spanish through the window opening, and the driver—whose name was Juan Ortega, according to his Hack Bureau placard—grinned happily and said, "Si, Señora," and we were off toward the dawn in a screech of burning rubber.

"Thanks for instructing our driver," I mumbled. "Want to carry my bag at the airport too?"

"It's too early in the morning to get all male-dominant," Jean said. Then she giggled. "Juan's funny. All the way up here he called me 'señorita.' But now that he sees I'm picking up a man, he's gone polite and I've become 'señora.'"

Juan must have originally been a fighter pilot for Castro. He got us to JFK in thirty-two minutes flat.

I got unsteadily out of the taxi, my knees feeling all macaroni. "I need a drink," I said.

Surprised, Jean asked, "At seven-thirty in the morning?"

"I aged nine hours in the last nine miles," I told her, "and that makes the sun well over the yardarm." I handed Juan a twenty and waved away the change. He thanked me profusely, insisted on carrying our bags inside, ignoring the irate Pan Am Skycaps, shook my hand, kissed Jean's, and bowed his way out.

Well, maybe there are *three* good ones. . . .

We checked our bags, showed the airline girl our proof of citizenship, and went upstairs to the coffee shop. The bar in the back wouldn't open until eight A.M. and I would just be able to hold out that long.

"Let me have your boarding pass," I said.

Jean gave it to me. "Why do you need it?"

"For the Duty Free Shop," I told her. "We're allowed to take a bottle of booze each, and a carton of cigarettes. What do you drink and what brand do you smoke?"

"I don't smoke at all," she said. "Scotch will be fine." Then, "What brand do *you* smoke?"

"Coronets," I said absently. I stopped. She'd trapped me. "Low blow," I said. "Come to think of it, I *don't* smoke Coronets. Always hated the goddamned things. Used to lock the doors and puff my way insanely through a pack of Pall Malls. Order me some black coffee, will you?

And be sure to say *black* or they'll put cream in it automatically."

"I'm sorry," she said. "I didn't mean to make fun of you."

"Forget it," I said. "It's our silly way of life, not yours."

"I meant the trick about the cigarettes, not the coffee."

"So did I," I said, and went off to find the Duty Free Shop.

INTERNATIONAL DUTY FREE SHOPS

Pan Am Concourse

John F. Kennedy International Airport

NOTE: *All merchandise must be delivered to you on board the aircraft after takeoff. Please show this receipt to your stewardess.*

M R M. Evans

FLIGHT TK 102

DESTINATION Montego Bay, Jamaica

No.	Item	Price	Total
2	Cartons Pall Mall	2.85	5.70
3	Fifths Demars White Label Scotch	3.15	9.45
1	1/2 oz. Chanel #5	6.80	6.80
		Total	21.95

Paid for Cash

"I can't accept this, Mike," Jean protested.

The stewardess had jumped the gun and delivered my package before we were airborne. But I'd cleverly held back opening it until we were somewhere over southern New Jersey and the nine-thirty Bloody Mary cart had been by. The perfume was in a little white paper bag taped to the outside of a heavy carton that held the liquor and cigarettes.

"Why the hell not?"

"Because you're not supposed to give me things."

"I give all my friends things. I'm going to smoke your Pall Malls. You can at least wear my perfume. *I'm* damned sure not going to wear it."

"Mike, you're making my position very difficult."

"Why? Can you be bribed off with half an ounce of Chanel?"

"Of course not."

"Then what's the big problem? I wasn't kidding. I give everything away. That's my schtick."

"Your what?"

73

"Schtick. That's phony show biz Yiddish for 'thing.' 'Routine.' 'Act.' "

She was interested. "Why do you use such a term?"

I shrugged. "I just do. It's supposed to be funny."

"Do your Jewish friends think it's funny?"

"They haven't complained."

"Have they laughed?"

I considered that one. Come to think about it. . . .

"Listen," I said, "from now on, I'll be good. But please take the perfume or I'm going to have to drink it. I can't stand waste. That's another one of my—"

"Schticks?"

"I was going to say compulsions."

She laughed. "All right, Mike. This one time. But no more. Please."

She broke the bottle's seal and dabbed a little behind her ears. "Mmmm," she said. "If I *could* be bribed, you'd be able to do it with Chanel. You've got a good nose for perfume, my friend."

I didn't say anything. I *should* have had a good nose for Chanel. Janice poured the stuff on like it was suntan lotion. I felt a sick lurch in my stomach as I suddenly remembered the last time I had been on the Pan Am jet on my way to Montego Bay.

"Mike! What's wrong?" Jean's voice was alarmed.

"Excuse me," I mumbled. I slipped out of my seatbelt and hurried up the aisle, past Ham Keyes and Howard Porter who looked up in surprise from their copies of *The New York Times,* and barricaded myself in the rest room, where I gave back the coffee and Danish I'd had earlier.

God, you are never free! The past wraps itself around your limbs with invisible little tendrils that, lax, allow you a sense of free movement. But just try to get away, buddy —try to slip the bonds and see how fast they bite into the flesh and bring you down in a heap.

I sat on the closed seat of the john and stared at my shaking hands. After a while my stomach settled down and I went back to my seat.

As I passed him Howard Porter asked, "What's the matter, Mike? A little of the mal de mer?"

"Mal de Pan Am," I said. "I damned near choked to death on the tabasco in my Bloody Mary."

Hamilton Keyes said nothing.

I stood there for a moment, but there wasn't anything further going to be said by any of us, so I continued along the aisle and buckled myself in beside Jean Patrick again.

"Are you all right?" she asked.

"Fine. Drink went down the wrong way."

"Oh."

The cabin loudspeaker clicked on, the pilot introduced himself, told us that his name was Taylor, that we had reached our cruising altitude of thirty-five thousand feet, and that we would continue down the Eastern coast, passing out over the ocean somewhere near South Carolina, thence over Nassau in the Bahamas, Cuba, and descend for our landing at Montego Bay. Total flying time, three hours and twenty-six minutes. He also managed a chuckle and said, "About Cuba, we don't anticipate landing there today. So have a pleasant flight."

"Funny bastard," I muttered.

We were served a fancy brunch, which I picked at, and then I had a couple of Scotch and waters. Jean drank coffee and dozed.

Somewhere over the Caribbean, Howard stood up in the aisle, caught my eye, and nodded toward the forward lounge. He and Keyes went up there and I followed.

"Let's get some work done," said Porter when I joined them.

I looked back toward Jean Patrick. Before I could say anything, Keyes said, "Nobody agreed she could follow us to the bathroom, Mike."

I shrugged. "It's your agency, Ham."

"Here's the routine," said Porter. "Mike and Miss Patrick will stay at Wexford Court. That's a moderately priced complex of apartments and motel rooms between the airport and Montego Bay."

"I hope you sprang for an extra room, Howard," I said. "I'm told I snore something terrible."

Keyes just stared at me.

"Ham and I," Porter went on, "will be just down the hill, at Hacton House. Another moderately priced place, both suited to the family traveler. No one would ever expect that these would be the choice of the representatives to two major American corporations."

I wanted to say that I hoped they had running water in these moderately priced places, but bit my tongue. Keyes was looking very uptight and my jokes weren't scoring with him today.

"Who's the other corporation?" I asked instead.

"What other corporation?"

"You mentioned two. MK&C is one. Who's the other?"

Howard looked at Keyes, who nodded.

"Coronet Tobacco," Howard said. "Colonel Haney is already down there. He's at Hacton House, registered as a salesman from Westinghouse."

I bit my tongue again. I just couldn't see anyone in the world, including the unsophisticated natives of Jamaica, mistaking Wild Bill Haney for a salesman from Westinghouse.

"Now," said Howard, "we get in at twelve-thirty, more or less. I've got a car rented for you from Dullum U-Drive. You'll find him at the Delta Airlines counter."

"Where's Hertz?" I asked. "In the men's room?"

Keyes spoke. "Mike, this isn't just some silly game we're playing."

"Sorry, Ham," I said. "I just get nervous when I don't know what the hell I'm talking about."

"Hopefully, we'll be able to let you in on what's happening tonight," he said.

"Is Uncle Norman with Haney?"

"I don't know."

Porter continued his instructions. "Drive up to Wexford Court. You've got a suite, Miss Patrick has a room in the motel part. We'll probably be using your suite for a meeting this evening. So keep in touch with the Wexford office. Don't try to look us up. We'll find you."

"Ham," I said, "please don't get mad at me. I just can't help it. I feel exactly like James Bond. Proceed to Point X, where you will be contacted by our representative, a homosexual dwarf, who will deliver the jewels."

"It is rather far out," Ham said smiling. "Sorry. I hate to act like Fu Manchu, but even Howard here doesn't know what's up. And that's the way it has to be for a while longer. But believe me, Mike, it's big."

"Well, forgive me for saying it," I said, "but this is sure

one hell of a time to have a member of McClintlock's Mob hanging around."

Ham said, "I don't think so. I pondered that problem when you brought it up before, and decided that having Miss Patrick here may even help us. I think we will be able to depend on her discretion—hers and the Professor's. And I have every reason to believe that he is in sympathy with the project we're down here to discuss."

"How much do you plan to level with her? When you start talking, that is."

"All the way," said Hamilton Keyes.

"You're starting out lousy, then. She'd have to be passed out cold not to know that we're up here conspiring without her."

"You can tell her what we discussed."

"That's not the same. Ham, I don't know this girl well, but I think I understand her. She's wound up tight as a clockspring. She's very well controlled, but somewhere there is a secret button that, if pressed, will set her off like a skyrocket."

Keyes thought about that for a while. "Very well, Mike. Apologize for me. Put the blame on my shoulders. And assure her she'll be a party to everything else that occurs."

"You don't have to worry about me dumping the rap on you, Ham. That's just what I had in mind. But about the rest. Scout's honor?"

He smiled again, raised three fingers and said, *"Sea Scout's* honor."

FOCUS ON JAMAICA
Complete Vacation and Shopping Guide

OUR ADVICE--STICK TO BOOZE

Like the young man whose girl was "real hot"
but not smoking, the vast majority of visitors to
Jamaica may burn in the sun but are advised not to
smoke our very fine locally-grown marijuana (known
here as Ganja)--it is very much against the law to
grow it, have it, or smoke it.

Ganja is very cheap in Jamaica and within
the past year an increasing number of Americans
have been smuggling it out of the island to make a
few thousand percent profit on its sale in the
U.S.A. Many of them have been caught and the
police are intensifying vigilance.

Many Jamaicans drink a brew of the leaves
which is claimed to be good for colds, flu, asthma,
and the like and, in this form, has no intoxicating
effect. But we advise: "Don't try it." The
mere possession of Ganja carries a minimum
sentence of 18 months in prison without option of
a fine.

Since the supply of marijuana from Mexico
has been virtually cut off, increasing numbers of
young people with very long hair have been coming
to Jamaica for trips--in more ways than one.
Jamaica's attraction for most of them is, of
course, Ganja.

These youngsters, when they go, hate to leave it all behind and often try to take some with them. Among the methods they have tried are, hiding the Ganja in bongo drums, stuffed into shoes (when they have them), hidden in the amplifiers for their guitars and once, in a hollowed out surf-board--which unfortunately came apart in front of police officers.

For their statistics, the Jamaica Tourist Board divides visitors into two categories: "short-stay," which means three nights or "long-stay," from three nights to three weeks or so. Perhaps soon they will have to add the category "extra-long stay"--18 months.

(from free guidebook given out at
Montego Bay airport)

"My God," I said. "It's like an advertisement. Come on down, kids, and get your cheap weed. It's like those postcards we used to get in the mail with the warning 'Under no circumstances apply lemon juice to these cards or the girls' clothing will disappear.' It's a big comeon, regardless of what they intended. 'Our very fine locally-grown marijuana'! It sounds like a Coronet sales pitch."

Jean and I were sitting in the Pelican Grill, just down the hill from Wexford Court, which turned out to be a modern complex of what looked like A-frames. My duplex suite was bright and clean. I hadn't seen the inside of Jean's room.

Clearing Jamaican customs had been easy. The immigrations official tore off the top copy of my landing card, scribbled the length of my stay and name of my hotel on the other half, handed it back to me, and we went out into the baggage area, where we were met by a handsome black girl wearing an armband that read "Jamaica Tourist Board Courtesy Corps."

"Rum punch?" she asked.

We took two, thanked her, and sipped from the stemware as a baggage man scooped up our suitcases and put them on the customs bench.

"Any liquor or cigarettes, sir?"

"A bottle apiece, same for cigarettes. Carton, that is, not bottle."

"Weapons? Firearms, knives, explosives?"

"No."

He scribbled a white chalkmark on each of our bags, grinned widely, and said, "Have a nice stay in Jamaica."

"Taxi, sah?" asked the baggage man.

"Dullum's U-Drive," I said.

"That's outside, at the Delta counter. Go that way. I'll follow."

Murf Dullum, a big friendly white man, rented us an English Ford Anglia at fifty-five U.S. dollars for the week, with unlimited mileage.

"Drive on the left," he warned. "And if a bus or truck is coming, *way* on the left. Down here, they say, 'de truck, he drive anywhere he *want* to,' and it's true."

We checked the spare and jack, loaded in the luggage, and I got in under the right-hand-drive steering wheel and played with the gearshift on the floor.

"Go out to the traffic circle just outside the airport," Dullum told me, "take the first right to Gloucester Avenue, drive along past a big hotel with a lot of little shops in a sort of arcade—you'll know it because all the airlines are there—and just after that watch for the Pelican Grill on the left. Go past it, turn up a little road, and you're at Wexford Court."

"How about gas?"

"There's a dollar's worth in the tank. That'll take you at least fifty miles. When you fill it up, be sure to use premium."

I thanked him, made sure Jean's door was closed, and off we went.

After the blustering cold of New York City it was odd to drive beneath tall palms and monkey pod trees, an eighty-five-degree sun streaming in the windows. The sides of the road were crowded with pedestrians—many of them children, who waved at us and shouted.

"What are they saying?" Jean asked.

"They're more or less shouting a challenge," I said.

"They almost never get to ride in a car, so they yell at anyone who does. There's no real malice in them, but the language is sometimes a little rough."

At the traffic circle I stopped beside a palm tree to let a bus pass. A little black girl in pigtails and wearing a blue school uniform stood waiting to cross the road, sucking on an orange.

"Hello, little girl," called Jean.

The little black girl stuck out her tongue and threw the orange at us. It splatted against the windshield. I drove on.

"No real malice in them?" Jean repeated.

We passed a big billboard that showed the face of an Afro-coiffed black woman and a big headline reading "You don't have to get pregnant." The logo at the bottom was the Jamaican Family Planning Association. I glanced at Jean. She was trying to look unconcerned.

We found Wexford Court easily enough, checked in, aided by a pleasant English lady who announced, "I'm Olive," and stowed our baggage. Then we went down the hill to the Pelican to cut some of the coral dust with a Red Stripe beer. I remembered Red Stripe pleasantly from my previous visit and it did not fail me today.

We drank two of the tall brown bottles, almost chugalug. When the second round came, I leafed through *Focus on Jamaica,* found the piece on marijuana, and read it to Jean.

"It's a comeon," I said. "What the hell would *you* do if you were an eighteen-year-old head and read that junk? And do you know what they do to those poor kids down here? It's the old entrapment game. The pusher sells to the kids, then turns them in to the police, and collects both ways. The Flying Squad busts the kids, and if they're holding, they may not get the full eighteen months, but sure as hell there'll be a whopper of a fine."

I expected her to argue moralistically with me. Instead, she said, "It's even worse than you paint it, Mike."

"What?" I said, surprised.

"We've been running a study on the whole drug thing, informally, not really part of the McClintlock Commission, but of course we have use of all the facilities. Naturally, we were interested in sources of supply. And the authorities' reactions. Remember back in Nixon's first term? Operation Intercept, when they closed the Mexican border? The CIA got into the act then, pumping money into local economies south of the border to make up for the income lost from marijuana that suddenly wasn't being delivered to the States. The Intercept operation itself was a failure, but when we dumped more than five million dollars below the border, suddenly it became more profitable to play ball with the authorities than to peddle marijuana wholesale. The officials who had been getting their rakeoff on marijuana crops now got it from the CIA, much safer and tax free. It worked, too. The big sources in Mexico dried up. The word is that the CIA tried the same deal here. In 1970, according to our records, the CIA expended two million dollars in Jamaica with the understanding that it would be spent directly on keeping marijuana from being smuggled out to the States. One CIA man who talked with us bragged that a million spent down here saved forty million in enforcement on the other end. So the Jamaican police ended up with brand-new Land Rovers and two-way radios and various other toys, and began carrying out their orders for Washington. It's just very interesting, and sad, that in a country where an extremely large part of the population smokes grass, the majority of the prisoners in ganja jail are foreigners, mostly under twenty-one."

"Such passion," I said. "The lady wouldn't by any chance be a pothead, would she?"

Flushed, she said, "No, but of course I've smoked. Almost everyone my age has. Naturally, you wouldn't—"

"Wouldn't what? Baby, don't—"

"Jean, dammit!" she said in a voice loud enough to turn the bartender's black face toward us.

I lowered my own voice. "Jean. Don't think that just because I've got ten years on you I spend my time sitting around in the old rocking chair, daydreaming fondly of the golden days back with the horse and carriage and the player piano. We puffed a little in my college days too, and we dropped acid, and worse. I think the drug scene stinks, honey. Jean. One of my best friends freaked out on LSD and spent four weeks in Payne Whitney. He was lucky, his father had money, otherwise he'd have ended up on the state farm in Rockland County."

"I'm sorry, Mike," she said, touching my hand. "I didn't mean that the way it sounded. I guess what upsets me so much is the injustice. The rich kids smoke and pop whatever and, like you said, they end up in Payne Whitney. While the poor kids—mostly black—get narcotics busts on their record."

"I agree," I said. "It's a lousy system. But since we have to live under it, can I suggest something while we're down here?"

"What?"

"Let's do like the magazine says and stick to booze."

WEXFORD COURT
Montego Bay
Jamaica, W.I.

INTERIM CALL REPORT

DATE: November 16

PLACE: Wexford Court, Montego Bay,
        Jamaica, West Indies

PRODUCT: C-900

PRESENT FOR CLIENT: W. Haney

PRESENT FOR AGENCY: H. Keyes, H. Porter, M. Evans

PRESENT FOR MC CLINTLOCK COMMITTEE: J. Patrick

Meeting convened at 5:00 p.m.

Miss Patrick was temporarily excused during discussion regarding her presence. At 5:10 she was readmitted and agreed to certain restrictions suggested by Client.

Client revealed nature of New Product C-900.

Agency agreed to assign top creative and account personnel and to work with all possible speed preparing:

1. Timetable.
2. Marketing plan.
3. Preliminary names and packaging suggestions.

All work on Product C-900 will be classified as Highly Confidential, and no memos, reports, research studies or other paperwork will be distributed or duplicated without signed approval by either Mr. Keyes or Mr. Porter.

Meeting adjourned at 6:10 p.m.

Reading between the lines of agency call reports has always been a favorite sport of mine. For instance, the one Howard Porter wrote describing our first meeting with William P. Haney in Jamaica indicates a quiet businesslike transacting of certain product and advertising matters. Nothing could be further from the truth.

The fireworks went off at exactly one minute past five, just after Wild Bill Haney had smiled at Jean Patrick and said, "I don't believe the young lady and I have met. A new copywriter? Mike's at it again, eh?"

Ham began to explain the situation, how he had offered the McClintlock Commission carte blanche, and that was as far as he got.

"Carte blanche?" Haney yelled. "Who the goddamned hell do you think you are, letting troublemaking spies have carte blanche on *my* business?" His face was contorted with anger. "I thought you had brains! Here I'm letting you in on the hottest new product of the century and you want to give it all away to a bunch of rabble-rousers?" His voice was echoing off the slate ceiling. "Get her out of here!"

"But, Bill," Keyes protested, "I promised—"

"Who the hell are *you* to promise? I said get her out of here or the whole thing's off. Do you know what Ted Bates would give to get their hands on this project? Or Y&R?"

Keyes sighed and turned to the girl. "Miss Patrick—"

She didn't let him finish. "I'm on my way," she said tightly, visibly trying to keep her anger under control. "If you . . . you big *executives!* . . . could only see the way you are now, you'd understand why everyone's suspicious of you. I'm going. Just don't rush me. I want to say something first to this—Southern gentleman!" She stepped up to Colonel William P. Haney, thrust her face up toward his—getting to his collarbone was the tallest she could manage—and said icily, "Mr. Haney, may I suggest that you take your Project C-900, whatever it is, and shove it up your fat ass!"

She broke for the door, stopped there and faced us again, and shouted, "And that goes for the rest of you, if you can get your brown noses out of the way!"

Her exit almost slammed the door off its hinges.

"Fiery little girl," Haney observed, unperturbed. "Not from the South, is she?"

Furious, Keyes said, "How the hell do I know? Listen, Haney, we've got a contract. If you think you can treat us like a couple of your redneck sharecroppers—"

"Simmer down, Ham," Haney said, his mercurial anger gone as suddenly as it had come. "You know exactly how much a contract is worth. If my handshake ain't good, what do you figure to get out of a contract except a big pain in the ass?" He laughed. "Ass. That filly *has* to be Southern. I'm sorry, Ham, I shouldn't have blown my cork, but you ought to know better than to bring an outsider into what we're planning. It could cave the whole thing in around our ears."

Stubbornly, Keyes said, "We don't have anything to be ashamed of."

"Nothing? Nothing except that what we're doing is illegal," Haney said blandly. "How would you like to spend a few months making little ones out of big ones over in Kingston Prison?"

"Kingston Prison?" I yelped. "What the hell for?"

Haney looked at me. "Didn't Ham tell you what C-900 is?"

I shook my head. Haney nodded his. "Well, at least he knows how to keep his mouth shut, even if he does go around making promises he shouldn't."

"Mr. Haney," said Howard Porter, "what *is* C-900?"

Savoring his moment, William P. Haney stretched in the bamboo chair, put his feet up on the coffee table, and said, smiling, "C-900 is what is going to make the Coronet Tobacco Company and Morton, Keyes and Cooper the two richest bastards in the business. Together we're going to introduce the first legal marijuana cigarette."

You could have cut the silence with a knife. Then a voice croaked. It was mine. "The *what?*"

"The first legal marijuana cigarette."

Calmly, Porter asked, "When?"

"Sometime in the next six months."

Porter's facade crumbled. "Holy shit," he said, and sat down.

"So," Haney said, "you can see why we don't need any crusaders hanging around. Listen, we'll have a full season's jump on the competition. They'll never catch up."

"How," I asked, "can you sell a marijuana cigarette? They're illegal."

"Not so long ago booze was illegal, and they're selling the hell out of it now," Haney said. "We handle it exactly like any other commodity. Make a good product, give it wide distribution and lots of advertising, and sit back like a pig in a garbage pail and get fat."

"I still don't think it's a good idea to send that girl back to Northwestern," said Ham Keyes. "It'd draw more attention down on us than if we let her stay."

"Stay, and send out weekly reports on what we're up to? Reports that anyone and his brother could get their paws on? Not damned likely." Haney put his feet firmly down on the floor and glared around.

"Wait a minute," I said, not sure why I was interfering. Was I trying to help Keyes—or Jean? "It all depends on what kind of crusader you're talking about. Remember back in 1970, when the President's Committee on Violence came right out and recommended that pot be legalized? They were crusaders, and yet—"

"Wait a minute, Mike," said Ham Keyes. "I've got it right here in the background file." He fumbled with a large brown folder, shuffling through papers and photographs. Triumphantly, he came up with a newspaper clipping. "This is it. From the *New York Daily News,* September 8, 1970."

"What the hell does the *Daily News* have to do with that girl?" Haney demanded.

Keyes read:

LEGALIZE POT FEDERAL
PANEL REPORT URGES

WASHINGTON, Sept. 7—A staff report to the National Commission on the Causes and Prevention of Violence released tonight recommended the legalization of marijuana.

The panel called for legalization of marijuana to persons over 18 years of age.

"By harsh criminal statutes on marijuana use and in light of evidence that alcohol abuse accounts for far more destruction than any known chemical substance today," the panel concluded, "we have caused large numbers of our youth to lose respect for our laws generally."

"So?" asked Haney. "I happen to agree. Between you and me and the gatepost, I'd a hell of a lot rather have my kid puffing marijuana than boozing it up and inhaling Coronet Cigarettes. But what's your point?"

"The point is," I said, "that Professor Harold McClintlock was chairman of the panel that did some of the original research for the National Commission. And I was talking to Jean—Miss Patrick—less than an hour ago when she told me that McClintlock's Mob is working right now to get some of those excessive marijuana laws off the books."

Haney put his feet back up on the table. "What you're trying to say is that you think we might get some backing from the academic community?"

Keyes looked at me. I nodded.

"Well," Haney said, "I been wrong before. You got to

be wrong sometimes if you play to win. If you never been wrong, you ain't doing your job. Okay, Ham. I apologize."

Keyes said, "I think it's Miss Patrick who deserves the apology."

Haney waved his hand. "Bring her on. I'll break my sword over my knee and everything. Too bad she's so skinny. I go for females with spunk like hers."

My face must have registered something, because he laughed and said, "Now don't you go getting riled up too, Mike. I'm just funning around. Why don't you go see if you can find our little lady and bring her back? We'll hold everything up until you get here."

"She may not come back," I warned, knowing it was true.

"You gentle her down, son," Haney said. "I'm depending on you."

Outside it was late afternoon and the clouds were coming down closer over the Caribbean, painted an orange and yellow along their tops and darker blue and violent purple on the bottoms. I went down the hill, past the office, and knocked on the door of Jean's room.

There wasn't any answer. I knocked again. The door opened a crack.

"What do you want?" she asked.

"Can I come in?"

"No. I'm packing."

"Please, Jean."

"I said no. Go away."

The door closed in my face. I didn't move. A minute went by. Two. I lit up a Coronet. It tasted like old sawdust. I threw it away. The door opened again.

"I said go away. Won't they miss you in the meeting?"

"Let me come in. Please."

She threw the door open. "Oh, all right. But make it fast. There's a seven-thirty plane I can catch."

Her clothes were piled neatly on the bed. She saw me looking, hurried to throw the spread over them. "What do you want?" she asked.

"We talked with Haney. He made a mistake. He's sorry."

"Too bad."

Anger touched me then. "Now wait just a goddamned

minute, Jean. The man made a mistake. He's sorry. He's worried about a multimillion dollar operation and we rang you in on him without warning. Also, he's got a short fuse. But no shorter than yours baby. Something tells me that Professor McClintlock would still be sitting over there in that meeting this very minute, with none of this crap about running home to mama. I think the good professor might have explained things in a way satisfactory to our itchy client, instead of telling the poor bastard to shove it up his ass."

I watched her face, where anger fought with outraged humor. Humor won. She laughed. "Mike, I'm afraid you're right. I lost my head."

"Then come on back and do your job. I think you're going to find it interesting. We finally learned why we're down here and it's right up your alley."

She started toward the door with me, stopped. "Oh, Mike," she whispered, "I can't. I made such a *fool* of myself."

"Forget it," I said, pulling her arm. "We *all* did."

She came toward me and her foot must have slipped on the rug, because she started to fall, and I caught her, and suddenly she was in my arms, and I found myself kissing her—gently at first and then, as she responded, deeply.

We broke for air, and she said thickly, "No," but she didn't pull away. I kissed her again and she made a kind of whimpering sound and almost collapsed in my arms. Then we were sitting on the bed and once again she whispered, "No," but again she made no move to get away.

I touched her breast and everything changed. With a hissing sound she threw herself across the bed and fell to the floor on the opposite side. Alarmed, I stood up, but by then she was on her feet.

"Jean, what—" I began, and she said, rapidly, "No, Mike, don't—" and I said, "I'm not going to hurt—" and she said, "Let's go now. Please. *Please!*" and the last "please" was on the ragged edge of hysteria, so I just opened the door and stepped outside onto the patio, into the humid air and the orange glow of the setting sun, and in a few seconds she joined me, artificially calm now, and we went up the hill to my suite and the meeting that was waiting for us.

Before Colonel William P. Haney could luxuriate in the complete disclosure of his Grand Plan, he had first to dispose of the matter of apologizing to Miss Jean Patrick.

Like everything else in his life, he did it big.

"Little lady," he said, when we had entered, somewhat sheepishly, both of us suddenly aware that I probably had lipstick on my mouth, "I have been considering the suggestion you made—and, justified as it might be, I find it physically impossible. However, if you would like to try, be my guest."

With that he bent over and aimed his ample rear end at the ceiling.

Jean choked. "I'll forget the suggestion if you will, Colonel," she managed between gasps of laughter.

Haney stood up and faced her. "Seriously, ma'am. I acted like a jackass. Am I truly forgiven?"

"Truly," she said.

"Sealed with a kiss?"

And so help me, she kissed him. On the cheek, though.

"Okay," said Haney. "Jean—I can call you Jean, can't

I?" (He could.) "Did Mike tell you what I was being so closemouthed about?"

"No."

"My company is going to manufacture and distribute the first legal marijuana cigarette in the United States." He held up the clipping from the *News*. "I got a basket full of clippings like this," he said. "From all over. We were thinking of this project even before this latest wave of public acceptance. Big companies are always looking for diversification. Back in the middle sixties a couple of the big tobacco companies were acquiring land in Kentucky and Mexico, holdings that were suited for raising marijuana. But then that man Nixon got in and pickings looked mighty slim."

"That's interesting," Jean said. "I heard that some of those companies were registering names like Mary Jane and Jamaica Red."

"False," said Haney. "You can't just register a name and hold it forever. You've got to *use* that name or you lose it. In addition, with all the heat the tobacco companies were coming under toward the end of the sixties, the last thing they needed was some subcommittee catching up with a thing like registering marijuana names. I don't deny that we all thought about the possibilities of a marijuana cigarette, but we did it privately and didn't put a damned thing down on paper."

"Why did you decide to take off the wraps and move now?" I asked.

"Because when that new man, Howard Foster, takes office next January, things are going to be different."

"How do you know?" Porter asked.

"Let's just say I *know*."

"All right," I said. "How many others *know*?"

"I'm not sure. Maybe one or two, maybe nobody. For all I know, right now there may be meetings like this going on in Guatemala or Kansas—where, incidentally, a pretty good grade of local marijuana grows wild. We're going to look into that source."

"Feeling extremely brilliant this evening," I said, "it occurs to me that *this* is why you took Coronets away from MK&C."

"Right. You're going to be too busy to think about any

standard tobacco cigarette. Besides, we intend to introduce this through a subsidiary corporation, but the agency of record has to be known."

"So if everything blows sky-high, the agency takes the rap and Coronet gets off with some minor money losses."

"Right again," Haney said. "Except that if you call twenty million bucks 'minor,' you must play with bigger marbles than I'm used to."

Hamilton Keyes, who had been silent, broke in: "Bill came to me three weeks ago and made a proposition. He felt that it was time to move and wanted to know if we'd come along. He'll guarantee cost-plus the first twenty months—out of pocket, overhead, and six-percent profit. From then on the account should be paying its own way on commission."

"Excuse me," said Jean. "Is this normal? Cost-plus, I mean? I thought the usual arrangement was fifteen percent of the billing."

"Smart little lady," said our now-genial client. I decided I didn't like the way he was looking at her. "Yes, Miss Patrick, until recent years that was the usual form of remuneration. But with new products in particular, an agency may spend a year in developing marketing and advertising, and then something will go wrong. The product just doesn't sell, or management at the client changes and they move the business to another shop, or a dozen other things can go wrong before a product begins paying its own way. So we, client and agency, sometimes work out one of these cost-plus things to be sure the client doesn't take unfair advantage of the agency, eating up their manpower and overhead and sticking them with a lot of bills for a product that may never fly."

Keyes said, "David Ogilvy was one of the first big shops to try the fee system, back in the sixties. He started with Shell Oil and it worked, so he expanded the method to a lot of his other clients."

"Oh," said Jean. Then, "If you know the new Administration's going to be more lenient toward drugs—or at least toward marijuana—doesn't everybody else in the cigarette business have the same information? So why all the secrecy?"

"Let's hope everybody else doesn't have the same information," Haney said. "You see, Artie Rand, the new Vice President, owes me one hell of a favor. It was a senator with whom I have a close relationship who stepped aside so President-elect Foster was able to nominate Rand at the convention without a floor fight. Men in politics have a way of remembering little good deeds like that. So Artie, who knows the profit squeeze we're in right now, with no radio or TV and with the health warnings they're making us put in the print ads, slipped me a little hint."

"That's terrible!" Jean said.

"Why?" asked Haney.

"The man's abusing his office, an office he doesn't even hold yet."

"Untrue," said Haney. "I asked him for his personal opinion as to what the new Administration's attitude is going to be toward the reform movement in the drug problem. He told me that as far as he knew Foster is going to be progressive. It was the eighteen-year-old vote that got Foster in office, remember, so he feels he owes those kids a little more understanding than they got from guys like Agnew. Arthur would have told the same thing to anyone else who asked him. But so far nobody has thought to pop the question except me, and I hope it stays that way."

He took out a foul-looking Jacci Jamaican cigar and set it afire. "Ah," he said. "I love these things. But naturally, I can't smoke them around Louisville. We don't even *make* cigars."

"Me, I like *these*," I said, lighting up a Pall Mall. Ham Keyes almost swallowed his dentures. Haney merely laughed.

"Silly goddamned world, ain't it?" he said. "Okay, don't get the idea that the USA's suddenly going to be dope heaven. Rand told me that Foster's death on the real hard stuff. Cocaine, heroin, the whole family of artificial hallucinogenics." He whirled on Jean. "Did you ever hear of dimethyltryptamine?"

"DMT," she said. "The kids soak it into tobacco and smoke it. Those who are afraid of getting cancer from the tobacco use parsley leaves."

Haney chortled. "Honey, you're some sketch."

"Thank you," she said. "What are you getting at?"

"That you're closer to the youth scene than any of the

rest of us except maybe Mike. Why do you think the kids are tripping out on amphetamines and mescaline? Why are they blowing their minds with psilocybin, LSD, and DMT? Why do they go on to hard drugs like cocaine and heroin?"

Calmly, Jean said "Because the Establishment keeps telling them that marijuana is dreadfully dangerous stuff, and yet they all have friends who use it and most of them have tried smoking themselves, and so they know the Establishment's lying about weed. Ergo, the Establishment is lying about speed and heroin too."

"Except," I said, "that speed and heroin and the other stuff are as bad as or worse than everyone says."

"You know that and I know that," she said, "but try convincing a rebellious eighteen-year-old whose parents get bombed every night on martinis. Try talking about honesty to a kid who watches his father cheating, week-in, week-out, on everything he touches—his expense account, his income tax, his wife."

Howard picked up the phone as she spoke, called the restaurant, and asked to have a dozen Red Stripes sent up.

Jean went on, "The net result is that they just don't trust *anything* you say."

"You?" I said. "Don't you mean 'we'?"

"Not me, Mike. I haven't passed that magic thirty marker yet."

"The guy who first said, 'Never trust anybody over thirty' is probably forty-one years old," I said. "I wonder how he feels about it today."

She shrugged. "You asked me what I thought. I told you."

"Okay," said Haney, "I heard what I wanted. And it's the truth, Mike. Now, you could make an argument that it's terrible to sell people something that might give them problems if misused—but that kind of reasoning would eliminate booze, cigarettes, cars, food, sex, and everything else that's fun. What I'm primarily concerned with is that we're mixed up with something that I'm virtually positive will be legal by next March, but which is illegal as hell right this minute. That's why we've got to be damned careful how we move around down here. You might as well know, Coronet has holdings in Mexico too, but the CIA fix is still pretty strong down there. It's faded in Jamaica, though, and that's why we're here. But we could still get our asses in a sling if we stumbled around making a mess. So that's the reason for the secrecy, other than keeping our competition in the dark. And, to apologize once more, Miss Patrick, that's why I hit the roof when these guys turned up with you, charming as you may be."

He held up sausagelike fingers and ticked off the points on them. "So, I'd appreciate it if you'd agree to a couple of restrictions. One: you can go anywhere within the project, see anything, ask anything. But any interim reports to Northwestern must *not* divulge the nature of C-900. Two: if you complete your study before we have introduced C-900, or at least broken publicity on it, and must make your final report, you will allow us to be present when it is turned over to Professor McClintlock. Maybe we'll be able to persuade him not to make any public announcement which might include C-900 until such time as an announcement would not damage our chances in the market. Three: all notes should refer to C-900 by that term, and none other, and if any typing has to be done, you will either do it yourself or have it done by a typist who has been cleared by the agency."

"What choice do I have?"

"None," he said.

"I know enough already to cause you a lot of trouble."

"You wouldn't play it that way."

Jean sighed. "No," she said. "I couldn't. All right, Colonel. You're on."

Legend on the
Shell Oil Company maps of Jamaica:

THE COCKPIT COUNTRY

Me no sen you no come

Land of Look Behind

"We've got two plantations down here at present," Haney said next morning as we had coffee at the Montego Bay airport. "One's over on the east end of the island, in Portland Parish, in the John Crow Mountains." His finger traced the location for us on a Shell Oil map. "The other's down here in the Cockpit Country, just south of Mo Bay. That's where we're going today. We'll file a flight plan for Appleton Estates, in the Nassau Mountains, and from there we'll make a little detour over through the towns of Crown Lands and Quick Step. That's Maroon country up there, but we have an understanding with the Colonel."

"What are Maroons?" Jean asked.

"Slaves who ran away from the Spanish when the English captured Jamaica in 1655," I said. "They went up in the hills and caused the new government so much trouble over the next hundred years that a treaty was finally signed giving the Maroons autonomy. They became virtually a nation of their own."

"Hold on there, boy," said Haney. "History lessons are *my* department." He turned to Jean. "You see, little lady, those Maroons were such rough old boys that the English soldiers had to ride two to a horse, back to back. That's how come the name 'Land of Look Behind.' Well, Mike here was right about England signing a treaty with the Maroons. What he didn't add was that at his first opportunity the Governor of Jamaica broke the treaty and shipped as many Maroons as he could capture back to Africa, by way of Halifax. The trip took four years and not many of those poor souls made it. But the ones remaining here in Jamaica held out, and now they're more or less on their own, although they're protected by the Commonwealth. That legend on the map, 'Me no sen, you no come,' means just what it says. If the Colonel, he's the boss man up there, didn't send for you, you'd better not go trespassing."

More curious than alarmed, Ham Keyes asked, "Could it be dangerous?"

"No, they'd just turn you around and escort you out of Cockpit Country," said Haney. "But like I said, the Colonel and me have an understanding. What you might call a fifty-thousand-dollar understanding. That's why I had to bring a change of clothes. We may be up there for the night."

A slim man wearing trim khakis and a bushy red mustache came over. "Mr. Haney?" he said in an English accent, "the plane is ready." He smiled down at Jean. "Good morning, mum."

"Hod Casey, our pilot," said Haney. He introduced us around the table. "Want some coffee, Hod?"

"I think not, sir. There's a front moving in from Cuba. I'd rather not be over the mountains when it arrives."

"In that case," Haney grunted, heaving himself up from the chair, "tally ho."

Hod Casey gave a strained smile at Haney's phony British accent and led us outside to an ungainly-looking plane parked on the ramp. The morning's rain was steaming off the asphalt in the sunlight.

Casey noticed my uneasiness about the plane and said, "Grumman Goose, Mr. Evans. All-around, she's the best aircraft I know for these flying conditions. She'll climb on one engine, you can put her down on land or water, and she can take a hell of a beating. Last May I had a job into Port Antonio, misjudged a takeoff run, and pranged into a great bloody rock off Navy Island. I got her across the bay, taxied up on the Reef Hotel's seaplane ramp, welded on some sheet metal, and we were back in the air by teatime."

Somehow his enthusiasm didn't soothe me.

We strapped in, Casey taxied the Goose out onto the strip, and with a great roar of engines we were airborne. He circled once over the bay. Montego was much as I had remembered it—the downtown area rundown and congested, the beach row of hotels toward the airport bright and clean in the morning sun. You pay a hundred bucks a night at one of those hotels for a place to sleep and two meals, with drinks costing extra. A first-rate chef at the same hotel earns around thirty dollars a week. You figure it out.

With enough altitude to pass over the range of hills girdling Montego Bay, the Goose headed southeast. Below us the matted jungle was a green sea.

Ten minutes out of Mo Bay Haney came back from the cockpit. He pointed out the window. "See that field down there? Kind of purplish?"

"What is it?"

"Ten acres of the best ganja in the world," he said. "There's another one over there to the left. Six acres. We've got them scattered all over this district."

"Colonel Haney," said Jean, "If *we* can see these fields from the air, can't the police?"

"Sure," he said. "But there are two things you have to remember. One, the police, even when they were all gung-ho with the CIA, were never really interested in stopping ganja production. They were only interested in making some highly visible arrests, and that meant there had to be a source of supply so the poor suckers from the States could get themselves entrapped. No ganja fields, no arrests. No arrests, no CIA funds."

Jean nodded. "What's the other reason?"

"The police couldn't do anything about those fields even if they wanted to. The police do not go into Cockpit Country. Ever."

We landed at a small airstrip near Appleton Estates, where the famous Appleton Rum originated.

"We'll be driving up to Quick Step," Haney told Hod

101

Casey. "We may get back this evening, we may not. If you don't see us by five, go ahead and get drunk, because we won't need you until morning."

"Good-o," said the pilot. "I'll get the Goose cleaned up a bit and set up HQ in the Tiger Lounge."

Haney laughed and pointed at a ramshackle building with a Red Stripe sign nailed over the glassless window. "That," he told us, "is the Tiger Lounge."

We followed him over to a waiting vehicle. It looked like an oversized jeep. A tall black man in neat shorts and a flowered shirt was sitting behind the wheel.

"Morning', mastah," he said. "De Col'nul, he say you com'."

"Our invitation," said Haney. He gestured toward the Land Rover. "Miss Patrick?"

While the driver piled our luggage on a rack atop the vehicle, we distributed ourselves inside it. The driver came back to the front of the Land Rover, slipped behind the right-hand-drive wheel, and honked the horn. A woman wearing a bright saronglike dress rushed out of the building Casey had called the Tiger Lounge. Balanced on her head was a case of Red Stripe beer.

"On de floor, woman," growled the driver. "You slower'n molasses."

The woman cackled happily, the driver gave her a mighty swat on the behind, and she hustled back inside.

"H'opener, he hang by de ash tray," said the driver, grinding the powerful engine into life and causing the Land Rover to lurch off down the edge of the airstrip.

Porter found the churchkey, popped two bottle caps. He gave one bottle to Jean and held the other himself. "Split these," he said. "They'll stay colder that way." He drank, politely wiped the neck of the bottle, and handed it to Ham Keyes, who regarded it with awe.

"Howard," said Keyes, "is there some red-dirt farmer in your background that I don't know about?"

Haney guffawed. "You boys are all right," he decided. "Wouldn't ever guess it, up there in them fancy Madison Avenue offices though. You know, if you'd take off those gray flannel suits a little more often and be just good old boys, we'd all make a hell of a lot more money. As it is, we spend so much time trying to impress each other, we ain't hardly got time left to work."

"Let me have that Red Stripe," Porter said. "It's getting warm." Keyes took another swig and handed the bottle to the account man.

To Haney, he said, "I'm not so sure you're correct, Bill. We're your white witch doctors. If we took off our juju suits and got rid of the fancy decorations, you wouldn't believe in our magic any more, and you'd probably go to someone who puts on a better show."

"Could be," Haney said jovially, "could just be."

We jounced over miles of incredibly bad road, heading uphill all the time, while Haney bantered with each of us in turn. Only Jean was immune to his gentle taunts. Finally she leaned forward, touched him on the arm, and said, "How about me, Colonel?"

"How about what, little miss?"

"Don't you have an opinion on college girls? Or crusaders? Modern youth?"

He seemed embarrassed. "Shucks, us men were just kidding around."

She shook her head. "You're pretending to joke, but it's the old pecking order. You're the boss, so everybody laughs just a little louder at *your* jokes. Then they tell one of their own, just to prove they're not completely under your thumb. But it's a one-sided game. You can keep it going as long as *you* want. Or you can stop it by just taking back your ball and refusing to play any more."

Haney's voice was hard. "You've got some fairly harsh opinions of us, haven't you, Miss Patrick?"

He seemed to have lost about ninety percent of his Southern accent.

"Hey," I said, "let's not—"

Haney didn't look at me. "You stay out of this, hear, boy?"

"See?" Jean said. "How big a man are you really, Colonel? Without your wallet, I mean?"

Haney turned angrily toward the driver, said, "Turn this goddamned thing around—" and Keyes cut in: "That's enough! Both of you are behaving like children. Miss Patrick, you are here to observe what we do, not comment on it. And as for you, Bill, when did you start beating up on little girls?"

There was a silence thick enough to spread peanut butter on, punctuated only by the smashing of the Land Rover's wheels in the road's multitudinous potholes. Then Haney laughed.

"You're right as always, Ham," he said. "A million apologies, little lady. Will you forgive old Willie?"

"On one condition," she said.

"Name it."

"Call me Jean. Or 'hey you.' Anything except 'little lady.' "

"That's a promise," he said.

Eight beers later we arrived at a collection of shacks that, according to Haney, was the town of Quick Step, last outpost of so-called civilization before the Cockpit Country.

We parked in front of a rundown church with the roof fallen in. The churchyard was filled with moss-covered tombstones, most leaning at an angle. Empty Red Stripe bottles were strewn between them, and a herd of small goats grazed on the lank grass.

"Com'," said the driver. "De Col'nul, he wait."

We followed him up the hill to a shack with a roof made of metal Red Stripe, Pepsi, and Dragon Stout signs. An old white-haired black man, barefooted and wearing khaki pants cut off at the knees and a white shirt with no arms, came out, blinking in the sunlight.

"Colonel Frazier," said Haney, thrusting out his hand, "good to see you again."

I don't know what I had been expecting when I'd heard that a "colonel" ran the Maroons. Probably a tall black man with faintly Arabic features and a trim uniform with red epaulets on the shoulders and at least a ceremonial sword. But a toothless old man in an armless shirt? Ah, cruel reality.

Haney introduced us as business friends, explained that he wanted to show us one of the plantations. "Things look pretty good, Colonel," he said. "I think we're going to be in business before long."

The old man showed his broken stumps of teeth and

bobbed his head. "Dat very good, Mistah Haney, very good indeed."

He said something rapidly in a dialect that I couldn't understand, and a young black man came out of the shack. "Dis Maurice," said the old man. "He show you ganja patch."

"See you later, Colonel," said Haney. "We'll drink us some good rum, yes?"

"Dat very fine, Mistah Haney," said the Colonel. And watching him, in his bare feet and rags, I realized that what he looked like didn't matter—he *was* the Colonel, and in his presence Haney was merely a civilian camp follower.

Jean sensed it too. As we stumbled along the rocky path, she whispered to me, "Up here Mr. Haney's definitely Number Two trying harder, isn't he?"

Without moving my lips, I muttered, in approved George Raft style, "That's about the size of it."

Haney was giving us a lecture on ganja.

"The hemp plant, Cannabis sativa," he said, to anyone who would listen, "has been around as long as mankind. It grows either wild or under cultivation, and has quite a few other uses than smoking."

"Such as?" asked Howard Porter.

"Hemp rope is the oldest. As early as 1662 Virginia paid a bounty to farmers who would grow it. And right up through the Korean War licenses were still being issued in Kentucky just in case our overseas supplies of hemp rope might dry up. And the seeds—sterilized, of course, so they can't be used for cultivation—go into birdseed. Oil from the raw seeds is used to make soap and for paint thinners."

"Useful little devil, our friend the weed," I said.

"That it is, son," said Haney. "And to make the situation even more interesting, the Cannabis plant is dioecious."

"Di-which?" asked Porter, beating me to it.

"Dioecious. Most plants have both sexual organs in the same flower. But Cannabis has a separate male and female plant. Two by two, just like humans."

"How nice for the Cannabis plants," said Jean.

105

We crossed a rushing stream on slippery steppingstones and went into a grove of bamboo.

"Well," Haney went on, "it's the male plant that has the strong fibers that you use to make hemp rope. But the female . . . aha, boys, she's the one who causes all the trouble. She's the one with the potent resin for smoking."

"I wonder if Women's Lib has heard about this," I muttered. Haney didn't hear me and went on with his lecture.

"Cannabis was in wide use all over the Middle East and Asia long before the Christian era," he said. "But it didn't penetrate into Europe until the eighteen hundreds, when Napoleon's soldiers brought it back from their Egyptian expedition. The French intellectuals copied the Arabs and drank a Cannabis mixture called bhang. But it wasn't until a hundred years later that Cannabis got over here. Here meaning North America, of course, not just Jamaica."

We paused for a breather. Haney took out a handkerchief and mopped his sweating forehead. "First time I ever heard of the stuff," he puffed, "was once back when I was just a tad. I overheard my great-aunt telling my mother about something called Queen Anne's lace, which was supposed to be a powerful love potion. Mix a little into your weary husband's coffee and get instant prick." He colored. "Pardon me, Miss Jean."

"Carry on," she said blandly.

"Well," Haney continued, "around 1910 Cannabis got to New Orleans, where jazz musicians and poor people in general started using it as a replacement for booze. And then, of course, the Eighteenth Amendment—Prohibition —pushed things along. The stuff spread north, up through the Mississippi River towns, and by the early thirties it was being smoked wherever there were poor people, especially Latins and Negroes. Then, in 1937, Congress got sold a bill of goods. With no actual scientific support to back up the claims of a few do-gooders who insisted marijuana was a 'killer drug' and a 'powerful narcotic,' our noble lawmakers were panicked. Their reaction was what you'd expect. The only witness with any scientific background was a representative of the American Medical Association, a Dr. William C. Woodward. He pointed out to Congress that they hadn't heard a word of scientific evidence either for or against Cannabis, and suggested that scientists who had done research on the plant be called. His reward was to be accused of throwing obstacles in the way of law and order, and the new law was railroaded through."

"That was the Marijuana Tax Act of 1937, wasn't it?" Jean asked.

"None other," said Haney. "Oh, they were sly ones. Congress knew that passing a law outlawing possession of Cannabis would probably be unconstitutional, so they pushed through a phony tax bill. It wasn't against Federal law to have Cannabis. You just had to fill out a million papers and pay a tax. That was for 'handling.' Then if you wanted to sell or give some away, you had to make out some more papers for 'transfer.' Whereupon the state cops, who *did* have laws against holding the stuff, moved in and busted you."

Our guide waved us on and we moved forward through the jungle again.

Jean said, "Mike and I were just talking about the enforcement of marijuana laws. As long as it was only poor people being busted, the public didn't worry too much about the 'problem.' The Law was catching those filthy dope addicts, and wasn't that nice? But then respectable middle-class white youngsters started getting picked up and that put a different light on things. Because some of those state laws you mention are *rough*. Society didn't worry about their harshness when they were enforced against people they didn't really want as neighbors anyway. But when it started happening to their own nice sons in college—"

"She's right, men," said Haney. "Do you know that not long ago in North Dakota the rap for a first offense of possession—not even selling—carried a penalty of ninety-nine years at hard labor? In Georgia selling meant life and a second offense could draw the rope. It's obvious that those laws were shoved through by folks who were scared to death of 'dope fiends' and were aimed at the hard drugs like heroin. But, hell, some of those laws are just insane. They don't make sense on any level. In Michigan, where the minimum sentence for second-degree murder is two years, the minimum sentence for possession of marijuana is *twenty*. And, by God, they don't stop there. That's twenty for each offense. In other words, one reefer, twenty years. Two reefers, forty years. And so on."

I waved a halt to take a stone out of my shoe. "But they don't enforce those penalties, do they?"

"Sometimes yes, sometimes no," said Haney.

We moved on through rows of banana trees. Haney continued what was obviously his prototype lecture for the many luncheons he would have to address if his legal marijuana cigarettes ever became a reality. "In 1969 the Supreme Court threw out the part of the 1937 Act that made it illegal to possess marijuana without filling out the tax forms. That, held the Court, constituted self-incrimination since, as they'd been doing for thirty years, the individual states could use the tax forms as evidence against whoever filled them out. But this new ruling didn't really help much, because the Court wasn't coming out in favor of marijuana, just pointing out that as it stood the Act was illegal. Our noble lawmen got to work immediately to rewrite it so it *would* be legal. And here's the kicker most people don't know about. There's still a tax of a hundred bucks an ounce on the stuff. So even if you beat the rap, the Feds can swoop down and demand that you pay the tax. Do you know that they nicked one college kid with a tab for almost nine thousand dollars? And because he was a minor, his parents were liable and lost their car and house, not to mention the old man's job. And this was for a kid who got off clean because his arrest was the result of illegal search and seizure."

"Listen," I said, "I know those laws are on the books, but isn't it true that most judges agree that they're outrageous and refuse to enforce them?"

"Sure," flared Jean, "if the offender is a nice respectable middle-class kid with pull. But what if he's poor or black or both?"

"Jean's right," said Haney. "The middle-class kids have a better chance. But even there, nobody's home free. Under Federal law a first offender can get from two to ten, and a twenty-thousand-dollar fine. But the judge is also allowed to impose a suspended sentence or probation. For a second offense, however, the minimum prison sentence is mandatory. The judge is boxed in. He *can't* let you off."

"What about state laws?" Howard Porter asked.

Haney answered, "Generally they're rougher than the Feds. I mentioned the ninety-nine years. Well, there are some other cuties around that are more likely to be imposed than a life sentence. For instance, to show you how kinked up they are, in Massachusetts if you have marijuana *knowingly*—you grew it or bought it or were caught smoking it—you can get three years. But if you have it unknowingly—for instance, a friend stashed it in your car without telling you—you can get *five* years."

Wonderingly, Porter said, "Blind Justice."

"In several states," Haney continued, "just entering a place where marijuana is being used without your consent or even your knowledge is a crime. One time out in San Francisco those ballet dancers—you know, the English one and the Russian who went over the wall?"

"Margot Fonteyn and Rudolf Nureyev," I said.

"That's them. Well, they went to a North Beach party with some hippies. The place got raided, the cops found pot, and it took a lot of fast footwork to keep our dancer friends from getting six months, even though they probably wouldn't know what a reefer looked like if it came up and bit them on the ankle."

I had a momentary vision of a reefer biting Rudolf Nureyev on the ankle. It was a frightening image.

We took another break. Around us, in the thinning jungle, goats grazed happily. I assumed they were in better shape than I was. My side was hurting.

Now Hamilton Keyes spoke for the first time.

"We tend to throw around a lot of polarized words and opinions," he said. "I don't smoke pot and I don't particularly approve of it. But people are free to do a lot of things I don't approve of." He turned to Jean. "Miss Patrick, I understand and sympathize with your concern for the deprived, and the repressive way these laws can be used against them. But since Bill brought this proposition to me, I've been doing some research on my own. And things aren't as simple for the middle-class kids as you think. Even when people try to make them so. Say the judge is a nice guy, or maybe he's even a racist who doesn't want to stick those nice young white girls in there with those nasty niggers." He glanced at our guide, who apparently hadn't heard the word. "Do you think that's the end of it?"

"Of course not," said Jean, "but—"

"Let me finish," he said quietly. "The district attorney agrees to let them plead guilty, avoid a trial, and draw a suspended sentence. Do you think that's such a good deal? Let me tell you what a suspended sentence means. It means that for the rest of her life that girl will have to write 'Yes' in those blank places on the form where it asks 'Were you ever arrested?' 'For what?' 'Narcotics.' Those forms are used for employment, for everything from credit applications to driver's licenses. As a matter of fact, in most states she'll *lose* her driver's license and never be able to get it back. She is branded a convicted felon, and that means she can never serve on a jury, never become an officer in one of the armed services—"

"Big loss," Jean said.

"Please, Miss Patrick," said Keyes, not raising his voice, "I've listened to your views. Do me the courtesy of hearing mine."

"I'm sorry," said Jean, and she was.

"She will be prevented from becoming a doctor or lawyer. She can never hold a job in which she must be bonded. In some states she must register with the local police every time she visits a strange town. All of this, mind you, for a suspended sentence. And in many cases she won't be that lucky. She *will* draw some kind of a prison sentence, even if it's only a short one. Do you know what the prisons are like today? I read recently where a judge was removed from the bench because he refused to send youthful offenders to prison. It was quite a scandal and he ruined his career, but I think I understand why he took his stand.

"Let's abandon our hypothetical young lady. Oh, she'll have it bad enough, closeted with prostitutes, many of them users of hard drugs, easily procurable even in prison, and eager for whatever reason including just plain destructiveness to addict newcomers. 'Fresh fish,' they call them. Forget the brutality she'll meet, probably for the first time in her life. Forget the callousness—at the hands of guards and other inmates, and ultimately in her own opinion of herself. Forget all this because she is, after all, a woman in society which grants women some measure of protection.

Things will be bad for her, but not as bad as they *could* be."

I had never seen Keyes worked up like this. Fascinated, I listened.

"Imagine, instead, a young man, eighteen or nineteen years old. Maybe he thought it was fun to do what the other kids were doing and so he let himself be talked into puffing a little grass. The next thing he knows, he's arrested at gunpoint and thrown into a tank with drunks and thieves and perverts. There are recorded cases where boys have been raped by homosexuals in a police van on their way to be booked.

"Is it any wonder that the judge I mentioned found himself unable to take boys who were basically guiltless of any real crime against society and subject them to such treatment? 'It's not a crime to be foolish,' he said the day he was removed from the bench. You see, he knew what even thirty days could do to a sensitive boy whose only crime was foolishness. I take my hat off to that judge, and if anything we can do with this project will help get those lousy laws off the books, I'm in there to the finish. Reformers haven't been able to pull it off. Maybe good old American free enterprise and the profit motive will succeed where morality has failed."

"I'm with you," I said. "Somebody wrote somewhere that the only thing prisons cure is heterosexuality."

"Somebody was right," Hamilton Keyes said.

BEWARE! Young and Old—People in All Walks of Life! This Marijuana Cigarette may be handed you by the *friendly stranger.* It contains the Killer Drug "Marijuana" —a powerful narcotic in which lurks

Murder! Insanity! Death!

WARNING! Dope peddlers are shrewd! They may put some of this drug in the teapot or in the Coca-Cola or in the tobacco cigarette.

Write for detailed information, enclosing 12 cents in postage—mailing cost. Address: THE INTER-STATE NARCOTIC ASSOCIATION

(Incorporated not for profit)

53 W. Jackson Blvd. Chicago, Illinois, U.S.A.

—A TYPICAL POSTER DISTRIBUTED IN THE 1930s

Until now the only marijuana I had ever seen growing was a scrawny little plant a New York friend was cultivating under a sunlamp in his closet. One day he made the insane error of putting it out on the fire escape for a little real sunlight, a passing narc—Narcotics Division policeman—spotted it, and in ten minutes my friend was in the station-house disclaiming any friendship with the erring plant. Luckily, that night the stationhouse cat, a gigantic neuter, consumed the plant, which had been placed in the Captain's office, and the case was dismissed for lack of evidence.

Here, on the fringes of Jamaica's Cockpit Country, the marijuana plants I saw were ten to twelve feet tall. Some, identified by Haney as the female plants, were even taller.

Each had a thick stalk, topped by a cluster of flowers. Along the stalks were dozens of smaller stems with long, jagged, sawtoothed leaves, and more flowers.

Haney beckoned us over to examine one monster of a plant that was at least fifteen feet tall.

He scraped his fingernail across the tops of some of the sawtoothed leaves. "See that yellow resin? That's the active ingredient. THC, tetrahydrocannabinol. It's found all through the plant, but it's most potent in the flowering tops. The leaves carry a good deal and so do the stalks. In the Middle East they scrape off this resin and press it into cakes of hashish."

"Is hash the same as marijuana?" I asked. "I thought it was a different drug."

"They're one and the same," Haney said. "Hashish is stronger because it's pure THC instead of being diluted with bits of organic matter." He indicated the sprawling field of towering plants. "This isn't the best way to grow Cannabis, by the way. These plants are mixed up, male and female. The resin is more profuse and more potent, too, from virginal females that have never been pollinated. When we go into operation on a wider scale, we'll have whole fields of nothing but female plants."

Porter asked, "Will you use Jamaica for a source of supply, or set up fields in the States?"

"That depends on what both governments have to say about our project," Haney said. I noticed that when he was talking serious business, his Southern accent and idiom were virtually gone. "The scientists believe that the resin is produced by the plants as protection against extremely hot sunlight. That's why plants grown in tropic climates are more powerful than those you find in temperate zones. So, if possible, we'd like to use tropical plants."

He wiped his sticky fingers on his pants. "Now, even with really good plants, the product comes in several grades. For instance, the pure resin itself is the strongest. That's hashish, or charas as they call it in India. You smoke it in a pipe, usually one of those hookah jobs. Waterpipes. Or mix a little with tobacco. Maybe put a little chunk inside a regular cigarette. In India they eat it too. You can mix up a mean bunch of brownies that way."

Maurice said, "All troo lookin', sah?"

"Yeah," said Haney. "We might as well get back."

We started down the hill.

"Ganja is the next strength," Haney said. "That's high-grade stuff made from the chopped tops and leaves. It's cured and cleaned by taking out the stems and seeds, and is usually smoked, although some cook with it too."

114

"What's the effect when eaten as opposed to being smoked?" asked Keyes.

"Less intense, but more prolonged. We're going to have to do a lot of work on this whole effect thing, men. After all, what are we actually going to promise the consumer? That he'll get stoned out of his mind? Or just get a gentle glow?" Haney looked around. "How many of you have actually smoked pot?"

At once Jean said, "I have." She looked at me.

I groaned inwardly, but said, "Me too." And, looking at Keyes, "A long time ago."

No one else spoke up.

Haney grunted. "About what I figured. Senior management doesn't have vices." His Kentucky accent was coming back. "Well, we'll take care of that."

Quickly, Porter said, "We don't have to smoke the stuff to find out how to sell it."

Haney grinned. "What's the matter, Howard? Scared of getting hooked?"

Porter didn't answer. We continued down the hill.

From a thicket just ahead of us came what sounded like a woman's terrified scream.

"What the hell was *that?*" Haney demanded.

Maurice bared two rows of flashing white teeth in a grin. "De Col'nul, he want pig dinner. Dey butcher him pig now."

The soaring scream came again as the frightened pig, seeing the knife, shrilled its terror to the listening jungle.

Jean had pressed both hands over her ears. "Please make them stop," she whispered.

Then it *did* stop, with a gurgling snort that told us the knife had done its work.

"What are the rest of the marijuana grades you mentioned?" Keyes asked—too obviously, I thought. But Haney picked it up.

"The weakest is bhang. That's the poor man's marijuana. They take dried leaves, stems, whatever they can get, usually with a low resin content, and mix it up with liquids to drink. Bhang is so weak that it doesn't even come under the 1961 Convention on Narcotic Drugs. It's to ganja what beer is to bourbon."

We passed the thicket. All was silent within.

Maurice grinned again. "De pig, him finish."

"Are we staying over tonight?" Keyes asked.

Haney shrugged. "If the Colonel's laying on a pig roast, I guess we have to. It's a real honor to be invited to one. You can't turn it down. He'd lose too much face."

"I don't mind eating pigs," said Jean. "I just don't like listening to them scream."

Haney laughed. "You get used to it down in farm country, girl."

"My name is Jean," she said, "and I grew up in farm country. You *never* get used to it."

We arrived back at the village named Quick Step. The sun was high overhead and very hot.

"Let's see if I can scare up some lunch," Haney said. He went into the Colonel's tiny shack and came out a few minutes later carrying five bottles of Red Stripe.

"All set," Haney said. "Anybody want a swim before lunch? There's a waterfall just around the bend in the road up there, and a deep pool underneath it."

"I didn't bring a suit," Jean said quickly.

Haney laughed. "Hell, neither did I. What's wrong with a little skinny-dipping among friends?" Jean didn't smile, and he hurried to add, "Just kidding, honey. But bra and panties are a hell of a lot less revealing than those bikinis you kids wear nowadays. And us men can wear our shorts. How about it?"

"You go ahead," she said. "I think I'll just sit down in the shade and get my notes organized."

He shrugged, half angry. "Suit yourself. How about the rest of you buzzards? If the little lady ain't around, we can swim the old-fashioned way."

I felt like a traitor for leaving her, but the humid heat made the thought of a swim delicious. I looked back. "Are you sure you won't change your mind, Jean?"

Without looking up from her notebook, she said, "No, thanks, Mike. But you have fun."

When we were out of earshot, Haney asked, "What's wrong with that girl?"

"Huh?"

"You heard me. There's something wrong with her. Is she a lez, or what?"

I heard a rushing in my ears and I must have stepped toward him, because Porter grabbed my arms and said, "Hold it, hold it!"

Haney moved back and said, "Simmer down, boy. I *like* her. But I done me a parcel of women-studying, and there's something funny with this one. I just can't put my finger on it, but I will, you can bet on that."

Furious, I said, "Why don't you just stick to peddling cancer and leave her alone?"

He stared at me. "Hoo-boy, you got it bad, ain't you? I'm right sorry, Mike. I mean it. I didn't know I was climbing any of your fences."

I didn't say anything. I felt silly. Why had I gone after him? What the hell did I care if he said things about a girl I'd met only three days before?

"Sorry," I mumbled. "Let's forget it."

The waterfall was more a series of rapids, cascading down over worn rocks. The pool was palm-shaded and icy-cold to the exploring toe. We stripped down, making an obvious point of not looking at each other, and slipped gasping into the chilly water.

"Ahhh," said Howard Porter. "This is true democracy."

Puzzled, Haney asked, "What are you talking about?" and Porter answered, "Where but in America could a peasant like me piss in a pool containing the presidents of two major corporations?"

DATE: November 18
PLACE: in field, Quick Step, Jamaica, W.I.
PRODUCT: C-900
PRESENT FOR CLIENT: W. Haney
PRESENT FOR AGENCY: H. Keyes, H. Porter,
                    M. Evans
PRESENT FOR McCLINTLOCK COMMITTEE: J. Patrick

Meeting convened during luncheon at
12:40 p.m.

Client suggested following timetable:

1. Product names, packaging suggestions and product descriptions due by
December 1.

2. Preliminary advertising in both
print and broadcast due by December 15.
Package designs due same date.

3. Dummy Sunday supplement advertising and "quick and rough" TV commercials
on either 16mm film or videotape will be
produced as soon as possible after receiving approval of copy from client. This
timetable will be moved back one day for
each day client approval is delayed.

4. Agency will present research
program for Client approval during week of
December 15. Suggested areas will probably include recall testing of print ads
in dummy Sunday supplement; recall testing
of TV commercials inserted in cable
transmission of regular programming via
a feed, such as is available in our present
captive test area of Norwich, New York;
and advertising effectiveness testing based
on captive theater situation, either
through projection or with Fairchild 8mm
or EVR tape cartridge system.

Meeting adjourned at 2:15 p.m.

Now at least we were getting some work done. The conference at lunch straightened out a lot of loose ends that had been bothering me. It was one thing to fly all over the boondocks, inspecting marijuana plantations, and another entirely to translate this seeming waste motion into an effective advertising project.

I am always ill-at-ease when there isn't work to be done. A certain Calvinistic streak in my character refuses to let me enjoy myself unless I have first paid for my fun with work. This has nothing to do with ambition—it doesn't seem to matter if the work is productive or not. It's just that I must *do* it or I fret at poolside, unable to enjoy my game of grabass with the vacationing airline stewardesses, or the run punches or even the sunset. This trait is probably one of the things that helped drive Janice away.

So, sitting on a rude log bench in a tiny Jamaican town named Quick Step, taking notes for the work to come during the next month, I felt at ease for the first time since Uncle Norman had dropped his bomb in Conference Room 661.

As for lunch itself, that was an experience. There was plenty of Red Stripe, of course. Also gin and Schweppes Tonic and Bitter Lemon.

We began with what Colonel Frazier called "patties." They looked like little apple turnovers. But instead of being filled with fruit, they were stuffed with ground meat, highly spiced with curry. They were steaming hot and the pastry dough was crisp and flaky. "I wonder if they used Crisco?" I said, thinking back to the days when I wrote glowingly of Crisco crusts that were "crisp on the outside, tender and flaky inside."

"Dey fry wid coconut oil," said the Colonel. I resisted a whim to mail Procter & Gamble a testimonial to the effect that in Quick Step it's coconut oil three to one.

Maurice brought out a platter of what looked like tiny bits of spareribs. Spread around the ribs were slices of pale gray sausage.

"Dis jerked pork," said the old man. "Him very hot. Eat wid bread."

Each of us was given half a loaf of white, extremely heavy unsliced bread.

"Hard-dough bread," said Maurice. He picked up a bit of pork, chewed it, then bit off a hunk of bread.

"He looks like a sunburned Italian eating salami," Porter said, trying it himself. He chewed silently on the pork for a while and then let out a surprised yelp and began gnawing at the hunk of bread in his other hand. "Holy shit!" he said, "That's *hot!*"

One by one we dared the jerked pork. It was rich with flavor, highly spiced, and totally delicious. It took a minute or so before the burning sensation began, and then it was time to munch on the heavy, doughy bread for relief. The little sausages were just as spicy.

"It's wonderful!" Jean gasped, her eyes watering.

I felt a sudden, almost overpowering urge to grab her in my arms and hug her until she yelled.

I shut my eyes and forced myself to remember William P. Haney's growling voice saying, "Simmer down, boy."

Like Effie said, she's too goddamned skinny.

What's more, she is out to nail our hides to the wall,

120

whatever she says and whatever Ham Keyes chooses to believe.

Keyes said something. "What?" I asked.

"I was saying that Bob mentioned he'd like to get together with you on some creative ideas," Keyes repeated. "Why don't you two get that out of the way after lunch? Meanwhile Howard and I can put down some preliminary media and budget suggestions."

"Fine with me," I said. I looked at Jean again. She didn't look *that* skinny, now that I thought of it. . . .

Two natives came down from the jungle hill, carrying a fifteen-pound suckling pig impaled on a stake.

Haney guffawed. "That must have been some surprised pig when they yelled 'whoa' and when he did that stake caught up with him."

He was glared at by Jean Patrick.

We sat around smoking thin brown cigars from a package marked Calypso and drinking Red Stripe until Haney got up, stretched, took an obvious look at his wristwatch, and said, "Well, Mike, boy, why don't we leave the businessmen to their adding machines and go do some brainstorming?"

"I don't see why not," I drawled through my Calypso.

"Jean," Haney said, leaning hard on the name, "I bet you can learn something from listening to these two figure out how to cut up my money. Mike and me'll be back in a couple of shakes."

She looked up sharply. "No," she said. "I'd rather stay with Mike."

"We're just going to bat around a couple of ideas," he said almost plaintively.

"Wonderful," she said, standing up. "I've always wanted to attend a brainstorming session."

"Shit!" said our dignified client and, without a backward glance, stormed off toward the waterfall.

The expression on Jean's face changed subtly, and she turned to Hamilton Keyes. "I'm sorry," she said. "I hope I'm not putting you in the middle. But once I've started with a subject, I'd rather stay with him all the way through. I'll apologize to Mr. Haney."

121

Ham smiled up at her. "Don't bother. Bill goes through life according to his own rules. It may do him good to meet someone else who also has a set."

I started liking Jean again. And, to my surprise, I found myself feeling very warm toward my boss.

As we walked along the potholed road I said to Jean, "Too bad you didn't have that swim this morning. Howard sent our eminent client boiling out of the water like a torpedoed whale."

"I know," she said. "Howard weeweed in the pool."

I stopped. "How do you know?"

"Howard told me. He thought it was very funny. So did I."

So good old Howard Porter was a secret swinger. The things you learn on location. . . .

Jean brushed against me as we turned onto the path that went down to the little stream.

"Aha!" I said.

She looked at me. "Aha what?"

"Aha, you're wearing my Chanel."

She smiled. "I warned you, Mike, if I could be bribed, it would be with Chanel."

"Are you bribed?"

The smile faded. "Of course not. I was only joking."

"So was I. Let's go down. Watch your step, immediate seating in the rear of the pool."

Haney, waiting by the falls, had regained his composure. "I've got a lousy temper, Jean," he said. "You're entitled to one free slug at my jaw or to a fancy dinner at the Rum Barrel back in Mo Bay."

"Is Mike included in the dinner offer?" she asked straightfaced.

"Reluctantly."

She stuck out her hand. "We'll take the dinner."

"Deal," he said. "Okay, listen. I know I don't have to say this ain't supposed to go no further than right here, but I'll say it anyway. We're playing around with a hell of a lot of money, but that ain't the most important thing. We're also playing around with maybe eighteen months on the rockpile, and that's why I wasn't too happy about you overhearing what I want to say to Mike."

A cold lump settled in my stomach. "What are you talking about, rockpile?"

"I need help," Haney said. "More help than I can ask those guys back there for. Look, Mike, maybe you don't like me and Christ knows there isn't any reason why you should. But there's one thing nobody ever said about me —that I sent other men out to do my dirty work. I'm a mean bastard, and I come from a family of mean bastards, and my *kids* are growing up to be mean bastards too. Because it's the mean bastards who will inherit this earth, in spite of what the preachers say."

"Bill," I said, "what the hell are you talking about?"

He waved back toward the village. "I wanted to get you away from those guys. They're okay, but they live in another world from me. They're too polite. They believe in rules that I never heard of. They'd shit a brick—'scuse me, Jean—if they knew what I was really up to down here."

In an amazed voice Jean said, "My God, you're going to smuggle marijuana back to the States."

"I *got* to," Haney said. "And I need Mike to help me. I didn't want to get you involved. I told you not to come over here with us. But you had to have your own way."

"I should have known we didn't fly two thousand miles just to have a pig roast," I said. "But why? You can buy grass all over Manhattan. The city is full of it. Or you can have fifty kilos shipped in from Mexico."

Haney shook his head. "That stuff isn't consistent. It's bad quality or else it's been cut. We can't count on it. We're prototyping a product that we have to be able to duplicate whenever we want to. That means quality control, and the only way to be sure we've got it is to start with our own stuff. We need at least five hundred pounds of weed to experiment with."

"Still," said Jean, "why you? You could hire a hundred experts to bring it in for you."

"I said, girl, I don't send others to do my dirty work. If I did and they got caught, what then? 'We were hired by that big businessman, William Haney'? Hell no, girl, I'd rather take my own risks. Less chance of getting in trouble that way."

123

Ignoring the two "girls," Jean said, "But why do you need Mike?"

"Let's say that as good a pilot as Hod Casey is, and despite the fact that he's a prince of a fellow, I'd feel much safer having a witness along when we head off into the wild blue yonder with a hundred thousand dollars' worth of ganja."

"Let me get this straight," I said. "Are you telling me that this limey is going to smuggle you out of Jamaica with a planeload of pot and try to sneak past the coastal defenses into the United States? You have to be kidding, and I'm not even mentioning the obvious idiocy of considering me any great shakes as a bodyguard."

"The flying part isn't as hard as you think, Mike. On this end, the only real chance of being busted is through an informant, and believe me, none of Colonel Frazier's people are going to shoot off their mouths. The Colonel's got his own system of finding out what's happening, and it would be kind of fatal for any of his men to get friendly with the Flying Squad."

"Okay, you get the stuff on the plane and head for Miami. What about U.S. Customs?"

"U.S. Customs? In Orlando?"

"How the hell do you get to Orlando? You've got to come in through a Port of Entry."

"Mike," Haney said patiently, "air traffic around Florida is high density. Sure, there's an ADIZ to get past, but—"

"A—what?" asked Jean.

"Air Defense Identification Zone. Air Force'll pick us up on their radar screens, all right. But hell, half of those bush planes coming in from the islands have radio problems. The chances of their sending a jet out to check on us are mighty slim. So when we're through the ADIZ, we mix ourselves up in the Miami traffic stack, then break out like we just took off, file a flight plan in the air for Orlando, and from then on, as far as Air Traffic is concerned, we are just another local flight."

"You were born twenty years too late," I said. "You'd have made a great rum-runner."

He smiled. "That's what my old pappy used to tell me. Well?"

124

He was pressing me for an answer and I wasn't ready to give it. "I'll assume you've got every chance of getting away with it," I told him. "But what the hell's the rush? You're risking jail—or at the least a hell of a fine. Why? Just to get a two- or three-month jump on the competition? How can it be worth it?"

"Mike, we're talking about a market situation that will go into the hundreds of millions almost overnight. Every day of lead time is another fifty thousand dollars in the till. Multiply that by even a ninety-day advantage, and we're talking about four and a half million dollars."

Sweetly, Jean said, "I would think that was just walking-around money for you, Mr. Haney."

"Go ahead," he said. "It's easy to make fun of money when you don't have any. But I'll take the real stuff any time and the respect that goes with it. Anyway, it ain't just the money. It's the leadership Coronet will have in the new market. If we catch those other bastards flatfooted, we'll have clear running for at least the first two years before they stand a chance to catch up. And even then, they'll have to buy every goddamned share point of market at top dollar. We'll be in the black from Day One, and it'll take the rest of them at least thirty-six months to get out of the red." He laughed. "That's worth a little risk."

"For you, maybe," I said, "but what makes you think I'll come along on the ride?"

Calmly, he said, "I don't know, Mike. Why *should* I think you'll come along?"

"I don't follow."

"I wouldn't insult you by just offering you money. But you must want something. What? A red Jaguar XKE on loan from Coronet so you don't have any tax problems with it? One of those new co-op apartments over by the park? Stock options? A chance at starting your own shop? Or maybe it *is* money. You tell me, Mike."

"I'm doing fine right now," I began.

Jean stopped me. "Mr. Haney," she said, "you're throwing around some awfully big pricetags just to have Mike riding shotgun with you."

"The job doesn't end there. I know Mike's a good advertising man. I need someone like him looking out for my interests over at MK&C. I couldn't tell Ham Keyes that

125

I'm going to smuggle in a planeload of pot. Maybe there'll be other decisions along the way that I won't be able to pass along to Ham. But somebody over there has to know the whole story and keep things moving in the right direction. That's why I told Ham to put you in charge of C-900, Mike. I know you better than *you* do. You like to be where the action is. Well, I can promise you enough action in the next two years to last you a lifetime. How about it?"

"I work for MK&C," I said. "Not you."

He shrugged. "I'm not asking you to be the company rat. All I want is someone watching out for the account with a realistic knowledge of what's going on."

"That's my job anyway," I said. "You don't need under-the-table deals to get me to do what I'm already being paid for."

"You're not being paid to fly a twin-engined Grumman Goose into the States illegally."

"And maybe I'm not doing it either."

"What's the matter, boy? Scared?"

I stared him down. "You bet your ass I'm scared."

When we got back to the village, the hapless pig was suspended from his pole over a bed of glowing coals. Maurice sat nearby, turning the pole every now and then. It was propped up between two forked sticks driven into the ground.

We paused for a moment and inhaled the rich odor of roasting pig.

I'd told Haney he would have his answer the next day, when we were back in Montego Bay. He grumbled a little, but accepted the inevitable.

"Rum punch, sah?" said Maurice, indicating a sweating metal pitcher on a shaded table.

"Sounds good," said Haney. "Jean? Mike?"

We both said no and I went over to the Colonel's little store for a pair of Red Stripes. Then we sat in the shade and watched the lengthening shadows move across the ravines between the hills.

"Something tells me," Jean said, as three naked black children ran, shrieking with laughter, across the road, "that I am not getting a completely representative picture of Madison Avenue meetings."

127

I choked on my Red Stripe. "Nonsense," I said. "This is the way it always is. We usually conduct our conferences in the old slave quarters back in the bush. Some of my best advertising campaigns were written with a pointed stick in the dust of Quick Step. Of course, it's a long commute from Westchester, but—"

Giggling, she waved me into silence. We sipped at our beers.

"I think I'm wasting my time and yours," she said finally. "I ought to disqualify myself from the project."

I stared at my half-empty beer and said nothing.

"I'm not going to, though," she said. "I'm going to see this thing through and then I'll decide whether or not I've got a report to turn in. I may end up with nothing. How does one justify participating in a smuggling operation?"

"You're not participating in anything," I said. "You're just an observer. I don't even think *I'm* going to participate in Haney's crazy goddamned scheme."

"Yes you are," she said. "And for the same reason I am."

"What reason is that?"

"Because it's fun."

"Some fun," I said. "Ten years in the pokey."

"Haney wouldn't let you take the blame," she said. "I don't know how he'd do it, and it might cost him a hundred thousand dollars, but if anything happened, he'd get you off."

"You're right," I admitted. "But it's still a crazy scheme. He's worth fifty million dollars if he's worth a dime. The *interest* compounds so fast he can't even count it, let alone spend it. What the hell's in this operation for him?"

"Winning," Jean said. "That's what's in it for all of you. The money isn't what drives you. The money is only an award proving you *won*. Did you notice how his eyes gleamed every time he talked about beating his competitors to the punch? That's what he's after, not the sales figures. He doesn't care if he only sells ten packages as long as that's one more package than anyone else sells. I think—"

I waited, but she was only staring at the green jungle.

"What do you think?" I asked, finally.

"I think I'm talking about things that we aren't going to solve this afternoon or any time in the next hundred years." She got up. "And I've had too much beer. Don't let anyone follow to protect me in the nasty jungle. I'm merely looking for a convenient palm tree."

"Your secret is safe with me," I said.

I finished my Red Stripe and rolled the bottle between the palms of my hands. For a moment I felt like going over and telling Haney that I'd fly with him to Orlando. There wasn't any point in kidding myself—I was hooked on the project. It was a chance to have some fun—and, as Jean had said, it was a way to win. Win big.

At no time did it enter my mind that we were conspiring to peddle a drug that, while it had not been proven harmful, had not been proven harmless either. If someone had questioned, I would have first been surprised—then, I suppose, I would have pointed out that if booze had just been invented, *it* would have a hard time getting certified by the Food and Drug Administration too. And aspirin wouldn't have had a chance. I had spent three years writing advertising for Coronet Cigarettes with the "Warning: The Surgeon General Has Determined That Cigarette Smoking Is Dangerous to Your Health" inscription on the side of each and every package. I even smoked the damned things myself, although Pall Malls were my secret vice. Like all smokers, I told myself that there was a risk in everything a person does, that the odds would never catch up with me, that crossing Fifth Avenue was more dangerous. So what was so new about trading new risks for the pleasures of marijuana? I didn't invent the stuff.

If the new Administration legalized pot, we would sell it. Period. Because if we didn't, somebody else would. I wasn't uptight about repressive laws the way Jean and Ham Keyes were. Mostly, I obeyed those laws—not because I was afraid of them, but because I had no great desire to use marijuana anyway. It was as if the government had made it illegal to eat Shredded Wheat. Since I don't particularly like Shredded Wheat, it couldn't matter less.

But if I ever got the Shredded Wheat account, I might *start* eating it. And I would certainly do everything I could to convince the world that Shredded Wheat was the sun and the moon and the four winds.

Why not? If I didn't, somebody else would, right?

I must have dozed for a while, because when I looked up it was blue twilight and the odor of roasting pork was heavy in the air. The tree lizards were chirping like crickets in the jungle.

"Well," said Haney, as I joined the group around the charcoal fire, "it's Sleeping Beauty. We were going to tie your shoelaces together, but your friend Jean wouldn't let us."

"Many thanks," I mumbled in her general direction. I am always stupefied when I wake up. I think that when I sleep, my metabolism must slow down to somewhere between hibernation and death.

"Here," said Keyes, handing me a tin cup. "Coffee."

"Many thanks," I repeated, sipping. The rim of the cup was fiercely hot. But the coffee was delicious. "Good," I managed to say.

"That's Blue Mountain Coffee," said Haney. "Best in the world. Made right here on the island. Cost you a couple of bucks a pound back in the States, if you could get it."

"You're too good to me," I said, feeling better.

"Just protecting my secret weapon," Haney said. "Incidentally, congratulations."

I blinked my still-swollen eyes. "Congratulations for what?

Haney looked toward Keyes, who stood up.

"Mike," he said, "you're still pretty young yet, but that's something time will take care of. I guess you already know that Bill insisted we bring you in on this project because of the great work you did on Coronet. But he wouldn't have had to ask, because you're the one we would have chosen anyway."

I swallowed some more coffee. "Well," I said, "either I'm getting a raise or you're building up to fire me."

"Bill has tentatively approved our estimated first-year budget," Keyes said. "We're going to launch C-900 with an eighteen-million-dollar appropriation. If we net six-percent profit out of media, fine. If not, Coronet'll make up the difference."

"What if we do all the work and then President Foster doesn't come through with legalization?"

"Coronet'll still cover us with the cost-plus deal."

I put down the tin cup. "So we're not going to have to fire people this time."

"No."

"Good." I bent over and sniffed at friend pig. He was going to be very tasty.

"Mike?" It was Keyes, obviously wanting to say something else.

"What is it, Ham?"

"Don't you want to know what's in it for you?"

"Okay, what's in it for me?"

"As of right now, you're a senior vice president. The board will have to meet, but that's just a formality."

"Hot dog," I said. "Now I can sign my own expense account. Boy, did *you* make a mistake."

Keyes added, "And of course you're creative director in charge of C-900."

"You mean creative group head."

"I mean creative director. This work isn't going through Charlie Stewart's office. C-900 is going to be a little agency within the agency."

This news took some getting used to. Like all creative directors, Charlie Stewart was very jealous of his prerogatives. I still remember one time when he looked at a bug spray commercial of mine and said, "I like it, Mike. But don't you think you ought to add a demo?" "The whole commercial's a demo, Charlie," I said, and he said, "Well, think about it, will you?" I agreed to think about it, and I did, one whole minute, and the commercial went on the air as I had planned, and sold a hell of a lot of bug spray, and that made it all the stranger that Charlie was going around glaring at me. Finally I braced him on it, and he almost snarled, "You lucked out, baby. I asked you to put a demonstration in that bug spray spot and you ignored what I told you." "You told me to think about it, and that's what I did," I came back, and Charlie answered, "Well, you're lucky it sold product, or you'd be out on your ass." It took six months for our relationship to return to normal—strained mutual respect. And now I was going to have a little duchy in competition with Charlie's. It would be very interesting.

"Charlie's not going to like that," I said slowly.

"Charlie's going to *have* to like it," Ham said. "From now on you're his associate creative director. Other shops work that way, and MK&C will too, or there'll be a few more changes around there."

"What about personnel?"

"You'll want to keep Mark Hedin and Phil McKenna, of course. I'd suggest that you let the junior writers move over onto some of the package goods in Bob Egan's group. This project is too sensitive for people we aren't completely sure of."

"Okay," I said. "I want more dough for Phil and Mark, though. I don't think I'll have to go outside to hire anyone else. But you ought to give Mark group head status. And the three of us will be doing the work of nine ordinary mortals."

"I'll see they're taken care of," Ham said. "How does forty sound for yourself?"

Playing it dumb, I said, "As retirement age? Great."

"I mean forty thousand for putting all of your time against C-900." I started to answer and Ham hurried to say, "*Plus* three thousand shares of MK&C preferred stock at today's book value. The reason I say today's value is because once the word hits the market about C-900, that stock is going to be worth double, maybe three times what it's booking for today."

"In other words, I can keep it for six months and unload for around two hundred thousand dollars in capital gains."

"Yes."

"Well, I'll be a dirty dog," I said. "It looks like I've hit the jackpot at last."

"Mike," Jean said softly, "you've *won*."

Puzzled, Haney said, "Won? Won what?"

"Just something we were talking about," I said. "Okay, Ham, what can I say? I hope I'm worth it to you. I'll do my best."

"I know that," he said. "And you *are* worth it."

With barely concealed double meaning, Haney added, "You're worth it, Mike, because *I* say you're worth it."

"In that case," I said, "keep talking."

We moved back as Maurice cut the roasted pig off the charred pole and slid it onto a huge platter that was piled

132

high with fried plantains, rice and red beans, and sliced to-matoes.

Everything had happened too fast for it to have any effect on me. All I knew was that I was somehow sorry that now I would never know if I had decided to go along with Haney because it was my decision or because I couldn't pass up all the goodies he'd laid out in front of me. As he had said earlier—maybe what turned me on *was* money.

I turned to Keyes. "Did Bill tell you that he and I are flying back to the States together?"

Keyes nodded. "We'll keep everything quiet at the shop until you get back to New York. Then we'll make the announcement. About you making senior v.p., I mean. We aren't going to announce what you're working on."

"I'll be flying back with them too," Jean said.

"Just a goddamned minute," I said. "Who says so?"

"I say so," Haney told me. "The way the little lady put it to me, I could hardly refuse." He did not sound at all happy about it.

Colonel Frazier came out and joined us. In honor of the occasion he had put on shoes—battered old blue suede loafers that looked as if they had once belonged to someone in a college orchestra.

Quietly, we filled our plates. I stood next to Haney. "You must have been pretty sure of me."

"I was," he said.

"How did Jean ace her way onto the plane?"

"She suggested that if she were aboard, it would remove any temptation she might feel toward being a good citizen and calling the Jamaican police."

"I'm surprised you didn't have the Colonel tell Maurice to fix her up like he did the pig."

Without smiling, Haney said, "I thought about it. But that might have made you unhappy."

"And right now my happiness is a business asset."

"That's the way it is," he agreed.

We sat on the rude coconut log benches again and wolfed down the meal. The pork was moist and tender, with bits of caramellike skin hanging from the meat. With the food we drank a coconut milk punch from shells that had been cut in half.

Afterward, feeling warm and lazy, we sat in the glare of

133

a single yellow bulb shining through the Colonel's open window and smoked the little Calypso cigars. Even Jean took one.

Without apparent reason, Haney asked, "How do you feel, Howard?"

Porter answered drowsily, "Happy as a cootie in a hound's ear, to coin a Haney. Why do you ask?"

"How about you, Mike?"

"Pretty good," I said. "Knowing you, is this when you pull out the reefers and 'suggest' we all give them a try?"

I couldn't see Haney's face, but I knew he was grinning. "No, Mike, not tonight. It isn't necessary."

I heard a gasp from Jean. Her hand tightened on my arm. "He's already done it," she said. "I know the feeling. I'm getting high."

"Bill—" Ham Keyes began.

"The little lady's right," said Haney. "Everybody relax and enjoy it. We're all going to be flying high tonight, because them rice and beans were seasoned with two ounces of top-grade marijuana."

AIRCRAFT DEPARTURE MANIFEST

Montego Bay, Jamaica, W.I.

November 18

AIRCRAFT: Twin Grumman Goose

PILOT: H. R. Casey, U.K.

DESTINATION: Nassau, Bahamas

PASSENGERS: Mr. Michael Evans, U.S.A.

Mr. William Haney, U.S.A.

Miss Jean Patrick, U.S.A.

CARGO: Personal belongings

ALL LANDING AND HANGAR FEES PAID

Somebody had been paid off, because aboard the Goose, theoretically loaded only with personal belongings, were nine cardboard boxes stenciled "National Lithographic Co. Wt. 63 lbs."

"Anyone asks," Haney had said, "those are copies of a book called *Beautiful Jamaica*."

Nine times sixty-three. That meant we had 567 pounds of compressed marijuana stashed in the tail of the Goose as it made its takeoff run.

It wasn't eleven yet. And we had gotten up before dawn to rejoin the plane at Appleton Estates. I don't know how anyone else felt, but I was still half high on the stuff I'd eaten the night before.

As soon as Haney had admitted what he'd done, I recognized the symptoms. I had never eaten marijuana before, but what I felt was similar to the reactions I had had from smoking it in college.

I wanted to slug him one, but there were more vital things to do.

"Ham," I said, "Howard. Tell me the truth. It's very

136

important. Has either of you ever used weed before?"

"Not me," said Porter. Keyes, apparently dazed, just shook his head.

I turned to Jean. "Help me with them."

She was already moving toward Keyes, and nodded.

As I passed Haney, I muttered, "This was stupid. What the hell were you trying to prove?"

He must have been smoking some on the side. He was already stoned higher than a kite, and he didn't answer me.

Although no two pot highs are the same, the user generally goes through certain predictable symptoms. The experienced smoker will have learned to moderate his reactions, disregarding the early anxiety that grips some beginners. For an inexperienced smoker the sensation can be terrifying.

I could feel the anxiety myself. After all, I was hardly an experienced smoker. This period of anxiety, which occurs in perhaps eighty percent of novice users, lasts from ten to thirty minutes, an eternity if you don't know what's happening. I was fighting down my own sensations, because I was worried about Howard.

"Come on, old buddy," I said. "Let's go up and look at the waterfall in the moonlight."

"I don't feel so good," he complained. Haney, obviously high, was laughing to himself. That's another frequent effect—unmotivated and often uncontrolled laughter. I felt a wave of fear sweep over me, and it took all my will-power to lead Porter away from the group. But I didn't want his anxiety to interact with Ham's and make both of them even worse.

"I think that roast pig may have been poisoned," Porter said, stumbling after me in the near-darkness. "Mike, I'm scared to death. What's happening?"

"Nothing's wrong, Howard," I told him. "Don't worry about a thing. Come on, let's go out and count the stars."

We blundered along the path. Then he stopped and let out a groan. "Mike," he whispered, *"my heart's going to stop!"*

"Like hell it is," I said, dragging him after me. Now we were far enough away from the others, and when the moonlight let us see a fallen coconut trunk, we sat down.

"You're feeling good, Howard," I told him. "Floating. And your arms and legs are light enough to fly."

"I'm scared," he said, the word coming strangely from his forty-three-year-old mouth.

"No you're not. You feel wonderful. Everything's beautiful. Whatever you see or feel or taste or smell is beautiful. You're floating in the ocean, and it's so comfortable you want to stay there forever. You're not afraid of anything."

Suddenly, he said, "I see flashing lights. They're all colored, like the Fourth of July."

"That's good, Howard,"

He giggled. "Hey, you're right. I feel great. And pot doesn't upset my stomach as aspirin often does."

He was reaching back for old advertising clichés. That was a favorable sign. I was feeling pretty good myself. My concentration on stopping him from having a bad trip had taken my mind off my own anxieties.

"Holy shit," Porter said, his voice filled with awe. "Mike—I can *see myself!* I'm standing here looking at both of us." He laughed. "Boy, am I getting fat. And you're not doing so good in the lard department yourself, boy."

I didn't answer. By then I had really started trying to count the stars. . . .

Anyway, we were lucky. Porter had a ball. He stood there outside his body (so he claimed), commenting on the physical shell that no longer seemed to have any connection with him. After an hour or so of that, he got sleepy, and I reluctantly abandoned my tabulation of the heavens to steer him back to a bed in a shack Maurice led us to.

Colonel Frazier rousted us out at five A.M. personally, on orders left by Haney. We stumbled down to a campfire and had some coffee, while Haney and the Colonel conferred earnestly inside the rundown store.

"Howard's okay," I told Jean. "How did you make out with Keyes?"

"No problems," she said. "He didn't even get anxious.

138

He went right on the stare and spent most of the night watching old movies on the inside of his head."

"That was a crazy stunt for Haney to pull."

She agreed. "It's like putting vodka in a child's orange juice. We're lucky nobody freaked out."

We were standing apart from the group, sipping our coffee.

"Jean," I said, "are you a head?"

"Is that any of your business?"

"No. I just wondered."

"I told you before, I smoke now and then, when it's around. But no, I'm not a pothead. Does that make you any happier?"

It did, although I don't know why. I was still high myself. The feeling was both pleasant and disturbing.

In the pale half-light Jean smiled. "You're still flying."

"You better believe it," I said.

"Me too," she said.

"First time I ever went the brownie route," I said. "I'll say this for it, this stuff stays with you."

"What's going to happen," she asked, "when a bunch of kids who never smoked before get hold of your C-900 or whatever you end up calling it? You know, Howard's lucky you were here last night."

"Something tells me," I said, without knowing if I believed it myself, "that whatever we put on the market won't be strong enough to blow the mind of a flea."

"So they'll puff five joints instead of one."

I shrugged. "Hell, I don't know what'll happen. I used to work on a booze account. I know there are alcoholics in the world. Some of them undoubtedly guzzled my booze. What was I supposed to do, personally accompany each and every bottle of Scotch and warn the consumer, 'Caution, if you drink too much of this stuff you will burn out your liver and probably wreck your car besides'? We ran seasonal campaigns warning about driving while under the influence and all that, but it didn't really do any good. I've done ninety on the Thruway myself with a can of Bud in my hand."

"Well," Jean said, "at least you're honest."

We connected with Hod Casey at Appleton Estates just after sunrise, and were back in Mo Bay by eight A.M. The silence during the flight was pronounced. No one mentioned anything about the previous night. But I felt Hamilton Keyes's eyes on me more than once.

I had just finished packing when a heavy knock rattled my Wexford Court door. When I opened it, Haney was there.

"I'm riding to the airport with you," he said. "Howard will drop Jean off."

"So she's still coming with us?"

He spread his hands. "I know she's bluffing, but we can't take the risk. Besides, I'll feel better having her where I can see what she's up to." He swore briefly, meanwhile opening the door to the refrigerator in the vain hope that there might be something to drink inside. There was. Water. He shut the door again. "You bastards really fixed me up when you dragged her in on this."

"I don't think we did her any favor either."

"Shit," he said, "I'm sorry about last night. I thought it would be funny. I'd blown a stick or two after lunch, and it seemed somehow unfair that the rest of you were so straight while I was flying. It was a kid stunt, and I've already apologized to the other guys."

"I don't think Ham likes you any more," I said. "You could have cut glass with the looks he was giving you this morning."

"Well, what the hell does he want?" Haney demanded. "He puts on this big act about wanting to break down the restrictions. He's willing to peddle the stuff and he's more than willing to make a buck on it. Where does he find cause to complain?"

"Maybe he'd like to choose when and if he uses it himself."

"My mouth is as dry as cowshit in August," Haney said. "Don't you have even one lousy beer around this place?"

"We can get one down at the Pelican. That's one of the fringe benefits of Cannabis sativa, you know."

"What is?"

"A mouth that's dry as cowshit in August. If I were you, I'd invest in a soft-drink company too. Potheads drink Coke like there's no tomorrow. But the bottom will drop out of the booze market. They don't dig the hard stuff."

"You think you're being funny," Haney said, "but that might not be such a bad idea."

We walked down the hill to the Pelican, swilled two bottles of Red Stripe each. I started to go back up to the hotel to tell Jean what was happening but Haney waved me back. "I already told her," he said.

"What did she have to say?"

He grinned sheepishly. "She cussed me out pretty good about last night. You know, boy, when I first started smoking pot, the first thing I noticed was that it got that old joint up a lot more often and kept it up a lot longer than before. I felt like that this morning. I don't think she's a lez after all. I couldn't get a hard on for her if she was."

"Somehow, I don't believe she knew what was on your evil old mind," I said.

Suspiciously, he asked. "What makes you say that?"

"Because you don't have a black eye."

He laughed. "I like you, you little bastard. And by Christ, you ought to like *me*. You're a quarter of a million bucks richer this morning than you were yesterday, because of what I set up for you. The least you could do is say thanks."

"Thanks," I said.

Haney swore again. "You're something else," he said. "Come on, let's go. I want to check out that plane."

I paid for the beers and we walked up the hill to the parked Anglia. The old black man who acted as caretaker had already put my bag in the trunk. I tipped him twenty cents Jamaican—a quarter in U.S. money. He was delighted.

"The bill's already taken care of," Haney said. "Come on, boy, let's get this heap on the road."

I backed down the hill by pushing in the clutch and releasing the hand brake. It's a tricky shift, getting an Anglia's gearbox into reverse, and whenever possible, I avoid it. I made a turn, passed the Pelican, and headed for the airport.

"What are we going to do about our Debarkation cards?" I asked.

141

"Get them checked out like always," Haney said. "As far as anyone knows, we're going to Nassau for a little gambling. What's wrong with that?"

"Nothing," I said, "except that they'll give us pitying looks as we depart. Everybody knows that people who gamble at Paradise Island have cinders in their heads. That place is the worst hustle in the western hemisphere."

"People must like it," Haney said. "They keep going back."

"Like the guy said when they asked him why he kept going back even though he knew the dice were crooked, 'It's the only game in town.' Sometimes people aren't too bright, Bill."

He grinned. "Don't knock it. If they were, we'd be out of business."

I stared at him. "Do you mean that?"

"Hell, no," he blustered. "Come on, kick this thing in the ass."

Instead, I pulled over to the side of the road at the White Sands Inn.

"Why are you stopping?" Haney said, sweat beading his upper lip.

"I'll only be a second," I said. "I saw something in the window here."

He started to complain, but by then I was already inside the little boutique and speaking to the halfbreed salesgirl. She was a mixture of Chinese and black, and had the best features of both.

"That bikini in the window?" I said.

"With the orange and yellow sunburst? Yes, sir?"

"Would that fit a girl who takes around a size ten—but she's tall for her age? I mean, tall for her build?"

"Of course, sir," said the salesgirl. "You see, both the top and the bottom have adjustable ties. I'll show you—"

"Never mind," I said. "I'm late for an airplane. Wrap it up."

Two minutes and ten Jamaican dollars—twelve U.S.— later, I was back in the car.

"Got everything you want?" Haney said sarcastically.

"Nearly everything," I said soberly. "But don't you worry, Bill. I'm going to get the rest, too."

The flight of the Goose took us directly over Cuba. This time we were low enough to see smoke from the cane-fields, and once a Russian MIG pulled up on our left wing and, lowering wing flaps and landing gear in order to fly slowly enough to stay with us, its pilot scrutinized us carefully. Then, retracting the flaps, snapping the gear up, and hauling back on the stick, the Cuban pilot disappeared straight up.

We flew over the Old Bahama Channel, crossed the Tropic of Cancer, and landed at Andros Island in the Bahamas for fuel. By now our flight plan had been altered to read "Miami," and since we were in transit and did not leave the flight line, there was no customs inspection.

After takeoff Haney came back to cheer us up. "Now comes the fun," he said. "In a couple of minutes Hod's going to start getting 'Identify' requests from Air Defense. Come on up and listen."

We were over the Straits of Florida when the pilot received the first call. He grinned at us and said, "Watch this."

Picking up the microphone, he said, "Air Defense, this

143

is Grumman Goose five zero niner zebra on local flight from—" and that was all. While he was speaking, he had been switching the microphone TALK button on and off rapidly, and the officer at ADC must have heard something like, "Air . . . is . . . Goose . . . zero . . . local . . ." and then silence.

"My impersonation of a radio shorting out," said Hod Casey. "Works every time. They only see one blip on their screen, we're slow and probably without communications. And I made sure they heard that word 'local.' They won't waste any time checking us out. They get a dozen a day like us. Although you'd think they'd learn. Hell, one time a little while back, a bloody MIG got through and landed at Homestead Air Base while your President and *Air Force One* were parked on the ramp. Luckily, the MIG pilot was a defector. But it created a proper flap."

We crossed the coastline at Fort Lauderdale, then flew up the interior of Florida, over Lake Okeechobee, along the Kissimmee River, and finally landed at Orlando without incident.

"What the hell are all those Air Force planes down there?" Haney yelped.

"No sweat," said Hod. "Civil facilities share the field with the Air Force. They won't bother us."

Casey had filed a flight plan with Miami Operations from the air, and unless the police had been tipped off by an informer, we were home free.

The police weren't waiting, but Uncle Norman Barnes was. He must have regained his good spirits, because he wore his big black cowboy hat and the high-heeled pointy-toed Texas boots.

"Gas up and tie her down over beyond the service hanger," Haney told Hod Casey. "Then keep yourself busy checking out the instruments or engines or painting the goddamned wings for all I care. Just stay close to that plane and don't let anyone aboard. Meet Norman Barnes, my righthand man. He'll watch the plane in case you have to go to the john." (And, I thought, in case you get any bright ideas about losing one or two of those *Beautiful Jamaica* boxes.) "He'll also supervise the offloading after it gets dark." Haney handed Casey a thick envelope. "Take a couple of weeks off. Will you have any trouble getting back to Mo Bay?"

The envelope disappeared as if by some feat of magic. Casey shook his head. "I sneaked the Goose out the last flight and we sneaked her *in* this time, so she's been here all the time, legally, and to leave I simply file an ordinary flight plan."

"All right," said Haney. "Thanks for all your help. I'll expect you to be on call in Mo Bay starting two weeks from today."

Casey touched the bulge in his jacket pocket. "Thank *you,* Colonel." Now that we were back on home turf, Haney was "Colonel" again.

I introduced Jean to Uncle Norman, who then hurried over to take up his job of keeping an eye on Hod Casey. Haney handed me a sheaf of twenty-dollar bills.

"The company Lodestar will be along in a while to fly me up to Louisville," he said. "I'd give you-all a lift, but there's no point to it. You can spend the night here and still get back to New York faster than I could get you there. And I want Mike in his office as soon as possible to get cracking on C-900. There's a direct flight out of here in the morning. So go out on the town, what there is of it, and have yourselves a ball. Go to Disney World. I owe it to you anyway, for that Rum Barrel dinner we didn't have. I'll be in touch, Mike, day after tomorrow."

"The day after tomorrow is Saturday," I reminded him.

Haney looked at me coldly. "Mr. Senior Vice President," he said, "something tells me that for the next four or five months there ain't going to *be* no Saturdays. Or Sundays, for that matter."

"The loneliness of command," I said.

He ignored me and gave a little bow toward Jean. "Mighty proud to have met you, Miss Patrick."

She curtseyed back. "Goodness sake," she said, in a voice remarkably like the Southern accent of Effie Fowlkes, "we're just *beginning* our acquaintanceship, Colonel Haney."

He played it all the way—kissed her hand and shook mine and helped us get a cab. As we pulled away from the curb, he called after me, "Good job, boy!"

145

I was acutely conscious of the sheaf of twenty-dollar bills in my pocket. There had to be at least three hundred dollars in the wad.

"Driver," I said, "is there a Holiday Inn near the airport?"

"Couple of miles up ahead," he said, "at the old Tampa junction."

"Take us there so we can check in," I said, "and wait. Then you can drive us downtown somewhere for a good steak."

"Well," the driver said slowly, "much as I hate to lose a good fare, I got to tell you that right across the road from the Holiday Inn is a place called Billy's that charbroils the best steak in the county."

"How much is the fare down to Orlando?"

" 'Bout two dollars."

"My friend," I said, settling back, "you have just earned yourself a two-dollar tip."

"Why did you pick the Holiday Inn?" Jean asked.

"Because," I told her, "six years of sleeping around this fair land of ours has taught me one thing: stay out of the fancy hotels with one exception: the Ambassador East, in Chicago, which is where all the famous movie stars and writers stay. If you don't, you will find yourself living in a broom closet at thirty bucks a night, paying sixty cents plus tip every time you want a little ice to make a drink, and the maids all have passkeys and burst in on you at seven in the morning while you are standing there in your shorts. Motels are the answer. But *good* ones. As often as not, in a place like Cincinnati I won't even have a car. But I'll stay at the Holiday Inn, because I've learned that wherever I go, one Holiday Inn is going to be pretty much like the next one. I won't get surprised by unexpected good taste and luxury, but I sure as hell won't get surprised by dirty showers and saggy mattresses either."

She seemed impressed, which pleased me. It reminded me that people of twenty-two do not necessarily know everything even if they *are* Northwestern graduate students who look like young Katharine Hepburns.

I gave the driver his promised two-dollar tip, and he thanked me three times and carried our bags into the desk, where we registered. It was six-thirty-five by the Western

146

Union clock over the teletype reservation machine in the corner.

Where the form asks for make and license number of your automobile, I wrote "Stutz Bearcat" and "Unlicensed" and nobody mentioned it, as they never do. I suppose motel people are used to clowns like me.

"Let's get cleaned up and meet in the bar around seven-fifteen," I suggested.

"Make it seven-thirty," said Jean. "I have a phone call to make."

"So do I," I remembered, wondering what *her* call was about.

The clever Holiday Inn folks had put us in opposite wings. Jean's bellman whisked her off in one direction while I followed mine in another. The room was exactly as I had expected: clean, bright, and looking as if it had been struck from the same mold that shaped a million other Holiday Inn rooms. I handed the bellman a dollar and asked, "Where's the ice machine?"

"I'll get it for you, sir," he said, taking the plastic ice bucket and ducking outside. He was back before I'd gotten the Scotch out of my canvas suitcase. "Down the sidewalk three rooms," he said, putting the ice down on the sink. "Turn right, you'll find the soft-drink machines, and the ice is just inside the door." I dug into my pocket and he waved his hand. "You already tipped me," he said. "Good night, sir."

"Good night," I said. He closed the door behind him.

I made a weak drink and sipped at it as I dug through the suitcase for my address book. Then I gave the operator the New York City number and waited, listening to the automatic switcher going *beep-ting-tweet*. At least tonight the machines weren't on strike.

"Hello?" said a voice on the other end.

"Effie?"

"Yes, who's this?"

"Mike."

"Mike! Where are you?"

"Would you believe in Orlando, Florida?"

"What are you doing in *Florida?*"

"It's a long story, sweetheart. Listen, try to get hold of Phil and Mark. Tell them—"

147

"Mike—"

"Don't interrupt, this is long distance. Tell them—"

"Mike! Mark doesn't work here anymore."

I paused and took a sip of my drink. "Say that again, Effie."

"He quit. Yesterday. I sent you a wire in Montego Bay, but I guess you didn't get it."

"Do you know *why* he quit?"

"He got another job over at Wells, Rich. Charlie Stewart was so upset he wouldn't even let Mark clean out his desk. That's what I've been doing all day. He's madder than a hoot owl."

"Who, Charlie?"

"No, Mark. He said he'd almost lost the Wells, Rich job by insisting on giving MK&C a month's notice. And then Charlie threw him out in ten minutes. Everybody else is pretty stirred up over it too. They think it all has something to do with losing Coronet."

"Try Mark at home," I said. "Or call his girlfriend, what's her name? The folksinger?"

"Lori Lewis?"

"That's the one. Tell Mark I've got to see him tomorrow night. Set up dinner at O'Henry's."

"I'll try," she said. "What should I tell Phil?"

"Tell him if *he's* looking for another job, I'll cram his T-square down his throat. And to wait for me in the office. I should be in sometime midafternoon tomorrow."

"I'll take care of it. Mike, you sound happy. Was it a good trip?"

"I'll tell you all about it when I get back. But can you keep one little piece of news under your bonnet?"

"Wild horses couldn't drag it out of me."

"You're working for the agency's newest and youngest senior vice president."

"Yoweee!" she shrieked.

"I'm glad you're happy for me," I said, "but you almost busted my eardrum."

"Who's happy for you?" she said. "I'm happy for *me*. Secretaries to senior vice presidents get another girl to help them out. And if their boss is anything of a gentleman, a sizable raise."

"And they say the South lost the war," I mumbled.

"Take care of yourself, y'hear? Don't have any wild parties until you get back here among your friends."

"Okay, Effie," I said. "Over and out."

"Good night, Mike."

Showering, shaving, and all the rest ate up half an hour, and then I went to the bar. Jean wasn't there yet. I ordered a martini. "Beefeater on the rocks, twist of lemon. Pour just a little vermouth over the ice, swish it around, and throw it out."

Friendly, but skeptical, the bartender said, "If you want straight gin, I'll give it to you."

"Trust me," I said.

He made the drink as I had ordered, put it before me.

"Taste it," I said.

"What?"

"Go ahead," I said.

He picked up the glass and sipped at the martini.

"I'll be a son of a bitch," he said. "It's *good.*" He started to ring up a check, then changed his mind. "No," he told me. "This one's on me. That's the best damned martini I've ever tasted. How did you learn to make it?"

"Out of necessity," I said. "I do so much traveling, it's a real problem to find a good martini. What you call 'dry' might be 'extra dry' to a bartender in St. Louis. This way there's no variation. Enough of the vermouth always sticks to the glass and the ice to gentle down the gin, and no matter where I go, it always tastes the same."

"What tastes the same?" asked Jean's voice. I turned. She had changed into a powder-blue pants suit. It was very flattering to her.

"The Michael Evans Miracle Martini," I said. "Want one?"

"Why not?" she said. "Let's celebrate."

The bartender went away to make the drink.

"Celebrate what?" I asked.

"The Professor's just canceled the advertising study. I'm out of a job."

"When did this happen? Why?"

The second martini came. She lifted it in a toast. "Yesterday. He's decided next year's big project will be Detroit."

Yesterday. As she drank I reflected that a lot of things had happened yesterday.

"In spite of controversy, two things about marijuana are clear: first, it is a sexual stimulant, and an effective one; second, it is an illegal drug. Setting new records in the bedroom is not worth doing time in the big house."

—Dr. David Reuben
Everything You Always Wanted to Know About Sex But Were Afraid to Ask

The steaks at Billy's were all the friendly cab driver had promised. Thick and tender, they were charred on the outside and blood-red within. We had a salad and some garlic bread with them, and that was all. We gnawed at the meat close to the bone too, and nobody even looked at us. It was that kind of place. The jukebox shook with old Hank Williams records, and we drank a good bottle of California red.

"How do you feel?" Jean asked me.

Stretching, I said, "Almost as good as I did last night. Don't tell me you sprinkled the salad with ganja."

She laughed and sipped her coffee. "No, but it's an idea.

151

It's been a long time since I was really high. I'd forgotten how nice it feels."

"It's been even longer for me," I said. "Not since college. I went the whole route then. But it was something else last night. The willies, the itches. I almost flipped out for a while. But then it was all right."

"Haney gave us too much," she said. "Eating isn't like smoking. You can't tell when you've reached the high and then take just enough to stay there. When you've eaten the stuff, you have to go all the way. That's why you and Howard had the anxiety. If you'd been puffing, you probably wouldn't have gotten past the euphoric stage. Of course, you have to train yourself to appreciate the effects. It's like anything else. It takes practice."

I finished my coffee and waved for the check. "And you say you're not a head?"

"Why does that bother you so much, Mike? I've told you I'm not, but you keep on with it. What difference does it make?"

"None, I guess. I just like to know where I am. How about some brandy?"

"No," she said. "I feel too good to want to get any higher. At least, on booze."

"There you go again," I said.

She tilted her head and looked at me for a long while, as if assessing some unknown value in me. Then, urgently, she said, "Pay up, Mike."

"What's your hurry?" I put a twenty on the check, which came to only $13.65, and Jean knew it, because she could see the figure written with a black crayon, but she stood up and said, "Be a big spender, leave the change," and started for the door without looking back.

What the hell? It was Haney's money anyway, right? I went after her.

We dodged a big Kroeger Supermarket truck getting across the highway, bypassed the lobby, and headed straight for her room. She was walking so fast that I had trouble staying up with her. Her hand shook so hard that she couldn't get the key into the lock, so I took it away from her and opened the door. She stepped inside, took my wrist and pulled me in too, and locked the door behind us.

152

I put my arms around her and bent forward to give her a kiss, but she twisted away from me and went over to the little stand where her suitcase was and snapped open the lid, nodded toward the suitcase. "I want to show you something, Mike."

She was fumbling with a brown manila envelope. It was distended, as if filled with crumpled balls of paper. But I knew it didn't contain paper. By then I'd caught a good whiff of the familiar musty odor.

"Damn it!" she said, scraping her finger on the metal clasp. Then she had the envelope open and was showing its contents to me.

Inside was a matted lump of cured marijuana, almost as big as a telephone book.

"Where the hell did you get that?" I asked.

"Colonel Frazier gave it to me last night," she said excitedly. "Mike, it's nothing but the flowering tips. You can get high just sitting in the same room with it. Smell?"

I pulled my head away. "How can I help but smell it?" I went over and closed the air-conditioner vent. Now at least the musty odor would remain in the room.

"Michael," she whispered, "I'm going to teach you to turn on."

"Come on, Jean," I said. "Grow up. I was turning on before you discovered Popsicles. And after last night, I'm not really interested—"

"Shhhh," she said, putting her finger against my lips. "You men. So proud of what you know. So independent, so stand-by-yourself. Oh, Mike, I'm *glad* the Professor canceled the study, because if he hadn't, I couldn't do this. I want us to be friends."

"So do we have to smoke pot together to be friends?"

"It might help," she said. "What are you so afraid of?"

"I'm afraid of the narcs busting that door down and hauling us off to the hoosegow, for one thing," I said. "My God, what a risk you took bringing that stuff in! There must be two pounds of it there."

"With almost six hundred pounds in the back of the airplane, what's a little envelope like this?" she asked. "And it's going to be legal next year. You said so yourself."

"Haney said so," I told her, but she had a point. And once I had gotten past the anxiety, last night had been

153

pleasant. Besides, although I knew that while marijuana was not strictly an aphrodisiac, we'd had a little rhyme at Columbia: "Candy is dandy, and liquor is quicker, but weed will succeed."

So I checked the door again, slipped the lock chain into place, and pulled the curtains all the way closed.

"What are you going to use for paper?" I asked.

"Give me one of your Pall Malls."

I shook one out of the pack for her and, with a pencil, she began poking the tobacco out of the paper cylinder. "I'll leave a little tobacco down here at one end to hold the grass in," she said. "Too bad you don't smoke filters. They're better."

"My oversight," I said.

She gathered up little particles of the Jamaican ganja and dropped them down the Pall-Mall tube, tamping them gently with the pencil eraser. Then she twisted the paper end closed, put the marijuana cigarette on top of the TV set.

"Are you making only one?" I asked.

"This is dynamite grass," she said. "You'd blow your head off if you smoked it like the stuff you probably get in New York. That's what happened last night. You got an overdose."

I was uneasy. Words like 'overdose' do that to me.

"Take off your tie," she said, hanging up my jacket. "Get comfortable."

Feeling the need to say something, I said, "Maybe when we go into production we can use old Coronet tubes for C-900."

She laughed. "What the hell's so funny?" I asked.

"C-900. You're talking about pot and you call it C-900."

"We're going to find a name. That's right on top of the project list. Maybe we'll call it Dynamite Grass."

"Jamaica Reds might be more accurate," she said. "Anyway, your idea of using old cigarette tubes won't work. You can't use regular-sized cigarettes."

"Why not?"

"What did they teach you at Columbia, anyway? There's too much waste with a regular cigarette size. More

154

of the stuff burns up in the air than gets inside you. You need a smaller, thinner cigarette."

"Why? Because it burns slower? That goes right in the face of modern merchandising. We *want* them to burn down fast. That's why they put saltpeter in cigarette paper, to keep the butts from going out in the ash tray. Conspicuous consumption, somebody called it."

"Well, conspicuous consumption won't work with weed, not if your product costs as much as I think it will," she said. "You'd better hope your buddy Haney's got a research team with a background of wild youth, or you're going to get laughed off every campus in the land."

Listening to what she said, I answered, "There's a lot of truth in that. Jean, what are you going to do now?"

"Now? I'm going to sit down and then we're going to take a match and light up this joint—"

"No, I mean now that the study's been canceled."

"I don't know. Go back to Chicago, I guess, and see if I can get in on the Detroit study."

"Do you think you can?"

She shook her head. "I hinted, but the Professor didn't pick me up on it. He's probably already got his team chosen."

"Then why don't you take some time off and come to work with us?"

She stared at me. "Who's 'us'?"

"MK&C. The C-900 group."

"Work for you, Mike?"

"Yes, if that's the way you have to put it."

"Doing what?"

"What you just did. Just helping. You're in touch with the scene. For instance, I can guarantee you that right this minute Haney's people *are* thinking in terms of a conventional cigarette size, only stuffed with marijuana instead of tobacco. Hell, even *I* was."

After a pause, she looked down at the floor. "So that's what you regard me as. Your marijuana expert. Damnit, Mike, I told you I'm not a pothead."

"I believe you. But you're aware of what young people are thinking and saying and doing. You've got a good brain, you can follow a problem through and come up

155

with sensible solutions. What do you think it takes to make advertising? Look, I'm not saying for you to make it your career, but you'd have an interesting four or five months."

The expression on her face became less strained, more questing. "And you really want me, Mike? *Me?*"

"More than wanting, I *need* you."

"I don't know. Let me think about it."

I knew better than to push further. "Okay," I said. "We'll talk about it tomorrow."

"Yes," she said, getting up. Then, to my surprise, she bent down and kissed me full on the mouth. Her lips parted, and I felt her tongue touching mine. She backed off.

Trying to joke, I said, "Why the sudden show of passion?"

She picked up the marijuana cigarette. "That was only so you wouldn't be disturbed when I did this." She put the entire cigarette in her mouth and brought it out glistening with saliva. The act should have been repulsive, but her soul kiss had done its work and I wasn't bothered at all. "You know," she said thoughtfully, "smoking pot is a group thing. A joint usually gets passed around to three or four people. You really ought to invent some kind of germicidal filter."

"See?" I said. "You're thinking already."

Calmly, she said, "We'll talk about it tomorrow."

Taking a book of Holiday Inn matches from an ashtray, she struck one and held the cigarette up at eye level a foot or so in front of her face. Turning the joint carefully, she let the flame ignite it evenly, just as a man would light a good cigar.

"It's important to get the joint burning evenly," she told me. "If it doesn't, it'll taste hot—and more than that, it'll burn too fast and waste the stuff."

Satisfied that the cigarette was burning right, she said, "Now watch how I inhale. You just barely touch your lips to the end of the joint, and draw the air in and around it. Imagine that you're staying 'Tfff, tfff,' only inhale the word. Don't try to taste the smoke. Keep your throat open and get it all the way down into your lungs and hold it there as long as you can. When you feel like you just *have* to exhale, go 'Tfff, tfff' again. That'll keep it in for a few more seconds."

As I watched, Jean did exactly what she had described to me. She was not smoking or inhaling the marijuana cigarette the way you do a tobacco one. When she went "Tfff, tfff," I could see that she was swallowing smoke from the outside as well as the inside of the reefer.

When her lungs were full, she handed the cigarette to me and nodded, without speaking. I copied her technique. The smoke was acrid and hot and rasped my throat. I felt an urge to cough and overcame it. Now my lungs were burning.

Jean and I sat there, holding our breaths, staring at each other. It was silly. I almost laughed.

She went "Tfff, tfff," inhaled deeply through her nose and then, redfaced from the effort, whooshed out her breath and reached for the cigarette which was burned down to half of its original length.

I was ready to exhale myself, but she shook her head and said, "Keep it in there. Give it a chance." So I sucked in some more air while she went through the smoking procedure a second time. When I finally let my breath out, I was giddy and not at all ready for the cigarette that she handed to me again. But she nodded vigorously and pushed it toward my lips. So I inhaled, cheating a little to get some fresh air down there along with the smoke.

Was I starting to feel effects? Or was my lightheadedness due to holding my breath?

I forgot to go "Tfff, tfff" a second time, and let the smoke escape before Jean had released hers.

When she did, she asked, "Feel anything yet?"

"A little giddy."

Jean mashed out the cigarette with the side of a pencil. "That's enough for now, then," she said. "It takes a while for the stuff to work. If you smoke until you feel high, then you've probably taken in too much."

She sat down on the floor with her back against the bed and stretched. "Just be still and let it do its stuff," she said.

I sat on the floor beside her. "This is pretty much the way we smoked it in college," I said. "Except we didn't suck in air that second time."

"You do that to overcome the imbalance of carbon dioxide in your system," she said. "It's the CO_2 that makes you want to gasp for breath, not lack of oxygen."

"Do tell, doctor."

She flushed. "I'm sorry. I *was* lecturing, wasn't I?"

Dreamily, I said, "Why did you save the roach?"

"For later," she said. "That's the best part. See how brown the paper turned? All the resin's down there."

"Got to get people away from that nonsense," I said. "We want them to buy lots of our product, not use up every tiny little bit. Conspicuous consumption."

"I knew a boy once," she went on, continuing her chain of thought as if I hadn't spoken, "claimed he knew every way of smoking a roach in the whole, whole world."

"How many is that?" I definitely felt good. I wasn't flying, but I could certainly be said to be floating. It was all warm and comfortable.

"Well, let's see," Jean said, ticking off her fingertips. "There's the cocktail. That's what we've got here, with the roach stuck down inside a regular cigarette." She laughed happily. "Except this time the regular cigarette *is* the roach."

Laughing with her, I said, "Doesn't seem right somehow. Regular cigarette being a roach."

"Then you can use a hairpin or tweezers." She picked up the half-smoked cigarette and held it between her thumb and forefinger. "Just *so*."

"What else?" I found that my eyes were dry from not blinking, and forced myself to close them for a moment.

"You can put the little old roach in a pipe."

"What kind of pipe?"

"*Roach* pipe, silly."

"I'm not silly, and there's no such thing as a roach pipe."

"It's what you call an opium pipe. Imitation opium pipe. Souvenir-store stuff. Buy one in all the tourist shops down in the Village. Little old ladies take it back to Kansas City, say, 'Look Myrtle, what I found in Greenwich Village. An *opium pipe*.' Just perfect for roaches, little old lady from Kansas City, if only you knew."

I didn't say anything. It was just too pleasant to move.

158

"Ever smoke a tin can, Mike?"

"Not that I remember."

"Take an old beer can. Got a hole in one end where you drank the beer out of, right?"

"Very right."

"Punch little hole in the other end. Just big enough for friend roach. Slip him in. Inhale the smoke from the drinking end. Very good. Cools it wonderful. Cover the beer hole with your thumb when you pass the can around the room."

It sounded so good that I found myself wishing we had a beer can. I even started to get up.

She pulled me back. "Where are you going?"

"Get a beer can."

"Forget it," she said. "Hey, how are you feeling?"

"Wonderful."

"Flying?"

"No. Just all dreamy."

"That's good. Let it work a while, and then we'll have some more."

"Jean," I said very seriously, "I love you."

"No you don't," she said, "but it's nice to hear you say it."

"I guess I know who I love," I said argumentatively.

"Mike," she warned, "don't take the edge off. Stay feeling good. If you start arguing, you'll come down."

"Don't want to come down," I said.

She giggled. "Neither do I."

Sadly, I asked, "But what are we going to do without a beer can?"

"Trust me."

"I do."

"I have a plan."

"What's your plan?"

Conspiratorially, she leaned toward me. "A California Crutch."

"Crutch? Can't you walk without one?"

"Why walk when you can fly."

I laughed. "Hey, hey, I feel good."

"I think I'm coming down a little," she said. She scooted over to the dresser, reached up without standing, and pulled down another book of Holiday Inn matches. "You've already got matches," I said, pointing to those on the end of the bed.

"Need these for the crutch," she said, tearing the matches away from the cardboard cover. She threw the matches into the wastebasket. "Watch," she said, rolling the cardboard into a cylinder just large enough to hold the remains of the Pall Mall. She inserted it and lit the end again, then, using the rolled cardboard as a cigarette holder, inhaled deeply with the now-familiar "Tfff, tfff" sounds. When she had filled her lungs again, she handed the improvised holder to me, and I did the same. Near the end of my drag, I tasted tobacco smoke.

Giggling, I said, "I think we're down to the cancer end."

"That's no fun," she said. She took the rolled-up matchbook cover from me, shucked the Pall Mall butt into an ash tray, then tore up the matchbook and flushed it and the butt down the toilet.

On the way back she turned on the TV set. I don't know what was being shown, but I remember sitting passively before the shifting images and sounds and letting my mind plunge wildly from one idea to another. Each new thought was so impelling and urgent that I wanted to communicate it to Jean, but I found it impossible to verbalize what I wanted to say.

"Now you're really flying," she said approvingly.

"I don't see any bright lights," I complained.

"You don't have to see bright lights. Why don't you *be* a bright light?"

So I concentrated on being a bright light for a while, and when I thought I had succeeded, I asked Jean, "Have you noticed the new bright light?" but she was staring intently at the television screen and did not answer. When I became tired of being a bright light, I tried watching television too, but it all happened too *slowly*. I could anticipate when Mr. Phelps was going to open the tape-recorder case, and long before the tape began to move I knew what it was going to say, and besides I already knew for certain that none of the IM force would ever be killed or captured and it would never be necessary for the Secretary to disavow all knowledge of their actions.

So I watched Jean instead. It was as if I were seeing her for the first time. I memorized the curve of her throat, and the long eyelashes, and the wisps of hair around her ears. I inhaled the many vapors in the air: her perfume—so tantalizingly familiar—and the slight soap-clean smell of her body, and the tiniest aroma of gin, and even the muskiness of the pot she had smoked.

She turned suddenly and found me watching her.

"What are you doing?"

"I'm absorbing you," I said. "I'm eating up every bit of you."

"How do I taste?"

"Like cunt." The word was out before I knew I was saying it.

She wasn't disturbed. "Are you horny?" she asked.

Although I had not really thought about it until then, I now realized that I was in a state of extreme sexual excitement. My trousers were painfully tight across my groin, where my erection strained against the cloth.

"Yes," I said.

Without moving, she said, "I am too. I'm all juicy."

I slid over and sat beside her. For a while we stared at the television screen, letting the drone of the soundtrack fill the empty silence.

She tilted her face up toward me. I kissed both her eyes, feeling their lids tremble under my lips. She put her hand on my thigh and I felt its warmth all up through my groin. When I kissed her mouth, it was full of so many hidden messages and intensities that it was as if we were both shouting with joy.

I don't know how long this went on. At last her hand found my engorged penis through the straining cloth of my trousers, and I knew that although I could ejaculate at that very second by just willing it, I could also hold off the orgasm indefinitely.

Nuzzling her cheek along my jaw, she whispered, "Did you ever screw on pot before?"

And despite the naughty little rhyme we had used at Columbia, I had to answer, "No."

"Let's get on the bed."

Dreamily, we lay down beside each other on the bright-yellow bedspread. I reached for her breasts but she pushed

161

my hands down her body until they cupped the tight little cheeks of her buttocks.

I pulled her up against me and she gasped, "Oh, harder, harder," and I pressed our bodies together until I could feel her pelvis grinding against the underside of my erect penis.

There was a distant *slowness* about everything. And while one part of me wanted to penetrate her and pound away until the world exploded, another part watched with amused tolerance and urged, "Slowly, slowly, there's so much to enjoy. Get it all."

We pulled apart slightly, and I traced the line of her jaw with my finger. It was as if my fingertip could *read* every pore, taste every tiny wisp of downy hair. When I kissed the palm of her hand, it took a conscious effort to keep from chewing at the fleshy mound between thumb and forefinger.

"Go ahead and bite me," she said throatily. "Hard."

I did. And she gasped with pleasure. When I took her hand away, there were white-and-red toothmarks in the flesh. I kissed them and tasted my own scent on her.

Perhaps we lay there for an hour exploring the little everyday parts of each other's bodies, perhaps only for a few minutes. Time was a distant stranger with no place in our world. Without removing our clothing, without petting to orgasm, without seeing any more than we might see of each other's bodies at a casual luncheon, I felt as if I had explored every part of this girl with an intimacy that months of marriage had never led to with Janice. I was conscious of deliberately putting off the final part of the act. Once, when Jean's hand cupped my erection through the fabric of my trousers, she whispered, "Do you want to come?" and I answered, "Not now. Not yet. It's like all this is one big come," and she replied, "Yes I know. That's what I tried to tell you."

Although time had vanished, I knew that we made love for more than an hour, because we were both still fully dressed when *Mission Impossible* went off. Twice I had tried to unbutton her blouse, and twice she had moved my hands down to her thighs, and now, as we lay pressed tightly against each other, my fingers had slipped down inside her waistband and were caressing the softness of her

162

buttocks through the slippery silkiness of her panties. She had unzipped my fly and her own fingers, butterflylike, fluttered through my pubic hair, alternately clasping the shaft of my erection and caressing the tight ball of my scrotum.

"So nice and big," she whispered. "And your balls are all tightened up."

"Everything's in my prick," I said.

Such foreplay would have ordinarily driven me to frenzied attempts to penetrate her. But there seemed to be all the time in the world. I was confident of lasting as long as I wanted to. I could not remember ever having been so excited, yet so in control. And as if I could read the responses of Jean's body, I knew that she too was trembling on the verge of orgasm—and that she would also control it as long as was necessary.

My fingers opened her and explored the moistness of her body. Their tips sought out the tiny little button and stroked it gently. As it swelled under their caresses, I felt what I would have thought impossible—my own organ growing even larger.

"Let's do it," I said softly.

She kissed me again, her tongue jabbing me with tiny, agonizingly sweet little flutters.

"Turn off the light," she whispered.

I did, and the room plunged into darkness. I had already taken off my shoes. Now I ripped away the socks, slipped down my trousers and shorts with the same motion, and shrugged out of my shirt. I groped my way to the bed and almost fell over it. When I sat down and felt with my hand, there was warmth where she had been, but Jean was gone.

"Jean?"

"I'm here," she said, and the bed sagged under her weight. I reached out toward her, and somehow her hand intercepted mine, and placed it on her waist. "Lie on your back," she said. I did, and she lowered herself, guiding me into her with her hand. She leaned back toward my knees, and I felt the full length of my organ in contact with her as she began to move.

"I could come right now," she gasped, "but I'm saving it."

"So am I," I said, enjoying the tingling delight of her motion. I put my fingers around her buttocks and felt the alternate tensing and relaxing as she rode me.

It seemed to last forever. I imagined that she was surrounding me, covering me with sweet honey and then nibbling it away with tiny birdlike pecks of her lips. We synchronized the motions of our bodies and each time she pulled back, the lips of her vagina trembled on the very tip of my swollen penis, and then she lowered herself again.

"This time," she sobbed, "roll over."

When our loins met, I clasped her tightly to me, and her own hands held the small of my back and we made the difficult motion without becoming uncoupled. Her legs tightened around my waist and her voice rasped, "Now, Mike! *Fuck me!*"

Savagely, I drove into her. Our bellies met with a meaty, smacking sound. Her fingernails clawed into my back, and I could feel each individual scratch and each was a tiny place where she had entered me and it was as if we were having sex in each wound.

"Harder!" she demanded, and began to convulse her legs with scissorslike movements. Then she began laughing wildly and I knew her orgasm was upon her, and allowed mine to happen too.

Jean was shrieking wordlessly, her voice mixed up with hysterical laughter, and I know that I cried out too, and mingled with the sounds of our voices was the wet slapping together of our flesh. I had never experienced such total sensation. As the spasm began I could feel the liquid spurting, and it seemed to take an eternity to move down the interstices of my body and into hers. "Throbbing, throbbing!" she cried, and I knew she could feel the contractions of my penis. Each new one was another flood of pleasure—and, after five, ten, how many—they didn't stop! I felt as if I could keep on coming for hours, and only the shuddering gasps of the girl under me brought me back to some kind of reality, and I consciously *willed* the spasms to cease and, with a groan, fell away from her, choking for breath.

"Oh my God," she whispered, "oh my God."

The marijuana high seemed to be gone now. I was wide awake and aware of everything around me.

"Jean," I said. "Baby. Are you all right?"

"Oh, it was so good," she said. "Wasn't it good?"

"I've never had anything like it," I said. "Is it always like that?"

"No, no," she gasped. "Sometimes it's better than others, and it's always good, but this was the best. I felt like I was all cunt, a huge receptacle, receiving you."

I knew what she was trying to say. In the height of our orgasm I had had a wild sensation that I was just a monstrous organ. Every inch of my body was sexually involved.

Her breathing smoothed. "Are you still high?" she asked.

"No. It's all gone."

"Do you want any more?"

"Not tonight," I said. "I couldn't hold my breath long enough."

She gave a deep, throaty laugh. "I shock you," she said.

"I shock myself," I told her. "It was never like that before."

"No guilt," she said. "That's what we're learning today, whenever something's good, take it and no guilt. When the hangups are gone, you can run free."

Then I remembered. "Listen," I said, ashamed, "I didn't use anything. I meant to, but I forgot."

She laughed again. "Don't worry, we learned that too. I'm a good Girl Scout. Always Prepared. Just let me use the bathroom first."

I felt the bed move as she slipped off it, then the bathroom door closed and a light went on under its crack, and I lay there in the darkness of the room, listening to the shower run. I got up and groped my way to the window and slipped the drapes open a little. Just outside the swimming pool was green with its underwater lighting and little wisps of steam rose from the surface. The water was probably heated. Suddenly I felt an urge to swim underwater for as long as I could hold my breath. I found my pants and shirt, slipped into them, stuck my feet into the bare leather of my shoes.

"I'll be right back," I yelled through the bathroom door, but I don't think Jean heard me. Then, trying to look like anything but a guy returning to his own room after getting banged somewhere else, I skirted the office and let myself into my own place. I pawed through my suitcase, found the old swimming trunks I'd taken to Jamaica and then the package from the Mo Bay boutique.

When I got back to Jean's room, the door which I had left slightly ajar was closed. I tapped on it.

She opened it and said, "Where did you go?" She was wearing the pants suit again.

"I wanted to get some stuff from my room." I held up my bathing suit. "It's swim-swim time."

"I don't have—" she began, and I said, "Yes, you do, present from the boss," and handed her the package. "Get in this and we'll hit the pool." She tore open the paper, held up the brief cloth of the bikini, bright in its orange and yellow pattern, burst into tears and threw the bathing suit on the floor. "Oh, Michael," she cried, "why did you have to ruin everything?" and slammed the door and locked it from the inside.

COPY DEPARTMENT

November 20

CONFIDENTIAL   DO NOT COPY

SUBJECT: Names for C-900

Agency has decided that the use of a traditional name for this product is preferred to creating a new one.

1. There is a large measure of acceptance for names that already exist, particularly among those who may already be users of a C-900 substance.

2. Such names, particularly those which we wish to research among consumers, imply potency and more importantly, delivery of the <u>traditional</u> product which certain consumers are already accustomed to using.

The names Agency suggests researching are:

Jamaica Red
Dynamite Grass
Acapulco Gold
Panama Red
Kansas Kings
Roo Blue
Poor Man's Heaven
Grass
Weed
Hay
Head Start
Top (Pot spelled backward)
Pot
High Time

Ganja Man
Boo
Sticks
Joints
Reefers
Tea
Sky Flier
Fancy's Leaf
Mary Jane

It is obvious that many of these names are
unsuitable for a quality product. But, if time
permits, we would research as many as possible. If
not, we believe several of them are ideal, and
recommend particularly that the first three names on
the list be researched. Acapulco Gold is perhaps
the best-known symbol of quality in the lore of the
product. Jamaica Red is a name well-known for
strength. Dynamite Grass has the same reputation, and
also has the advantage of being generic, instead of
pertaining only to one growth region. The drawback,
for instance, of having to use Mexican product
exclusively in a product named Acapulco Gold may
outweigh the advantages of the name. Dynamite Grass
has none of these problems, since the product can grow
anywhere.

This memo is being hand delivered to Mr. Norman
Barnes. It has not been copied, nor are there any
carbons or earlier drafts.

Michael Evans,
Associate Creative Director

Morton, Keyes and Cooper

Advertising

629 Madison Avenue

<u>PERSONAL</u>

TO: Hamilton Keyes

FROM: Michael Evans

Come on. Enough already. Anybody who
intercepts our C-900 memos and reads all about how
we're thinking of calling it Acapulco Gold or Mary
Jane would have to be feeble-minded not to know what
we're talking about. So let's stop this code
name jazz in our private dealings and talk about what
it is we're going to sell, which is plain old
marijuana, right?

Mike

Mike

(Better known as Roo Blue)

Morton, Keyes and Cooper
Advertising
629 Madison Avenue

EXECUTIVE OFFICE

TO: Mike Evans

FROM: Ham Keyes

You're right.

Ham

(Better known as Sky Flier)

It took me until Saturday noon to get that first memo out on C-900. For one thing, I didn't get much sleep Thursday night. I didn't know what had set Jean off, and after what had happened between us I was wound up tighter than a rubber band. I knocked on her door a few times, until somebody next door opened a window and growled, "Come on, buddy, listening to you two screw was fun, but I don't go for door pounding." So I hurried back to my room and got her once on the phone, and she said, "It isn't your fault, Mike, but please don't call me again tonight. I'll see you in the morning."

My high had worn off, and I tried to refresh it with Scotch, which didn't do any good, and I dozed in the chair and woke up in the dawn hours to the organ strains of *Sermonette* and showered and got ready to leave, and it still wasn't seven A.M. At seven sharp, I phoned her again and this time when she answered it was as if we were merely traveling companions.

"Thank you, Mike, but I'm not going to have any breakfast. Let's meet in the lobby at eight-fifteen."

I agreed. I didn't know what else to do.

171

We flew back to New York in strained silence, and when the cab let me off at the office, she kept it to go down to the Village. I asked her several times if she had thought over my offer to work at the agency, and she said no, she hadn't, but she would be in touch, and the last thing I saw of her was a back view of the short hair through the window of the taxi as it drove down Park Avenue.

I went right up to the executive floor to check in with Ham Keyes, but he wasn't back yet from Jamaica, nor was Howard Porter, so I went down to six and closed the door to Phil McKenna's office.

"How was the trip?" he asked, doodling on a Coronet layout.

"Pretty good. What the hell are you working on that thing for? Let the guys over at Esty worry about it."

"You know how it is," he said. "I started this. I'd kind of like to finish up, even if they don't use it."

"You wouldn't be putting a sample book together, would you?" I asked.

"You wouldn't be acting like management all of a sudden instead of the lazy old Mike Evans I know and love, would you?"

"I don't know," I said. "What the hell got into Mark?"

"He didn't believe the crap Keyes passed out about the new account taking up the slack. He had a good offer, so he took it."

"He should have talked with me first."

"Come on, Mike. You know he's been ready for a bigger job for quite a while. You should have done something about getting him made a group head."

"What about you, Phil? Are you ready for a bigger job, too? Level with me. Are you bailing out?"

"Something's up," he said thoughtfully.

"You bet your ass something's up. How about an answer. Are you staying?"

He sighed. "Yeah, I guess I'm sticking around. I'm too lazy to start hiding my sample book in a coin locker at Grand Central so I can zip out for quickie noon interviews. I guess I'll remain at my post and go down with the ship."

172

I doublechecked to be sure the door was locked, then I told him, "Old buddy, the ship ain't going down. Ham Keyes was telling the truth. We've got us an eighteen-million-dollar hunk of billing."

He whistled. "Who's 'we'?"

"You and me, that's who. Mark too, if I can talk that stupid bastard into getting his tail back here. Jesus, Phil, why couldn't he have waited? He didn't know it, but until he walked in and quit he *was* a group head. I had it all settled with Ham."

"Charlie Stewart didn't say anything to him about it."

"Charlie Stewart doesn't have anything to do with this new account. It's our baby and we work directly through Ham."

"That's a kick in the balls for Charlie," Phil said thoughtfully.

"So? What's Charlie ever done for you?"

"Did you stop to consider what might be behind it all?"

"Phil, I've been moving so fast I haven't had time to take a crap, let alone think about intrigue and all that jazz."

"It might just be, Mike, that if this account goes well, Ham could have you in mind as the next creative director of this shop."

I thought about that for a moment. Certainly stranger things had happened. If the C-900 project succeeded, I would be the fair-haired boy with MK&C's biggest client. Charlie Stewart might be promoted upstairs in charge of something or other, and I might get a chance to see how that corner office felt. Of course, if the C-900 project bombed out—well, nobody wants a loser around.

Phil interrupted my thoughts. "Is it a secret, or can you tell just what *is* this new account? It might help my layouts if I knew what I was drawing."

I laid it right on him. "Coronet is going to introduce the first legal marijuana cigarette."

He took it calmly. "It was bound to happen. When?"

"Early spring. Haney claims he's got the word straight from the horse's ass that the new Administration is going to loosen up on the whole soft-drug thing."

Phil shrugged. "We sell them cigarettes and booze, so

173

why not pot? It can't be any worse than bourbon, which incidentally isn't much of a recommendation. When do we start?"

"We've started. Better take a good look at your kids this weekend, because you may not be home much for a while."

"I'm tired of the little snappers anyway." He looked down at the Coronet layout and, with a sudden motion, tore it in half. "What am I working on this crap for?"

I got up. "Right now we need names. You know, like Top, which is Pot spelled backward."

"How about Grass?"

"Not very classy."

Phil nodded. "But look at it this way—when we bring out the menthol version, we could call it Green Grass."

I groaned. "Keep at it. No memos, nothing written down. Don't talk about it, not to anyone, not Effie, not even your wife."

"I never talk to Agnes about anything except sex," he said, "which keeps me pretty busy. The day she hit forty that woman became a nympho. Hey, Mike, is it true that weed will help you keep it up?"

"I wouldn't know," I said shortly, and left.

Effie had a stack of messages for me. None of them was important, especially the ones from mutual fund salesmen.

"I tracked down Mark," she said. "Dinner's fine, except he said to tell you it's on him because he wants to celebrate his new job, which, and this is a quote, is 'with a shop that knows how to treat creative people right, particularly on payday.' "

"Thanks," I said. "Effie—"

"Coffee's already on its way. I saw you go into Phil's office."

"Thanks."

I had been about to ask her to look up the number of the Claremont Hotel, but the coffee would taste good, and anyway it might be smarter for me to get the number myself.

No, Miss Patrick wasn't in. I left a message for her to call me at the agency. It was only three, so I spent the rest of the afternoon piling my Coronet Cigarette files up on

174

top of my taboret. A little after four the phone rang and it was Norman Barnes.

"Can you talk?" he asked.

"Sure. Go ahead."

"Not on the phone."

I checked my watch. "Norm, I'm waiting for Keyes and Porter to get in from Jamaica. And I've got a dinner date I can't get out of. How about five-thirty at Charley O's? I can stay there until I have to jump on a subway around seven-thirty."

"Charley O's," he said, and hung up.

Drinking places for ad men and people in publishing, the communications industry, and the rest of the glamour jobs around town run in cycles. Somebody opens a great joint, the hip guys find it, the word passes, the less hip start pouring in, the prices go up and the size of the drinks goes down, the tourists finally penetrate, and then it's time for someone else to open a great new joint. So far, Charley O's, around the corner from Radio City, had managed to withstand the inroads of success.

At ten after five Stella called me from Ham's office and said, "I just heard from Mr. Keyes. He and Mr. Porter are taking a limo straight home from the airport. But they'll both be in around ten tomorrow if you can make it. It's Saturday, you know."

"I can make it," I said.

She laughed. "I told him you could."

I tried the Claremont again. No, Miss Patrick had been in, but she was out again. I left another message. "Ask her if she'll join Mr. Evans for dinner at O'Henry's on Sixth Avenue and West Fourth Street. Eight P.M. No, I can't be reached anywhere before then."

I couldn't get a cab, so I walked over to Charley O's. It seemed strangely cold and foreign to be topcoated after having been in steamy Jamaica just yesterday.

Norman was waiting inside the door. He had on his black cowboy hat.

"Welcome," he said. "Bastard! What a kick seeing you down in Florida yesterday."

We shook hands. "Have any trouble unloading?" I asked.

175

"No problem. Wild Bill had hired a station wagon with a driver. We got the stuff unloaded and on its way five minutes after the wagon drove onto the field. Which was fine with me. That limey pilot made me nervous. He looks *hungry*. The shipment ought to be in Louisville sometimes tonight."

"Why didn't Haney just fly everything up on the company plane?"

"No way. It's one thing to risk a fifty-thousand-dollar Goose. But who the hell wants to have a two-million-dollar jet confiscated? What are you drinking?"

"Mug of beer," I said. "I've been going pretty hard lately."

"So I heard." Norman bellied his way up to the bar and came back with a dripping mug of beer for me and a martini for himself. He toasted. "To the old team. Shit, I was happy when Haney finally told me. I was leveling with you Monday, you know that. I just didn't know what the hell was up. I only got the full scoop myself last night."

"What do you think about it?"

"I think we are all going to be one rich batch of bastards."

"No hangups?"

"About what? Oh, I see what you mean. No, Mike, why the hell should I worry about that? If the stuff's legal, we'll sell it. Why not? Shit, if it wasn't us, it'd just be somebody else."

His words sounded strangely familiar. . . .

Jean didn't show up at O'Henry's.

Norman and I had gotten a pleasant buzz on by seven-thirty. I had switched from beer to martinis after the first mug. We conversed without any real fear of being overheard—Charley O's at six in the evening is so noisy you have to stick your mouth right to your buddy's ear and bellow, and even then he catches only two words out of five.

We set an early lunch for tomorrow, Saturday, at which time I promised him he would have a list of proposed names to take back to Louisville on the late-afternoon flight to show to Haney.

"If you think you've got problems," Norman bellowed, "you ought to see the poor production guys down there. They don't know what kind of machines they'll need, whether or not they can use existing production lines—not even whether the paper we use is any good for the new product."

Remembering what Jean had told me, I said (shouted, actually), "It won't be. You have to take out the saltpeter."

"WHAT?" he yelled.

And, just as I yelled back, the room took on the coincidental quietness that sometimes occurs in a crowded place, and my voice echoed off the bar mirror as I shouted, "TAKE OUT THE SALTPETER!"

"Buddy," said the bartender, a new one whom I did not know, "if you don't like our drinks, why don't you go around the corner to the Blarney Stone?"

Norman and I had one more martini each to restore the peace, and then I did go around the corner, to the IND subway.

As I stood in the crowded car, up to my ankles in tattered copies of the *New York Post,* I wondered if ancient Rome had a Transit Authority, just before the end. . . .

O'Henry's used to be a meat market. Now it is a steak joint with waiters who wear straw hats and butchers' aprons. Meals are served on tables made from old butchers' blocks. The steaks are good and the drinks ample—as is, however, the check. But the ambience is pleasant, and now that the cashier will accept credit cards, at least you can share the tab with Uncle Sam.

Mark Hedin was already there when I arrived. He sat at a table near the window, two drinks before him.

"Is one of those mine?" I asked.

"Lori's with me," he said. "Sit down."

"I prefer to stand, traitor." But I sat.

"How was Jamaica?"

"Shall I sing you a chorus of 'Island in the Sun'?"

"Still vicious as ever." A waiter arrived and put a martini down before me. I raised my eyebrows. Mark explained, "I told them that when a fat advertising executive sat down, they were to rush gin."

"Thank you," I said. "Although the part about being fat is a lie, I *am* an executive." I looked around. "Where's Lori?"

"I told her to powder her nose for a few minutes when I saw you coming. Just in case you wanted to punch me in the jaw. You know how women hate the sight of blood."

"No punching, Mark. I just wish you'd waited until I got back."

"I meant to. But Wells, Rich was pressuring me. And I

178

wanted to give the shop a month's notice." He laughed harshly. "Ten minutes was more like it."

"Charlie was out of line. He hadn't been brought into the picture."

"Too bad for Charlie. But I thought of locking his door from the inside and giving him a few minutes of something he's never encountered in that pleasant little cocoon he inhabits."

"Really? Such as?"

"Raw, naked violence. You know, just beat him down to the floor and stomp on him a little." Mark gulped some of his drink. "Ah, shit. What would that accomplish?"

"Charlie may have some troubles of his own, so let him lie. What are you getting over at the new place?"

"Twenty-six. But more important, Mike, I'll have my own group."

"What brand?"

"A little chunk of the automobile business."

"Little is right. They keep that one pretty much upstairs."

"Hey, buddy, what are you trying to do, destroy my morale? Let's celebrate—who knows, they might make drinking illegal tomorrow."

"I doubt it. But I'll tell you one thing they're making *legal.*"

"Pot?"

I stared at him. "That's right. How did you know?"

He stiffened in his chair. "Wait a minute, I was only joking."

"I wasn't."

Mark put his glass down. "And that's what the new business is?"

I nodded. "You're the group head on it."

"I can't, Mike. But, Jesus, what a gas!"

"Sure you can. I'll pay you thirty."

"Mike—"

"Wait a minute," I said. "You didn't enter any contract of slavery with Wells, Rich. Are you telling me that once you're working there, you'd turn down a four-thousand-dollar raise if someone else came after you?"

"But, Mike, I haven't even started yet."

179

"What difference does that make? I'm offering you four grand more, plus your own group on a swinging product."

He shook his head. "It isn't fair."

"Why not? They hired you away from us with a raise, didn't they? Well, I'm hiring you away from them with another one. You've got nothing to feel guilty about. I came after you, you didn't blackjack me to match their offer. And this is just the beginning. We're all going to be a bunch of rich bastards when we get through."

"You sound just like Uncle Norman," he said.

"Yeah," I agreed, "I guess I do."

He stared at his drink for a while. Then, "Okay. Shit, I can't pass it up. But what will I tell Wells, Rich?"

"Tell them you got a better offer. They've had it happen before."

"What if they want to make another offer themselves?"

I grinned at him. "In that case, come back and beat the shit out of me with it."

He lifted his glass. "Okay, boss."

I touched it with mine. "We're going to have a lot of fun."

"When do I start?"

"Tomorrow."

"Saturday?"

"Wild Bill Haney spelled it out for me down in Jamaica. There just aren't going to be any Saturdays for a few months, or Sundays either."

"The schedule's that tight?"

"We're talking about copy testing the first week in January."

"Lori's going to love this," Mark said. "We were going to take the next two weeks down in San Juan."

"Give her a raincheck," I said. "But for Christ's sake, don't mention what the product is. Code name is C-900. That's all anyone has to know. When you give Wells, Rich the word, don't even mention that you're working on a new product. Security's tight on this one."

"What do we do first?"

"I want some names. What do we call the stuff? Something snappy. Let me have a list around noon tomorrow. Phil's coming in. Work with him on it. And start thinking of copy lines, promises, the usual."

"How about 'fly the friendly skies of C-900'?"

I started to make a sarcastic reply, but just then Lori Lewis arrived. "Mike!" she said, genuinely glad to see me. And, to Mark, "Honey, if I sat on the pot any longer, I'd have developed hemorrhoids."

At twenty-eight, Lori had achieved a sizable following with her slightly slick versions of standard folk numbers, had done two Carnegie Hall appearances, and was a frequent guest on the *Tonight* type shows. On stage she had the composure of a nun, and offstage the vocabulary of a Hell's Angels mama.

"When the fuck are we going to eat?" she demanded, and Mark said something but I wasn't listening. Instead, I was remembering sitting beside Jean Patrick in the Delta jet that morning, staring at her profile silhouetted against the window, at the gentle curve of her throat and the softness of her lips, and wondering if last night had been a wild dream.

After all, girls with the clean, fresh-scrubbed face of a young Katharine Hepburn do not scream "Fuck me!" in the sweaty bed of a Florida motel through the darkness of a humid night.

"Hey, Mike," said Mark Hedin, "wake up. What do you want to order?"

I looked up. "You two go ahead," I said. "I'll just have another drink. I'm not very hungry tonight."

I came up the stairs to my apartment, slow and drunk and after midnight, and she was sitting on a garbage can outside my door, waiting.

"Jean!" I said, sobering instantly. "Where the hell have you been? I've been calling you all night."

She giggled. I looked at her with suspicion. "Are you high?"

"You're drunk," she said.

"All right," I said, unlocking the door. Wordlessly, she followed me inside.

While I was putting the coffeepot on to heat up some water for instant, she wandered into the bedroom.

"You didn't make your bed," she called.

"I didn't have time the other morning," I said, "and I haven't been home since."

She didn't answer, but I heard the radio go on. It was tuned to WQXR, the classical music station of the *New York Times.*

"How do you want your coffee?" I called. She said

182

something that I didn't make out, and I said, "What?" and she yelled, "Black!"

I put two spoonfuls of Yuban into two heavy mugs with a replica of the Maxwell House package stenciled on them, poured in the boiling water, stirred, and went back to the bedroom.

My apartment is what they call a two-and-a-half, which is to say that as you enter, you find yourself in a long, narrow room that serves as entrance hall, living room, and dining area. A little alcove off to one side is an efficiency kitchen. That's the "half" in the rent scheme of things. Through a door near the end of the room is my bedroom, fairly big, with two windows, that open onto a courtyard filled with garbage cans. A tiny bathroom off the bedroom completes the accomodations, $249.50 a month, thank you, sir.

Jean had just finished making the bed, and was now gathering up my dirty shorts and an even dirtier pair of socks that I had kicked off before leaping into the shower Tuesday night.

"Come on," I said, "leave that for the maid. Here's your coffee."

Putting the soiled clothing in the bamboo hamper, she said, "You don't have a maid."

"How do you know?"

"Because people clean up for their maids. You knew nobody was coming in here until you got back, so you didn't hide your dirty underwear." She took the coffee. "Thank you."

"You're welcome. Didn't you get any of my messages?"

"I got all of them. Or at least two. Did you leave more?"

"Wasn't two enough? Why didn't you call me back?"

"I don't know," she said. "Hey, let's watch *The Late Show*."

"Goddammit, you're high," I said.

"Don't be a squirch. Where's your TV?"

I followed her out into the main room and watched as, with a squeal of delight, she found an old Alan Ladd movie on Channel 4.

My feelings were ambivalent. I was so glad to see her that it hurt. Yet I felt a vague anger, a shifting uneasiness because she was obviously high. I knew that I shouldn't keep harping on it, but it was like a scab on your knee, that you must keep picking at.

"Who were you smoking with?" I asked.

"Nobody."

"You're lying. You told me that you always smoke with someone else."

"All right, I was smoking with you."

"Like hell you were! I haven't seen you since I got out of that goddamned cab!"

"Michael," she said, making three syllables out of it. Mike-ay-el. "I came here to tell you something that you don't understand."

"Tell me how I was smoking with you when I've been somewhere else. That's one thing I don't understand."

(Why did I strike out at her? Why didn't I simply accept that she was here and let the rest lie buried?)

"I want to talk about last night," she said.

"I want to talk about tonight," I said.

"Me first."

"All right!" I shouted. "Go ahead!"

Softly, "Mike—it doesn't always happen that way."

Angrily, "What doesn't?"

"You don't just automatically fall into bed with someone because you're stoned. You've got to *want* to first. Being high only makes it better. Don't you see?"

"No."

"What happened last night wasn't just because we got high together. Getting high just made it more good."

"What the hell kind of English is 'more good'? I thought you went to college."

"Marijuana doesn't turn you on sexually. It only opens up the way for you to do more easily what you already *want* to do. That's what I'm trying to say."

"Fine. You've said it. Now, who were you smoking with tonight?"

"With *you*, Mike."

I almost hit her. "You're a liar."

"Mike," she said, "I sat there alone in my room trying to figure out what to do. Your calls came and I told the switchboard to say that I was out. And after a while you didn't call any more, and I felt lonely. Oh, Mike, I was so lonely. But then I had a joint, and it was as if you were there with me, and that's all I meant when I said I was smoking with you. I *wanted* you to be there, so you were." She fumbled in her purse and pulled out a plastic Baggie filled with cured marijuana. "Here. This is for you. It's half of what I have."

I knocked it to the floor. The brown and yellow leaves scattered. "I don't want that crap," I said.

"I'm sorry, Mike," she said. "Everything went wrong last night when you came back. I wanted to talk with you, but I was afraid."

"Sure. I was going to rape you with a bathing suit."

"I was afraid you wouldn't love me."

"Why the hell should I? How many other times have you blasted off with whoever just happened to be in the room and then given them a quick ball because it was *so good* that way?"

"But that was before I knew you."

"Does that make everything all right?"

She shook her head, and got down on her hands and knees and started trying to push the marijuana back into the plastic bag. I shoved her and she fell on her side. "Leave that goddamned stuff alone!" I shouted.

She crept away from me and sat with her head pressed up against the tube of the GE color set, and the static electricity plastered her hair against Alan Ladd's frozen face. She cried softly amidst the gunshots.

Love is such an invisible thing. It is such a furtive, hiding thing. It must be surprised when you come around a corner and find it there, frightened and vulnerable. It must not be grabbed for, or it will flee. It must not be shouted after, or it will shrivel and vanish.

So, when I came upon it again, after all this time, I grabbed, I shouted, I tried to drive it away.

But Jean would not go.

Slowly, my anger receded. It washed around the silent room for what seemed an eternity, but eventually the anger left us and we were two alone again.

"Jean," I said, "I'm sorry."

"It's my fault," she said. "I tricked you."

"No, you didn't," I said. "It wasn't the goddamned weed. I wanted you too. I wanted you from the first second I saw you. You're just lucky that you didn't get thrown down and raped in my office Monday afternoon."

"I wish you had," she cried. "Then you would have known."

"I wanted you," I repeated.

"You don't know what I am," she said, standing unsteadily. "Or you would have run away like the rest once you saw me——"

Angry again, I yelled, "What the hell are you talking about?"

"Michael," she whispered, "why do you think I wouldn't let you touch me? Why do you think I had to have the lights out? Don't you know what I am?"

Cruelly, because I was furious, I answered, "No, what *are* you? What in hell are you?"

"This!" she said, ripping at her clothing. Her blouse tore under the assault of her fingernails. "This!" she cried again. "Nothing! Only a piece of a woman! Scraps! Leftovers! I cheated you, Michael, I cheated you."

Her blouse fluttered to the rug, and her bra was half off, hanging strangely from one side of her body, and then she ripped at it and broke the strap and it tumbled to the floor, abnormally heavy in one padded cup, and I saw what she wanted to show me.

Tonelessly, she said, "I told you I had an operation. For cancer, Mike. This is what's left. It's all right, you don't have to look at me, you don't have to love me, but I couldn't cheat you any more."

When I reached for her, I could scarcely understand my own voice, because I was crying.

"Oh, Jean, my poor darling . . . is *that* all? It's nothing, it's only a little scar; you've magnified it all out of proportion in your mind."

She wanted to leave now, I kept her, we cried together, we sat closely for hours, we talked quietly, we crept to bed like two lost children, we made love softly and silently and deliciously, we slept nestled like two spoons in each other's curves, we sighed in the darkness of the night and held

186

each other for warmth, and then I woke at eight and she was gone, and when I called her hotel, they told me she had checked out and left no forwarding address.

You can always work.

When I got to the office, Mark and Phil were laughing it up, throwing crazy names for the product back and forth. It was funny for a while, then I warned, "Listen, I know you guys are just kidding, but this is something we're going to have to watch. If we give in, even subconsciously, to the natural inclination to gag up this product, we'll all be on unemployment."

Then I went up and had a brief meeting with Ham Keyes and Howard Porter. They didn't ask me what had happened on my mysterious flight with Haney and I didn't volunteer the information. I did tell Ham about the mixup with Mark Hedin, and how much it was costing us to keep him on the team, and Ham swore quietly, then said, "We can't blame Charlie Stewart. I didn't let him in on what I was doing."

"Nobody's blaming Charlie," I said, "but it might be a good idea for you to cue him in over the weekend so that he doesn't come in Monday morning and accidentally run into Mark in the john and blow a fuse."

Ham agreed, and we set another meeting for Monday

afternoon, and I went back downstairs. The boys had compiled a huge list of names on yellow pads. Mark said, "Listen, we've got a bunch of names that mean nothing in particular, like Breeze and Bright Leaf, and I think that's the wrong way to go. Our name should come right out and tell people, "Hey, here it is, the real stuff!' What do you think?"

I thought it was a good idea, and so we put together the list. I typed up the memo personally, warned them to tear up all their notes and put them through the paper shredder down in Research. We would have to get one for our own use on Monday. Then I went down to meet Norman Barnes.

Luncheon opportunities are limited in New York City on a Saturday. Most of the places catering to the business crowd close on weekends. But a little Continental restaurant called the Venus was open over on West Fifty-Eighth Street, and we went there.

As we sipped Bloody Marys, Norman skimmed the menu. "I agree about the traditional names," he said. "I'll catch Wild Bill tomorrow with these, and we'll have an approval first thing Monday morning. But how do you figure on testing them?"

"Flash cards. We'll mix the three we're really interested in up with a batch of dummy names. Then we'll show the cards to respondents one at a time and ask them to say the first thing that comes to their mind."

"Like an ink-blot test?"

"Sort of. And naturally we'll try to get a good mix to simulate the entire market spectrum."

Norman whistled. "Here I've been telling everybody you're a writer and now you start talking like a research consultant."

"Don't you believe in research, Norman?"

He spread his hands. "I can't afford *not* to believe in it," he said. "If I go out and spend twenty million bucks on a campaign based on my own reasoning and, admit it, hunches, and it bombs out, I'm up Shit Creek without a paddle. But if I research it before and it still bombs, then at least I can spread the blame."

Privately, I agreed with Norman about research. If I had my way, it would be used merely to suggest possible

189

strengths or weaknesses in an approach. The operative word here is "suggest." Instead, since such vast sums of money are involved, clients—and agencies too— try to use research as a "scientific" procedure to insure success. A commercial will be "air-tested" by being run once in a selected market, and next morning the housewife will get a phone-call inviting her to describe the "new shortening commercial" she saw the previous night. My God, I have a hard time even remembering where I *was* last night, let alone the specific details of one commercial out of several hundred. But, amazingly, women *do* remember and do give answers that can be tabulated. Sometime in January we would be subjecting C-900 to this scrutiny, although I hoped to avoid the telephone interview because it is so biased in favor of the woman viewer. After all, when you call a house at ten-thirty in the morning, it's unusual to find the husband there.

The fallacy in the whole research system is the assumption that advertising is a *science*. Science usually operates on predictable, repeatable actions. An art, on the other hand, is seldom predictable, often not repeatable. But who wants to hand someone eighteen million bucks and say, 'Okay, Mike, go out and do your thing"? No, clients with that sort of bread demand assurance that it isn't going to be wasted. So the agencies themselves have fostered the "science" myth. "Oh, yes, Mr. Haney, don't worry about your eighteen million scoots. We'll use the same proven copy-testing system that helped us sell ninety jillion boxes of Zilch, the soap with the suds on the bottom," But what it really comes right down to in the end is a couple of guys like Mark Hedin and Phil McKenna sitting in their offices, telling dirty jokes and drawing pictures and hoping that one of the many approaches they put on paper will score with the reader or the viewer.

Norman had said something. "What?" I asked.

"I like that third name," he said. "Acapulco Gold. I'm going to recommend it to Wild Bill no matter what your research shows. Dynamite Grass is too rough and Jamaica Red sounds like a folk singer. Acapulco Gold has class. It sounds nice, like you wouldn't be afraid to smoke it yourself."

"Would you be able to get enough Mexican grass to

manufacture it? I mean, won't the FTC force you to use an all-Mexican product if you go with that name?"

Norman laughed. "What the hell's the name got to do with it? Hell, you don't think 'the beer that made Milwaukee famous' is really *made* only in Milwaukee, do you? Or that Chun King is produced in China? Mike, save yourself some effort. We'll be going with Gold, so get ready for it."

"In that case, why waste money doing the research?"

"Like I said, buddy—"

"I know. Spread the blame."

We had lunch and a few more drinks, and around two-thirty I poured him into a taxi headed for La Guardia and went back to the office. I padded down the empty halls, listening for the sound of a distant typewriter, the whir of an approaching elevator, the hum of a copying machine.

Nothing.

There was nothing to do but work.

I sat down and rolled a sheet of paper into my typewriter.

COPY DEPARTMENT

ACAPULCO GOLD — COPY STRATEGY

The purpose of Acapulco Gold advertising will be to convince the maximum number of consumers that, of all marijuana cigarettes, Acapulco Gold is:

1. The traditional standard of quality by which all others are judged.

2. A <u>genuine</u> marijuana cigarette which, although manufactured under exacting hygienic and scientific procedures, will deliver those benefits the consumer desires in such a product.

3. A superior product in effectiveness, consistency of results, and lack of aftereffects.

The tone of the advertising will be competitive, modern in concept and execution, and responsive to the consumer's quest for products that do not pollute the atmosphere or upset the ecology in any way. Mention will be made of the natural origin of the product, unaltered by additives or chemicals.

Good. It would do. The copy strategy was broad enough to allow us plenty of leeway in our claims and executions.

It should have been. I had written at least twenty such strategies, all practically identical except for the name of the product. Crisco, Black Flag, Coronet Cigarettes, Kaboom Breakfast Cereal—they all had their own nifty little copy strategies to protect us from the danger of ever doing something that wasn't previously planned out.

I locked the strategy in my center desk drawer and went over to look out my lovely windows at the emptiness of Madison Avenue. The only traffic was half a dozen taxis, darting up the half-deserted street six flights below like little yellow bugs.

It was only four P.M. At least eight hours until I would be able to sleep even if I did the pub-crawling bit and dosed myself with double Scotches.

I had been able to spend the entire day without thinking of her, and now I knew that in reality I had been thinking of nothing else.

"Screw it," I said, and rolled another sheet of paper into my typewriter.

You can always work.

Norman called me at home Sunday afternoon with the go-ahead for Acapulco Gold. "Test the other names," he said, "but make sure Gold wins."

"I can't promise that," I said. "You know we don't rig our research, Norm."

"I didn't say you did. Just make sure that Gold wins."

So, first thing Monday, hungover and dragged out from doing the swinging-singles bit on Second Avenue until three A.M., I sat down with Phil McKenna and talked packaging.

"I see it in very bright poster colors, Mike," he said. "Something like Peter Max. Artwork. No photos."

"Could be. But keep in mind that whatever we come up with, it's probably going to have to work in several sizes. I imagine the smallest pack will be five cigarettes. Like one of those little packs you get on airplanes. I mean, how many reefers can you smoke in one day?"

"That depends on how strong they are."

"I guess we'll have to have a place on the package for details about the potency. Like the proof of booze. Oh, and some kind of health disclaimer."

" 'Caution, use of this product may send you into orbit'?"

"Come on, Phil."

"Sorry, sorry, I lost my head. Okay, what about the product itself? What will it look like?"

"Like a regular cigarette, I guess. No, wait, some kind of filter. Not to screen the smoke, but to make it a little more sanitary for passing around from person to person. Jean says smoking is a group thing—"

"Jean? Oh, that broad from Northwestern. Whatever happened to her, anyway?"

"I think she went home," I said.

If she had, Professor McClintlock's office wasn't talking. I'd had them on the phone at eight-thirty their time that morning. Luckily, schools open early. But all McClintlock's secretary would tell me was that, yes, they had Miss Patrick's home address, but they weren't allowed to give it out. I explained that Jean had left some papers in her office, and McClintlock's secretary suggested that I send them to Northwestern for forwarding. I asked her to take a message and was told that while the university would forward mail, they would not engage in handling oral messages. I told her what I suggested that the university do and hung up.

"What color paper?" asked Phil, yanking me back to the present.

"White?"

He shook his head. "Ordinary. How about different colors in the same pack?"

"No. Somebody tried that with a cigarette a few years ago. Instant death. Make it brown—but not cigar brown, make it paper-bag brown."

"Crazy."

I left Phil to work and typed up a list of names:

ACAPULCO GOLD

JAMAICA RED

DYNAMITE GRASS

BREEZE

196

and took them down to Herb Samson, MK&C's Director of Research.

"Herb, has Ham talked with you about C-900?"

"Yeah," he answered. "That's something, isn't it? A new product category for the first time since they came along with detergents back in the forties. It ought to be fun."

I gave him the list of names. "We need some flash reactions on these product names," I said.

Blandly, he said, "Which one do you like?"

"Acapulco Gold would do just fine."

"I like that one too," he said. "It has character. It's memorable. It's pleasant. I wouldn't be very surprised if it came back high on the response curve."

"How are you going to do it? I mean, you just can't set up a booth in Grand Central, Herb."

"We'll use panels from NYU and Hunter for the urban college segment. I'll TWX the list to Kansas City for a combination housewife study and rural college. For the general thirty-to-fifty age category, how about Philadelphia, Atlanta, and Sacramento? We'll get a good spread fast."

"Fast is better than good," I said. "But we've got to maintain security. How do you do that with names like Acapulco Gold and Dynamite Grass?"

He thought for a moment. "Chewing gum."

"Chewing gum?"

"We'll mix in a couple of good chewing gum names like 'Banana Stripe' and tell the respondents we're researching a new flavor."

"Jesus, Herb, that wouldn't fool a ten-year-old. They'll see through us."

Almost sadly, he shook his head and said, "No, Mike. Somehow, they never do."

I went back to my office, had Mark come in, and showed him the copy strategy. He read it and laughed.

"Gets better every time," he said. "I especially like that part about ecology."

"It's a pretty safe bet that we're going with Acapulco Gold as a name," I told him. "Why don't you start working on some claims and copy lines?"

"How strong do we want to go?"

"Let's hit the spectrum. 'Get Stoned' on one end and 'Fresher than Springtime' on the other."

"Are they really going to let us put this stuff on TV?"

"Your guess is as good as mine," I said. "We'll assume they will until we hear otherwise."

Mark left and I phoned Porter. He was free, so I went up and put the copy strategy on his desk.

He read it and said, "Great. I was going to ask you to write one. I like it. Especially the name."

Dryly, I said, "Herb Samson thinks it'll come back good in the research."

Porter laughed. "I wouldn't be surprised." He handed me a typewritten memo. "Take a look at this. First shot at the media plan. John Cross just brought it up to me. What do you think?"

I sat down and read my way through the maze of figures.

MEDIA DEPARTMENT

MK&C OFFICE MEMO

TO: Howard Porter,   DATE: November 21
                Management Supervisor
FROM: John Cross, Media Director
SUBJECT: Media Plan For Acapulco Gold

Dear Howard:

This is to recommend a basic media plan for
introducing Acapulco Gold nationally. The plan
reflects the agreed upon media budget and the
exclusive use of local media to maintain secrecy and
timing flexibility. A copy of the approved media
strategy is attached to this recommendation.

Recommendation

The basic plan calls for expending the entire
introductory advertising budget in a one-week
saturation blitz. A plan for sustaining level
advertising will be forwarded at a later date.

The recommended plan allocates Acapulco Gold media
spending as follows:

Spot TV (96% of U.S.)	$12.6MM	(70)
Radio (66% of U.S.)	2.7MM	(15)
Newspaper (90% of U.S.)	2.7MM	(15)
	$18.0MM	(100)

Rationale

The recommended plan will best achieve the primary
media objective of maximum advertising reach among all
U.S. adults. We estimate that the average U.S.
household will see our message nearly four times a
day during the introductory week. Reach and frequency
estimates by media are detailed below:

	Estimated Reach	Average Frequency
TV	90%	16.4
Radio	58%	15.6
Newspapers	83%	3.2
Total U.S.	96%	27.6

Discussion

The specific elements of the recommended plan are discussed below:

1. Television — The recommended plan calls for the extensive use of minute commercials as the basic advertising vehicle (approximately 75% of TV dollars). However, :30 and :20 second commercial lengths will be available for use in prime time period station breaks which cannot accommodate the longer commercial length. Our media buying policy calls for the use of prime time on all television stations in a market. However, the bulk of the expenditures will be placed in prime time (7:30-11:00 P.M. E.S.T.) on the network affiliated stations where ratings are highest. Late night fringe time may also be used. To maximize advertising reach, we will try to buy horizontal spots (same time on several stations) in order to reach all adults watching television during the peak viewing hours. On the average, we will be scheduling 3-4 commercials per station per night.

2. Radio — The recommended plan calls for the use of the major radio stations in the top 50 U.S. markets accounting for approximately two-thirds of the U.S. adult population. Radio is being used primarily to increase the frequency of our advertising effort in key metropolitan markets which we expect to account for most of Acapulco Gold sales. Approximately 100 announcements per station (14 per day) will be scheduled throughout the week. The schedules will be concentrated during the auto drive hours (7:00 - 9:00 A.M. and 4:00 - 6:00 P.M.) to reach adult males and during the prime housewife listening hours to reach adult females.

3. <u>Newspapers</u> – An extensive newspaper schedule is recommended for all major U.S. markets. Five (5) full page ads are scheduled for the week. We are recommending that the last two ads be ROP (Run of Paper) color to maximize impact and enhance awareness (studies show ROP ads are recalled an average of 30% better than black and white). Scheduling of ROP ads last is based on the production requirements of the newspapers who need the materials two to three days in advance for ROP versus the next day timing for black and white ads. We will seek to obtain back of paper or back of section positions for our ads whenever possible.

The attached budget summary is based on our Media Department estimates. Once you have approved the plan, we will establish market by market budgets for each medium and begin negotiating with the local stations and newspapers.

We will await your comments on the recommended plan.

Best regards,

John Cross

ACAPULCO GOLD MEDIA STRATEGY

The overall media objective of Acapulco Gold
will be to achieve immediate and total advertising
reach among all U.S. adults with the maximum
affordable frequency.

Media Strategy

To accomplish the media objective, the media effort
for Acapulco Gold will:

1. Concentrate all available media dollars within
a one-week introductory period to achieve the
advertising dominance necessary to achieve maximum
immediate product awareness.

2. Provide broad national reach as effectively as
possible through the use of several media, and
by utilizing the largest possible number of outlets
within each medium.

3. Purchase only prime time periods and print
positions that deliver the broadest possible
advertising reach.

4. Select individual media vehicles that concentrate
advertising messages against adults and avoid
vehicles that deliver a disproportionate number of
children or teenagers.

5. Use local media only in order to maintain
maximum security and timing flexibility.

MK&C 11/21

ACAPULCO GOLD MEDIA BUDGET SUMMARY

Spot TV

Average # of Announcements/Week	Markets	% U.S. TV Homes	Budget ($000)
150	NY, LA, Chi.	(19.4)	$ 2,100
125	Markets 4 - 25	(32.3)	3,650
100	Markets 26 - 50	(16.9)	2,525
75	Markets 51 - 75	(11.2)	1,960
50	Markets 76 - 150	(16.5)	2,380
	TOTAL TV	(96.3)	$12,615

Radio

# of Stations Bought (100 anncts/station)	Markets	U.S. Population	Budget ($000)
7	NY, L.A., Chi.	(19%)	$ 825
5	Markets 4 - 10	(16%)	650
4	Markets 11 - 25	(15%)	500
3	Markets 26 - 50	(16%)	675
	TOTAL RADIO	(66%)	$ 2,650

Newspapers

Major daily newspapers all markets – 50M plus

Three insertions – page, black & white	$ 1,470
Two insertions – page, ROP	1,255
TOTAL NEWSPAPERS	$ 2,725
TOTAL	$17,990

MK&C – 11/21

I handed it back. "Isn't that spot schedule pretty heavy?"

"Insurance, in case the networks give us a hard time."

"What about the NAB?" The National Association of Broadcasters had kept hard liquor advertising off the airwaves for a long time despite the fact that, under existing laws, it was perfectly legal to run such advertising.

"We're getting an informal ruling from them this week."

"Won't that let the cat out?"

"C-900 is mixed in with a bunch of other 'what-ifs' including the new birth-control pill and phone-in horoscope services."

Remembering what Herb had said, I repeated, "And somehow they never catch us."

Porter looked up sharply. "What's that?"

"Nothing, just thinking out loud. Okay, Phil's working up package layouts. Why don't we have a look at them this afternoon?"

"Four-thirty?"

"Good. I'll call you if there's any delay."

I left him to his task of slicing up eighteen million dollars.

"Any calls?" I asked Effie.

"Just the library, wanting to know when you're going to return their copy of *TV Graphics.*"

"Tell them I lost it."

"Did you?"

As a matter of fact, I had cut the magazine up into little pieces. The issue featured the latest outpourings of what I refer to as the *Fruit Boot* Gang.

Back in the late sixties, with population experts screaming "pretty soon, more than half of this country is going to be under the age of twenty-five," many agencies decided they needed a bunch of wild kids to write advertising for the other wild kids they hoped to sell their products to. Long hair, wide neckties (if any), bell-bottom trousers and, above all, *fruit boots,* became the uniform of the day. Anybody over thirty was old-fashioned and had good reason to fear for his job. So grandpas of fifty started combing their hair forward in bangs and wearing purple doublebreasted suits. As for the *Fruit Boot* Gang themselves, their principal mark was arrogance. Craftsmanship experience, logic, planning—these became dirty words. You had to "do your thing," and if you sat down and asked one of these geniuses just what his thing was, your answer would be, "Baby, if you can't *see* it, how can I ever explain?"

The fad passed soon enough. Demanding complete authority without responsibility, the Gang ran prices up to where a one-minute commercial that should have cost around $25,000 often came in for more than $100,000. As their wild excursions into fantasy won award after award from other *Fruit Booters,* product sales went down.

Me? Well, I was young enough then to qualify as a *Fruit Booter,* but I must have been born old. The wide neckties never really looked right on me and I kept asking questions like, "Who am I aiming this message toward? Where is my market?" I didn't win as many awards, but we sold a hell of a lot more product that way.

So when *TV Graphics* devoted an entire issue to the latest *Fruit Boot* output, I got mad and cut the expensively printed pages into little paper dolls engaged in unspeakable acts.

"It's gone forevermore," I told Effie.

"They're going to want us to pay for it."

"So pay. Where's my coffee?"

"You drank it."

"You should have ordered more. We senior vice presidents need our wits about us."

"We secretaries to senior vice presidents have two hands. Why don't you buy a coffeepot and then we can have fresh coffee all the time."

"And start the 'Let's drop in on Mike and have a cup of coffee' club? No deal. Dial, woman."

"Tyrant," she said.

At least we were back to normal again.

I rummaged around in my desk, looking for some paper clips, and when I couldn't find them, I called, without thinking, "Jean?"

Effie appeared. "Who did you say?"

I shook my head. "No one. I guess I made a mistake."

COPY DEPARTMENT

C-900 -- EXPERIMENTAL PRODUCT

1. PRODUCT DESCRIPTION

C-900 will be a cigarette 60mm in length, just about half the length of a king-sized tobacco cigarette. It will be somewhat smaller in diameter than ordinary tobacco cigarettes. The paper will be a brown color, very similar to the color of a paper bag. There will be a special germicidal filter, not to filter smoke, but to prevent germs from being passed along as the cigarette is handed from smoker to smoker. The filler will be cannabis sativa, commonly known as marijuana.

2. PRODUCT PACKAGING

C-900 will be sold in three package sizes. The five-pack, containing five cigarettes; the ten-pack, and the conventional pack containing twenty. Each package will display the product name, mandatory manufacturer's identity information, and a health disclaimer:

CAUTION--use of this product may result in drowsiness. The user should not operate machinery or drive a vehicle during or shortly after smoking it. Excessive use of this product may cause chemical changes in the system which can be harmful to bodily function and health.

3. PRODUCT NAME

C-900 will be merchandised under the name ACAPULCO GOLD.

"These are the packages," I said, putting Phil's sketches up on the chalk tray. "The two on the end seemed best at first, but then we settled on this one." I pointed to the simplest of the three.

Norman Barnes frowned. "I don't know, Mike," he said. "It seems—well, cruder than the others. I kind of like that Peter Max style."

"So did we, at first," I said. "But watch." The color monitor at the end of the room flickered. Mark Hedin, on the telephone, said, "Roll the tape, Harry."

Down in the MK&C recording room, the reels of a Sony Color Videotape machine began to turn and a picture appeared on our monitor.

We saw the three packages, first in sequence, then all three lined up together. The one I'd recommended was easily the most visible on the TV screen.

"I'm convinced," Norman said. "Why the hell haven't we done this videotape bit before, instead of taking half-assed packages and paying a fortune to have them color-corrected so they'll look good on camera?"

I shrugged. "It's so simple that everybody must have

figured someone else had already tried it. We've never worked with you on package design before. You brought in packages that you were already locked in to. But this is something we always do at MK&C when we get into design." I was looking directly at Hamilton Keyes when I said this and he had the honesty to wince, because what I had just told Uncle Norman was an out-and-out lie. I had gone to Ham just the month before and pleaded for the videotape unit, and this was the first practical use it had ever been put to.

But it *was* something art directors should have been doing. Perhaps some were—but if so, they had been keeping it very quiet.

It was late afternoon Tuesday, and the meeting had been going since early that morning when Norman flew back from Louisville with final approval from Haney for the name Acapulco Gold.

"We'll have to run it through the trademark office," Norman said, "but Wild Bill's got a friend there who already gave us a quick unofficial okay."

"The Colonel seems to have friends everywhere," I said. Norman's eyes narrowed, but he didn't come back with anything.

Instead, he said, "This eliminates the research project on names. We don't want to take any chance of it leaking out."

So I called Herb Samson and canceled the "chewing gum" names.

Norman was less enthusiastic about the product description I'd written.

"I guess this filter's all right, but who the hell's going to pass a cigarette from mouth to mouth? It's disgusting."

"Too bad," I said. "That's the way they smoke the stuff, so there's no point in fighting the problem. This way, we make a plus out of it."

"Are we going to *show* people passing the goddamned things around?"

"Not specifically. It'll be enough to make a hard mention of the filter's germicidal action. They'll get the idea."

"I sure in hell wouldn't," he grumbled.

"You're not our principal market. The kids don't have

to be educated on how to puff a joint. They've already had their basic training."

"That's another thing," Norman said. "This product isn't supposed to be just for kids. I'm up to my ass with that under-twenty-five crap. How are we going to get those folks in their thirties and forties? That's where the dough is."

"We hit them below the belt," I said.

"What do you mean by that?"

"Acapulco Gold can really give them what all the regular cigarette advertising always promised but never delivered. Sex. Remember all those boy-girl commercials, with two great-looking models puffing a Hit Parade and sighing like they were both creaming in their jeans? Well, Acapulco Gold can deliver, my friend. We won't come right out and say it in the advertising, of course, but we can push all the right buttons so our adult viewers will know exactly what we're promising. A great roll in the hay."

"Mike," Ham said quietly, "are we sure this is the approach we want to take?"

I got mad. Polite as his question had been, it amounted to telling me that he didn't like what I was doing, and you don't say things like that in front of the client. "Ham, this is just one side of an overall plan," I told him. "We're going to be hitting them from all directions. But, yes, this *is* the approach that we want for the over-thirty segment of the market."

In other words, Boss, go fuck yourself.

"About the size of the cigarettes," Norman said. "We'll have to modify our machines to get that smaller diameter. Why can't these things be the same size around as a regular cigarette?"

"Because there's too much waste that way," I said. "That's why you also won't use any burning agent like saltpeter in the paper. If a Gold's put down for a few minutes, we want it to go out, not burn up in the ashtray."

"Cigarettes are *supposed* to burn up in the ashtray!" Norman protested. "Shit, that's where eighty percent of our product goes. Most people take three, four puffs and the rest gets wasted. If it didn't, we'd only sell a pack a week."

211

"Norman," I said patiently, "we're not selling cigarettes any more. This is a whole new ballgame. Acapulco Gold is high-priced merchandise. Those joints will cost thirty or forty cents each. You just don't let them burn up in the ashtray—not at those prices."

Angrily, he said, "How come all of a sudden you're the marijuana expert? Where do you get all this information? Are you the local pusher or something?"

Ham began, "All right, both of you, this has gone far enough—" and I cut him off with, "Norman, do you realize what you just said?" and Norman came back with, "Okay, I lost my temper, I apologize."

"No apologies necessary, Uncle Norman," I told him. "What I meant was your choice of words."

"I *said* I got mad—"

"And you called me a pusher."

"I didn't mean it, Mike. Shit."

"No, let me finish, Norman. That's a subconscious attitude we've all got to overcome if this product is ever to succeed. Look, I'm not mad. I'm just trying to get something straight inside *all* our heads."

Quietly, Ham said, "What's that, Mike?"

I looked around the room before answering. Phil McKenna was twiddling with the cardboard mockup of the Acapulco Gold package he'd put together overnight. Mark Hedin doodled on his copy of the Product Description, drawing clouds of smoke. Howard Porter's face was tense. He didn't like to see copywriters defying clients. Norman was obviously curious and Ham's reactions were masked.

I said, "Do we secretly believe we're peddling dope?"

It seemed an eternity before anyone answered. Then the room was filled with a jumble of voices.

Norman's overrode them all. "Hell, no, we're not peddling dope. Where did you get that idea?"

"I'm only asking. Because no matter how much we justify it by comparisons with tobacco and booze and other products that can be harmful if used immoderately, if any of us feels that marijuana is dope, then he ought to get off this account right now. And that includes you, Norm."

I waited. No one answered.

"Well?" I said.

Howard Porter cleared his throat. "I guess," he said, "that all depends on what dope is."

"Don't you know?"

He spread his hands. "I honestly never thought much about it. To me, dope is something you can become addicted to. That you can't help yourself with, once you get started."

"Oh?" I said. "How about the roster of lushes, not to mention true alcoholics, I could list right in this very agency? They're addicted to something about liquor. To its effects, if not chemically. And what about Jeff Ward? He goes up the wall if he can't drink at least five Cokes a day. Does that make Coca-Cola dope? And what about the aspirin-eaters we all know, and the compulsive smokers, and the coffee hounds? Are all those things dope?"

"Obviously not," said Ham Keyes. "And in my opinion, neither is marijuana. It doesn't happen to be *my* pleasure, but I don't see any virtue in denying it to others who do enjoy its effects. I don't maintain those effects are completely harmless, but neither are the effects of all those other things you mentioned. What do *you* think, Mike?"

"My mind is open," I said. "Ever since I got on this project, I've tried to find out as much as possible about what we're going to sell. So far, I don't see any reason not to market it. My definition of 'dope' is something that one or two experiences with can lead the user to progressive overindulgence in—and the action word here is 'progressive.' So far as I know, the marijuana user doesn't have to keep using more and more to get the same effect—which isn't true of many other products, including liquor. Morally, I know that people out there *are* going to misuse the product—but that will be the result of their own compulsions, which aren't under our control, nor are they our responsibility. They're the people who eat candy bars until they hit three hundred pounds or who can't put a liquor bottle down while there's still a drink left in it. So, no, I don't think we're peddling dope. If I did, I wouldn't be associated with Acapulco Gold. I don't have to work on products that are harmful. None of us do."

Norman, his composure regained, said, "Hoo, boy, when you get going, you really fly. Okay, I buy your proposals. We'll make the product the way you suggest because I have to admit you probably know a hell of a lot more about it than a bunch of Kentucky tobacco planters. And we ain't got time to argue, because we've got to be ready to jump that third week in January. That's when Wild Bill wants to announce the new product."

Not thinking, I said, "What happens the third week in January?"

Norman laughed. "Hell, that's when the new President gets swore in and makes his Inaugural Address. Haney figures that by tying in with Foster's speech, we'll get network coverage as a news item."

"Who says Foster is going to give us anything to tie in with?"

Norman winked. "He will. Don't worry, he will. Leave that up to Wild Bill."

"Well," I said, "we're ahead of schedule now. Today's the twenty-second. We can have advertising ready to look at a week from today. Say November thirteenth. That puts us two weeks ahead of the schedule we worked out down in Jamaica. We can produce the commercials during the weeks before Christmas, finish them up over the holidays, and test right after New Year's Day."

"What if the advertising doesn't work? We won't have time to try again."

"We'll have at least two viable approaches. Frankly, I don't have the concern about the advertising that I do about your distribution. You may find yourself running up against all kinds of local opposition and get boxed out of the stores. I remember a few years ago, right here in New York, it practically took an Act of Congress to permit the newsdealers to sell lottery tickets."

"We're working on the distribution," said Norman. "It's not as tough as you think."

"Especially when you've got the President of the United States on your side," Mark Hedin said dryly.

Norman laughed. "That sure don't hurt." He looked at his watch. "Five o'clock. I'm late for a meeting at Esty."

Surprised, Ham said, "Are you still on the Coronet account?"

"Only for another couple of weeks. Just to muddy up the water. We don't want that smartass down at the *Times*

214

wondering in print whatever happened to Norman Barnes. But I've got a new assistant, Jim Grymes from National Tobacco, and he's going to take over when Wild Bill gives the word."

He shook hands all around, thanked us, and hurried out, his high-heeled cowboy boots clicking on the hall tiles.

"Mike," Ham Keyes said, "come on up to my office when you're through."

"I'm through now," I said. "The boys can put the work away. Let's go."

We didn't speak as we waited for the elevator, rode it upstairs, walked silently down the hall to his office. Inside, he closed the door and locked it.

"Mike," he said, "I don't want to throw my weight around, but you're all wrong about that sex approach."

"Ham," I told him tightly, "the next time you contradict me in front of a client, you're going to be looking for a new boy to run Acapulco Gold."

"That is not the point—"

"Like hell it's not! If you have any problems with what I'm doing, let me know before the goddamned meeting, not *during* it! If that had been anyone but Uncle Norman in there, we could be in bad trouble, and you know it."

He smiled. "You're really taking hold of the job, aren't you?"

"You handed it to me," I said. "I intend to do it, and that means doing it my way. If you don't like my way, fine. Fire me. But don't get between me and my client again."

"You're right," he said. "I was out of line in there, and I apologize. I won't do it again. But I still don't agree with your approach."

"Why not? We don't have to educate the kids to the effects of pot. They already know it, either from having tried it themselves or from listening to their buddies. It's the older market whom we have to provide with a reason, an urge to buy."

He shook his head. "There's plenty of market out there already. The ones who already use marijuana will make us rich. We don't have to attract new users. I'm only concerned with making it safe for those who already have the

215

habit, to try to keep *them* out of jail. I'm not interested in creating additional users."

I stared at him. He seemed tense and nervous, and his eyes couldn't meet mine.

"Ham," I said, "What the hell are you up to? Do I hear you right? Are you saying that you don't really care whether or not you sell this product, that your only concern is in getting those laws off the books so the present potheads won't get locked up? What have you suckered us into, anyway?"

Dully, he said, "Check that lock, Mike. And let's have a drink."

I tried the door. It stayed shut. Meanwhile, Ham poured out two stiff shots of Scotch.

"Thanks," I said, taking mine. We drank.

He opened his wallet and took out a snapshot. I looked at it. It was the usual group shot, with Ham and his wife and three teen-aged boys standing in front of his swimming pool.

"That's my family," Ham said. "The two younger boys are in college. One's at Princeton because he said he wouldn't be caught dead at Harvard. David. John, the middle boy, is in his first year up in Boston. He wants to be an accountant." He sipped his drink again.

Because it was expected, I said, "How about the third boy?"

"Collin. Well, he's right here in town."

I waited. Ham drew a ragged breath. "Mike, a couple of years ago Collin got mixed up with a bad crowd down in the East Village. He was in his second year at Harvard, and two Septembers ago I put him on a train and that was the last I heard from him for more than three months. He never got to Boston—just left the train at a Hundred and Twenty-fifth Street and came back to the city with the allowance money I'd given him. When I found out, I was furious. I tracked him down—in one of those crash pads, they call them. It was disgusting. He was half-naked when I walked in, sharing a waterpipe with four other . . . creatures. If their breasts hadn't been naked I wouldn't have been able to tell the girls from the boys. Collin himself was bearded and dirty, and when I asked him to come home, he gave me a long speech in that filthy hippie talk and essentially laughed in my face."

"Ham," I said, "I don't need to know all this—"

"I want you to know it! My God, I want *somebody* to know it. Even his mother doesn't know the whole truth. So, please, let me finish." I waited, and after a while he went on. "He insulted me. My own son, whom I had always loved best. He rejected me. He was high on that stuff he was smoking—and had the impudence to suggest that *I* try it, that I might understand him better if I 'turned on' with him and his disgusting friends. Well, Mike, I was incensed. I struck him. He didn't resist. He didn't even try to defend himself. He just lay there on a filthy bare mattress and laughed at me."

Ham held his glass in both hands and stared down into it. "I left. I was ready to kill. And, in a way, I suppose I did."

I tried not to look at him. He was crying.

But he didn't speak. The pause was too long. I asked, "What did you do, Ham?"

Without looking at me, he said tonelessly, "I went around the corner to the police station, told them what I'd seen, and gave them the address. Then I waited." He dumped more Scotch into our glasses. "Jesus Christ, I must have been insane! I thought I could bring my son back that way. I thought, with my position and my money, that I'd give him a good scare and the police would understand and release him to me. But it didn't work out that way. When the apartment was raided, someone started swinging and two of the boys were seriously injured. Collin was one of them. He spent five weeks in the hospital and then was found guilty on counts of narcotics possession and assault. I hired the best lawyers. They did everything they could. We got him off with thirty days and two years on probation."

Trembling, he rubbed one hand over his eyes. "But, Mike, those thirty days were too much. I don't know what they did to him in there, but Collin emerged from jail a hardened deviate. Collin, my *son,* flaunts his homosexuality. My son! A gentle and quiet boy, who got in trouble, and instead of helping him, I turned him into—that! And

217

I did it with a law that shouldn't exist, a law that murders the young because they're immature and foolish! God, Mike, I've thought of that night a thousand times, reliving it until dawn comes or the pills start working. That's why I was so receptive to Haney's idea. What happened to Collin must never happen again to other boys. I don't know what the answer will be in the last analysis, but punishment isn't it."

We sat in silence for a few minutes. Then I got up and put my hand on his shoulder.

"You poor tortured bastard," I said. "Why the hell do you beat up on yourself? You did no more and no less than a lot of other fathers. It isn't your fault that this is a lousy world. But, Ham—you can't buy your conscience off this way. You can't go into this project half-assed, figuring you're just going to straighten out some bad laws without getting further involved yourself."

Without looking at me, he said, "Why not?"

"Because it wasn't marijuana that hurt your son. It was the law. And, yes, you. I asked you before, and I'll ask it again—do you think marijuana is dope?"

Muffled, he said, "No."

"Then sell it as hard as you would any other respectable product! You're responsible to a hell of a lot of people. If we aren't going to handle Acapulco Gold the best we can, we ought to resign the business. Because we'll only end up losing our asses anyway, and it'll be in a dishonest way that doesn't rub off easily. Ham, my job is to believe in my product and sell it to whoever I can, not pick and choose my buyer by some private system of morality. If pot is bad, we shouldn't be selling it. If it isn't bad, what the hell sense is there in tiptoeing around? Let's get the stuff out there and *sell* it."

"It's not that simple."

"Yes it is. Is marijuana dope?"

"I said it isn't."

"I know what you said. I repeat, is marijuana dope?"

"No."

"If you really believe that, then we've got to do a job for this product. Or else resign it."

He sighed. "All right, Mike. You're right. We took on the job. And I took on you. So do it the way you have to."

Leaving him was embarrassing after what had happened, because I wanted, in a helpless, masculine way, to comfort him, and he was ashamed of having broken up before me, so we kind of sidestepped around each other toward the door, mumbling about having lunch one day soon, and then I was outside in the empty hall.

Downstairs, I checked in with Phil and Mark, who were worried, and assured them that I was still their lord and master who wanted at least a dozen good product promises by ten A.M. Wednesday, which, as I pointed out, was tomorrow.

I turned down an offer of dinner with Mark and Lori, had a pair of martinis at the Beef and Brew, caught a cab home, found to my surprise that my apartment door was unlocked, and went in expecting to find I'd been burglarized and discovered, instead—sitting on the sofa with two suitcases pressed against her feet—Jean, who said, "I came back.

"The sensation of pain is distinctly lessened or entirely absent and the sense of touch is less acute than normally. Hence a woman in labor may have a more or less painless labor. If a sufficient amount of the drug is taken, the patient may fall into a tranquil sleep from which she will awaken refreshed. . . . As far as is known, a baby born of a mother intoxicated with Cannabis will not be abnormal in any way."

—*Journal of the American Medical Association*

"I ran," Jean said, as we sat on the floor, our backs against the couch. WQXR filled the room with Tchaikovsky, and we drank hot tea with rum in it. "I ran because I was afraid you were only sorry for me, so I went home and spent a day in our big old living room surrounded by the faded photographs of my grandparents and of my big fat old self. No one bothered me, no one asked me why I was content to sit there and stare out the window at the new snow. And when night came, I knew that it didn't matter— even if you were only sorry for me, it was more than I'd ever had before, and so I spent a day in Chicago rearranging my class schedule for the next half, and then I got fogged in at O'Hare, but anyway, here I am."

"What do you want to do?" I asked.

She touched my arm. "Oh, don't be alarmed," she said, smiling. "I didn't come back with my father's shotgun packed in my suitcase. I don't ask for any commitment from you, Michael. I just want to be with you for a while, if that's all right with you."

"It's all right with me," I said.

"And if you still want me to, I'll work with you on the cigarette."

"Are you sure?"

"Yes. I think it's a good thing to do."

"Okay, I'll set it up." I told her about the tight schedule we were on, about President Foster's anticipated Inaugural Address, and she laughed. "If Bill Haney hadn't turned to smuggling," she said, "I wouldn't have been surprised if he had big eyes for the White House himself."

"Don't be too sure he doesn't," I said, and I was only half-joking.

When I showed her the product description and the copy strategy I had written, she nodded. "That's good, Mike. It sounds like you don't even need me."

"Don't joke," I said. "Listen, what do we do about dinner? I don't have anything to eat here."

"I'd like to go to Minetta's again, if you want to."

So we went to Minetta's, and ate linguine with white clam sauce and the richly seasoned salad they serve, and drank a bottle of the inexpensive house wine. Afterward, we had a drink at the Surf Maid, where a big black man played a tantalizingly delicate series of piano numbers, then caught a cab home and, without a word, went to bed.

Later, in the darkness, I whispered, "I'm sorry."

She hugged me to her and kissed my face and neck with quick, moist lips. "It was good," she said.

"No it wasn't. I guess I've been drinking too much."

"Go to sleep."

"I'm sorry."

"Hush."

We lay there for a long while. I listened to her breathing. She was not sleeping, although she was pretending to. Finally I got up and went to the bathroom. When I came back, the bedroom light was on, and she was sitting up. For a second, when I came into the room, she reacted and started to pull the sheet up over her scarred chest, but then she let it fall away. I went over and sat beside her, then I bent and kissed the ridged scar tissue. She shuddered and put both hands against my temples.

"Michael," she whispered, "does it disgust you?"

"No," I said, still kissing her tortured flesh. "It's just—you. I love all of it because I love you."

She moved my head toward the other, perfectly formed breast. "Don't you love this one too?"

I kissed the rosy nipple. "I love it very much."

Then I moved my lips down to her stomach. "I love your tummy, and I love—"

She pulled me back until our faces were close together. "Not yet," she said. "Here."

She handed me a reefer.

"You're tense and nervous," she said. "This will relax you. It will relax both of us." She lit it, and I took the first puff. "Did I ever tell you when I first started smoking?" she asked.

"No."

"It was in the hospital after my operation. There was a young doctor there who had been experimenting with the use of marijuana for childbirth. He persuaded me to try some, and it seemed to work. I was in such pain—mostly mental—but when he turned me on, I can't describe how much it helped. I forgot that I was a fat, lumpy thing with a hole in my chest. It was a way to get out of myself for a few hours, and when they caught him and had him dismissed from the hospital, I cried for two days. But once I got out, I made a connection, and all the way through high school I smoked a couple of times a week."

She passed the reefer back to me. I inhaled it and held my breath. A slight dizziness was beginning to encircle my mind.

"Whatever good times," she said, "whatever nice that I can remember happening to me always seemed to be connected with weed. And I wasn't the only one. The whole class was full of potheads."

Dreamily, I said, "I thought you said you weren't one."

"One what?"

"One pothead."

"I'm not. I *was,* but when I left home for college, I don't know, somehow the urge left me. Oh, I still smoked if someone was holding, but there was so much else to do that I just got out of the scene." She crushed out the roach and put it in the ash tray, then pulled my head down against her body. "Now you just lie still, darling, don't fight it, let yourself drift off." Her voice was gentle and soothing. "I won't let anyone hurt you, there's no one to be afraid of, I'll protect my baby, just relax and let it all happen to you." My body seemed to be floating in warm water. It was almost painfully pleasant. Her voice droned on, "You don't have to move, you don't have to do anything except just be happy. Be happy."

I remember nothing more.

I left early the next morning. She promised to meet me for lunch at Sun Luck East. Effie looked at me in surprise as I sauntered into the office.

"You're becoming an early bird, Mr. Senior Vice President," she said. "Are you sure you didn't sleep here last night?"

"Silence, wench," I said. "Order my coffee."

"It is done, oh master." Then, quietly, "She's back?"

"Who?"

"You know who."

I sighed. "Yes, she's back. Are you going to start yelling at me again?"

"No, Mike. I'm sorry. I shouldn't have carried on like that before. I won't do it again."

I touched her shoulder and went into my office. It looked bare and empty. All of the work we'd done on Acapulco Gold was locked up.

At nine-thirty I called Ham Keyes and told him that I'd hired Jean Patrick.

"All right," he said. No reference to the previous day's meeting, no mention of our private session in his office.

I called Mark then, and asked him to come in with Phil. They arrived, carrying their own coffee and a sheaf of papers.

"How are we doing?" I asked.

"Lousy," said Mark, "but with luck, we may come up with something."

"That's good," I said, "because we're having a little contest here, and the winner gets to keep his job."

"Our problem," Mark began, "is to try to guess how strong they're going to let us work."

"Let's go for the best stuff we can get," I said, "and worry about pulling back later."

"Fair enough," he said. He picked up a sheet of paper. "How about, 'Acapulco Gold gives you more of what you're smoking for'?"

"Put it in the 'maybe' stack," I said. "Next?"

Phil read, "Take a trip, a beautiful trip, with Acapulco Gold."

I thought for a while. "It's not complete," I said finally. "But it has a good beat. Maybe we can use it in a jingle. Put it in the 'good' pile."

"Acapulco Gold," said Mark. "It's out of sight."

"Yeccch," I said. "Some hip talk is hipper than other hip talk."

"You're right," he said, crumpling the paper and tossing it on the floor.

"Acapulco Gold," recited Phil. "It's the real thing."

"Great," I said. "Except Coke used it first."

"Turn on with Acapulco Gold," said Mark. I shook my head. He deep-sixed it, read another. "Acapulco Gold—it's here at last."

"Maybe. Hold it."

Phil read, "Acapulco Gold—it's a blast."

"Lousy."

"What about, 'Come fly with Acapulco Gold'?"

"Pan Am would sue us."

Mark read, "Acapulco Gold—you never had it so good."

"Maybe."

Phil said, "Only the best is good enough for Acapulco Gold."

"Not bad. Keep it."

We went on like this for another half-hour. The suggestions the guys had brought in sparked other ideas, and when the meeting ended, we had several ideas that we liked well enough to work on further. They were:

TAKE A TRIP, A BEAUTIFUL TRIP, WITH ACAPULCO GOLD

ACAPULCO GOLD GIVES YOU MORE OF WHAT YOU'RE SMOK-
   ING FOR
ONLY THE BEST IS GOOD ENOUGH FOR ACAPULCO GOLD
ACAPULCO GOLD——YOU NEVER HAD IT SO GOOD
ACAPULCO GOLD. THAT SAYS IT ALL

"Okay," I said, "this gives us a start. Mark, let's shoot
for a prototype commercial as soon as you can get it out."

"Thirty seconds or a minute?"

Since the late sixties, the thirty-second length had become almost standard for a television commercial, particularly in prime network time. The one-minute length,
which had once seemed so confining, had now assumed
the comparative proportions of a Eugene O'Neill drama.

"Shoot the works," I said. "Go for a minute."

One minute. A hundred and twenty to a hundred and
thirty-five words of copy. Less, if there was music to take
up time. Shakespeare had it easier with his sonnets. And
he didn't have a ten-man committee second-guessing every
rhyme and every word.

"Phil," I said to the art director, "let's see some rough
layouts using these lines."

"Photos or graphics?"

"Try both. Just remember to get that pack up there big
—and in particular, let's take a good look at that brown-
paper wrapper and our fancy new filter."

Phil sighed. "That reminds me of when I worked on the
True Cigarette introduction. That lousy filter was everywhere."

"You don't have to sleep with the filter, Phil. Just draw
it."

We gathered up the discarded ideas and fed them into
the new paper shredder that had been installed under one
of my windows. It made satisfied grinding noises.

"Mike," said Phil, "are we going to have to work tomorrow?"

"Probably. Why?"

He shrugged. "It's Thanksgiving. My kids like the turkey
carving bit."

"I forgot. Okay, let's be lazy. We'll take tomorrow off.
But no long weekend. We have to be in Friday and maybe
Saturday too."

Phil looked relieved. "Just so tomorrow's loose."

"Have a cranberry for me," I said.

"Do you want to come out?"

"Thanks," I said, "but I've got something on. Okay, good work. Mark, you start thinking copy. Phil, hang around a few minutes. I want to talk production."

Mark got up. "My cue," he said. "I'll check in as soon as I've got something."

"Good." He left and I turned to Phil. "Listen, we're going to have to move like the wind when we get the word. How long will it take you to produce an ad for the dummy supplement?"

The dummy supplement was a phony Sunday magazine section that contained articles supposedly of interest to newspaper readers, quite a few genuine ads, and room to tip-in specially printed ads we wanted to test. The dummy would be left in homes overnight with the explanation that this was a new magazine section the local newspaper was thinking of adding and we wanted the reader's reactions to it. A lie? Sure. Was anyone hurt by it? How the hell do I know? No mention would be made of the ads—but next morning, when the researcher returned, most of the questions would relate to the advertising, particularly the ad we wanted to get a reading on. If the ad worked, the respondent would probably remember it and be able to play its message back. If not . . . well, back to the old drawing board.

"Do I have to get the offset printing done too?" Phil asked.

"Can you do it faster than Herb Samson?"

"At least two days faster. I know a little offset shop that'll work all night for an extra fifty bucks."

"Then you handle the printing too. How long?"

He pursed his lips. "I've got an idea. Why don't we put some extra work into the layouts? We've got the time on this end. Once we get beyond roughs, I'll hire a couple of the best renderers in the business to comp up the artwork, and then when we get the go-ahead, instead of blowing a week shooting photographs or having new comps made, we'll get color separations directly from the layouts and use them for the test."

"Are you sure they'll be tight enough?"

"Positive."

"Okay. That saves us what? A week?"

"Five days at the least."

"Go, man."

"I'll need two days after approval, then," he said. "Assuming we get approval during business hours, the color separation people'll shoot the negatives overnight, we burn plates the next morning, go on press that afternoon, let the printing dry that night, and tip them into the supplement the following morning."

"Beautiful," I said. "Did you ever think of going into advertising?"

"What are you going to do about TV?" he asked.

"It's either videotape or cheap-and-dirty sixteen-millimeter film," I said. "We won't have time for anything else."

"Can I make a suggestion?"

"Suggest."

"Remember the outfit we used in Hollywood that named themselves 'The Spaghetti Factory' because every producer out there calls sixteen-millimeter film 'spaghetti'?"

"Yeah," I said. "They did a good job for us on the Coronet sales film last year."

"If we use someone like them for the film job, and put the pressure on, we can probably end up with shots good enough to use in the finished commercials in case we have to go on the air fast. We could A-B the original Ektachrome low-contrast camera stock and roll right onto videotape. Remember that cop show with Jack Warden— *N.Y.P.D.?* That's how they did it, shot sixteen-millimeter color and rolled the good takes onto videotape for broadcast. They never even saw the inside of a film lab once they got their original footage back."

It was worth considering. Although 16mm film stock cost only half the price of the more professionally accepted 35mm, the cost saving itself wasn't great enough to warrant going to the smaller size just for that reason. The convenience, the portability, and versatility of the 16mm equipment *was.* One man could hand-hold a 16mm Eclair, with a Nagra tape recorder over his shoulder and a microphone mounted on top of the camera, and shoot a scene singlehanded, that might, in the good old golden days of Hollywood, have taken a nine-man technical crew. Ordinarily, we would shoot test commercials on 16mm "quick-and-dirty," meaning that we wouldn't bother to go for really slick production values, since the only purpose of the commercial was to test its basic idea. But in this case, with the genuine possibility that we might find ourselves having to rush finished commercials into production overnight, it might be wise to spend the extra few days and an additional several thousand dollars on the quick-and-dirties to end up with footage that we could use in the final commercials if necessary.

"Does The Spaghetti Factory have an East Coast rep?" I asked.

"I'll find out," Phil promised, and left.

I have always had a theory about advertising and clients. Of Procter & Gamble I used to mutter, "The Procters never buy until the buying flag is up," which meant that work expanded to fit the time available for it. If you didn't actually *have* to shoot a P&G commercial until October, lots of luck in selling a storyboard to them in July. This is true of many clients, who believe that a little extra work can make something good into something better. Sometimes this is true—but sometimes you also get so tired of a project that the very life is fine-stroked out of it.

On the other hand, some clients are always in a state of emergency. When they ask for a commercial, yesterday is the desired delivery date. Corners are cut, vast sums of money spent, haste necessitates accepting less than is really possible. My mutter about these clients goes, "There's never time to do it right, but there's always time to do it over again."

Hopefully, our Acapulco Gold project fell between the two extremes. We had more than a month to produce acceptable work. That was enough time, but not so much that we were in danger of going stale.

I finished my coffee and went upstairs to talk budget with Howard Porter. That was one of the nice things about this business—to have the illusion, however brief, that you were in the position to throw around eighteen million bucks.

"Effects which appear especially after repeated administration and as more experience is acquired by the user
include: lowering of the sensory threshold, especially for
optical and acoustical stimuli, thereby resulting in an
intensified appreciation of works of art, paintings, and
music."

—*World Health Organization Bulletin*
32:721—733, 1965

Jean and I spent Thanksgiving stoned.

We'd had dinner the night before at a little Japanese
restaurant on Sixty-ninth street and Columbus Avenue,
the Sakura, then had drunk several tankards of ale at the
O'Neal Brothers Pub and gotten home limp from a session
of heavy petting in the taxi.

Jean had used her first afternoon at the office as an em-
ployee of MK&C in making her peace with Effie and having a knockdown dragout fight with Phil McKenna over one
of his layouts.

"You know," he told me later, "she was right. Maybe it
was subconscious, but I was portraying the user as a semi-

hippie. She spotted it and let me have one right between the eyes. She said those way-out types make up less than one percent of the campus crowd, and most of the rest of the kids want nothing to do with them. I was on the wrong track. But I wish she could be a little more diplomatic."

"Forget it," I said. "Diplomacy they ain't got at NWU."

The day was a long one for both Jean and myself, and when we got home after dinner, my principal goal was bed, although not necessarily for sleep.

But Jean paid no attention. She must have spent part of the morning rolling marijuana joints, because she produced one already made and lit it up.

"Honey," I groaned, "if you'll look over here, you will see ample evidence that I don't need that stuff tonight. Barkis is willin'."

"Shush," she said, passing me the joint.

We smoked it, made love, smoked, made love again, and then again. It was dawn before we slept.

When I woke, the acrid smell was in the room once more. I sat up. Jean was sitting on the edge of the bed, smoking.

She saw me and smiled. "No work today, so enjoy. Happy Thanksgiving." She handed me the skinny, twisted cigarette.

"What time is it?"

"Noon."

I took a deep draw of the cigarette, held it in. Almost instantly, I felt the effects. It now took less time for me to achieve them.

"Getting there?" Jean asked.

"Yes. All the way."

We smoked without speaking again until the cigarette had dwindled down to a roach and was wrapped up in a matchbook cover, the California Crutch, and consumed down to its very ashes.

"Ahhh," Jean said, stretching out beside me. "That feels good." She stroked my stomach. "Want to screw?"

"Not particularly," I said lazily. "Do you?"

"Not if you don't. Let's just dig the music." The radio was playing WPAT, the background music station which I often let go all night so that I wake up the following morning aware that there are terrible problems occurring in the world and not really knowing where I learned the details. Where, of course, was through the hourly news broadcasts all night, a confirmation of the theory of sleep-teaching.

WPAT often takes a particular song—say, "The Rain in Spain"—gathers all the available recordings from around the world, then plays them all at once, intercutting from the English version to the Japanese to the Spanish. The effect, when you are high on pot, is mind-blowing.

Rambling, I said, "We had an argument."

"Who's we?"

"Uncle Norman 'n' Ham 'n' Eggs."

"Eggs?"

I laughed. It seemed very funny. "I meant Howard. Told them that if they thought grass was dope, they'd have to get the hell off the account. Laid it right out there. Senior vice-president. Stockholder. Put it right to them."

"Put what?"

"Dope."

"Who, me?"

More laughter.

"No, silly. Grass. Is it dope?"

"Sure it is," she said.

I laughed. "Sure it is," I repeated, "Then you have to quit."

"Quit what?"

"I don't remember."

"Neither do I."

"Then why are you asking?"

"Asking what?"

"I don't know."

We giggled together. This was fun.

Thanksgiving evening passed slowly, in a haze of sleepy laughter and, twice, sex. We did not go out to eat, but around midnight I opened a can of tuna and we ate from the can with our fingers.

Then, as we lay in the darkness with our legs intertwined, we talked again. The high was gone now, and we had agreed not to smoke again because tomorrow was a work day.

"Did you say pot was dope?" I asked.

"I don't know. Did I?"

"I thought you did. I vaguely remember it."

231

"Maybe I did then. Sometimes I think it is."

"If that's what you think, why do you smoke it?"

"What do I care what they *call* it? I know what it *is*. That's why I smoke. But, yes, I suppose they're right. Yes, they are right. Pot is dope."

"I don't think it is."

She giggled and kissed my cheek. "What do *you* know? Poor Mike, you've been out of it for ten years."

"I still want to know why you think it's dope."

"Because if it looks like dope, and smells like dope, and tastes like dope, and acts like dope, then it probably *is* dope."

"That's no answer."

"Then try this one. In our research for the McClintlock Commission we found evidence that tetrahydrocannabinol —THC—extracts from marijuana can produce all the effects of LSD-Twenty-five, which is the most powerful drug science knows of. And real potheads have a day-in, day-out upset of the alimentary tract. They can't assimilate food properly and they don't excrete it properly either. The whole system becomes poisoned. They lose weight, and their skin goes gray, and sometimes it's covered with scales. Their nails and teeth decay, and even their hair loses its luster. Like I said, if it looks like dope, and smells like—"

I sat up and turned on the light.

"Holy Christ, Jean, where did you hear that?"

She looked up at me, blinking. "I read it in a bulletin from the World Health Organization. Dated 1965, I believe."

"I read a quote from that same report," I said. "All it commented on was how much pot lowered your sensory threshold."

"Oh, it said that too. It all depends on what kind of a quote you're looking for. You just didn't read far enough. And like I said, anything that can cause that much purely physical damage, never mind about possible mental effects, probably has to be classified as dope."

"Yet you want it legalized?"

"So do you, Mike. You're the one who's gung-ho to sell it on the open market."

"Because I don't consider it to be dope. And I don't be-

232

lieve you do either. Otherwise why would you be using it?"

"Because it's not dope to *me*. I don't misuse it, Mike. I drink moderately, and I smoke pot moderately too. But I don't underestimate the dangers of either liquor *or* pot."

"But that's just the point," I said. "Booze isn't dope."

"Tell that to the five million alcoholics we've got in this country."

"I'm trying to understand you," I said, "and somehow all of a sudden we're not communicating. Putting aside the effects of overindulgence—which, I'll agree, can be serious—my definition of 'dope' is something that produces an actual physical addiction, not merely a dependence. You can depend on something, and yet do without it if you have to. But if you're addicted, you have physical withdrawal symptoms if you try to stop using it."

"Michael," she said, "what does it matter? You're always trying to put labels on things. Well, if you simply must have a label on marijuana, I say you've got to label it dope. But why do you need the label at all? It's what it *is,* and what it is for you and me is something very wonderful. Why mess up your enjoyment with polarized words like 'dope' and 'addiction'?"

"I said dependence, not addiction. And it's important to me. Jesus, I can't justify selling dope, if that's what this stuff really is."

Jean sighed and turned over. Her bare shoulder blades were sharp points, soft and rosy in the lamplight. Her voice was muffled. "I don't want to fight, Mike. Good night."

"Good night," I said. But it was a very long time before I slept myself.

ACAPULCO GOLD — "RICARDO" 1:00 TV

VIDEO	AUDIO
SMALL BOY RUNNING UP BEACH	ANNOUNCER (MEXICAN ACCENT) Thees is Ricardo . . .
BOY CLIMBS MOUNTAIN TRAIL	Every morning he climbs to the hills overlooking the Bay of Acapulco. . . .
BEAUTY SHOTS OF MOUNTAIN SCENERY AS BOY PASSES	Here, the fresh trade winds meet the mountain monsoons . . .
CLOSEUP OF MARIJUANA PLANT	Here, and only here, grows the giant plant, cannabis sativa. . . .
WIDEN TO SHOW MAN IN MARIJUANA FIELD LIGHTING CIGARETTE	from which is made the world's finest marijuana cigarette . . .
ZOOM IN ON BEAUTY CLOSEUP OF PACK	ACAPULCO GOLD
PICKING SEQUENCE	Ricardo helps hees father pick the ripe marijuana . . .
CU OF HANDS SHREDDING LEAVES	and only the richest leaves are chosen . . .
ZOOM IN ON CLOSEUP OF PACK	because for Acapulco Gold, only the best is good enough.

MATCH DISSOLVE PACK TO ANOTHER PACK IN WOMAN'S HAND. WIDEN TO DREAM SEQUENCE OF BEAUTIFUL WOMAN AND HANDSOME MAN DANCING ON HILLTOP	JINGLE ("Barcarolle") Only the best is good enough for ACAPULCO GOLD . . .
SHE AND MAN LIGHT UP CIGARETTES	It stands the test, never smokes rough,
THEY "DANCE ON AIR"	That's ACAPULCO GOLD . . .
DISSOLVE TO TWO IN BEACH SCENE	ANNOUNCER (REGULAR VOICE) So don't settle for second best. . . .
THEY SMOKE	get the marijuana cigarette that delivers what it promises . . .
PASSIONATE KISS	all the way!
GIRL GRIPS MAN'S ERECT, NAKED WRIST	Remember, Acapulco Gold in the morning keeps you up all day.
THEY EMBRACE IN SURF WHICH WASHES OVER THEM	So come up to flavor that stands the test, time and time again.
PACK WASHES AWAY. MAN'S HAND GRABS IT IN TIGHT CLOSEUP	Germicidal filter, too. Remember, only the best is good enough for ACAPULCO GOLD.

There are very few strokes of genius in the advertising business. Almost everything worthwhile is accomplished by long, tedious, and often boring work. That's why I was astonished when I put down the script Mark Hedin had handed me and found myself saying, "Mark, you're a goddamned genius. You've got it. We'll sell the stuff faster than they can make it."

Pleased, he said, "You don't think it's too close to that coffee stuff they ran a few years ago?"

"Sure it's close. That's the stroke of genius. It's so close, it's respectable."

"Want to see a storyboard on it?"

"You bet your ass I do. Get Phil off whatever he's doing and hop right on it. Wait. Knock off a Xerox first. I want to show this to Jean."

It was only a few minutes before ten in the morning. Our coffee was still hot. The phone hadn't even begun ringing yet. And it looked as if we were off the hook already on the script. I was suspicious. It isn't supposed to be that easy.

My conversation with Jean last night was still in the back of my mind. I had Effie, who had been cleared to work on the project, make a personal trip to the library to gather up whatever material she could find on the subject of marijuana.

Her own reaction, the day before, when I had told her what we were working on, was strange.

"This is the foot in the door," she said. "It's only a matter of time."

"What's a matter of time?"

"Until we start peddling euthanasia to old people with ads. Can't you see the headline? 'Why wait in line for eternal peace? Go now and avoid the rush.' She looked at me for a moment. "Mike, you're not serious about this one, are you?"

"Effie," I said, "it's coming. If I don't sell it, someone else will."

"Let someone else."

"You don't have to work on it," I said.

"No," she decided, "I'll do my bit in the crusade. My folks are getting pretty old, anyway, and maybe I can get them a discount when we get the euthanasia account."

She'd plopped the research material down on my desk without comment, and when I finished rummaging through it, I was just as confused as ever. The net result was that nobody was really sure what marijuana is or what it does. For every authority condemning it, another well-endorsed source insisted that pot is relatively harmless.

Mark Hedin came in while I was finishing the last pages of *The Sexual Power of Marijuana* by Barbara Lewis, a report on two hundred and eight middle-class users which substantiated my own sexual reactions to the weed.

"Homework?" Mark leered, reading the title over my shoulder.

"Sort of. Mark, what do you think, truthfully, about peddling this stuff? Are we doing something wrong?"

"Wrong like what?"

"Like pushing dope."

"If weed is dope, I personally know around two million dope fiends. I even live with one."

"Lori?"

"Sure. She turns on. For that matter, so do I. I never mentioned it to you before, because I didn't know how you'd take it."

"I still don't know how I take it," I said. "Shit, I've been blasting off myself recently. But I still don't know if it's right."

"What's right? Right is when you don't end up in jail. Right is when you ball your chick and you both have more fun than you ever heard of. Listen, Mike, if pot can relax the wound-up American male, we'll have done more good than Jonas Salk and Louis Pasteur put together, not to mention the cheers we'll get from the babes who start swinging too. Anyway, it's not my job or yours either to decide whether or not we can sell the stuff. The Law's going to tell us that, right? If they say it's a no-no, we fade. If not—"

"Okay," I said. "What's up?"

"Phil and I are going to lay out the storyboard. Do you want to look in?"

"Thanks," I said. It was an indication of the close working relationship I had with Mark and Phil that they would ask me to join in on a basic working level, instead of perfecting their thinking and then presenting it to me as a completed project.

A storyboard has two purposes. The first is to visualize, for internal and client meetings, what we intend to show on the television screen. Even the best board is a mere indication, however, and therefore I like to keep them simple. It is not unheard of for a client to take a dislike to a particular commercial simply because he doesn't like the face of the character who has been drawn on the storyboard, forgetting that actors will be hired and that the board is only an artist's rendering. So the storyboards that come out of my group concentrate on demonstrating the relationship of human figures to the product and sets or backgrounds, leaving details of costume and personal appearance to the imagination. The second purpose is to guide the production house in the actual filming.

We went down the hall to Phil's office and closed the door.

"Got one for you," Mark said, handing the script to Phil, who glanced at it.

"We'd better do miniboards," Phil said, taking a sheaf of 8½-x-11 inch paper with five TV frames printed down its center from his taboret. "Then we can duplicate them ourselves on the Xerox without going through mimeo."

"Okay," I said. "No reason why I can't present the small size to the client." Usually, for meetings, we had oversized boards around two feet long, easily visible from anywhere in the room.

"I'm just going to rough this out," Phil said, drawing black lines with slashes of his Pentel felt-tipped pen across the script, indicating which words would be included in each storyboard frame. "Once we like the direction, I'll render it up tight."

He and Mark conferred on each frame, tracking the story slowly through to its conclusion. Occasionally, I suggested a change or a new idea.

In less than an hour I said, "I like it. Mark, why don't you type up the words, or have Effie do them. Let's finish it off."

"I'll do them myself," he said. We went back to our own offices. In mine I found Jean waiting.

"I've been thinking about what I told you last night," she said, leafing through one of the reference books.

"So have I," I said. "I still don't agree with you. There's too much confusion. People seem to read into this problem whatever they want it, so I'm getting out of that game. Let somebody smarter than me decide what's right or wrong. If pot's made legal, I'll sell it. If it isn't, I won't."

"I didn't mean to upset you. Maybe it isn't such a good idea for us to be working together."

"Don't be silly," I said. "I need your thinking. I just have to do my own too. I'm okay now. Listen, what did you think of Mark's commercial?"

"It's brilliant," she said. "The young people'll think it's a gas, taking off on that old Colombian Coffee commercial, yet it won't turn off the parents because they'll find it vaguely familiar."

"That's funny," I said.

"What's funny?"

"You named them right. Here I've been thinking of part of our market as over-thirties or over-forties, and that's

239

true enough. But what's more of a common denominator is that they're most of them parents. Which means that no matter how self-centered they may be, a part of their concern is directed toward others, toward their children. That's something we're going to have to watch in the messages aimed at them. There's always a danger of their subscribing to the old 'do as I say, not as I do' philosophy."

"How would that affect the advertising?"

"They might be uneasy about their children 'finding out.' Or about setting a bad example. It's a problem we always run into on liquor accounts. We have to find some way to give the parent *permission* to indulge."

Jean shook her head. "And you still resent being called 'hidden persuaders'? What are you talking about, if not mind-bending?"

"Changing anyone's opinion can always be called mind-bending. It's sad but true, honey, that since the dawn of time, when Ooog tried to trade an old club to Uggg for one of Uggg's extra fish, the seller has emphasized the best side of his product. You don't think Ooog said, 'This is a pretty good club except it pulls to the left, which can be dangerous when you're fighting giant tsetse flies' do you? Like hell he did. He said, 'This is the best club in the jungle. It's the latest model, and it's improved to get more meat than any other club you can buy.' "

Jean laughed. I went on: "As for Uggg, he wasn't about to tell Ooog that his fish was two days old and that he'd been on the way to the bear cave to use it as bait. I bet he said, 'We've discovered a new way to flavor fish. Smell that? That's *cool aging;* only the best fish are aged that way to bring out all the delicious fishy aroma. Uggg's fish may cost a little more, because they take two extra days of care, but they're worth it!' That's what old Uggg said."

"What happened then?"

"Uggg went home with Ooog's club and Ooog got the fish, and they were both convinced they got the best of the deal."

She had stopped laughing. "But all they both got was cheated."

"Both—or neither. Depends on how you look at it. After all, they each knew the rules."

Phil came in and handed me a slip of paper. "That's

the name and phone number of the New York rep of The Spaghetti Factory. He's expecting your call."

Jean looked surprised. "Spaghetti? Is that another one of your accounts?"

Phil explained while I slipped the paper under my desk blotter.

"Why would you go all the way to California to make a commercial?" Jean asked. "Doesn't that cost an awful lot of money?"

"It does," I said, "but this time of the year, you'd play hell shooting a beach sequence out on Fire Island."

"Couldn't you use Florida?"

"Costs almost as much to get there as it does to fly to the Coast," I said, "and while they've been trying to build up a film industry down in Miami, Florida doesn't touch the Coast for facilities or personnel. When you shoot in Hollywood, you can get some of the best film people in the world working on your commercial. I made one once with a cameramen who had won two Academy Awards."

"But you don't need all that elaborate preparation, do you? I mean, it's only a commercial."

Phil and I both stared at her. He started to say something, but I waved him aside.

"Jean," I said, "some of the finest technicians in the world do their best work in what you refer to as 'only a commercial.' Do you know what we spend producing a one-minute spot? Anywhere from twenty to fifty thousand dollars. For *one minute*. We'll shoot a full day, sometimes two or three, to get those sixty seconds of 'only a commercial.' More care and thought and effort are put into most commercials than into a twenty-million-dollar feature film."

"But when it's all over," she said, "you're still just selling soap."

"Or pot," I said, getting up. I was so angry that I had to get out of there. "Phil, is the storyboard ready yet?"

"They were just pasting it up. It ought to be in my office by now."

"Let's go look at it."

Jean made a move to follow us, but she looked at my face and said instead, "I've got some minor suggestions on the script. I'll go put them on paper."

241

"You might just do that," I said, and led Phil down the hall.

"Hey," he said, "what are you so hot about?"

"Nothing."

"Look, she's just breaking into the business. Give her time."

"Drop it," I said.

"She thinks good," he persisted. "And she stands up for what she believes in."

"Damn it, Phil, I said drop it."

In a different voice, he said, "Okay, Mike. It's dropped."

The storyboard was waiting on his drawing table. I picked it up.

SMALL BOY RUNNING UP BEACH		ANNOUNCER (MEXICAN ACCENT) Thees is Ricardo. . . .
BOY CLIMBS MOUNTAIN TRAIL		Every morning he climbs to the hills overlooking the Bay of Acapulco . . .
BEAUTY SHOTS OF MOUNTAIN SCENERY AS BOY PASSES		Here, and only here, the fresh trade winds meet the mountain monsoons . .
CLOSEUP OF MARIJUANA PLANT		And only here grows the giant plant, <u>cannabis sativa</u>
WIDEN TO SHOW MAN IN MARIJUANA FIELD LIGHTING CIGARETTE		FROM which is made the world's finest marijuana cigarette . . .

ZOOM IN ON BEAUTY CLOSEUP OF PACK		ACAPULCO GOLD.
PICKING SEQUENCE		Ricardo helps hees father pick the ripe marijuana . . .
CLOSEUP OF HANDS SHREDDING LEAVES		and only the richest leaves are chosen . . .
ZOOM IN ON CLOSEUP OF PACK		because for Acapulco Gold, only the best is good enough.
MATCH DISSOLVE PACK TO ANOTHER PACK IN WOMAN'S HAND. WIDEN TO DREAM SEQUENCE OF BEAUTIFUL WOMAN AND HANDSOME MAN DANCING ON HILLTOP		JINGLE ("Barcarolle") Only the best is good enough for ACAPULCO GOLD. . . .

THEY LIGHT UP
CIGARETTE

It stands the test,
never smokes rough,

THEY "DANCE ON AIR"

That's ACAPULCO
GOLD . . . .

DISSOLVE TO TWO IN
BEACH SCENE

ANNOUNCER
(REGULAR VOICE)
So, don't settle for
second best . . . .

THEY SMOKE

get the marijuana
cigarette that
delivers what it
promises . . . .

PASSIONATE KISS

all the way!

GIRL GRIPS MAN'S
NAKED, ERECT WRIST

Remember,
Acapulco Gold in
the morning keeps
you up all day.

THEY EMBRACE IN
SURF, WHICH WASHES
OVER THEM

So come, come up
to flavor that
stands the ultimate
test . . . time and
time again.

PACK WASHES AWAY,
MAN'S HAND GRABS IT
IN TIGHT CLOSEUP

Germicidal filter,
too. Remember, only
the best is good
enough for ACAPULCO
GOLD.

"It looks damned good," I said.

"Thanks," Phil said coldly. He was still miffed.

I punched his shoulder. "Hell, I'm sorry. I didn't mean to take it out on you. Listen, get a dozen stats—no, better Xerox them yourself. I'll call Howard and set up an agency meeting this afternoon. Can you make three o'clock?"

"Sure," he said. "But is anyone else in? Most of the shop took the long weekend. You could shoot a cannonball down the hall and not hit a secretary."

"Howard's in," I said. "I don't know about Ham."

"I'll be ready," Phil promised.

I went back and peeked into Jean's office. She was huddled over a yellow pad, scribbling.

"I'm sorry," I said.

Without looking up she said, "So am I."

I waited, but she said nothing more, nor did she look at me. So I went to my own office and phoned Howard Porter.

247

The Spaghetti Factory

Creative Films
1812 Melrose Avenue
Hollywood, California

Mr. Michael Evans,
Morton, Keyes & Cooper,
629 Madison Avenue,
New York, New York

December 9th

Dear Mike:

It's our pleasure to submit the following bid
for three (3) 1-minute television commercials, to be
filmed at our studios and locations in California, in
16mm color sound on film. You understand, as we
indicated in our phone conversation, that these are
actual costs, which will be marked up 40%.

We will deliver four (4) 16mm prints to you no
later than January 5, for your air test. Our editing
will be zero cut, with A&B rolls which will be
provided to you for subsequent rolling-in to
videotape if you so request. We recommend Reeves:
we've had very good luck with them. But there's no
obligation for you to go there if you have another
supplier in mind.

Here's our breakdown:

Conferences, Location Scouting, Equipment and
Material Preparation

Category	Days	Rate	Total
003 Assistant Director	16	125	2,300
163 Auto rentals			400
		SUB TOTAL:	2,700

Set Construction, Dressing and Preparation

016	Carpenters (3)	3	70	630
017	Grips (2)	6	70	840
020	Outside Prop Man	6	70	420
024	Special Effects Man	2	75	150
059	Payroll Taxes and Union Payments			204
			SUB TOTAL	2,240

Set Materials and Props

202	Lumber, Hardware, Capentry Mat'l	600
205	Props -- Studio	900
205	Props -- Location, Use	1,400
241	Studio Rental, Building	450
	SUB TOTAL	2,350

Shooting Labor

001	Director	10	400	4,000
003	Assistant Director	10	125	1,250
005	Script Clerk	10	70	700
007	Cameraman	10	350	3,500
009	Ass't Cameraman	10	85	850
012	Sound Crew (3)	10	200	2,000
017	Grips (2)	10	70	1,400
021	Inside Props	10	70	700

026	Electricians	10	70	700
034	Teamsters, location	5	60	300
059	Payroll Taxes and Union Payments			1,540

SUB TOTAL 16,940

Shooting Equipment, Materials and Services

301	Film: Raw Stock	30,000 feet	35 per 1,000	1,050
302	Film: Develop and Print Dailies	9,000 feet	25 per 1,000	225
305	Cameras			2,700
320	Sound Equipment Rental			900
321	Sound Tape Stock			800
327	Wardrobe Rentals and Purchases			1,500
344	Location Site Rentals			3,000
348	Helicopter, Airplane, Boat, Camera Car rentals			2,200
352	Grip: Equipment rental, Supplies			3,400
361	Per Diems, Food, etc. (including gratuities)			6,100
371	Shipping & Freight Charges In/Out			1,200
373	Sundry			1,500

SUB TOTAL 24,575

Striking Sets, Equipment, Etc.

017	Grips (1) 4	70	280
020	Props (1) 4	70	280
059	Payroll Taxes & Union Payments		56

SUB TOTAL 616

Completion Labor

052	Editor and Assistant Editor	3,600
059	Payroll Taxes & Union Payments	360
	SUB TOTAL	3,960

Completion Materials & Services

505	Sound: Studio rental, Mix, Transfer, Etc.	1,500
512	Interpositives/Internegatives	3,000
514	Optical Effects & Optical Negative	3,600
	SUB TOTAL	8,100
	NET TOTAL	61,481
	40% Markup	24,582
	GROSS TOTAL	86,063

Now, we realize that this is somewhat higher than our usual rate for 16mm, but you have stressed that you must have air quality footage and so we have budgeted accordingly. We can promise first class work throughout.

Let us know if we got the job.

Cordially,

Ian Harper, Executive Producer

BK/ih

I flew to California the day before Christmas to supervise the shooting of the three Acapulco Gold TV commercials with The Spaghetti Factory.

"I don't want to go with you," Jean told me.

"Why the hell not? We can have a ball. Listen, it's warm out there."

"And Janice is out there too."

I stared at her. "What the hell does that have to do with it?"

"This is something you have to do by yourself," she told me. "You know you're going to see her."

"I hadn't even thought of it," I said.

"Is that why you still keep her picture in your taboret?"

"That picture was supposed to be a dartboard. Hey, what's with this jealousy bit all of a sudden? I thought you agreed that this wasn't anything serious. Agreed, hell. You *insisted*. I tried to tell you it was different with me, but—"

"Michael," she said, making it "Mike-ay-el" again in that special way, "you don't love me. Maybe it's soothing to your romantic nature to pretend that you do, but—"

"*You're* the one who keeps saying I don't—"

"Will you let me finish—"

"No, goddammit, you let *me*—"

"Shit!" she yelled, and ran out of the room. When I went into the bedroom half an hour later, she was packing.

"What's this all about?" I asked.

"You go to California," she said. "I'll go home, and we'll let things settle for a while."

A sinking sensation invaded my stomach. "Come on," I said. "I don't want to fight with you, baby."

"*Jean,* goddamn it!"

I pulled her to me and kissed her stiff, unresponding lips. "Please," I said. "All I wanted was for you to be with me on the trip."

"You've got to do it alone," she said. "Mike, it was a mistake for me to take the job with the agency. I didn't tell you, but I handed in my notice today."

"You what?"

"It's *wrong!*" she said hotly. "You can't go out and peddle dope on streetcorners and pretend it's merely business as usual."

"Look who's talking! Little Miss Pothead herself. Who spent the past month turning me on every chance she got? Who—"

"You *liked* it!" she challenged.

"Sure I liked it! And why the hell not? I never got laid so often or so well in my whole life. But that doesn't make pot into dope. For Christ's sake, honey—"

"JEAN!"

"—you're screaming for the laws to be changed so you can smoke without being busted. But you figure *you're* the only one in town who can handle the stuff? Let's keep it away from anyone else who doesn't have your iron will? It doesn't work that way. What's good for one is good for all, unless you want to take on the responsibility of deciding who's fit to exercise their own independent judgment and who isn't. And my personal judgment tells me that pot is just another mild substance that can bring pleasure to a world that doesn't have nearly enough of it these days, and, by God, if it's made legal, I'm going to sell the stuff, and I'm going to sell a hell of a lot of it, and how do you like them apples, baby?"

She sat on the edge of the bed for a long time before

253

answering. When her voice came, it was soft and hesitant.

"This was all wrong from the beginning, Mike. I was foolish to think I could have . . . this . . . without our loving each other. I let my own need dominate me. I'm sorry, Michael. It wasn't fair to you. When you say you love me, perhaps you think you do, but I am able to see us without illusion, and there just isn't anything there. There—"

"Oh, bullshit!" I shouted. "Why must you dissect every moment we spend together? I don't know what the hell you're looking for, or for that matter what I'm looking for myself, but I've been happy these past few weeks and I thought you were too."

"In a way I was," she admitted. "But—"

"Shut up. You can't take something beautiful and cut it up to see what makes it tick, because when you do, you kill it." I pulled her to me and this time when I kissed her, she responded. "Jean, if you want to go home for the holidays, that's all right, but let's not let this rotten business of saying goodbye balloon out of proportion. I'll be out there until the week after New Year's, and then I'll be back, and I want you waiting for me. Waiting. Here."

She pressed my hand against her jaw, rubbing it back and forth.

"All right," she said. "But I'm not going back to work at the agency."

"You don't have to," I said, and then we kicked her suitcase onto the floor and made love slowly and deliciously, and neither of us had smoked a joint for more than two days. "You see?" I said as we lay naked on the bedspread, our sweat cooling in the chill of the underheated room. "It *can* be good without pot."

She didn't answer, just hugged me to her, and when I lifted my hand to fondle her breast, I felt the hardness of the scar tissue for a second before she tensed and pulled away.

Jet travel has become so commonplace that it's hard to remember when going across the country was a major decision. Today you board a TWA jet at eleven in the morning, drink your way across three thousand miles, and arrive at noon California time. I've often wondered what would happen if they got the jet speeds up a little faster to overcome that last hour of time lag. Can you imagine arriving before you left?

As usual I was staying at a hotel-apartment called, for God knows what reason, the Hollywood Hawaiian. I drove my rented car up from the airport, checked in, and collected my waiting messages, including two bottles of booze that had been sent over by the producer at The Spaghetti Factory.

Uncle Norman had left word for me to call him at the Regency, another of the unusual resting places for itinerant ad men. Unusual, because for the twenty-five bucks or so a day that you'd pay for a broom closet at the Beverly Hilton, you get a suite consisting of bedroom, kitchen, living room, terrace, and swimming pool right outside. I have always wondered what strange magic the Hilton exercises over its guests, who cheerfully pay through the nose for such extras as ice, glasses, snacks—all available at the Regency in your very own kitchen for nothing.

The Regency's operator rang Norman's room and he answered, "Mike?"

"Yeah. Just got in. What's on the agenda."

"Are you sober?"

"Reasonably so."

"We'll fix that. Meet me at the Phone Booth and we'll spend some of Wild Bill's expense money."

"Let me take a shower. Three-thirty okay?"

"Yeah,'" he said, and hung up.

My body was still perfumed with Jean's scent—Chanel No. Five, of course. We had slept entwined in each other's arms, and with morning came the choice between breakfast and a shower or making love against the relentless ticking of the alarm clock. Breakfast and shower lost.

Washed and changed into my California uniform—plaid sports shirt and jacket, khaki pants, and soft Hush Puppies loafers—I drove up Sunset Boulevard to the Phone Booth, which had been one of the town's original topless joints and had recently graduated into total nudity. While expensive, it was no clip joint, and there was a curious titilation in gabbing with a young waitress while she served you a drink, knowing that in a few moments she would be up on one of the tiny stages showing you everything she had. Like most other tourists, I let it end there. I didn't know what would have happened if I tried to pick up one of the girls, but I had a sneaking suspicion that I would have found myself instantly seated outside on the sidewalk.

Norman Barnes had already started on his first drink when I arrived. He waved a dark Negro girl over and nodded toward me. "Scotch and water," I said. She went away and Norman stared after her switching behind with admiration.

"If I could import this place to Louisville," he said, "I would make a fortune."

"You may make a fortune anyway," I said. "We test the Acapulco Gold commercials on the ninth of January. I presume you have stock in the Coronet Tobacco Company."

"A bundle," he said. "Oh, Wild Bill sends his regards. Especially to Jean. Where is she? I thought she'd be coming out with you."

"She went home to see her folks."

He started to say something, and I knew it was going to be "Getting any of that?" and I didn't know if I would hit him or just get up and leave, and somehow he sensed it, because his lips opened and then closed and he turned his attention to the girl dancing on a platform just a few feet away from us.

She was young, with long blonde hair that swirled around her waist. Her body was glistening with sweat, and I could smell her perfume as she gyrated to the rock beat of the music. She tilted her pelvis in our direction and gave a series of marvelously coordinated bumps, her pelt of pubic hair scattering tiny droplets of perspiration with every movement.

"I never thought I'd see this in a public place," Norman said. "The good old world's sure come to something."

"What?" I turned to him. "What did you say, Norm? I wasn't listening."

He guffawed. "Don't blame you. I was saying that a couple of years ago the only place you'd see something like this was at a Legion smoker."

"A couple of years ago you wouldn't have been able to buy a pack of Acapulco Golds either."

He frowned. "It's not the same thing."

Recklessly, I said, "Like hell it's not. Maybe nobody planned it out, but everything we've been going through in this project is a direct result of the so-called new freedom the country's experiencing. Although sometimes I feel like substituting the term 'license' for freedom."

His tone of voice was disapproving. "What do you want, Mike? Prohibition and Comstock morality?"

"Of course not. But occasionally I wonder what's going to be left when we've finished disposing of such old-fashioned institutions as the family and marriage and the kind of morality that kept you from doing something wrong simply because it was *wrong*, not because you were only afraid of being caught."

"Morality?" Norman said slowly. "I didn't know you had that word in your vocabulary. You've managed to hide it pretty well up to now."

"What the hell are we arguing about, Norm?" I asked.

He stared at his drink. "I don't know," he admitted. "Maybe I have a touch of that old morality bug myself. Mike, my wife is highly pissed about me being on this account. Mona thinks I ought to quit the company rather than be a part of it."

"What do you think?"

He shrugged. "Somebody's going to market the stuff. Why not us?"

"That's the problem right there," I said. "Men have souls, but corporations don't. If you and I both resigned this very moment and destroyed every Acapulco Gold storyboard in existence, we'd slow down the timetable by exactly two hours, which is all the time it would take to replace us. And besides, if it makes you feel any better, I don't happen to think we're doing anything wrong."

"Don't throw words like 'morality' around, then," he said. "They make me nervous."

"Do you think it's wrong, Norm?"

"No," he said glumly. "But Mona sure in hell does."

The Negro girl who had served us now mounted the tiny stage and discarded her bikini bottom. Her eyes met mine and she gave me a slow wink as she aimed her curly black pelvic bush at me and began to move it in that slow, ageless motion. . . .

The Spaghetti Factory

Creative Films
1812 Melrose Avenue
Hollywood, California

CASTING CALL

PLACE: The Spaghetti Factory
TIME: 9:00 -- 11:00 a.m. December 22nd
PRODUCT: C-900

PRESENT FOR AGENCY: M. Evans
PRESENT FOR CLIENT: N. Barnes
PRESENT FOR PRODUCER: C. Marmocci, casting
                                   director

MALE MODELS

Harry White
Sam Pollack
Whitney Harper
Jerry Gross
Peter Woodford
Pat McGrady

FEMALE MODELS

Haley Brown
June Berrey
Alice Rusk
Martha Freeman
Lauren Moore
Elizabeth Winslow
Sally Heath
Janine Joseph

VOICE-OVER ANNOUNCERS

Samuel Westbrook
Robert Spencer
David Spotiswoodie

The casting call—cattle call, most of us call it—is one of the most degrading procedures in modern advertising. No one escapes unscathed. Certainly not we clients, who must endure the agony of watching half-desperate performers try to appear unconcerned and show their best features, when from the moment they enter the room, we know they are wrong for the part. Nor do the actors and actresses escape, some nervous and openly showing it, some concealing it with flip remarks and tired jokes. They are asked to parade their bodies and their voices for the approval or disapproval of a committee who often do not know precisely for what they are looking. As for the actors who are auditioning for a voice-over commercial, such as we were casting today, they are deprived of what may be their best feature, their own speaking voices. Instead, they will be asked to move across the room, to smile, to frown, to demonstrate that they are capable of the most basic of human reactions—and then advised, "Thank you very much, dear. We'll let you know," and forced to depart, sensing that they have been rejected once more because of a pug nose, or too many freckles, or thick ankles, or some other insane disqualification.

The casting director of The Spaghetti Factory, Carla Marmocci, had drawn on her own knowledge of the business—she had been a successful young leading woman in a series of television programs before abandoning the twenty-one-inch-screen for the behind-the-scenes job she now had—to present us with the most difficult of choices: picking one person from a group of six or eight, or three, any one of whom would probably have been excellent in the commercial. We auditioned the group of six male models, one at a time, and they all fitted the role physically, so it then became a matter of personal prejudice.

"I don't like blond men," said Norman.

That took care of two of the six.

"He ought to have a mustache kind of face, if you know what I mean," I said, "so when he plays the part of the Mexican we can make him up. You need a long upper lip to handle a mustache."

There went two more. Sorry, fellows.

Unable to agree which of the remaining two to choose, we simply tossed a coin. The tall outdoor man who won might, if Acapulco Gold proved successful, earn more than a hundred thousand dollars because of the way the coin fell, while the loser would never know how close he had come to a fortune.

The first of the female models, which is what we call actresses who don't have to speak lines, came in.

"This is Haley Brown," Carla said. We nodded at the girl, who bobbed a mock curtsey back and said, "I can wear my hair down too."

"It doesn't matter," I said. "Can you dance, dear?"

"I had two years with the American Ballet Theatre," she said. Leave it to Carla to be sure all the applicants had good backgrounds.

"Ever do any record miming?" Norman asked. "You know, mouth the words to a prerecorded number?" He turned to me. "We might want her to do a line from the jingle in sync."

"Sure," said the girl. "I do all the old Betty Hutton stuff. Want to hear 'Doin' What Comes Naturally'? I've got it on a cassette. . . ."

"That's okay," I said. "Just walk over to the window and then give me a slow turn on point."

She did, making the turn on one stiffened foot.

Carla looked at us. I nodded. She said to the girl, "Thank you, dear. We'll let you know."

At the door, Haley Brown turned and said, "I'll work in undies too. I mean bra, that kind of thing, if you need it."

"Thanks, dear," I said. "You'll be hearing from us."

When she was gone, Norman said, "Too skinny."

Where had I heard that before?

Carla said, "She's a very good little comedienne. I've seen her on Mike Douglas."

"Too skinny," Norman repeated. We scratched Haley Brown's name off the list and moved on to the next model.

After the first seven, we had found two whom both Norman and I agreed would fit the role of the girl in the dream sequence.

Carla brought the last candidate in.

"This is Janine Joseph," she said.

I stared at the new girl.

Janine Joseph was my ex-wife, Janice Stanford.

I had promised myself—and Jean—that I would not contact Janice. I'd made several other California trips without doing it, and so, seeing her standing there in the producer's office, it was as if some pursuing fate had hounded my tracks, steadily driving me to this time and place in spite of myself.

Janice stared back and said, turning, "I'm sorry. I didn't know. I'll go."

"Hold on there," said Norman. "What's the matter?"

Janice looked at me. "Uh—" I said, "Miss Joseph and I have worked together before."

"Good," said Norman, "because I think she's got just what we want."

You do not say such words in front of talent. If things work out, it drives their price up. If things don't, you've been unnecessarily cruel, holding up hope that does not exist.

Janice knew this. She said, "I'd better go."

"Turn around," said Norman.

Janice turned, still saying, "I don't think—"

"She'll do," Norman told the casting director. "Send the

261

rest our thank you's." I had the right to be angry with him over his singlehanded decision, but I was still too numbed by seeing Janice after all these months to say anything. He got up and shook Janice's hand, making an obvious survey of her ring finger, which was bare. "Yes, ma'am, you'll do just fine."

Carla Marmocci handed me a folded brochure—Janice's "composite," showing her in a series of poses and costumes, and listing her major credits, which, I noticed, included the Duncan Hines commercial she had done when we first met in San Francisco. Nowhere on the composite did it mention that she had ever been married, particularly to one Michael Evans.

"Thank you," I said, still looking at Janice. She hadn't changed much. Her hair was lighter and shorter, and her dress was a little more chic than those she used to wear, but she was still much as I remembered. With a sense of embarrassment, I realized that my thirty-eight-inch belt was considerably more than she had bidden farewell to.

"I'll send in the voice-over announcers," Carla said, leading Janice out of the room.

"How about that?" Norman said softly. "Can I pick them?"

"Yes," I said, "you can pick them."

We had concocted a phony script for the voice-over announcers to use for the audition, with a section to try out their Mexican accents, so that the losers would not know what they had been reading for and have a chance to broadcast it all over town. Norman's original plan to try for Orson Welles or some other "name" had been vetoed early in the game. "It'd cost too much," I said, "and besides, how do we keep a name quiet if the deal folds up? Take some good voice who works for scale and show him how he can make fifty thou if he keeps his lip buttoned and he'll be quiet as a mouse."

So three excellent announcers came in one at a time and stood before us, reading from a script that extolled the merits of Honda trail bikes on the Baja Peninsula, and we picked one because both his Mexican voice and his straight announcer's voice were good, and then, promising to meet everyone on the set next morning, Norman and I parted—I to take my rented car to the nearest gin mill for a much-needed martini, and Norman to the outer desk, where I heard him asking in a heavy whisper for Janine Joseph's telephone number.

One of the civilized things about Los Angeles—alone except for New Orleans, as far as I know—is that it is a twenty-four-hour-a-day bar town. Somewhere, maybe on a sidestreet, and maybe hidden behind painted windows, you will always find a bartender willing to serve your every need. My every need was a lot of gin and a very little vermouth, which I found a few doors off Hollywood Boulevard and sipped slowly, wondering how I was going to get through the next few days. I could have vetoed Janice's selection, but that would have caused more fuss than going ahead and making the best of the situation. Besides, she *was* right for the part, and I wasn't vindictive enough to do her out of a job, although with all her trust funds and blue chips, it was doubtful that she needed the money. Bitterly, I reflected that my own two hundred bucks a month alimony probably paid her apartment rent.

Two of the silver bullets refreshed me enough to send me back to the Hollywood Hawaiian, where I intended to look over the scripts one more time before committing them to the evil eye of the motion picture camera. I sneaked in the back way—one of the nice features of places like the Hawaiian is that guests do not have to submit to the scrutiny of the desk clerk. But today's must have been using a periscope, because I had just finished popping the top of a can of Coors Beer when my phone rang.

"Mr. Evans? I thought I saw you come in. You have a visitor, sir."

"Oh? Who is it?"

"A Miss Stanford."

Zappo. Jean, why the hell didn't you come with me?

"Mr. Evans?"

"Oh, all right. Send her back."

I opened the door so that she wouldn't have to knock at it and have me answer. Somehow that seemed a little *too* Noel Cowardish. "Hullo, pet. S'nice t'see you again. Won't you come in. 'S been a long time." "Thenk you for asking, Piggy. Yes, it's been a very long time." No thank you, Noel. I'd just play it the boorish American way.

Janice knocked anyway, but I was making a big point of rummaging through the refrigerator and yelled over my shoulder, "It's open, come in," and she did, and we looked at each other over the formica breakfast bar.

"How about a beer?" I asked. "It's all I've got right now. I was going to order some Scotch, but—"

The two bottles of booze the producer from The Spaghetti Factory had sent over were hidden under the counter. And I knew Janice didn't like beer.

"No, thank you," she said. "Mike, I'm sorry about the audition. I didn't even know you were in town."

"It doesn't matter," I said. "Besides, Norman likes you. He's the client. You'll probably be hearing from him when you get home tonight.

She laughed. "I already have. I checked my service about an hour after I left the audition. His message was already waiting. He wonders if I'd like to get together with him for a drink this evening and talk about the script." She studied my face. "Should I?"

"It all depends on whether or not you want to get laid."

"You didn't have to say that."

"No," I said, "I guess I didn't. Sorry."

"I think I'll take that beer after all," she said. I popped one for her and she sipped it from the can. "You're looking well," she told me.

"Fat, you mean. It's the booze. I don't eat that much."

"You never did," she said. "That's why it's so strange that you'd put on weight."

"Budweiser'll do it every time. Listen, Janice, this is awkward as hell. What do you want?"

Her lips tightened, but her voice stayed under control. "I know things didn't work out between us, Mike, but I wasn't aware that we'd sworn vows of eternal hatred."

"Baby," I said, "one of the things that developed my fondness for Budweiser was a couple of years there when all of my free cash took the first plane for California while I had to live in a furnished room and drink beer because I couldn't afford the good stuff. Now my accountant signs your checks, so I don't have to puke over them the way I used to. Does that answer your question?"

"No," she said. "I just don't believe you'd get that disturbed over money. You don't like money—that's what helped break us up, your attitude about it."

"Correction," I said. "It was your money that I didn't like. I was very fond of my own and it made me sad to wave goodbye to it."

Her eyes blinked. "I only insisted on the alimony to hurt you."

"You succeeded. It hurt me very badly in the hip pocket."

"I thought after a month or two you'd see how silly it was and come back to me."

"You thought wrong."

"Yes, I know that now. Look, Mike, let's forget that I turned up. I'll call Carla and tell her I broke my ankle or something."

"Don't do that for my sake. I don't mind working with you again. You're a pretty good performer."

She blinked again. "Well, thank you for that, anyway."

"Don't mention it."

"I won't!" she flared. At the door, she turned and said, "Any messages for your friend Norman?"

"Tell him I suggested that you're best in the female-dominant position."

"You lousy bastard!" she said, and slammed the door.

I went into the bathroom and looked at myself in the mirror.

"You lousy bastard," I repeated slowly, and then I was violently sick.

On the set next morning I found Norman Barnes at the coffee wagon.

"How was it last night?" I asked.

He gave me a knowing wink and circled his thumb and forefinger, and I knew then that he was lying, that whatever else had happened, he hadn't scored with Janice, and I don't know why, perhaps out of dog-in-the manger jealousy, I was pleased.

In New York, more often than not, the first two hours of a shooting day will be occupied in finishing the set, dressing it with props and decorations, adjusting the lighting. Not so on the Coast. All of that has been done the night before by craftsmen who learned their trade in the days of the big feature film, when every hour spent standing around cost tens of thousands of dollars in talent fees. Standing around waiting for a television commercial to be shot can cost a thousand dollars an hour, but that's not in the same league. The technicians still perform at the old level, though. The story is told of an agency producer from New York who arrived on his first Hollywood set at nine-thirty, clapping his hands together and shouting,

"Okay, let's go. I want to get a shot by eleven," only to be told, "Buddy, we're on the third shot already, and if you'd waited much longer, you'd have missed the whole commercial."

Commercials, just like films, are shot out of sequence to take the best advantage of your sets, your talent pool, and technical staff. You don't really save any money by sending people home before the eight hours are up, but after then each body waiting around costs money and if, heaven forbid, you should shoot past midnight—as often happens with producers who do not preplan their work carefully enough—the crew goes into what's known as "golden time": triple pay. So the usual shooting day is set up to get rid of as many people as possible, then if things go wrong you are down to the shots that use the fewest cast and crew. If there are silent sequences, they're saved for last, because that way you can wrap sound without going into overtime for the sound crew.

We spent the morning doing the dream sequence, with Janice and the male model dancing on clouds and puffing like mad on cigarettes in brown wrappers. We hadn't told anyone what the product really was.

"It's going to be good," Norman said, watching Janice whirl across the sound stage in step with the recorded music. "Doesn't she swing that ass?"

"She has experience," I said. "Are you seeing her tonight?"

"Why bother?" he said. Then, remembering that he'd fibbed to me this morning about last night, he added quickly, "Look, I'm a married man. I don't mind boffing them once for a little change of scenery, but I don't want to get nothing serious started, you know what I mean?"

"Sure," I said. "If a girl like that fell for a married man like you, she could cause you a lot of grief."

Relieved, he said, "Yeah, you're right there. So listen, boy, if you want to take a shot at it, be my guest."

"I might just do that," I said.

Up until now, we had been using a package that said nothing about the product. Its lettering had been "Greeked"—that is, from a distance, it looked as if there were a label on the package. This prevents lawsuits when you're showing an enemy package for comparison; in our case, it preserved secrecy. All of our shots so far had been from a distance, but close up the camera would have seen that the label was merely gibberish.

The director came over. "Mike," he said, "we've got our dream sequence. We'll do the surf scene tomorrow out at Malibu. So we can wrap sound playback and release the actors."

"Good," I said.

"Not so good. We've got trouble."

"What's wrong?"

"The hand model I booked for you is in the hospital with a bad case of stopping short on the freeway. We just got the call."

"Hurt bad?"

"Bad enough to keep her out of action for at least a month. Frankly, I picked her because I knew she'd keep her mouth shut about the product. I don't know anyone else I'd trust on something as big as this."

"What about one of your production assistants?"

He shook his head. "Denise is the only one with hands good enough, and I wouldn't even trust her with my un-listed home number. She's not malicious—just stupid and talkative."

"How about our star?" asked Norman.

The director looked around. "Miss Joseph?" He shook his head. "I've never worked with her before. I couldn't guarantee anything."

"Mike's worked with her before," Norman said. "How about it, Mike? Can we trust her?" I hesitated, and he said sharply, "Well, don't you know?"

"No," I said. "I *don't* know. Can you shoot around her for an hour or so?"

"We can do the man's hand shots," said the director. "I'm going to model them myself. And we can pick up the product beauty shots and the filter closeups. I guess that'll take at least two hours, especially since I'm releasing all the crew except for my cameraman so there won't be any-body else in the shop to see what we're filming."

"I'll take her across the street for a drink and let you know," I said.

Worried, Norman said, "Can't you just ask her?"

"No," I said. "Why don't you ask her, Norman?"

He spread his hands. "She's mad at me," he said. "She'd tell me to go shit in my hat."

I was tempted to zing him with how well he'd claimed to have made out with her, but things were too serious for that, so I just slipped on my jacket and went over to the portable makeup bench where Janice was fixing her face and said, "Crisis time. Put on something and I'll buy you a drink."

She started to say something, then shrugged and put on a light blue jacket and followed me out of the studio. Across Highland Avenue was a cocktail lounge with a painting of a bucking bronco painted across the front window. The Old Corral was the joint's name, and from the smell that greeted us as we entered, someone had forgotten to clean up after the horses.

We sat in a booth and, without asking Janice, I ordered two stingers. "White crème de menthe, not green," I told the waitress.

"You remembered," Janice said.

"I remember all too well," I said. "My limit on these things is two, so we'll have to talk fast."

"I thought you said everything rather well yesterday," she said. "What is there left to discuss?"

"Baby, this is business."

"Of course. Everything is business with you, isn't it, Mike? No place for plain old human frailties and concerns. In the Mike Evans scheme of things, everyone must work for their money and the job comes first. All right, Mike. What is it this time? Am I under orders to be nicer to your client?"

I laughed. "Any nicer and he'd poison your coffee. What did you do to the poor bastard? He gave me the old finger this morning, but his heart wasn't in it. That's the first time I've ever known Norm to strike out when he really went after something. How'd you do it?"

"When your 'something' has enough money of her own to be able to laugh at the little favors your Normans can deliver, it creates a certain independence."

"That's one of the advantages of money," I agreed.

Our drinks came and we waited until the waitress had gone to continue our conversation.

"I think you've learned the advantages of money rather

well yourself, Mike," Janice said. "You're not exactly Mr. Poor any more, are you?"

"No," I said, "but the difference is, I worked for every dime of mine." I lifted my glass. "Let's stop sniping at each other. Peace?"

"Did you?" she asked, not touching her glass.

"Did I what?"

"Did you work for every dime of it?"

"Well, Daddy sure didn't leave it to me."

"How about Wild Bill Haney?"

I put my drink down. "How much did Loudmouth Barnes tell you last night?"

"Just that one minute it looked as if you were on your way out of the advertising business and the next you had Haney by a ring in his nose, a bigger job at the agency, and a stock deal that ought to return you a couple of hundred thousand dollars in capital gains. My friend, working stiffs don't get that kind of payday. You were lucky, that's what Norman said. You lucked in, by being in the right place at the right time when the moneysacks started falling from the sky. Which is approximately what happened to me too—so you see, Mike, there's no longer that much difference between us."

"How did you and your new boyfriend come to be talking about poor little Mike?"

She shuddered and took a hefty swig of her drink. "He's not *my* boyfriend. I've had some hard times since you and I split up, but not that hard. Not that there haven't been plenty of chances. What is it with your Normans? When they get away from Louisville, they forget what the mirror tells them and go around like they're Cary Grant and Steve McQueen all in one, with all us little starlets just aching to fall down and spread our legs. Don't they have the sense to realize that even when they *do* score, it's just a business deal, no more, and they'd have gotten more for their money if they stood down on the corner of Wilshire Boulevard waving a fifty-dollar bill?"

"They're victims of the very dream they created," I said. "They spend so much time in the fantasy world of the boob tube, they've come to believe it themselves."

"But not you, Mike?"

"Not me. You didn't answer my question. Does Norman know you and I were married?"

"Not from me. I got him started on Mike Evans because—well, I wanted to know what you've been doing since I heard from you last. And I'm not being snide. I'm really glad for you."

"All right," I said. "Like I said, peace. Well, back to our problem. Our hand model got clobbered on the freeway and didn't show up. Norman wants you to do the shots."

"All right," she said. "I don't have the best fingernails in the business, but I get by. What's the big deal about it?"

"The big deal is that you've got to keep quiet about the product," I said. "It's a security problem that makes the atom bomb look like *Town Meeting of the Air*. So if you're mad enough at me, or are likely to get mad enough at some later date, to figure you might want to get back at me by blowing the whistle on our product, then I don't want you to do the shot. I—"

"Oh, come off it," she said. "I'm a professional and I don't mix personal feelings with the job. That's one thing I learned from you. If you want me to do the shot, I will, and I won't even tell my shrink. Okay?"

"Fine," I said. We worked on our drinks for a while, and then I asked, "Do you really have one?"

"Have one what?"

"One shrink?"

She laughed. "No, but sometimes because I don't, I feel deprived. Every girl I know in the business is going to one at least twice a week. There's one block in Beverly Hills with more than fifty psychiatrists doing business there. It's a riot in the dressing room, sometimes, to hear the chicks holding forth with psychological doubletalk about their roles—hidden motivations and character substrata. And then they go out and say their piece for posterity: 'Nap cleans diapers three ways better.' It'd be laughable if it weren't so sad." She held up her empty glass. "Do we have time for another one of these?"

I caught the waitress's eye and held up two fingers. Then, to Janice, I said, "So that's what you've been doing? Commercials?"

271

"Scads. Haven't you seen any of them?"

"I don't watch the tube much."

"Too bad. That destroys my beautiful vision."

"What vision is that?"

Janice smiled. "Oh, I pictured you viewing my little triumphs and admitting to yourself that I was finally doing what you'd always wanted me to—earning my own way in the cold, cruel world. And now it turns out you never even saw the goddamned things."

Our drinks came and this time we clinked glasses. "Here's to visions," I said. "At least yours was a good one. That's more than I can say for some of the daydreams *I* was having those days."

"It was a flawed vision, though," she admitted. "There were months when I didn't have a dime. Your money came in very handy. And I slipped a couple of times and called up the folks for rent money."

"It's hard to imagine you with holes in your shoes," I said. "Have you been here all that time?"

"I was in New York for a while. I almost called you a couple of times, but it didn't feel right. Once I saw you on Fifth Avenue. You walked right past me, scowling at the sidewalk like you were kicking it with your shoes."

"It's just as well you didn't call," I said. "I probably wouldn't have been very nice."

"You're not so bad now," she said.

"I've had more time to get over it."

"Good," she said, "because I never did."

"Did what?"

"Get over it." She looked straight at me. "I blew it, Mike. I never thought you'd let me leave. And once I'd gone, I thought you'd come and get me. I wanted you to come and get me."

"Sorry," I said. "I didn't receive the message."

"You're receiving it now."

I shook my head. "No, Janice. We're two different people these days. I guess you're better now than I used to think you were. And it's no secret that I'm worse. But it's just too late for us."

"What you're really saying is that you've found another girl."

I shrugged. "I'm not claiming I've been living in a monastery, if that what you mean."

"That's not what I mean. You have the look of a man who's getting it regularly, without having to play the field."

"Your years of self-sufficiency have coarsened you, my fair lady," I said.

"Do you love her?"

"I don't love anyone," I said, and hearing the words now, I knew it was true.

M LA DEC 10 LLAO48 XLT4068 TB NL LOS ANGELES CALIF 10

HOWARD PORTER MORTON KEYES & COOPER
629 MADISON AVE NEW YORK NY

LEAVING TOMORROW AM FOR NORWICH WITH FILMS. WILL MEET YOU
THERE ALL IS WELL.   MIKE

WU 1201 (R 5-69)

Of course, *all* is never well. My wire to Porter was true enough, as far as it went. The films had turned out fine, and I thought we had a good chance at attracting a high percentage of viewers, particularly with the "Ricardo" commercial, and even of selling them some of our new product.

Things were less well on the Mike Evans front, however. As Jean had sensed even before I left New York, I ended up back in the sack with Janice before the first week was out. It began that first day in the Old Corral when I showed her the sample package of Acapulco Gold.

"This is our product," I said. "And the reason we've got to keep it quiet is—"

I stopped then, because she was laughing so loud that everyone was looking at us.

Hiding the package with my hand, I said, "What the hell's so funny? You've got the whole place staring at us."

"I—I'm—sorry . . ." she choked. "It's just so—so—ludicrous!"

"What is?"

She tapped my hand, the one that cupped the dummy

package. "This! Here I've been building you up in my mind as Mr. Straight-and-True, who's made it by being good and pure, thereby proving you were right and I was wrong—and how the hell are you doing it? By peddling dope! Am I wrong, or is that funny?"

"I'm glad you think it's funny. We've only got around twenty million bucks riding on this product, and it *isn't* dope. Janice, this stuff's going to be legal next year when the new President gets in office. We're just jumping the gun so we'll be ready when we get the word."

She went on as if I hadn't spoken. "So this is how you got your big new job and all that wonderful stock! I've been wrong—there *must* be a God, and He's got a sense of humor too." She pried my hand away from the package and looked at it. "Acapulco Gold! I can see why you were worried, Mike. Can you guess what would happen if I hustled down to the *Hollywood Reporter* and gave an interview about the sharpies from the East who are out here filming pot commercials? Why, I'd have my picture on the front page of every newspaper in the country. Now *that* would be a break for an aspiring young actress."

Worried, I said, "That's why I wanted to be sure you'd be quiet. The wrong kind of publicity right now—"

"What if I told you that all bets are off? What if I told you that when I took this job, nobody informed me I was filming a commercial for an illegal drug, and that I want no part of it? What if I told you to take your kite out in the middle of the Pasadena Freeway and fly it?"

I put the dummy package back in my pocket. "Is that what you're telling me?"

"Mike, if only you could see your face!" She touched my hand. "No, you fool, of course I'm not telling you that. I'm just so glad to see that you're *human,* it seems to have affected my funnybone. Don't worry. I'll do your silly hand shots for you. And I won't run down to the *Hollywood Reporter*. But don't expect any more brownie points from me for your sterling character—because as I have just discovered, chum, you ain't got any."

She did the hand shots well enough, and that night after we'd wrapped shooting, we had dinner at the Villa Capri, and then we parked her car in the public lot in front of Don the Beachcomber's, and after a Navy Grog each drove my rental back to the the Hollywood Hawaiian, sneaked in the back door, and scattered our clothing all the way from the living room to the big king-sized bed.

The next ten days were blurred booze-filled episodes between sweaty nights that mounted in tempo as my departure date came closer. Somehow, in between, I supervised the shooting of three television commercials and their editing behind closed doors. One night after we had worn each other down to two gasping, twitching wrecks, Janice whispered, "It's more fun when it's sin, isn't it?"

"You're so right," I said. And she was.

I hadn't called Jean or written. I meant to every morning, but I was busy at the studio, and there were business luncheons, and of course there was Janice.

Christmas Day I had checked in at the Hawaiian front desk and there was a wire reading:

YULE BE GLAD TO KNOW, JOSEPH, THAT I'M IN TROUBLE.
MARY

I had a momentary spell of panic before I realized she was playing some kind of joke, and told myself I'd write that night, but I didn't, and then it was almost time to fly back to New York anyway, and I decided to save everything for when I saw her.

Our last night Janice was more frenzied and persistent in her lovemaking than ever before. Later, as we lay in the darkness, I heard her crying.

"What's wrong?" I asked.

"Shut up," she said.

I lit up a Pall Mall and, as I puffed it, I realized I hadn't smoked pot since coming to California.

"Did you ever screw on pot?" I asked.

Janice sat up and said, "What?"

I repeated it, and she said, "Of course not. Why would I want to?"

"It makes it better sometimes," I said.

"So that's what I lack?" she said. "Why didn't you tell me sooner? I could have gone down to Hollywood and Vine and made a buy. Or, for that matter, I could have begged some from Uncle Norman. If he got sloppy seconds, that is. I'm so awfully sorry that I'm not up to your

277

high standards, and if I'd only known how simple it was to meet specifications, I would have leaped at the chance."

"That's not what I meant at all," I said. "But anyway, you've stopped crying."

"I stopped crying because I'm *mad!*" she said. Then: "It didn't work, did it?"

"What didn't?"

"My campaign to get you back."

There wasn't any sense in lying. "No," I said.

"What did I do wrong?"

"Nothing."

"Then why didn't it work? Is it because of her? Mary?"

"Who?" I asked, surprised.

"Mary. I saw that telegram you were carrying around."

I inhaled too much cigarette smoke and started choking. "Her name's not Mary, it's Jean, and that telegram was just a joke, and I think I'm suffocating."

She pounded my back. "I hope I break your spine," she said.

"You're halfway there." I stopped choking and caught her bare warm arm and bit it. "You taste good."

Quietly, she said, "You really *are* a bastard, aren't you? After everything we've said tonight, you'd screw me again to get just one more good come before you leave for keeps."

"It works both ways," I said. "I haven't noticed you pining away for lack of orgasms."

"I was faking them."

"Sure you were."

"No, I wasn't," she admitted. "Oh, Mike, it's been so good. Why can't it go on?"

"Because I'm not willing to admit to myself that's all there is."

"What's all there is?"

"Haven't you heard that Peggy Lee song? She goes to the circus and afterward asks, 'Is *that* all there is to a circus?' And it's the same for love, and even life, because the girl in the song will die asking, 'Is *that* all there is?' Well, I don't think that's all there is. I don't think I've had it all yet, and I'm not quitting until I have. I'm not talking about you, Janice, not you as a person. But I remember that bitched-up relationship we had, and the way I haven't really seen anything better since then. I won't settle for that. I won't go back to the old things, not while I can still hope that there's something *more* somewhere. Maybe one day I'll call you up and say that I've finally seen the light, that there *isn't* any more and to break out the booze—"

"Don't waste the dime, you louse," she said, sliding out of bed. "I keep peeling off layers of the Evans hide, hoping to find new depths underneath, and all I locate is the same old selfish crap. And believe me, baby, that's *all* there is!"

I didn't try to talk her out of dressing and leaving. There wasn't any point. When I offered to walk her to her car, she shook her head. "Save the energy, Mike," she said. "You may need it some day."

So next morning I drove to the airport alone, hungover, vaguely dissatisfied with the way things had gone, and wondering why I even gave her a second thought. The 16mm composite prints of the Acapulco Gold commercials were in my briefcase—four copies of each. I dropped the car at Budget, and they drove me out to the TWA terminal, where I checked in and went to the bar to wait for my flight.

Early that morning I had tried to call my apartment in New York. No one answered. So I phoned Mark Hedin and asked him to locate Jean and ask her to fly up to Norwich, New York, to meet me.

"I'll be coming in to Newark and taking a chopper over to Teterboro to catch the air taxi up to Norwich," I said. "It'll be simpler if she goes direct."

"It'll be simpler if I can find her," he said. "She hasn't been around."

I told him to do his best and hung up.

Flying east from the Coast is very different from going the other way. The plane takes off at eleven in the morning, and by the time you've finished eating lunch, the sun is setting behind you, because you have picked up the jet stream and are hurtling away from the Western horizon at seven hundred miles an hour. There is an unreality about seeing the sun dip below the mountains when your watch reads two-thirty.

It was pitch-dark when I got to Newark, and the helicopter was late, and the air taxi ride was bumpy, so I arrived at Norwich sweating at the palms and urgently in need of a martini.

We had chosen the small town of Norwich as the locale for our television testing because the cable system there allowed us to pipe one commercial to the north side of town and at the same time send a different commercial to the south side. And since there were two major shopping centers in town—one north, one south—that gave us a good way of checking how many viewers went to the drugstore at each and asked for the product. Thus we could evaluate the strength of one commercial versus the other.

I took a cab up the hill to Stefanelli's Motel and went to the bar, where you also had to check in. Howard Porter was already there, sipping a martini.

"I'll have one of those," I said. "How goes it, Howard?"

"So-so," he said. "You didn't get a tan."

"The bars out there don't have sunlamps. What's wrong, buddy? You look down at the mouth."

"Have some of your drink first."

"That bad?"

The bartender handed me a hefty martini. "Are you Mr. Evans?"

"Yeah. I'll be checking in when I get through here."

"No rush, your room's reserved. But there's a message for you."

He rummaged under the bar and came up with a small notepad and read from it: "Miss Patrick called to say she'll be late because she's driving up and she ran into snow over near Roscoe." He looked up at me. "I'm holding her room for late arrival."

"Thanks," I said. "How late do you serve dinner?"

"Ten-thirty tonight."

It was just after eight now. I'd give Jean another couple of hours before ordering. Suddenly, I wanted to see her very much. While I had been on the other side of the continent with another woman pressed against me, Jean's face and voice had faded into that timeless past that holds all your memories—but now that we were within a few miles of each other, her presence had become strong in my consciousness. I thought I smelled her perfume, and to my surprise, there in the brightly lighted bar I began to feel the first stirrings of sexual excitement.

"Hey, tiger," said Howard Porter, "are you going to sit there all night? Your silver bullet's getting warm."

"Right you are," I said, sipping. "Where are the clients? Aren't there any around?"

"Negative. They're all down in Washington."

"Why Washington?"

"It seems that we've run into a little snag. Somehow the new Vice President, Arthur Rand, got wind of what we've been up to, and he's called Wild Bill Haney on the carpet."

"Ouch."

"Ouch and double ouch. This could blow the whole deal, Mike. Haney may have been taking too much for granted. I don't see how Foster would dare go on record for marijuana legalization if it appeared that he or anyone in his Administration were mixed up in some way with a plan to commercialize his decision. Haney's down there now, trying to convince Artie Rand that all we're doing is following the lead of several other tobacco companies, merely readying ourselves for the *possible* legalization."

"Doubletalk. Don't tell me you think Rand'll buy those worms?"

"He doesn't have to. All he has to do is be convinced that the Congress and the public will."

"Will they?"

Porter spread his hands. "Why shouldn't they? After all, we're not doing anything wrong. Are we?"

I gulped down the rest of my martini and said, "No. Of course we're not."

INTERVIEWER: Good morning. This is the National Television Research Service. Is this Mrs. Burke?

HOUSEWIFE: Yes.—Honey, it's somebody from the TV!

INT: Do you mind telling me if you were watching television last night?

HW: Yes. Yes, we were. Honey, pick up the extension!

INT: Did you by chance watch the program *Ironside* last evening?

HUSBAND: Hello, this is Mr. Burke. *Lee* Burke, not Allan Burke, he's my brother-in-law. Yes, we watched. Why do you want to know?

INT: Do you remember any of the commercials?

HW: Well, there were so many of them. I think I saw one of those Ajax Cleansers. Or was it Comet?

INT: Do you remember the part of the program when Raymond Burr, who plays Chief Ironside, is in his wheelchair at the top of the stairs and someone gives him a shove?

HW: Oh, yes! Why, my heart absolutely stopped. I—

INT: Then there was a commercial? It was for a new product.

HUS: Hey, I remember that one. It was for some kind of cigarette. What was it named, Helen?

HW: Mexico something. No, it was Acapulco.

HUS: Acapulco Gold. Yeah, it was one of those new things. You know, what the kids call pot?

HW: Marijuana! That's what it was. Honestly, I never thought—

INT: Do you remember anything about the product?

HUS: Well, they said it was the real stuff, you know what I mean?

HW: The people smoking it seemed to be having fun. And I remember now, there was a little boy. He was smoking it too. I think they said it was safe even for children.

HUS: Take a trip, that's what they said. Take a wonderful trip with Acapulco Gold. *(laughter)* If they meant the kind of trip I think they meant, I'm going to buy a carton today.

HW: Lee, she can hear you!

HUS: So what? If they're selling the stuff, what's wrong with—

INT: Mrs. Burke, do you remember anything about the package?

HW: Oh, it was very pretty. We have a color set, you know, and I remember it had a lovely picture on the label, all bright and golden. And there was a picture of a palm tree.

INT: Did you say palm tree?

HW: Yes, that's what I said. Isn't that right? Did I miss the question?

INT: Well, Mrs. Burke, thank you very much for your assistance. We—

HW: Do I win something?

Jean did not mention California or my silence from there, except to say, "You didn't get a tan."

Porter laughed. "I said the same thing. He told me the bars out there don't have sunlamps."

It was almost ten when she finally arrived, and the snow was falling heavily. The bartender had said, half an hour before, "If it keeps coming down like this, I hope your friend doesn't get caught between South New Berlin and Norwich. Those hills get mighty slippery before the sanders and the plows get out."

A few minutes before Jean arrived the phone rang. It was for Howard. He listened a lot and kept saying, "I see" and "We'll take care of it." When he hung up, he waited until the bartender was out of sight and said, "Everything's been cleared up down in Washington. But what happened was no accident. Somebody's stirring up trouble for us."

"What kind of trouble?"

"Rand has been given a complete report on what we're doing. Right down to the Jamaican trip."

"Anonymous?"

Howard shook his head. "According to Haney, Rand knows who his source is. But he's protecting it."

"In that case, how can you say everything's all right?"

"Because whoever the source was, he misjudged Rand. Rand *wants* to see marijuana legalized. Not just relaxed, but sold commercially, otherwise the rackets will still be handling it and the kids will be just as bad off as before."

"How's that? If they can't be busted for smoking, what does it matter who sells it to them?"

"Because our friendly neighborhood pushers have come up with a new gimmick. Did you ever hear of dirty pot?"

I resisted the temptation to joke. "No. What's that?"

"A lot of it's been coming in from Vietnam. Dirty pot is marijuana that's been treated with heroin. Let someone puff a few of *those* joints and he can wind up addicted to heroin without even knowing it. And heroin will remain illegal, and that means the kids will still be in the grips of the pushers."

I stared at him in wonder. "I'll be damned. Is this really square, straight old Howard Porter? How come you know so much about the drug underground all of a sudden?"

"You're not the only one who does research, Mike. And you're not the only one who's been worried about the morality of what we're doing. So I checked out everything I could. Anyway, that's why Arthur Rand wants to see marijuana sold on the open market, cheaper than any pusher can sell it. He wants pot taken out of the hands of the syndicate to remove the easy way for the hoods to addict kids onto something stronger."

We had given up on Jean and were reading the huge menu when she pulled into the driveway, her bright-red Karmann Ghia glistening between the snowflakes.

"Sorry I'm late," she said, pecking my cheek. "I stopped in Walton and had snow tires put on." Then she asked me about my tan and we made small talk through dinner. Outside, the snow fell heavily and the passing traffic was muffled and shadowy.

Around eleven Porter yawned and looked at his watch. "Hibernation time for the old folks," he said. "Mike, Haney's flying up here in the morning, and then we'll go down and check the cable feed. Tenish okay?"

"Tenish is fine," I said. "But the jet lag's got me. I think

I'm going to sit here for a while and look at the snow. Jean?"

"Why not?" she answered.

Our little charade didn't fool Howard for a second, but it was part of the game, and he went off to his motel room just as indicated in the script.

"Brandy?" I asked Jean.

"Coffee with Irish whiskey."

I nodded at the genial bartender. Then I looked out the window at the red Karmann Ghia. "I didn't know you drove a bug."

"I brought it back from Iowa. It belongs to my brother." Our drinks came. She sipped her Irish-laced coffee. "This is a bad habit you've given me," she said.

I stroked her forearm. "You've given me a couple too."

"Did she want you to stay out there with her?"

"Yes."

"Why didn't you?"

"I didn't want to."

"Are you sure?"

"Absolutely sure."

Jean sighed. "I wasn't positive you'd come back. I think I hoped that you wouldn't."

"That's a hell of a thing to say."

"I'm sorry, Mike. I wish things could be like they are in the movies. There the lovers have a fight and break up and that's it. Period, no more. In life it never happens so clean. It drags on. They prolong their misery."

"I'm not miserable. I'm as happy as a clam. Being with you does that to me."

"Were you happy as a clam in California?"

"That was different."

"You haven't answered me. Not that I have any right to an answer. But I wish you would."

I sipped some of my brandy. "Let's just say that there's always a certain amount of pleasure in—revisiting something you've left behind. But that doesn't mean that you want to spend the rest of your life there."

"I think those are just words that you use."

"What words?"

"Words like 'rest of your life.' Mike, you haven't even *thought* about the rest of your life. You haven't even

286

thought beyond tomorrow, except vaguely. Where do you want to *be* five years from now? Twenty?"

"Is that so important?"

"It is when you start asking someone else to share those tomorrows. Mike, I don't want to hurt you, really I don't. That's why I almost wish you hadn't come back and why I shouldn't have come up here to be with you. I wasn't going to, but I'm weak, and it's wrong because it's inevitable that I *am* going to hurt you."

"I can take it."

"Can you?"

I almost said, "Try me," but I didn't, because I was afraid she might.

Instead, I finished my brandy and said, "Let's go over to your room and watch TV."

She hesitated, then said, "All right."

"Do you want some beer?"

She shook her head. "I've got—something else."

A tiny thrill of excitement tickled my stomach. "Okay."

I paid the check and collected both our room keys. We stopped at the red car, took her suitcase from the back seat, jammed in among the two summer tires, and then found her room and unlocked the door.

Jean switched on the TV set. I stood behind her and put my arms around her. She leaned back against me and gave a deep trembling sigh. I started to tell her that I loved her, but she cut me off. "Don't talk, Mike. Please. Just take off your shoes and get comfortable. Let's turn out the lights and look through the window at the snow and not say anything to each other."

We watched the falling snowflakes for a while, and when she took out a joint and lit it, I accepted it without a word, and we sat there in the silent gloomy motel room, smoking marijuana and staring at the snow swirling outside the big plate-glass window.

When we started on the second marijuana cigarette, I said, "I can *hear* the snow."

"Shhhh."

"It sounds like little tinkling bells."

"Please don't say anything, Mike."

So I didn't. I leaned against the side of the bed and listened to the tiny chimes of the falling snowflakes.

287

Jean moved closer to me. Her questing hand found mine and we pressed together, then, in the snow-filled darkness. My whole body was filled with such a tender yearning warmth that I almost cried out. Her cheek pressed against my thighs, and I felt myself stir toward her.

Her hand unzipped me. I reached for her slacks, and she whispered, "No. Don't move. Let me do it all."

I let her. It may have lasted a moment, or an hour, or a lifetime. I came back to sensibility with my own choking gasps still rasping in my throat. Her hair was tendriled around my fingers and her breath was hot against my bare legs.

The marijuana high was gone now. Stiffly, I got up and helped Jean to her feet. "Let's go to bed," I said.

Wordlessly, she undressed. I finished taking off my own clothes and we crawled under the blankets.

Her body was warm and moist against mine. I hugged her to me.

"Mike," she said softly, "why didn't you stay with Janice? She turned out to be nicer than you remembered, didn't she?"

"That's not the point," I said. "I couldn't admit to myself that that's all there is."

"What do you mean, that's all there is?"

"That I've reached my limits. That there's never going to be any great American novel, or any *King Lear,* or any hit play, or even any more to *life* than just more sex and moderate comfort and a few beers on Saturday afternoon. It's like saying that all happiness is is when you don't have a broken leg."

"Isn't it?"

"I'm happy now."

"But you don't have a broken leg either."

"I've got a broken something else. Are you aware, woman, that when you're passionate, you *bite?*"

"Shhh," she said. "Please don't make jokes."

"All right, no jokes. But don't try to convince me that I'm not happy."

"Ahhh," she sighed, "Mike, don't depend on me. Please don't trust me. Because I'll only hurt you."

"It sounds like you're warning me."

"I am. Please believe me, I am."

"I believe you," I said, "but I don't care. I honestly don't."

"You should," she told me. "You really should."

N.T.R.S. TV REPORT

TITLES:	BLUE SKIES,TRAVELOGUE, RICARDO
LENGTH:	1:00
POSITIONS:	Fifth/Sixth, Middle/Closing
PURPOSE:	To measure ability of these commercials to communicate the following messages:

1. New.

2. Description of pleasure and enjoyment.

3. Reassurance of safety of ingredients and that this is a quality product.

4. Implication that product may be used to secure same effects as liquor.

5. Superiority over other brands.

INTERVIEWING DATE:
   January 9

LOCATION:
   Norwich, N.Y.

PROGRAM:
   "Ironside" (Color)

DATE OF
TELECAST:
   Thursday, January 8

METHOD:
On the day following airing of the test
program, telephone interviews were conducted
by the National Television Research Service
with consumers in the test area. Survey
procedure followed the standard TV testing
method. A total of 8,489 dialings was made to
obtain 185 interviews with consumers who had
seen some part of "Ironside." Of these, 156
(84%) were at the set during some part of the
Acapulco Gold commercials.

SAMPLE: Completed interviews were distributed
          as follows:

                    185 = 100%

          By City By Age

Norwich   100   Under 35   29
                   35 - 50   23
                   51 and over 45
                   No answer   3

            -----   -----
            100%   100%

By number in By Sets
Household
----------   -------
1-2   41   Color   18
3-4   31   B&W   65
5 & over 24   Both   15
No answer 4   No answer   2

            -----   -----
            100%   100%

NATIONAL TELEVISION RESEARCH SERVICE SUMMARY

COMMERCIALS
TESTED: C-900 ACAPULCO GOLD "BLUE SKIES"
        (1:00 Fifth/Sixth Positions)
        C-900 ACAPULCO GOLD "TRAVELOGUE"
        (1:00 Fifth/Sixth Positions)
        C-900 ACAPULCO GOLD "RICARDO"
        (1:00 Middle/closing)

PERFORMANCE	BLUE SKIES	TRAVELOGUE	RICARDO
Related Recall	31	37	53
New	4	11	24
For/told about enjoyment/pleasure	17	13	29
Safe ingredients/ quality product/ natural	8	8	21
Use in place of liquor	4	7	23
Better than others/ best/standard of quality	3	2	19
Showed man/men/ woman/women/ child/someone	18	17	33

PAST EXPERIENCE

(NOTE: Since this is a totally new product
category, it has been related to the averages of
beer/wine/cigarette commercials previously tested)

	Median %	Total Range %
All 1:00 commercials in above categories tested with consumers (242)	27	7 - 49
All 1:00 commercials tested with consumers this year (106)	20	4 - 46

"I'll be a son of a bitch," said Bill Haney. "That 'Ricardo' spot went right through the roof."

We were all sitting in Conference Room 661. Ham Keyes was at the end of the long table. Howard Porter and Norman Barnes were on one side, I was on the other, and Wild Bill Haney was standing against the chalk tray. We had just screened the three commercials to refresh our memories, and now Haney was reading the research report aloud.

"How do we know this thing isn't biased in favor of the housewives?" he asked. "Did we get enough buys?"

Porter consulted a thick folder. "We deliberately made our calls in the evening and on every second dialing asked specifically for the man of the house. We lost a few here and there who had gone bowling, but it averages out."

Haney read from the summary. "Twenty-four out of fifty-three remembered that we said the stuff was new. Twenty-nine—more than half—remembered that it'd give them a good time. We got twenty-one, over a third, who remembered it was safe, and around half who got the message that you use it instead of booze. Men, we're home free."

"If Washington doesn't call us out at third base," Ham Keyes commented dryly.

Haney didn't even hear him. "Listen to these verbatim playbacks. One babe gave us back the whole goddamned commercial. She said, quote, 'It's a new cigarette that gives you more fun than the old ones. They're safe, and the government says they're legal now, and even children can use them. There's no hangover, like you get from whiskey.' God bless you, lady! And these verbatims are fat, boys. They've all got five or six recall points in every one. We've got ourselves a commercial that'll penetrate those bone heads out there like a hunting arrow."

"What do you think, Mike?" Ham asked.

Carefully, I said, "Ham, I always had a leaning toward 'Ricardo.'"

"Why?"

"Because it covered the board. Look, it isn't any trick to switch the kids who are already smoking pot from the underground weed and onto our product. One, we're legal. Two, we're going to be cheaper. All we have to do is let them know that we're around and they'll line up. The hardest sale will be to those who haven't used marijuana before, at least not regularly. And this research indicates what I hoped for has happened. We're getting through to that group. Maybe the kid did it, maybe the takeoff on the old coffee commercial, maybe the appeal to sex. Maybe all three. Anyway, it's working, and I think we're in good shape."

"My opinion exactly," said Haney. "If Artie Rand holds his water, we're in fat city."

"What exactly is the picture down in Washington?" Ham asked. "Are we still in serious trouble? I thought all that was cleared up."

"Someone," said Haney, "has been feeding our future Vice President chapter and verse of our operation. When I find out who it is, I intend to hand him his head."

Mildly, Ham asked, "Do you suspect one of us?"

"Hell, no. Listen, I knew there wasn't much of a chance that we could keep this whole project under wraps for

295

more than a few weeks. Guys all over the country are already calling me up trying to get a piece of the action. I only hoped that we'd be able to get past Foster's Inaugural Address without making any headlines, and so far, thanks to Artie Rand, we're staying on that schedule. Rand's disturbed by what we're up to, no doubt about that, but it fits in with his own long-range plans, so he's going along with us."

"So long as it fits in with his long-range plans," Ham Keyes said.

"Well, what more can you expect?" Haney asked. "Do you expect the poor bastard to put his career on the line for us? He owed me a favor and he paid off. I don't own him."

"Listen to this verbatim," said Norman Barnes. "She got the whole message. 'A boy and a girl were dancing. They said that Acapulco Gold makes you sexy. They said it improves your love life. There was a package with a picture of a palm tree on it.' A *palm* tree?"

I shrugged. "Most people don't know what marijuana looks like. I guess that without anything on the pack to give size to the leaves, people imagine they're palm fronds."

"Who gives a shit?" said Haney. "The important thing is that we've got a vehicle that'll carry our message. I've got the plant working overtime. On Inauguration Day we'll be ready to ship."

"Isn't that premature?" Keyes asked. "Even if Foster does ask for legalization, it'll take time to put it through committee and—"

"Bullshit on that stuff," said Haney. "We'd end up waiting around for months while everyone from American Tobacco to the A&P got into the act. I figure that once we've got the Man's go-ahead, we GO! We may hit a few minor busts in Republican towns, but what are they going to do? Lock storekeepers up for an offense that everyone knows is going to be outlawed? I've got two million bucks budgeted just to fight those cases. The dealers will go along with us, because we'll guarantee to protect them."

"What do you think, Mike?" Ham said.

"I was still considering that last verbatim. We never said that Acapulco Gold makes *women* sexy."

"The implication was that they'd have a ball in the sack," said Norman Barnes. "That's making *someone* sexy."

"Look," I said, "when we get a bad test score, I have to bleed for it, so I guess I have a right to lie back and rejoice when we get a good one. But sometimes I think that we let the research methodology use *us* instead of the other way around. I agree that the aphrodisiac angle is a good one for the product, but this particular respondent got it all turned around. She thought Acapulco Gold was something like a lipstick that would make her become more sexy *outwardly* instead of enhancing whatever sexuality she's already got."

"Who gives a shit?" said Haney. "Let her think whatever she wants as long as she buys the product."

"Right," said Norman Barnes.

"Speaking of sexy," said Haney, "where's that little stringbean of yours? I thought you and her were just like that." He held up two crossed fingers and guffawed: "That's her on the bottom, of course."

"I haven't seen her since Norwich," I said. "She brought up some things that I needed."

"I'll bet," said Haney. "A pair of size thirty-eights, hey, boy?"

Getting up, I said, "Go fuck yourself."

Quietly, Keyes said, "Mike, you're out of line."

"Could be," I said. "Why don't you go fuck yourself too?"

As I started for the door, behind me I heard Howard Porter say, "Mike, don't be a fool."

But by then there was the all-too-familiar red noise in my head, and I slammed the door as I left.

ACCOUNT DEPARTMENT

MEDIA ORDER

TO: All time and space buyers.

1. Book all avaiable A and B television time for
week starting January 22 for 1:00 TV Commercial ROP
68 - 191 (Desert Inn Wine). Prints of this commercial
will be provided to stations with flag warning that
there may be last-minute substitution of another
commercial. On morning of January 22, prints of RPO
68 - 178 (C-900 "Ricardo") will be delivered to
substitute for previously scheduled spot.

2. Full page newspaper space will be booked for print
ad. Mats will be supplied on the morning of January
22. Booking will be for five insertions, two of which
will be ROP color, and one of the latter must include
weekend editions.

3. Radio spots will be booked as indicated for TV,
except that dummy tapes will not be supplied. Please
advise stations that they will receive program material
on the morning of January 22. Material will be
provided in choice of disc, cassette or reel-to-reel
tape.

4. The information contained in this memo is highly
confidential and should not be discussed in any way
with space salesmen.

h Porter

Howard Porter
Management Supervisor

HP:rj

If anyone but Wild Bill Haney had come after me, it wouldn't have worked. Actually, he—as head client—was the only one who could extend the olive branch anyway, because if he wanted me out on my ass, I was long gone.

He came into my office without knocking. I was rummaging aimlessly through my desk drawer, trying to find the piece of paper I'd written Jean's Chicago number on. The day we finished up in Norwich she had driven back out there. I wanted desperately to talk with her.

Haney closed the door. "I shot off my mouth and I'm sorry," he said. "Hell, boy, I don't mean anything. It's just my way."

"You've gone down that route once too often," I said.

"Simmer down, Mike. I'm apologizing to you. Now don't open your mouth. Don't say one goddamned word. Just listen."

He put his hand in front of my face and began to tick off points on his fingers. "One, I like what you've done on this project and I want you to keep running it. Two, we're still not out of the woods, but things are looking mighty hopeful. That means we're all going to get well, old buddy, *real* well. You don't want to blow that just because of a little flareup. And, three, I'm ashamed of what I said. I didn't really mean it. It's just my way. But the truth is, I think the world of that girl, and you too, and I'll try to hold down the noise in the future. Finally—"

I couldn't keep from laughing. "Enough, already. I'm sorry too, Bill. I guess I've been pushing too hard. Sometimes my nerves feel like a popcorn machine."

"Forget it. And don't worry. All is forgiven. I've already squared things with Ham. He chewed *me* out, if you want to know. Listen, kid, why don't you take a few days off? Hey, I've got an idea. Kind of a celebration. You and Jean join me as guests at the Inauguration. I've got a couple of extra seats at the ceremony, and a box for the parade, and invitations to a couple of the fancy balls."

"What did you do? Hold a gun on the Democratic National Committee?"

Haney winked. "I'll tell you some day. Well? Is it a deal?"

He held out his hand. I took it. "Yes," I said. "It's a deal."

"Okay, you ain't got any work to do until after the Inauguration. Don't let us see you around here. Go off somewhere and drink up some booze. And catch up with me in Washington. That's when our partnership really begins, Mike."

He shook my hand again and left. I dialed Porter's number and said, "Howard? This is Loudmouth."

"Welcome back to the team," he said. "You have more lives than a calico cat."

"I'm heading for the hills," I said. "Haney practically ordered me to. Anyway, there's nothing more for me to do around here until Coronet starts shipping the product."

Worried, Porter said, "I don't know, Mike. Did Bill—"

"I *said* he suggested it, Howard."

"Oh. Well, no one can deny you've earned it. What hills did you have in mind?"

"How about the Blue Mountains in Jamaica?"

"Bastard."

"I'll think of you, up here in the snow and ice."

"Yeah, you'll think of me when you have to wire for money."

"Anyway, I'll be back for the Inauguration. Haney wants me down there as his guest."

There was a short silence. Then he said, and I wasn't sure if he was joking, "Mike, when you get your own shop, I hope you remember your old buddies."

"Have no fear. I carry a little black book of trustworthy empty suits. Your name heads the list."

"Well, have fun."

"Thanks."

It took three calls, being referred from number to number, to track Jean down in Chicago. "Get on a plane for Montego Bay," I told her. "I'll meet you there tomorrow morning."

"What?"

"Don't argue. The prisoner is being given a week off."

Seriously, she said, "Mike, don't do this to yourself. It's better this way—"

"Please, Jean. It wouldn't be any fun without you."

"But I can't just take off. I've started classes again and—"

"Screw the classes. Do I have to come out there and get you?"

There was a pause. Then: "You would, wouldn't you? You really would."

"Try me."

"I shouldn't. It's not a good idea."

"Let's do it anyway, though."

She hesitated. "All right. But I'm being weak. I'll hate myself in the morning."

"In the morning you can hate yourself in Montego Bay."

"I miss you," she said softly.

"I miss you too."

"Tomorrow?" she said.

"Tomorrow."

"Mike?"

"What?"

"I've got a bathing suit that works. I'll bring it this time."

"Good. I love you."

She waited, then said, "I'll remember that."

"I'll remember it too," I said.

301

I broke the connection and got Effie busy lining up reservations and drawing money from the cashier.

"You sound awful happy," she said, handing me a thick envelope full of cash and tickets.

"I *am* awful happy," I said. "What can I bring you back from the exotic Caribbean?"

"Would it be too pushy to ask for one of those big straw bags?"

"I'll swish it through customs myself, baby." I kissed her cheek.

"Mike," she said.

"Yes?"

"I'm glad you're getting away. I wish it could be for longer."

"Thanks for the good wishes."

"Just doing my job, master."

"Speaking of your lowly job——"

"It is done, oh mighty one," she said. From behind her back, she produced a cup of steaming coffee. "Watch it. That little booger is *hot*."

I sipped at it. "You weren't so dumb, Effie, taking the secretary route. From where you sit, you see it all. What are you going to say about us poor mortals on Madison Avenue when you write your book?"

"I don't think I'm going to be writing any book, Mike," she said.

"Why not?"

Her lip trembled. "Because I can't stand sad stories."

It is a very long way from the beaches of Jamaica to the steps of the Capitol in Washington, D.C. It is long in distance and longer in the way you look at things.

During our week on the island, Jean and I tried to forget about Acapulco Gold. It was just something that had united us during the past weeks. We smoked pot only twice—both times in the company of a young English couple who were staying at a cottage near our own in Port Antonio. This is a little fishing town at the far end of the island more than a hundred miles from Montego Bay. Here there were virtually no tourists; the beaches were empty; almost every night we had no choice of entertainment—it was always one of the parties being thrown in one of the thatch-roofed cottages on Navy Island, the small palm-shaded one in the middle of Port Antonio harbor. Navy Island was famous for two historical events: in the eighteenth century Captain Bligh landed there with his ill-fated load of breadfruit trees; and in the twentieth century Errol Flynn won the whole island in a crap game. Now sold to a group of vacation-minded Americans, it was being developed into a cottage colony, and the thatch-roofed huts all had refrigerators and tiles on the floor. I am sure, however, that the ghost of Errol Flynn was never very far from the various open-walled bedrooms.

Jean and I drank overproof Appleton Rum, and reminisced about Quick Step and the Colonel's famous pig roast, and tried to ignore what was terribly obvious to both of us: we were in a downhill spiral, rushing toward some as yet unseen catastrophe and powerless to stop the plunge. We made love in its presence, and tried to drink it under the table, and yet it was always with us.

We attended one pig roast while in Port Antonio, at the Blue Lagoon Club which was owned by American writer Robin Moore, who wrote *The French Connection,* and delicious as the meal was, there seemed to be something missing.

"What's missing," Jean whispered, "is two ounces of ganja sprinkled over the rice and beans."

We water-skiied in the Blue Hole, the lagoon nestled beneath the sharply rising hills. Jean did fine. I fell off twice and gave up.

A young man from the Jamaican Tourist Board had attached himself to us, and between bouts with the water skis and the rum bottle he gave us a continuous travelogue of the island. About Blue Lagoon itself, he confided, "It's called 'the bottomless hole.' But that's absurd. It has a bottom."

"I should hope so," said Jean.

"Yes," the young man continued relentlessly. "Of course, in places it is around a hundred and eighty feet down. You're Americans, aren't you?"

"Occasionally," I said.

He gave me a sharp look. "Oh. You're joking. Very good. Then you must be familiar with James Jones, the novelist."

"Could be."

"You're pulling my leg, Mr. Evans."

"I'm familiar with his work," I said. "Somehow, our personal paths never crossed."

The young man gave me a faint smile. "Well, it seems Mr. Jones was down this way researching a book about skin-diving. Perhaps you read it?"

"If it was called *Go to the Widow Maker,* I did."

The smile flickered. "At that time, Mr. Robin Moore was living up the hill here in his cottage, Bamboo San. Having heard of Mr. Jones's prowess underwater, Mr. Moore invited him out for a bit of diving. Mr. Moore went first—without an aqualung, mind you—stayed under for some time and came up blue in the face, but clutching a handful of mud from the bottom. One hundred and eighty feet down, remember. Mr. Jones was impressed. He tried himself, and failed to reach bottom. Once again Mr. Moore succeeded, and once again Mr. Jones failed. All he got for his pains was a badly bleeding nose. Finally, Mr. Moore revealed the joke."

"It sounds uproarious," I said. "Bleeding noses always tickle me."

The young man kept on. "It seems that there is a volcanic cone out there, and if one knows precisely where it is, one can dive just fifteen feet or so and find bottom. But the person going off the other side of the boat has to swim through more than a hundred feet of water. Mr. Moore had merely been lowering himself a few feet and holding onto the bottom until he ran out of breath. While poor Mr. Jones had been trying to do the impossible."

He finished his rum punch. I prayed that he would not order another. My prayers were answered. The young man from the Tourist Board was finally going to leave us. He stood up, saying, "Mr. Moore said later that he became afraid we were going to lose a major novelist in the Blue Hole, and that is why he called the sport off."

Jean asked, "Did Mr. Jones punch Mr. Moore in the nose?"

The young man stared at her. "Whatever for?"

"Just for the sport of it," she said sweetly.

He got the idea and left, wishing us a pleasant vacation. His voice sounded as if he were wishing us in the place of James Jones and his nosebleed.

"What do you think about the vacation?" I asked when he had roared off in his Land Rover. "Do *you* think it's been pleasant?"

"Yes," she said. "I'm glad we came away together. Because there is something I've been trying to tell you for weeks and—"

"Hey, two rum punches," I called. The bartender began

305

mixing them up. I turned back to Jean. "Look, let's not have any confessions to spoil this last afternoon. If you start confessing to something, then I'll have to trade you one, and that makes for a lousy vacation."

"You're going to have to know," she said. "Sooner or later."

"Then let's make it later."

Our drinks came and she stared down at hers. "Later," she said.

"How about Navy Island tonight?" I asked.

She tried to smile. It was wan and pale. "All right. But let's stay away from the Gordons' place. I think they're trying to line up an orgy."

"I thought you liked orgies."

"Only two by two," she said. She looked up at me. "Do you like orgies, Mr. de Sade?"

"Why do you think I brought you down here?"

She blinked. "I don't know. Why *did* you?"

"The Gordons are trying to line up—"

"Mike, please. What are you trying to tell me?"

"All right. I brought you down here to ask you something important."

"What?"

"Will you marry me?"

Her eyes squinched up. "Please don't!"

"I meant what I said, Jean. I don't know when I started meaning it, but I do."

She stared at the now-empty glass on the table before her and said, "I can't, Mike."

"Why? Is that your confession? There's a husband hidden out in North Chicago?"

"I only wish it were that simple."

"Jean, I love you." She started to speak and I wouldn't let her. "Listen to me. I know the whole thing has been wacky, and I sure as hell didn't go out of my way looking for it to happen, but—"

"Mike! You're making it so hard for me!"

"All I want to do is love you. Is that so hard for you?"

"Yes! Michael, you don't love me. We've been all through that—"

"How the hell do you know what I—"

"—and what's more, what's important, is that *I* don't

306

love *you*. I'm sorry, but that's the way it is. I need you, and I wish I didn't, that's why I didn't want to take this trip with you, but I've already admitted I'm weak and I hate myself for it—"

"Why do we have to keep putting words around it? Jean, I'm happy when I'm with you and I'm unhappy when I'm not."

"Were you unhappy in California?"

"Yes! Look, don't answer now. Wait until this whole goddamned Acapulco God project is out of the way. Then we can—"

"Mike," she said, starting to cry, "do you know what we're doing? Both of us? We're lying to each other and to ourselves. You're telling me what you think I want to hear . . . and as for myself, God help me, I'm not telling you what I should. I want so much to tell you the truth, and I can only tell you part of it, and I'm all sick and empty inside." She got up. "I want to go back to the cottage."

"I'll drive you."

"I don't *want* you to drive me. Stay here. Get drunk. Go over to the Gordons' place and get laid. I don't care. Just give me the car keys."

"Jean, what's wrong?"

"Give me those keys or I'll start walking."

"All right," I said. I handed her the keys to the little Anglia. "I'll see you later."

"Maybe you will and maybe you won't," she said, taking them.

"Hey, wait a minute."

"Oh, go to hell!" she said, and stumbled away.

I did just as she had suggested. I sat there and got myself quietly plastered on Jamaican rum. I remember playing checkers with a very pleasant black man, who listened patiently as I discoursed on the stupidities of women and who eventually helped me into his car and drove me home.

The white Anglia was parked outside of the cottage. But Jean wasn't there when I went inside. A suitcase was opened on the bed, but her clothes still hung in the closet.

"Good," I said, and opened a Red Stripe.

I wandered through the cottage again. It was dark outside, and I passed the portable clothesline hung in the bathroom several times before I noticed that while my bathing suit was still there, Jean's was gone.

The beach was just a few yards below the cottage. It was a gentle sloping bay that was fed by waves breaking over the reef a few hundred yards out from shore.

Moonlight scattered silver bursts over the water's edge as I picked my way carefully through the stones and driftwood.

"Jean?" I called.

The waves answered, making a sighing, swooshing whisper against my feet.

The clouds parted and the moonlight blazed yellow.

Far out, on the reef, I thought I saw something move among the breakers.

"Jean?" I called.

Did I hear an answer? Or was it only the waves, ending their two-thousand-mile journey from the far shore of Africa?

I kicked off my shoes and stepped out of my trousers.

The water was blood-warm. I waded, the salt of the Caribbean lapping at my knees. Then it was waist-deep, and soon I had to swim.

Ahead the reef shimmered white in the moonlight.

I was out of shape. When I tried to call "Jean?" again, it emerged as a wheezing gasp. But this time there was an answer.

"Oh, Mike!"

"Where are you?"

"Over here."

I lowered my legs into the water and found the reef just three feet under the surface. Later, I would discover that its coral had cut violent patterns into the soles of my feet, but at that moment I felt nothing.

The clouds cooperated by parting again and I saw Jean, lying in the water atop the reef.

I splashed toward her.

Her upper body was bare, where the bathing suit had been ripped away. Black swirls of blood coated her arms and shoulders.

"My God!" I said. "What happened?"

"Oh, Mike," she cried, "take me home."

Somehow we swam the hundred yards to where we

could crawl up onto the shore. When I got my breath back, I picked her up and carried her the rest of the way to the cottage.

Inside, under the light, I could see how badly she had gashed herself on the coral.

"What the hell did you think you were doing?" I asked, dabbing her with a washcloth soaked in Appleton Rum. She turned her face away from me and shook her head. "Damn it, answer me!"

"No, Mike. Don't make me."

"Talk."

She sat up and pulled a bloody towel around herself and in a dead, toneless voice told me: "It isn't easy to drown, Mike. So don't try it. I thought that all I had to do was swim out until I was so tired I'd never have the strength to make it back. But I don't know where the energy came from, when I felt the water deep under me and it frothed down my throat, I couldn't help myself. I began to swim back, toward safety—and then I was thrown up on the reef and the waves began to roll me back and forth. I don't know how long I was there. Then I heard your voice. And I didn't *want* to answer, but I had to. Oh, Mike, it hurts!"

I reached for the phone. "I'll call a doctor."

She stopped me. "I don't mean the cuts. They'll heal. What hurts is what I've done to you. And after all that, you wanted to marry me."

"It's all right," I said. "You're back and that's all that matters to me."

"Is *that* what you think? How can you be glad to have me back? Mike, don't you know that I've been spying on you?"

Numbly, I said, "What do you mean, spying?"

"You and those people from Louisville—you want to sell dope to kids."

"What the hell are you talking about?"

"I'm talking about Acapulco Gold. I told you it was *wrong,* but you wouldn't listen to me. I told you it was dope, but you wouldn't believe me. I had to do something to stop you."

Coldly, I said, "What did you do, Jean?"

"I'm the one who leaked your marketing plan to Arthur Rand. I thought that would stop you, but it didn't. Somehow your Mr. Haney talked him out of heading you off. And then when you called me and asked me to come to Jamaica with you, I knew I'd have to do something else."

She stopped, crying. I shook her by the shoulders. "What else? What did you do next?"

"I had my father call the chairman of the Democratic National Committee. Daddy's only a delegate, but he thought he'd be able to get through, and I thought that by keeping you down here out of touch—"

"Is that why you came?"

"Yes! I spoke with Daddy yesterday, and he said there have been secret meetings with the President-elect and that the project was going to be stopped, because—"

I sat down. All of the blood seemed to have drained from my legs. "Why, Jean? What the hell reason did you have?"

She was sobbing so hard that I almost couldn't understand her. "I told you, Mike. Marijuana is *dope!* I ought to know. I'm hooked on it. You called me right when you said I was a pothead. I've been smoking all these years and I can't function without it. I can't come alive unless I'm high. You know that. How could I sit back and let you do that to other kids? I *had* to do something. Mike, I'm sorry. I had to."

I reached for my wallet and remembered that it was in my trousers on the beach somewhere. Without speaking, I went out and found my clothes. When I got back to the cottage, Jean had dressed herself in a robe.

Her eyes misting, she said, "What are you going to do?"

I fumbled a piece of paper out of my wallet and said, "I'm going to call Bill Haney. What the hell do you think I'm going to do?"

But I didn't. Very sorry, there were no overseas lines available for at least two days. And the cable people were on strike again.

I got dressed and started to pack. When I found the gift wrapped package in my suitcase, I tossed it to Jean.

"What's that?" she asked, still sobbing.

"That was supposed to be my engagement present to you," I said. "Now you can call it a goodbye gift."

Numbly, she stripped off the wrappings and when she

310

saw the two-ounce bottle of Chanel No. Five, she began to cry harder.

"Baby," I said, "I'm sorry you're crying, but the minute I'm out of that door, I'm going to forget it. I'm going to forget you too. For your future information, you're some kind of nut and you're dangerous for people to be around."

It was a great exit line, and I had charged out of the cottage and hiked more than a half a mile toward town before I started to cry myself.

I caught the next plane to New York, took the shuttle down to Washington, and found Bill Haney at the Diplomat Hotel. There I told him exactly what Jean had done.

"So it was her all along," he said calmly. "Well, it doesn't come as any surprise, Mike. I knew someone was japping us, and it had to be someone on the inside. Just so it wasn't you."

"Why? You can't keep me around after this."

"Like hell I can't. Boy, I need you worse than ever now. Listen, I already knew about the Committee's meeting with Foster. I've got spies all over this town. It's too bad—this means that we're going to have to do it the hard way instead of easy."

"But I'm to blame."

"Nobody's to blame. Not even that poor girl down there. Shit, boy, don't take it so hard. Who ever said it was going to be easy? If it was easy to make a million bucks, everybody would be doing it. It's hard, and it takes guts, and it takes pain too. You don't get anything for nothing, Mike. You have to pay for it, with sweat and with worry and with heartache."

"Is it worth it, Bill?"

"I don't honestly know. But it's all I know how to do."

"But what are you going to do now? They'll never let Foster legalize marijuana after this."

He spread his hands. "Boy, I already *did* it. As soon as I found out that we were getting the plug pulled, I ordered shipments to begin. The carloads started moving out yesterday. We're going on sale day after tomorrow, no matter *what* President Foster says. But don't get too upset—my guys inform me that even with all the flak we've had, he's still going to recommend reducing the penalties. He just won't go quite as far as we'd hoped."

"Then it's still illegal. We'll be committing a crime."

"If it's a crime when two hundred thousand outlets start selling something at the same time, after a new President has said the penalties ought to be relaxed, then we're going to be committing a crime. But who's going to lock all those people up?"

"You'll never get away with it," I said.

"Maybe I will and maybe I won't," he said coldly. "But I'll tell you one thing, Mike: when it's all over, they're going to know Bill Haney was *there*. The question is, are you going to be there with me? Or do I have to carry the whole load myself?"

"No," I said. "I'll help you carry it. I don't have anything else to do."

"Thanks, boy. I knew you would. Listen, don't think I blame you. You ain't the first one who went down the track after a piece of cunt and wound up with a cowcatcher stuck up his ass. Now, find yourself another girlfriend and let's have us some fun. We got us a President's Inauguration to attend, and a parade to watch, and a barrel of champagne to drink. Let's enjoy it. This may be the first twenty-million-dollar party in history."

"Let me get organized, will you, Bill?"

"Sure, you get straightened out. Catch up with me down in the bar around seven."

"Okay."

I started for the door. He stopped me. "Mike?"

"Yeah?"

"I wish I had a boy like you."

I went to my room and sat on the bed, staring at the telephone.

Why was I going along with him? Why was I being his *boy?*

Jean was right. We were going to peddle dope. I felt a quiet craving for it at this very moment.

So why didn't I get off the train?

And, out loud, I gave the answer: "Because this is all I'm any good at."

This was all I'd ever be any good at. And now that it was there before me, what was so hard about saying that?

I picked up the phone and direct-dialed Los Angeles.

She answered, "Hello?"

"This is Mike. How about flying to Washington tomorrow to be guests of the President at his Inauguration, and afterward we'll drink up all the champagne in town."

"The Inauguration?" Janice said. "What are you doing there?"

"It's a long story," I said. "But it starts when you admit to yourself that that's all there is. We only go around this track once, so let's stop fighting the odds and have a blast."

"Meet the first plane from L.A.," she said. Then she added, "And break out the booze."

"That," I said, "or something else."

I took a shot of Appleton Rum straight from my traveling flask and went out to buy myself some new clothes so I would look good at the Inauguration of our new President.

The elevator door was closing. I ran for it, pried it open, and squeezed in.

A tall white-haired man looked at me in wonder.

"Where are you going in such a hurry, young man?" he asked.

"Nowhere," I told him. "Nowhere at all."